For Simon

OFFICER QUALITY

With best wishes

from

Roberts

November 1994

Also by Rosemary Enright

Alexa's Vineyard
The Walled Garden
Signed by the Artist

Officer Quality

Rosemary Enright

Hodder & Stoughton

First published in 1994 by
Hodder and Stoughton
A division of Hodder Headline PLC

10 9 8 7 6 5 4 3 2 1

British Library Cataloguing in Publication Data

Enright, Rosemary
Officer Quality
I. Title
823.914 [F]

ISBN 0-450-61005-5

Typeset by Avon Dataset Ltd, Bidford-on-Avon

Printed and bound in Great Britain by
Mackays of Chatham, Chatham, Kent

Hodder and Stoughton Ltd
A division of Hodder Headline PLC
338 Euston Road
London NW1 3BH

For Nancy

1

1943

It was pitch-black in the derelict shepherd's hut. But Alice, who had prepared this new transmission post several days ago, knew the spaces by heart and by touch. The attaché case containing her radio lay open and ready on a bale of dusty straw, with the storm lantern, wick trimmed, hanging from a rafter above. Matches in one jacket pocket, Browning automatic, safety catch off, nestling comfortingly in the other.

Earlier, Alice had swept the floor of impacted earth so that her feet should not crunch on charred wood or cinder spilled from the hearth. Not so much as rustle in stray wisps of hay. Unnecessary noise was unnecessary risk. Even here, where nobody came.

Pushing the crude shutter with her forefinger, it yielded instantly and silently to her touch. A little work with an oilcan had done the trick. There was a sliver of moon and the view of the village down below was good. It had been necessary to scythe some brushwood away to ensure a clear line of sight between the hut and the Epicerie Darges. Enough to see when the third-floor window at the gable end was illuminated.

A dim light there, they had agreed, would arouse no comment if it were observed. And it would be observed. In a community of six hundred or so, there was always some busybody up and about so close to cock-crow. But a baby in the house explained nocturnal activity. Two months old now, and waking every four hours for her ration of goat's milk. Mothers on active service couldn't breast feed. It wasn't as if Veronica had any milk of her own anyway. Not on a wartime diet of nervous excitement and root-vegetable stew. The

Germans took most of the available food.

Peering at the luminous dial on her watch, Alice inwardly cursed the recklessness of her sister and Free French brother-in-law. The child was a complication they didn't need. London would explode if they knew. Or at any rate, their SOE section chief, Brigadier Drummond, would.

The marriage itself, which had taken place one weekend during training in Scotland, had caused enough of a furore. The Nightjar operation, so long in preparation, had come close to being cancelled. Current F Section policy was against sending married agents into operational theatres together. But, as Drummond sourly observed to Alice in a private interview, beggars couldn't be choosers. Lately there had been too much of what the Brigadier preferred to call 'wastage' . . . Or, on that fraught occasion, 'probable mortalities'. Arrests, executions, betrayals, disappearances. Nightjar would have to go ahead. Too many Resistance leaders had been promised London's support, Hubert Darges among them.

The supply of volunteer officers who spoke fluent French and could use a parachute was not limitless. Alice and Veronica Winstanley had been brought up in a Belgian convent school, while their father, a widowed foreign correspondent, pursued his career in Paris. Alice, at a loose end after leaving school, had stayed on and off with distant relatives in London, joining the FANYs before hostilities broke out. That exclusive, supremely self-confident crew of Mayfair soldierettes, adept at horsemanship, first aid, driving staff cars and giving cocktail parties, had been suppressed, outgeneralled by the meritocratic, rank-conscious ATS ladies and their champions in the War Office. Veronica, who'd been hanging listlessly around a civilian-run transport depot in hope of war work, joined the ATS in 1941. All that was left of the amalgamated FANYs was the red shoulder flash Alice and her friends were permitted to wear on their new khaki uniforms. A source of immense, bitter pride.

But here, in the Forêt de Palante, outside the village of Saint Estèphe les deux Fontaines, in the Département of Haute-Saône, forty miles from the German frontier and the lightly garrisoned town of Belcourt, there were no British uniforms. No room, either, for intricate rivalries between one formation and another.

Only one loyalty, one invisible hierarchy mattered in this area of prehensile townships, of narrow, wooded gorges and tunnelled hillsides which carried miles and miles of railway track. Nightjar, commanded by Alice as co-ordinator and radio-op., had a simple, well-defined objective.

"To disrupt enemy schedules," Alice murmured the official words like a soothing mantra to herself, "to destroy or render useless enemy war material; to harry, demoralise and preoccupy enemy personnel." Beautiful. It rhymed.

Nightjar was a well-established network now. Successful too. After eight months, a long-running show. Esme Hansard, a natural with explosives, had accounted for a startling tonnage of enemy transport. Code-named Crow, he was apt, in Alice's view, to linger too long near the scenes of his triumphs. A debonair, devil-may-care kind of cove, as Drummond had described him to a colleague in SOE's Baker Street headquarters, Hansard was unpredictable. As likely to help free an injured civilian from the cruel wreck of tangled steel he had himself created, speaking the pure *hoch deutsch* he'd learned at his Prussian grandfather's knee, as to vanish, dryad-like, with his band of *maquis* into the trees.

And yet, Alice recalled, sucking a precious square of chocolate to quieten her nervously squealing gut, Esme Hansard's file marked him down as unsuitable for infiltration operations. Vouchsafed a sight of that file, as she would be responsible for the safety and performance of its subject, Alice had seen her brother-in-law summed up as being commonplace as a mermaid in a trawlful of haddock. Yes and no, Alice demurred inwardly. It all depended what role he was playing today. And there was no way of knowing what that would be.

He had a daughter now, named for himself. Sometimes Alice's tidy mind toyed with the idea of issuing her infant niece with a code name, a call sign like that of her own and her parents. But Baby Bird had no status. London did not know her. Odd that her own call sign should be Mother Bird. Veronica's was Swallow, a name mildly descriptive of her high velocity message-carrying role.

"Careless, selfish . . . *inefficient.*" Alice had bellowed furiously at her sister, once she knew about the pregnancy. "Don't you realise I shall have to send you home? At the very least a pilot's life will be in jeopardy because of you . . ."

But Veronica had argued convincingly against quitting her post.

"Nonsense, Ally. The village will adore pursing its lips over my fatherless mite. Me and my shameful bundle will be jolly good for Nightjar. With my bastard at my breast, where can I be at nights but home?"

Not that the pregnancy had hampered Veronica over much until the last week. And it had certainly reinforced the neighbourhood view that Hubert Darges' younger 'daughter' was a slut who conferred intimate favours on soldiers of the occupying force for fripperies like lipstick and chocolate.

Seven minutes to go, Alice noted, interrupting her thoughts. She wished she could smoke. Anything to loosen the knots in her stomach. It didn't matter how many times she went through this, the tension never diminished. But a cigarette made a pin-point of needless, premature light. And a flying spark from one of the coarse, loose-packed French products could ignite the straw. Then there'd be a beacon visible for miles around. Alice swallowed her saliva.

Six minutes. Plenty of time. The sky was lightening a little. A rim of gold around the hilltops. Casually, a bird experimented with a note or two and then fell silent again. Too early for crickets.

The earth, richly fecund, smelled damp with the dew.

Deliberately Alice stopped herself staring winklessly in the direction of the critical window. It was pointless and tiring. The signal would come and she wouldn't miss it. One candle, to be exposed for five seconds precisely. Any variation and there was trouble. So far, Alice touched the wooden shutter in a reluctant obeisance to superstition, Nightjar had been remarkably trouble-free. Almost too free. Too relaxed. At what point, Alice wondered, did boldness degenerate into hubris?

From time to time Esme strolled into the village, wearing a uniform pulled off some German soldier killed in a derailment. It hardly seemed possible that slender, patrician Esme could manage to look so much the ranker.

The ill-fitting uniform helped, along with Esme's assumed slouching gait and cocksure affability. A pat for a dog, a caress for a schoolchild . . . banter in convincingly broken French, spattered with the odd word of German. He breezed through Saint Estèphe, every inch the common soldier out on a forty-eight-hour pass. Out for a good time with his girl. He strode into Epicerie Darges, all hail-fellow-well-met, chaffing the customers and awkwardly presenting the younger 'Mademoiselle Darges' with a posy of wild flowers. Meanwhile Hubert, sullenly sharpening knives, played the outraged father and glowered at the man with the flowers.

Veronica always received them with just the right tone of greedy, coquettish sarcasm. *"Charmant!"* she shrilled. *"Un cadeau tout simple."* And all eyes would stray to her convex belly where the simple gift thus obliquely mentioned, lay enlarging. Nowadays the same eyes looked aloft, up the stairs which rose from the shop to the living-quarters. The gift had been delivered in a long night of groaning.

There was no doubt in Saint Estèphe where Mademoiselle Darges' illegitimate infant came from. And equally, no realisation that her parents were other than they seemed to be, or legally married. In some respects, it was safer that way.

4

The scandal was the subject of endless bawdy conversation down at the open-air laundry. There were some places in the world, it was darkly remarked, where a girl like that would have her head shaved . . . be feathered and tarred. Hereabouts, they were too tolerant. Then each toiling woman would fall into a sensual, private reverie about the pleasure that shearing Veronique's sumptuous, buttery tresses would give her. Rubbing and wringing and dreaming of violence.

In Saint Estèphe's polite parlours, schemes for ostracisation were projected and abandoned on a regular basis. Darges' was the only moderately well-stocked general grocery for miles around. Always a precious, delicious little something under the counter for good customers.

Darges himself was a frail widower. A veteran of Verdun . . . and he needed the services of both his daughters. Hadn't he recalled them from their work as housemaids in Paris eight months ago? Before that, they hadn't been seen in the village for years. Sent off to earn their crust at a very early age, the Darges girls had been. The shop had been less prosperous in peacetime. War had brought the entrepreneur out in Hubert Darges.

Still, he might conceal that trollope's shame from decently patriotic eyes, it was thought. A nice enough lad, though, her tow-headed *Boche* sweetheart. *Gentil*, if that could ever be said of one of those murderers. Where did he say he was stationed? No one could remember. Oh yes, Paris. Must be. That's where he'd met the Darges girl. The filthy little *putan*. But boys, especially boys away from home, went up the motherly sigh, *would* be boys.

The general absolution for Esme himself in this character made Alice uneasy. The spinsters and matrons of Saint Estèphe compensated for their treachery in liking him by despising her sister all the more. Hate was not too strong a word, Alice mused.

"Excuse me, Mademoiselle," Joséphine Despard, the retired notary's wife had said only yesterday, "I prefer to be served by Monsieur, your father. Or by your sister. Your hands, I see, are not clean."

Veronica shrugged and pouted in a magnificent parody of the fresh, fruitful woman's disdain for her menopausal senior.

"Just as you wish, *Madame la Notaire*," she purred insolently, "although there's some as is pleased enough to let me handle their sausage."

A claret-wine stain climbed the older woman's neck. But she stood her ground. She had a regular arrangement with Darges' for an eighth of a kilo of *boudin*.

Later, when the shop shutters were up, Veronica had laughed. A

5

cadenza of mockery. The sound of liquid silver seeping past every sill of the house. Dangerous, dangerous.

Given an opportunity, Alice feared, the community would turn on her. Even the child was at risk. It would never be possible to tell Veronica's detractors that the suppressed glee they felt at the nearby German's garrison's mounting frustration was in large part due to her.

Three minutes. A profound quiet wrapped the valley. Distinct shapes were beginning to emerge from the massed huddle of buildings in the distance. Four o'clock was really too late for the summer time. Alice made a note to advise London of a change. One hour earlier in future, until the nights lengthened again. How many more times would the year turn before the war was over?

Two minutes. The skin on Alice's face felt moistly waxen and lumpy. It was always like this. Waiting. Most of war was waiting. Even infantry soldiers said that. At least they had companionship. Swatting that momentary weakness in herself, Alice looked again at her watch. The seconds crawled. So fast and so slow. The only thing to do was to throw the mind forward, over the fence, past the bad moment. It would pass.

Think of breakfast, of baby Esme's tiny, wise face. Already, it was so like her father's . . . Of the ripening tomatoes in Darges' *potager*. Night soil worked well as a fertiliser . . . After the war, Alice promised herself, I shall be a farmer . . . Veronica would be back now with the news.

Alice pictured her sister, cradling her baby in that upper room, flushed with triumph and love. Breathless, perhaps, from her six-mile hurdle through fields, gardens, farmyards and small family vineyards. She would be telling Darges all about it whilst she gave little Esme her bottle.

The derailment of the ammunition transport would have been over and done with an hour ago. Sometimes the commotion could be heard in the village, but not always.

Esme kept his activities as far distant from Saint Estèphe itself as he could, but elsewhere in other villages innocent hostages had been taken. Some of them denounced to the Gestapo to settle old scores. Nobody could be trusted. In occupied territory there was no unity. Summary executions made cowards of most people. Individual survival was the universal imperative. Nature, ignoble, irrepressibly selfish, conquered all but a few. Alice prayed that if ever need arose, she would be one of those few. One minute.

Alice's ears detected the sound of a petrol engine far below. Not a tractor. Too smooth. Few peasant farmers could get their hands on petrol these days, anyway. No, a black car, headlights shining as it crossed the bridge over the Saône's narrow, gurgling tributary which ran through the village. Germans! Forty seconds. And now a truck. A troop transport . . . soldiers leaning out of the back. Another. Twenty seconds. Blood rushing in the ears, pounding every pulse. Ten seconds. Alice flicked her eyes back and forth between her watch and that gable-end window in the valley.

Zero hour . . . but no light.

Afraid many times in the past, Alice commenced her invariable technique of self-treatment. Breathe deeply several times. Aerate the brain. Think reasonably. Think reasonably optimistically. Half the mistakes made in this business arose out of the pessimism of panic.

Darges may have failed to make the five-second signal because the derailment had not taken place . . . was delayed. The ammunition train itself, travelling south-west from the Ruhr, might have been cancelled . . . or was running late.

The signal was delayed because Veronica was still waiting for the chain of prearranged animal cries and bird calls to reach her. And there had been no variation in the signal which spelled danger . . . only a complete absence . . . which meant nothing. So, Alice told herself firmly, nothing had happened. Those soldiers were bound for some other place.

There was a system for aborting an operation but Esme had decided not to abort. This meant the train was not far away. Would fall into the trap before dawn broke. He was cutting it fine. Any moment now, that light would appear. London must do their share of the waiting. War was all waiting.

Alice waited an hour and a half. At the end, there was only sunlight. Beside it, no candles stood a chance of being seen. Veronica was probably back. A muddle . . . but almost certainly harmless.

Watching the village, it seemed to Alice to be busier than usual at this hour. Specks of humanity moved swiftly along the riverside walk. Men? Surely not. All the menfolk, young or in their prime, had been taken away to slave in German labour camps. Those who wouldn't go joined the *maquis* and hid like foxes in caves in the hills. Saint Estèphe had no men but the old.

There was somebody at the end of the bridge. A group? Difficult to make out from here . . .

Rival cocks were crowing. Their diurnal contest for vocal supremacy came earlier each day as the summer advanced. Alice could imagine . . . rationalise, Saint Estèphe's early morning scene. Where only a few days ago there were blank rectangles of faded red, blue and green, now there were hollow-eyed apertures in their stead . . . which signified housewives throwing open their shutters and grandfathers yawning in their braces on the doorsteps. Early rising got earlier in

7

the summer. It was in the nature of countryside things.

Or was the village in a state of alarm? It had to be considered.

Looking around at the pile of old hay and straw in the corner, Alice was tempted for a long moment to crawl on to it and sleep. Hide herself from hideous reality. Those two trucks in the Place de l' Hôtel de Ville were just ordinary vans freighting merchandise. Zinc pails and flowered wrap-around overalls . . . Wednesday was market day. The trucks had arrived early from somewhere, ready for tomorrow . . .

A dream.

Concealing the radio rather than herself, under the straw, Alice left the hut and began to thread her way down through the trees, grabbing saplings for support as she went.

The radio was best left behind. To be caught with it would mean immediate arrest. She would come back later and transmit to London. And new radio positions were not two a penny. Use any one twice and it invited German intelligence to trace the source of the signal. Abwehr was ceaselessly vigilant for unauthorised radio traffic.

Pausing a moment in her descent, Alice saw a ruby glinting up in the shredded, woodland light. It lay close to her coarse, lace-up shoe. A wild strawberry. Here and there, there were more, spangling the grass. Stooping to pick them, Alice crammed the fruits into her dry, unhungry mouth. They tasted of nothing but her body badly needed the sucrose.

Further down there was a hamlet of toadstools. The sort that made such delightful housing for story-book elves. Humpy scarlet roofs with white dots. Extremely poisonous. Taking out her handkerchief, Alice plucked the largest and put it in her pocket, not knowing quite why she did so.

"I'm on the mayor's list," Veronica stamped her foot pettishly on the bare, scrubbed boards, "and I'll be the one to go."

"No you won't," snapped Alice, "you'll do as I say. Listen carefully . . . Where's Hubert, by the way?"

"He's gone out. Something about trying to find out what's going on. He'll offer himself as a substitute. It's no good. It's me they want."

"Will you be *quiet*?" Alice hissed. "It's not you they want. Don't be so vain. The mayor will just have closed his eyes and stabbed a pin in the electoral roll. Twenty times. What else could he do?"

Veronica, leaning against the polished, cherry-wood counter with her arms folded, eyed her sister cynically. They were so inured to lying now . . . But did they have to lie to each other?

"Don't be stupid, Ally. The mayor may have stabbed nineteen times with his pin but not twenty. Somebody suggested my name to him. It must have been a relief to have one responsibility taken off him. Poor old goat. A German squaddie's bit of skirt is fair game.

"If you think about it," she added, loosening the top button of her limp cotton dress, "it's all worked terribly well. Nobody's going to point a finger at me for being a Resistance worker. No, I'm just some tart who got into bed with the enemy. They won't interrogate me."

"No, they'll just hang you instead," Alice said, truth bursting painfully from her lips. "Or shoot you."

"Steady on. I thought it was you who believed in thinking optimistically. We're a long way from shootings or hangings."

But Veronica did not believe that and knew that Alice didn't either. The baby upstairs began to wail.

"I'll fetch her down," Veronica said steadily. "Might as well give her this feed. You'll do the next one, won't you?"

Alice looked away, feeling a stone in her chest. Where did stupidity begin and gallantry end? It was all so obvious to Alice. Some people are expendable, she thought, and others are not. Mothers never are. Hadn't she and Veronica grown up without one?

Hearing her sister's bedroom door close, Alice looked out of the window. There was a German soldier outside with a rifle and another one further up the street. They were smoking. It was the same, she discovered, in the yard at the back. Two of them there, searching the hencoops for eggs. The Germans must have drafted in yet more reinforcements. Overhead Veronica was crooning to Esme.

Sloppy men, Alice sized up the opposition's strength for a moment. Hardly alert. But too numerous to make escape feasible. Saint Estèphe was surrounded, and under curfew. Only the named hostages were allowed to emerge, to surrender themselves.

The idea of making a run for it, she and Veronica together, represented itself to Alice yet again. No good. They'd be gunned down in their tracks, both of them. Then Hubert Darges' life would be forfeit. Or they'd interrogate him. No one could predict if his fortitude would prove sufficient to protect the rest of the Nightjar network. Too long a shot. Too many other lives thrown away . . . And what would happen to the child that was their own flesh and blood?

Someone had better go and go quietly. Nightjar then could melt away safely, the Germans none the wiser.

Mounting the spiral staircase, Alice was certain of what she must do. There was nothing to fear. Everything had gone very well. Nightjar had achieved enough and would look very cheap with only one casualty. She would have liked to have seen Paris again. That was all. Otherwise, no regrets.

In the small kitchen Alice took a pan down from the rack, melted some butter and sliced the toadstool into it. Then she quartered a *baguette*, split one piece, spread the two halves with the fungus mixture, and put them together again before wrapping the sandwich in a piece of paper. She walked back down the stairs and put it in her old jacket pocket.

She felt peaceful.

Veronica came down with the baby. Alice drew herself up. She was the senior officer here when all was said and done. Her sister, fortunately, had taken the King's shilling too, and was bound to obey her.

"Funny smell . . ." Veronica started.

"Pay attention, Veronique," Alice spoke in French as always. "There's little time for this. Very soon, if one of us does not report to the Hôtel de Ville, someone will come and get . . . one of us. I shall spare them the trouble. You will stay here and keep out of sight with my niece."

Veronica started to argue again. Alice silenced her furiously.

"That's *enough*, Junior Commander! You're out of order. Do you hear me?

"Later," she went on more calmly, "as soon as the racket dies down you will go up to the hut *with* the baby . . . I'll give you the grid reference. You will first contact Drummond and ask for immediate evacuation. Say the cover's blown. Say anything you like. Then radio your husband and get him to meet you at Tintagel. You know it? It's where we came in. Local name Champs de Paradis. Tell him they've got Hubert and me. He'll want to know why it's not me transmitting . . . He knows my Morse style . . . And for God's sake keep it short. The longer the message the greater the danger."

Alice was forced to say the same thing several times over. Commanding, reasoning, and snarling by turn.

Finally, Veronica looked down at her baby. There was no sound to be heard in the empty house except the child's sucking.

"I'm giving you an order. Do you understand?" Alice lunged at her sister, shaking her shoulders. "You must save yourself and the baby. Esme too, if you can. You're a family. I'm just a soldier."

"And I'm not, I suppose." Veronica looked up coolly from her infant. "Take your hands off me, Ally. If we're going to talk military niceties, you're not entitled to touch me."

Repelled by a blast of vapourised ice, Alice stumbled back.

"Look, *chérie*," Veronica said gently after a pause. "This one's got my number on it. I'm going to go and you can't stop me. Veronique Darges, the *Wehrmacht* mattress, was my idea, not yours. I'll pick up the tab for it. OK?"

"I can't get through to you, you little fool, can I?" Alice clenched her fists. If Veronica hadn't been holding the baby, she honestly believed she would have hit her. "This isn't one of your games . . ."

"They'll probably just send us all off to labour camps," Veronica cut across her. "And if not, well, I'll think of something. Don't I always? I'll survive. It's Esme I feel sorry for. I'll probably wind up as some Gestapo swine's mistress. Don't tell him, will you? After the war, we'll give him an edited version."

As Alice remembered that moment later, her sister had never looked more lovely. Rounded, completed. Unearthly. Already detached from the life she had so vehemently loved. It was the moment in which Alice knew Veronica had won the right to make the sacrifice. By sheer force of will. Alice had nothing left with which to fight. They couldn't both go. The baby needed someone.

The sacks of beans on the floor and sparsely-populated shelves all around them suddenly seemed what they had always been. Ephemeral. Even Hubert Darges' black and white cat, Marthe, dozing indifferently on a flour bin. None of it was more than a rickety stage set for a drama, the last act of which had been known in advance. Eight months had been too long. Too many scenes. But they had acted well together, the three of them.

"Here," Veronica thrust the child into Alice's arms. "Take care of your Aunt Ally, darling, until I get back."

"There's a sandwich in my coat pocket," Alice said bleakly. "I made it for myself. You may need it . . . to help you sleep."

"Thanks, Ally," Veronica responded briskly. "You're a pal."

Wonderingly, Alice found herself wishing that Veronica wouldn't use such appalling slang. It was the ATS, of course. They could be so common. Anyway, she should never speak in English. There was something to be gained, even now, by maintaining the cover. No point in torturing an ignorant peasant girl. How was it possible even to think such thoughts as these? Training.

The sisters kissed then, something they had never, ever done before. Veronica smelled of cheap scent.

She opened the street door and walked out into the sunshine. Alice watched her through the window. The German soldier said something sharply, Veronica said something in return, smiling warmly. The soldier threw away his cigarette and had the grace to look embarrassed. His gaze followed her, hips swinging from side to side as she went, tottering seductively on high-heeled red shoes. Tarty, scutted-looking things. Keeping everything in character till the end.

Quite right, the operational part of Alice's mind ticked automatically. People, unseen, would be watching. Vindictive people who could do

11

yet more harm to Veronica. Let them be satisfied with her quick, close-mouthed death. Let it be easy.

The baby stirred, restive in Alice's arms. A pair of solemn grey eyes looked up enquiringly.

2

The twenty hostages were shot at six o'clock the following morning in the Place de l' Hôtel de Ville. Nobody talked before the massacre or was asked to. To the German army and Gestapo, their victims were just a handful of French rustics with nothing to talk about. If any of them had had anything to say, terror would have shaken it out of them. This was just another random reprisal. Twenty lives for some rolling stock, a few tonnes of bullets and some shells.

Hubert Darges was detained briefly on charges of defying the curfew. He was not, therefore, amongst those who brought themselves to witness the scene in the square.

An elderly chemist took a photograph from a crack in his *salon* shutters directly overlooking the firing squad line-up. He hid the film, taking it after the war, to the Allied commander in Belcourt. Evidence of an atrocity.

Alice had no means of knowing whether the sandwich she gave her sister had been eaten or if it had helped. Maybe it drugged her . . . At the worst, it may have given her a night of gastric agony which made her glad to be put out of her misery.

Practical compassion, measured regret, was all there was time for.

A day later, most of the soldiers went away. Naturally, the Epicerie Darges did not open for business. Hubert, who had aged twenty years in a day, helped Alice make a papoose for the baby out of an old grape-harvester's pannier. The obvious thing, since it strapped on the back. Napkins, feed bottles and her pistol, Alice would carry in her pockets. Nightlights, a torch and well-padded jam jars went in a bag hooked on to the pannier.

13

Just before seeing her off in the dark through the yard gate, Hubert straightened his stiff old body. With an effort he brought his heels together and bowed.

"*Bonne chance, ma chère Commandante.*"

That formal compliment from a comrade in arms lightened Alice's heart for a moment. Everything else was so heavy.

"*Yes!* It's her. Mother Bird." The duty sparks plucked at Vaughan's arm. "Wake up, sir. She's coming through loud and clear."

Groggily, Major Vaughan raised his head from the desk. He and Drummond had been taking it turn and turn about, every four hours for two whole days and a half.

"Are you sure?"

"I'd know her touch anywhere."

The sparks let his earphones snap back close to his head. For some moments he gave his undivided attention to the crackling dits and dahs. Beautiful Morse. Mother Bird was an artist. A near-perfect linear pattern. An inimitable signature. Irrefutable evidence that she was safe.

Coming to himself, Vaughan staggered out of the room with his service dress tunic all undone. "Brigadier, sir! We've got Nightjar. Mother Bird calling."

Drummond came in beaming, immaculate and soldierly as usual.

"What did I tell you? No faith, that's your trouble, dear boy. Mother Bird's always been reliable."

They had to wait until the message was taken to the decoding section for processing. When it came back the few words were convoluted and whimsical. Their meaning, however, was stark. Mother Bird was a master of safety-conscious brevity:

Swallow down. Crow flying. Mother Bird homing. Nightjar must terminate. Request urgent migration in double formation. Confirm.

"Get on to Tempsford," Drummond rapped. "We want a Lysander out to Tintagel soonest. Priority."

Vaughan met some opposition at first. The aircraft and crew allocated to the SOE sections were savagely overworked during the moonlit phase of the month. The base commander gave in after a tussle. A weary "OK, wilco," signalled the RAF capitulation.

Relevant information streaked between Tempsford and Baker Street. Minds moving fast.

A Lysander would take off within thirty minutes. An armed specimen, not yet converted to A Flight's use. It would be the lone pilot's first pick-up run. Guns but no gunner or navigator. All the cabin space would be needed. No enemy action was anticipated. Three minutes waiting time on the ground . . . maximum. That was the RAF rule. Agents in place to make the usual arrangements for landing. A report on ground conditions was needed. Four hours' flying time to Tintagel. Yes, yes, Tempsford had the map reference.

Had Mother Bird given her position? No, she hadn't. Ever cautious. Could she make the rendezvous in time? And Crow . . . where the bloody hell was Crow?

Further communication with Alice in the hut established that she could walk to the improvised landing strip in approximately three and a half hours. The ground was dry and hard. No rain for many days. Good landing conditions. Hansard's exact position, resolutely withheld by his sister-in-law for fear of Abwehr eavesdropping, sounded less favourable. He would have to walk further, Mother Bird admitted. But then he was faster. She would answer for Crow.

Esme was setting a rabbit snare when he picked up the signal. *Merde!* More of Mother Bird's interminable nagging. But no . . . This was his wife's amateurish, hesitant, up and down style of sending. *Qu'est qui se passe?* Listening intently, he decoded the message simultaneously. The hair on his body stood erect:

Baby Bird and Swallow in danger. Nightjar recalled. All migrate from Tintagel.

She gave the estimated time of departure in a routine SOE code.

Plain enough, thought Alice, even for a foolhardy numbskull like Esme. With any luck at all, whoever was listening didn't know who was broadcasting to whom or where or what 'Tintagel' was. It was the timing that bothered her. That code had been in use quite a while.

Squatting on his haunches, Esme uttered the clattering, chattering song of the nightjar. A snatch only. Then another followed by the bloodcurdling, pitiful death scream of a rabbit. It was the signal to his *maquis* to disperse. It had to come one day. Nightjar had ceased to exist. It was every man for himself.

Marksman's rifle slung over his shoulder, Esme began to bound through the forest in an oblique, ascending line to the upland meadow above the treeline, seven miles away. Considering the distance, the incline was steep. But the sharp goad of concern for his wife and child lent powerful wings to the Frenchman's feet.

The first half-mile at this gruelling pace was hard. His rhythm, Esme knew, would come in a moment. Leaping and springing, his heart and lungs expanded in the face of the challenge. Ah, good. He was past the pain barrier now.

In London, he decided, the three of them would put up at the Ritz. The best place to make love and laugh and play with the baby. It was where angels danced . . . Where *exactly* had he left his *smoking* . . . Uniform was restricting. How good it was to run so fast . . . To feel this intoxication of fear. To feel so acutely and live so intensely.

Esme never once thought of Alice. She was plain and reliable. That was all.

Lying face down in the long grass at the edge of the meadow, Alice blessed the deep trusting sleep of infants. Probably the papoose arrangement had helped, rocking little Esme, lulling her into longer slumbers than usual.

She had cried only once and that very briefly. Stopping to change her and feed her promptly had paid dividends. Before the bottle was finished, the baby was sleeping again. Shouldering her burden once more, Alice had reminded herself that a pack of twenty-five pounds was less than half of what was expected of infantrymen. She wasn't tired. Her legs didn't ache, nor did her back. All pain was an illusion of weaklings.

Where, in God's name, *where* was Esme? The aircraft's engines should be audible any moment.

Here it came. A murmuring in the distance . . . getting louder. A Lysander, probably. They usually were. Yes. She recognised it briefly, silhouetted against a moon-brightened cumulus cloud. A single engine, high, stubby wings and fixed landing gear. Better be careful. German counter-intelligence might have acquired some RAF planes. Take nothing for granted. Relief can be the cruellest of traps . . .

The ugly voice of the nightjar, away to the right, flooded the whole of Alice's being with gratitude. Esme!

"Darling," in spite of herself, Alice whispered softly to the oblivious child on her back, "your daddy is here."

Wait now, wait for it to come once more. To be sure. Another burst of tuneless nattering. Alice answered the call in the same fashion. She hated doing it. She wasn't as good at this sort of thing as her brother-in-law . . . or as Veronica had been.

He confirmed. Two hoots of an owl. Good. The aircraft was circling. A flash from the cockpit . . . Time to light the candles in the jam jars. A pity Esme couldn't do it but he hadn't laid out the landing strip.

He saw her, taking her back load for a rucksack. Once he

understood the strip's orientation, he broke out from some bushes, running at a crouch to help her with the flarepath.

With the sound of safety throbbing so close now, some conversation was unavoidable. They were standing out in the open.

"Where's Veronica?"

Alice's ruse began to unravel. She took a torch from her pocket and flashed the agreed 'all clear' signal to the pilot. Esme dashed the torch from her hand.

"I asked you where my wife is . . ."

"She's here. She's coming. Slow. That's why I'm carrying your daughter."

Honed by many months of living on the edge of a precipice, Hansard's mental warning systems flashed on like high wattage light-bulbs. He grabbed his sister-in-law by the lapel of her jacket.

"Slow? You lie. My wife is like me. A *chamois*. Where is she?"

Alice had feared this all along. If Esme knew his wife had been killed by the Germans he would try and take some suicidal revenge on her murderers. He would refuse absolutely to leave. Alice knew him. She didn't much like him. He had always been a liability in her eyes. A cool customer, yes. But flashy. A wild card. Lacking in everyday common sense. Not a good team man. A *prima donna*.

"Esme," she improvised, shouting now, above the noise of the propeller, "I can't tell you . . . Too long. Veronica's been taken out. Drummond will brief you. For God's sake, just get on that plane . . ."

It was down now. The pilot threw open the hood of the cockpit and beckoned them urgently. A frantic gesture. It didn't look as though he intended to kill the engine.

"Come on! Let's get out of here. It stinks."

"Windy bugger," Esme said in English.

It was as if he believed Alice's story. She felt some of the tension go out of his body. He took her arm and ran with her towards the Lysander. That's when a searchlight sliced up the darkness.

"*Halte!*"

A machine-gun started chattering. There were figures all around. Bowl-headed demons rising up from the meadow's deep-shadowed margins, spitting flames from their guns.

Esme pushed Alice up the ladder to the cockpit. The pilot wrenched her in by the arms. The baby was crying. Turning to help her brother-in-law in turn, Alice's hand closed on air. Esme was standing back waving, kissing his fingers. Making a cradling motion with his arms. Look after our child. Then he ran, weaving and dodging the fire.

17

"Man that bloody gun, if you know how," the pilot screamed, revving the engine. "At the back, damn you!"

Alice crawled to the tail of the aircraft, the child still crying in the papoose. Mind racing, she tried to make sense of the rear armaments. Two 303 calibre machine-guns. She'd seen the type before and got one of them moving somehow. At least she could give Esme some cover.

"Sorry," the pilot yelled over his shoulder, "Your chum's bought it. Let's go."

The Lysander climbed and banked steeply, leaving the chaos below. "That a kiddie you got there?"

"My niece," said Alice. She couldn't understand why her face was all wet. Slowly, unutterably tired, she started to unstrap the papoose. Esme Hansard's daughter needed changing and feeding.

"Christ," the pilot jerked his head round. "You people!"

He saw the glint of grief on her cheeks. He spoke again.

"More room up here. Come on." His accent was Canadian. He reached for something under his seat, careful not to look at her. "Guess you need this more than I do."

He handed a hip flask across. Brandy. Alice stared at him. Liquor was strictly forbidden to pilots on duty, surely. Suddenly he flashed her a broad, friendly grin.

"Just kidding. It's for you. Brigadier Drummond's treat."

Alice drank it, every drop.

She reported next morning to Baker Street in uniform. She had lost weight and it sagged on her angular frame. But Alice was glad to be reunited with her identity again, particularly her FANY flash.

And Esme made her first official appearance in a very stylish carry-cot, borrowed from a third cousin's Curzon Street nursery. Empty now. Those children had gone to the country for safety.

"This is Esme Hansard," Alice saluted her section chief, left-handedly hefting the carry-cot on to the desk. "The only one left. My niece."

Drummond and Vaughan were thunderstruck. Vaughan recovered first and pulled out a chair for Alice, who removed her leather gloves, primly matter of fact as an old-fashioned nursemaid. She was rather pleased with the way that little introduction had gone.

The debriefing was quite quickly over. Alice would need rest, and to grieve. There were just a few stray ends to tie up.

"Have you any idea, Alice, my dear," Drummond said, tapping his pen on a blotter, "who blew the gaffe on Nightjar? You said it was all right until *after* your sister . . . Do please forgive me but . . ."

18

"I did," Alice interrupted him quickly. "I gave Nightjar away."

The two men looked aghast.

"Not deliberately," she reassured them, reading their thought. "It was the Estimated Time of Departure I gave Esme. We're still using the same old code. The Krauts picked it up, threaded it together with the rest of the stuff. They didn't know about Tintagel, of course, so they must have spread out in force all along the ridge on that side of the valley. They may have got a bead on Esme's approach . . . But they were greedy. So they waited until the plane landed, hoping to get the jackpot. They overreached themselves. In the end, they didn't really get anything. No information, gentlemen. I'm quite certain. At any rate, not from us. But with respect, we *must* change that code."

Drummond nodded gravely. Alice's composure was extremely impressive. Most professional. But this all called for a great deal of tact. Congratulation seemed out of place. Thanks . . . obscenely inadequate. Wholly insufficient for this bereaved woman who was managing to speak of her family as if they were coloured drawing-pins on a map in the ops room.

"Tell me something," Vaughan began tentatively. "There's an aspect of all this I still don't quite understand. The child's mother . . . I mean, why did she really think that it was her job to . . . I'm sorry. Perhaps I shouldn't . . ."

"That's quite all right, Major Vaughan," Alice replied. "I'm sure it was partly this. My sister was aware that her husband was . . . How shall I put it? Rash is the best word I can think of. And that he was fast exhausting his credit with what's generally regarded as luck. It would have been over for him sooner or later and I don't think Veronica could face living without him. She loved him, you see, to the point of insanity."

"Yes," Vaughan conceded the point, "But her child . . . You'd have thought . . ."

"That's as I told you. Veronica, as you know, proposed her own extra layer of cover and developed it her own way. It was very successful. I would never have thought of it. And could never have brought it off. I am not, you see, gentlemen, as she was, a desirable woman. I shall never bear a child of my own . . ."

Vaughan cleared his throat but Alice waved his sympathetic demurral aside.

"Sorry. Wandering off the point. The truth is that my sister was a passionately responsible officer. I was inclined to forget that myself. Living day in and day out with someone who'd become a tawdry little guttersnipe . . . But *she* never forgot who she really was or what she owed to the service. She felt her masquerade had endangered the

19

mission . . . and me. She took the responsibility. An officer's privilege, you'll agree."

Alice looked up, her eyes desert dry.

"And I," she grated, "take responsibility for the loss of Captain Hansard. I misjudged the situation, gentlemen."

There was silence in the room.

Responsible? Well, technically speaking, yes, of course. Acting as scapegoat for unattributable blame was an officer's job. But Alice had misjudged nothing. There was absolutely no question, thought Drummond, of her carrying the can. She had done all she could to save Hansard.

Desirable? Vaughan asked himself. In the ordinary sense . . . no. He looked down at the photographs of Alice and her sister, affixed to the inside covers of their respective files. The same features in each case rendered a different sum. Veronica's total had been delicate beauty. Her elder sister's was a comfortable, puggish ugliness. But in her sturdily considerate self-control she was dear, immeasurably so. And honourable beyond admiration. Bletchley had better get on to that bloody code.

A glance passed between the two men.

Brigadier Drummond, late of the Grenadier Guards, and Major Vaughan of the Royal Fusiliers, rose to their feet and stood to attention for a full fifteen seconds. It was the only possible thing they could do.

Alice was not overawed. She remained still, accepting graciously, on their behalf, the tribute to the parents of the child who lay sleeping before her. It didn't cross her mind that the compliment was intended primarily for herself.

"Thank you, gentlemen," she said quietly. "My sister and brother-in-law would have been honoured."

"And now," smiled Drummond, lifting Esme out of the cot without further ceremony, like the competent grandfather he already was, "are we likely to be taking this young lady on the strength?"

"For the duration, Brigadier, yes," Alice said stoutly. "I think that would be best. We've been through a lot together. I can't lose her now."

Army rules are rigid and brittle. Most can be broken when special circumstances dictate.

Alice Winstanley spent the rest of the war up in Kincardineshire, at Strathlairn Castle, one of SOE's secret training establishments. She had a great deal to teach. Skills she passed on effectively, defending her privacy with an increasingly crusty demeanour.

She was allocated a spacious flat in the castle itself and had an ATS girl put at her disposal who made an excellent batwoman and nanny to Esme. Such arrangements were highly unusual, if not unique.

Esme's own memories of those days were non-existent apart from two or three flickering impressions. She retained a vague consciousness of having been venerated by an endless stream of khaki-clad visitors to her nursery, as some sort of relic. Something left over from an important event.

3

1964

"Esme! Esme! You have *five minutes!*"

A smile of satisfaction brushed over Esme's sleeping features. Five minutes to spare. Her syndicate would finish first. She launched herself off the vaulting horse, feet dangling like a crane's . . . She should tuck them up . . . The crocodiles in the coconut-matting torrent below might jump up and bite them off . . . The others had got across safely thanks to her astute bridging arrangement with boxes, stick and rope . . . But she would have to fly. They had all listened to her in the end. Did leaders who finished the exercise without feet lose marks . . . The scribble of the DS major's pen racing over his clip-board was deafening.

Esme woke. Exhilaration and anxiety died away in seconds. Her aunt's Jack Russell bitch, Gimlet, was worrying her toes, emitting deep-throated growls of mock aggression. Twitching her feet under the candlewick counterpane for the dog's further amusement, Esme watched her impassively whilst restoring the events of the past few days to their proper chronology.

The Regular Commissions Board, held at a large, grey country house near Westbury in Wiltshire, was over two days since. A hundred or so boys and girls, mostly direct from public and grammar schools, along with a few serving soldiers from the ranks and fewer still from universities, had shown their paces to the army in a series of tests, exercises and interviews, and within forty-eight hours, dispersed to every corner of Britain to await the army's verdict.

There would be no news today, Esme was sure. Officer candidates left behind them such a plethora of notes, of scores, of myriad

23

impressions; it would take time for the Directing Staff to compile them, distil them and make comparisons. To offset a brilliant 'lecturette' against a lumbering performance on the assault course . . . Not the same one for boys as girls, of course.

Recollecting the girls' set of a dozen obstacles erected in the gym, Esme grinned. Daunting as it had looked, it had turned out to be a stroll. More to do with mind than muscle . . .

"Oh, well *done*, Number One," the Women's Royal Army Corps colonel with the exciting red patches on her collar had enthused, as Esme had plopped, leisurely as a cat, from the last swinging rope. 'Well done, indeed."

For a moment, Esme had half expected to be offered a congratulatory lump of sugar on the flat of the colonel's leather-clad palm.

"Did I have a clear round?" she remembered asking pertly, inspired as much as anything by the bystanding cavalry major's butterfly-cut riding breeches. There came no immediate answer but energetic pen scratching on the major's clip-board. Then, lips quirking, he had remarked, "I think we needn't keep Miss Hansard from her haynet any longer."

Flushing at the memory of herself exiting at a collected, high-stepping trot, Esme wondered if she hadn't overcooked that joke somewhat. The whole thing had been such a tempting opportunity for showing off. Too late to worry now. And too early. It would be ages and ages before a massive government department like the Ministry of Defence could get itself into gear, she reasoned. There would be weeks, yet, of peaceful ignorance to enjoy.

Gimlet was licking her paws now, only her legs were so short she always missed and merely succeeded in wetting the counterpane instead . . .

"*Esme!*" Alice Winstanley's voice bellowed irately from the foot of the broad, stone stairs. "Get up! Is this the way you carried on in Edinburgh, slummocking in bed like some dockside trollope at eight o'clock in the morning? And I hope you haven't got that damned dog on your bed again."

The more Alice loved a creature, the more she cursed it.

Rolling out of bed, Esme snatched her dressing-gown and pounded as noisily as possible along the wainscoted corridor to the bathroom, wondering for the umpteenth time what Aunt Alice could possibly know of the behaviour of dockside prostitutes. Nothing, she suspected, but argument was fruitless. The few notions Alice cherished, extraneous to her actual experience, were only reinforced by repetition.

And one of these calcified ideas, Esme was thinking as, once back in her plainly furnished bedroom, she wriggled into a jersey and moleskin slacks, was that the wartime ATS's successor, the Women's Royal Army Corps, which Alice herself had resolutely refused to give any help in forming, would have no peacetime job to do.

"Corps? Hah! Corpse, more like."

This opinion, freely expressed at the time, hadn't increased her popularity with her female colleagues, or enhanced her prospects of further promotion. With more medal ribbons on her breast than most other officers in her service, this hadn't troubled Alice. She had already purchased her farm in Westmorland and sent her papers in the day she got the deeds. The projected WRAC, she announced to all and sundry, would soon be out of business whereas there would always be a market for wool and mutton.

Nor had Aunt Alice ever wavered in her view, Esme shudderingly reflected, brushing her hair hurriedly with one of the silver-backed brushes her father had given her mother as a wedding present and which Veronica had not lived to use. And whilst it was a decade since Alice had penned her last letter to the *Telegraph* denouncing the government's weakness in pandering extravagantly to women's vanity, it occurred to Esme now, that the blood tie between herself and her famously outspoken relative might be more injurious to her own candidature than helpful. Oh, well. One couldn't help those things.

Maybe nobody at Westbury knew who she was . . . At least her name wasn't Winstanley . . . There had been a book written about SOE with a whole chapter on Nightjar . . . But it was out of print . . .

"*Esme!*" Alice hollered again, just as her niece was thinking crossly that Joan of Arc had had a very easy time of it. Family connections hadn't stood in her way of going down in history.

Throughout her life to date, Esme had oscillated between ferocious pride in being who she was and a passionate resentment that she had not been born in an ordinary way to ordinary parents. There wasn't much to choose between being the child of heroic, dead parents and being the offspring of fictional characters. From time to time it made her feel detached from any organic, biological reality. Someone who really had been brought by a stork . . . Aunt Alice, tall and rangy, was the nicest possible stork, of course.

But the army – and this was something Esme could not explain to anyone, least of all herself – was the living institution under whose auspices her parents had met, married and given birth to her. And the army, unlike her parents, was still there. Inside it, she would feel in touch with all her roots. After all, Aunt Alice had come from so many different places. She had talked of selling Lowlough Farm when Esme was grown up . . . There had to be a place that couldn't change or go away . . .

"*Esme!* How many more times, darling?"

"Yours," Aunt Alice flipped the thick, white envelope from the sheaf of mail she was opening. "Get *down*, Gimlet! I do wish you wouldn't feed her at the table, Esme."

Esme turned her letter over once or twice apprehensively, the toast she was eating turning to sand in her mouth. It bore the MOD frank. Three days wasn't long. She must have failed. Obviously they were clearing the definite 'no's' out of the way first. So she was second rate, after all. Not wanted.

Swallowing, Esme thought she might just be able to adjust to that knowledge if it weren't for Aunt Alice. She'd made it fearfully plain that she didn't care two hoots whether Esme joined the army or not. But that she shouldn't be invited to would be a stigma past bearing. Aunt Alice would take it personally. Because, it *was* personal, wasn't it? You were good enough to hold the Queen's commission or you weren't.

"Well?" Alice abandoned her attempt to appear fully absorbed by a catalogue from her agricultural suppliers. "Aren't you going to open it? If they don't want you, it'll be their loss, not yours. And certainly not mine. Blithering idiots."

Slipping her thumb under the flap, Esme smiled wanly at the way Aunt Alice met any half-anticipated slight to herself with a pre-emptive attack. She was always like that, fiercely protective and not always helpfully so.

Every school report, once analysed and dissected, had become in turn the subject of an intensive typewritten critique by Dame Alice Winstanley, directed to the headmistress, copied to hapless members of staff and the Chairman of the Board of Governors.

If Esme was unsatisfactory in any degree, maintained Alice, it was the task of the establishment favoured with her custom to rectify those defects without whining. That's what they were paid for. And come Speech Day, Alice was to be seen impressing an emphatic sense of their pedagogic inadequacies on Esme's schoolmistresses with the sharp end of her shooting-stick.

Having an embarrassing guardian did tend to toughen one, Esme had once remarked to a friend.

"Come *along*, Esme," Alice badgered whilst Esme took a moment to digest the briefly-worded contents of the envelope. "What do those nicompoops have to say for themselves? I'm too busy for mysteries today."

"They say I'll be a second lieutenant from 7 January 1965, subject to satisfactory completion of six months probation prior to something called gazetting . . . And I'm to report to the WRAC College, Camberley the day before to start an eight-week commissioning course . . . Is that a Direct Commission?"

"Certainly it is," Alice made an unsuccessful stab at smoothing the rictus of pride and pleasure from her face. "No more than I expected. Congratulations," she added gruffly, seizing the better part of a rasher of bacon from her plate and bestowing it on her terrier. "Good job, too. I can't see you putting up with being an officer cadet. Dog's life. Once an intelligent gel's cleaned a lav she's cleaned 'em all in my book. Your mother had it to do, of course. There wasn't any such thing as fast track entry in our day. All that time wasted wrecking shoe leather with spit and red-hot spoon handles . . . A load of rubbish."

"What was? I don't know what you mean."

"Say, 'Please could you explain that, Aunt Alice'," Alice reproved absently, insincerely. Bringing Esme up nicely, as she put it, had always been something she did on automatic pilot. She was apt to forget, too, that Esme was twenty-one years old and a classics graduate of Edinburgh University. Long past the deportment lesson stage.

But Aunt Alice was suddenly in full flood, describing the time-honoured, officially winked at method soldiers had of attaining the mandatory but otherwise unachievable standard of diamond-bright footwear thought essential to the smartness of other ranks. Officer cadets were classed as such and obliged to spend as many hours ruining the tax payers' shoes as any ordinary soldier.

Sheer, bloody hysteria, Alice told herself, listening to her own voice rabbiting on about shoe polish. Probably all out of date anyway. It was difficult to remember, sometimes, that she'd resigned her commission eighteen years ago. Nearly a lifetime to someone as young as Esme. The very thought of her niece in uniform made her feel queasy. Brought too many bad memories back. Her own fault, of course. She'd talked so much about those old days. The best and worst of times in her otherwise uneventful life. There was far too much of her old junk in Esme's head. But reminiscence had painted the winter evenings when Esme was home on holiday from school. Chased away worries when the farm books wouldn't balance. Until a few years ago there'd been no television at Lowlough. No mains electricity either. Too remote.

"Never," Alice stuck out her lower lip, tapping the toast rack with the tip of her knife peremptorily, "go around in bulled-up shoes. It shows a brutish preoccupation with small matters. That's the best advice I can give you."

"Thank you, Aunt Alice," Esme said demurely.

27

"Yes, well," Alice regarded her niece through narrowed eyes. "It's lucky you have a sense of humour. You'll need it. Mind you keep it on a short rein. Not everyone's as lenient with young people as I am. I suppose," she added almost wistfully, "you'll have to get this thing out of your system, won't you? Pleased with yourself?"

"Very," confirmed Esme cheerfully.

"You've a right to be. They're taking one in forty at the moment. I checked."

Esme allowed this new garment of adulthood to settle around her. To her, this news . . . this commission represented a rite of passage as essential as confirmation or coming of age. The mark of twenty-four carat adulthood. Election to a superior state of existence.

"Six months," Alice cut across these transports prosaically. "You've got some time to fill in. What do you want to do with it? I suppose you'd like some cash to travel with . . ."

Hastily Esme disavowed any desire to travel at her aunt's expense. Sheep-rearing on the Westmorland fells barely produced a living some years, never mind a profit. Although these things had always been kept from her, she was aware that, at times, the balancing act between paying the shepherd's wages and meeting the school fees had been precarious.

Fortunately, for university there had been a government grant. But Aunt Alice's best coat and skirt, the lugubrious outfit she wore for attending stock auctions, judging sheep at the local agricultural show and appearing on the Bench, had been her best for seven years past. Nor did she possess anything in the way of personal transport besides the Land Rover, whereas Esme had been given a second-hand Hillman Imp for her nineteenth birthday.

Purely a safety measure, Alice had explained her own generosity away. Better for Esme to leave a party under her own steam than rely on the whim of some inebriated escort. *Youths*, as Aunt Alice called all members of the opposite sex under thirty, were not to be trusted.

"I'll get a job," Esme said suddenly. "The Copper Kettle tea rooms in Kirkby Lonsdale want a waitress . . ."

"Hmm," Alice replied repressively. "Well, we'll see. In the meantime you might get Oberon up from the field and give him some walking exercise. Poor old boy hasn't seen hide nor hair of me for a fortnight. Quarter him first. He's been rolling. He'll have sheep dung in his tail. I've got things to do in the office. And jolly well done, by the way. Clear the breakfast things, won't you, darling?"

Aunt Alice never allowed celebration to get out of hand.

Opening the sideboard cupboard to put preserve jars away, Esme touched the drawer which was always kept locked. She could visualise the contents, lying there in the dark. She yielded to an impulse to look at them. Today of all days, she must see them, touch them.

The key was kept in the Bedermeir bureau, which, like the table and sideboard itself, had furnished Grandpa Winstanley's apartment in Paris. The pale, exotic wood looked strange in this low, black-beamed room. All wrong with the dim winks of light from the mullioned windows. Aunt Alice had talked of sending it to a sale room many times, since it was evidently worth something. Esme had begged her not to. The furniture and a few leather-bound scrapbooks of cuttings were all they had left of her grandfather. Things meant a lot, when the people who had owned them were permanently absent.

Grandpa had been a newsporter reporter. Esme knew that much. It never occurred to Alice, who had seen so little of him herself, that journalist, even distinguished journalist, might have been a fairer description. Sustained by a literary diet of *Farmers' Weekly*, and the Court page of the *Telegraph*, with an occasional assault on that journal's leader, Alice remembered her father as a selfish Bohemian scribbler. They had never been close.

Esme had met her grandfather only once, when she went to collect her parents' *Croix de Guerre* from a French general. Waiting with other people in that windswept courtyard outside Les Invalides had been tedious. Esme, three years old at the time, hating her grey, double breasted coat with its navy velvet collar, had wanted to go home.

Afterwards, Esme and her aunt had gone to lunch with Grandpa Winstanley, who was too feeble to attend the ceremony. He sat at the table, she remembered, with a rug over his knees, a bottle of whisky at his elbow. They had eaten a long parade of dishes which the old man, as he seemed to Esme, had only picked at. And then Esme had wanted to show him the two crosses the general had given her that morning. Unaccountably, Grandpa had begun to cry. Esme had been hustled away from the table for a nap. Poor Grandpa.

He died of an intractable pulmonary disorder a few months later. Internment in Fresnes prison followed by starvation and ill treatment in La Verte concentration camp had put paid to his powers of recovery.

After a lifetime's attachment to his typewriter and the malt whisky he preferred, he'd left nothing behind save the remainder of his lease, his furniture and the scrapbooks. Esme's fingers closed on the key to other memorials.

The sideboard drawer, which had once contained Grandpa's cigars, still smelled faintly of Havana tobacco. Unconsciously, Esme recognised this odour as that of her parents. The incense which perfumed their relics. The scent rushed up at her now, as she slid open the small household shrine. Always there was this feeling of heightened emotion. Excitement and longing.

Everything was there. The two Croix de Guerre . . . the two Military Crosses. Photographs of her parents in uniform . . . of herself holding their decorations. Esme had also been to the investiture at Buckingham Palace. A nice place full of red carpets, good for sliding on in her new patent shoes. Nobody stopped her.

For a long time after that day, Esme had regarded herself as being quite on terms with the King. He had thanked her for having such a brave Mummy and Daddy. It had, he said, been a very lucky thing for England.

"I was brave too," Esme had pointed out firmly. "I came a very long way in a basket."

This had made the King's tired, drawn features light up. He laughed, Esme distinctly remembered. She'd found herself bounced away from the Presence rather smartly. It had often been the same when she was little. One of those interminable naps intervened just when things began to get interesting.

Today, Esme picked out her mother's commission. The King, dead himself now, had signed it. Her mother had been his *trusty and well beloved* . . . The words brought a lump to her daughter's throat. Words that had made Veronica Winstanley somebody special. Someone, like her father, who'd proved that specialness beyond any dispute.

Holding each citation, commission, each medal . . . all intrinsically valueless, Esme communicated with her parents. Told them her news, solicited their blessing and support. Caressed by fragments of paper and metal that trailed clouds of glory from regions not quite reachable. Too distant by a short handspan to touch. But the breath of Esme Hansard and Veronica Winstanley blew warm on their only child's skin.

Esme shut the drawer and locked it, tears pricking at her eyes. She swallowed hard. Aunt Alice must never know about these excursions into pre-remembered existence. Practical, commonsensical, unsentimental, she would never understand . . . Might be hurt by her niece's longing for what could never be. Esme owed her everything.

At the far end of the long, low house, Esme could hear her now. The usual sounds of auntish business. A slamming of antiquated steel filing-cabinet drawers, exasperated expletives and bangings down of the telephone. Nobody ever got to their desk early enough for Aunt Alice. The magistrates' clerk, the veterinary surgeon's receptionist . . . the slaughterhouse directors and the hunt secretary. Slovenly layabouts, every one of them.

"Good heavens, Esme," she said a moment later, catching sight of her niece through the open office door as she joggled the trolley down

30

the hall's uneven flags. 'Still here? Leave that for Mrs Fairbairn. Can't have you stuffing inside like this. Lovely day. Get outside and see to Oberon, can't you? Take Gimlet with you. She could do with running off some fat."

At eleven o'clock, Esme came indoors again after a desultory ride on her aunt's elderly hunter. He was grass fat and disinclined to contribute much to any blood-stirring fantasy of Esme's about cavalry actions. No, definitely not a charger this morning. Gimlet had covered more ground than they had.

They had gone as far as the next homestead up the fell, a derelict pile of stones now. Aunt Alice owned it but when the last tenant had died, she'd taken the bracken-infested hill pasture under management for her own stock. You needed four acres of that stuff to support a single ewe.

A copse or two of deciduous trees flourished on the bottom land but up there, on the thin soil, little survived but the short, coarse grass the Dales sheep managed to thrive on.

Poor but pretty, in its wild and woolly way, that was Lowlough. At least it was on a summery sun-lapped day like this. In winter it could be a savage, storm-raked wilderness, tormented by wind and rain. When snow came, as late as May, it banked high against the dry stone walls, covering the huddling sheep. Esme had helped to dig them out once or twice. It was all right for the ewes. They could generally take it, but not the lambs. Aunt Alice and her shepherd thought they could smell snow but they couldn't always, or not in time. Some years it had been too late to fold the stock.

Further up there was heather. Good for nothing but a fluctuating population of grouse, it bloomed gloriously in August, making an oceanscape of amethyst.

Alice let the shooting, prudently retaining a half-gun for the future use of any nice young man of Esme's. Esme herself had no idea this facility existed. Dame Alice, a judicious guardian, knew what kind of courtship she wished to encourage and which she didn't. Leather-jacketed undergraduates found little favour in her eyes.

Lowlough's farmhouse, joined to its barn, shippon and single stable, which made it seem much more extensive than it was, sat a third of a mile above the valley bottom road. It perched snugly enough, thick walls clothed in whitewashed render, stone-slated and lavishly fenestrated for its date. Early eighteenth century, it looked older. Architectural fashions had taken a century or more to travel this far north. The storm porch, an addition of Aunt Alice's, had blended in fairly well, with its own matching rooflet and miniature mullioned windows to the side. As well as being useful for shrugging off raincoats and gumboots, it protected the carved initials of some proud yeoman and his wife, which decorated the original front-door lintel, from further weathering.

Often enough, Esme had suggested that her aunt add her own initials. Agreeing, Alice never had. There always seemed to be something more urgent that needed doing. When she had bought Lowlough in 1947 as a self-financing home for herself and Esme, she had been attracted, so she claimed, by the place's austere nature which matched her own. There was some truth in that, no doubt, but the low cost per acre compared with lush, southern water meadows had encouraged the preference.

Leaving Oberon to pick his own way down the fell side, Esme noticed the stand of spruce her aunt had planted soon after coming to Lowlough. Had the timber price picked up lately? It must be nearly ready for cutting now. She didn't know that the small plantation was earmarked to pay for her own wedding. Alice, who spoke often of the past, was reticent about future plans.

Wrenching off her boots with the iron jack in the porch, Esme reviewed her own short-term prospects with mild concern. Dear as it was, summer, autumn and the beginning of winter at Lowlough promised to be achingly slow. Unless, that was, she could borrow a mount to compete on at the Lakeland Show . . . That was one possibility, Esme realised ruefully, more likely to cost than pay. There would be a share of shoeing, boxing . . . And her old black jacket had been rained on till it was blue-green with age. Not fit for an appearance in smart showing circles . . . And no self-respecting show-jumping woman wore anything but navy, these days.

After lunch, Esme decided, she would change and go and see about that waitressing job. She would be very efficient, write things down and use a tray. The service at the Copper Kettle was badly in need of reform.

"Well, I never," Mrs Fairbairn lifted the battered steel coffee percolator off the Rayburn hot plate at Esme's appearance. "Going for a soldier, then. That's what your auntie says. You'll be off to foreign parts like as not . . ."

"Thank you, Mrs Fairbairn," Aunt Alice put her head round the door with her glasses on. "We'll have that in my office. Come along, Esme. Don't go holding poor Mrs Fairbairn up. She's got the bedrooms to do."

Sighing, Esme followed her aunt out of the kitchen. She recognised the signs. Aunt Alice in her spectacles was dangerous and the usual vacation enquiry into her overdraft was due. A severe dressing down followed by a lecture about responsibility, rounded off with a bailing out cheque. This time, Esme promised herself, she would refuse. She wasn't a child any longer. Not even a student. On the contrary, she was about to be trusty and well beloved . . .

"I've been on to the War House," Alice announced from the cratch chair she did her office work in. "I've told them you're going on the next Camberley course, or you're not going at all. Can't have a young girl lounging about here all summer. Not suitable. Naturally, they saw the point. First time my Widow Twankey title's been the slightest bit of good."

"Oh," Esme said, taken aback, "When is the next course?"

"The day after tomorrow. You'd better take the Bean Can into Kirkby Lonsdale and get the oil and so forth seen to. And get the thing washed and waxed while you're at it. Tell Briggs to put it on my account. Can't have my niece showing up in muck order. Well." Alice fixed Esme with a belligerent stare, "Hurry along with you."

Kissing her aunt lightly, Esme resisted the impulse to hug her. Aunt Alice wasn't good at that sort of thing. Just at giving everything you wanted.

Later in the day, when Esme was absent from the house. Alice opened the drawer in the dining-room sideboard herself.

"Well," she addressed the assemblage of objects here. 'It's the last thing I wanted. But safe enough, I must say. That lot haven't got their fingernails grubby since formation. De-clawed, non-combatant kitties. Not like you and me, dears. Still, she'll come to no harm."

Alice flip-flapped away down the hall, chippering the notes of the nightjar under her breath. She still wasn't very good at it. Maddening.

4

"*Squaaad . . . Halt!*"

Conscious of a trailing shoe-lace, Esme gave her best efforts to attaining an heroically vertical stance. Shoulders back, head erect, bottom and chin tucked in. The army was indifferent to the graceful alignment of the female jaw and neck. It would, in fact, be happy to dispense with this inconvenient junction in human anatomy altogether, according to the RSM. Dedicated drill sergeants all had double chins. But, Miss Blenkinsop had added kindly, officers need not strive for this.

"*Aaat . . . ease!*"

Executing the spine-jarring transfer from one uncomfortably rigid posture to the next, Esme regretted the manoeuvre gave no opportunity for a glance at her wrist-watch. The parade ground was baking hot and storming up and down it had gone on long enough. Nor was the corrugated-iron structure, the only vision available to her strictly focused eyes, in any way refreshing. Quite unredeemed by a single aesthetic virtue.

"Be so good as to enlighten us, Miss Hansard," the RSM's voice carried clear across the asphalt wastes. "What is it about the drill shed that draws you like a magnet?"

Hoping the unauthorised muscular twitch would escape notice, Esme smiled. These tirades of Miss Blenkinsop's, astringent but devoid of malice, were a feature of life at Camberley. "I really wish I knew, Miss Blenkinsop," Esme fluted disingenuously. To get the best out of the RSM, you had to play along. She had to have a straight man.

"Miss Hansard cannot help us, ladies," the RSM's celebrated sigh

35

fanned the sweltering air. "Latin and Greek have spoiled Miss Hansard for plain, common or garden English. I say 'left turn' and as night follows day, Miss Hansard does the opposite. Polarity overcomes her . . . *Stand still!*"

Almost helpless with suppressed laughter herself, Esme heard the giggling some distance away. Judging by what the RSM said, Caroline Clough, Joan Simmonds and the rest were facing the officers' mess.

True, a sense of isolation had overtaken her during the brisk march towards the drill shed, but by then, she had been committed. At Camberley they told you that any decision, even the wrong one, was better than no decision at all. Vacillation was not an officer quality. Single-minded error was preferable to wavering.

"*Squaaad . . . 'tenshun!* . . . Not you, Miss Hansard. As you were . . . Pick up your dressing now . . ."

Miss Blenkinsop went through the routines of dismissal, saluting her troop of Student Officers off the square with profound if ironic courtesy.

Approaching Esme, still rooted to her distant spot, she said, "Captain Mayhew's compliments, ma'am. Would you be good enough to wait on her in her office at your earliest convenience?"

"In other words, now," Esme construed aloud.

"That would be the normal interpretation, ma'am," replied the RSM smoothly. "Nothing obstructs your meeting with Captain Mayhew, I take it?"

"Except that you haven't yet given me permission to move, Miss Blenkinsop. I'm still under your wicked spell, remember."

Released by the RSM, whose mouth never once betrayed the laughter shining in her eyes, Esme strode towards the administration block with a jauntier step than experience of these arbitrary summonses would naturally promote. But grace under pressure, gaiety in adversity, were the hallmarks of an officer. So Colonel Camilla Crump, the Commandant, had stressed in her inaugural harangue, delivered in a ringing baritone. And who, Esme had asked herself a dozen times since then, should know this better than she did herself? She had been born to that inheritance.

It was the last period before luncheon, which would normally be occupied with Pay. A subject Esme disliked even more than the arid personality of Captain Deirdre Verity who taught it. But Caroline Clough, whose degree was in Applied Mathematics (an achievement for which Esme honoured her, believing it took uncommon steadfastness of character to pursue a subject so dull), would explain it to her later. Imprest and PRI accounts were child's play to Caroline. She was a better teacher than dreary Deirdre any day.

36

"Esme," Major Mortlake Rankine-Burke rounded a corner, touching the bull's-pizzle whip he kept clamped under his arm to the peak of his cap in response to her salute. "My word, that was a good effort of yours yesterday. Well done."

One of only two male members of the Directing Staff at Camberley, Rankine-Burke's sole function was to teach map reading to what he jocularly termed a pack of cartographically illiterate girls. That and to help out with discussion groups and seminars on less specific topics like Leadership. His compliment, Esme presumed, glowing with pleasure, referred to her performance at the previous day's set piece symposium on that very subject.

Regarded as a figure of fun in some quarters, Esme appreciated this middle-aged Hussar. She was good at his subject for one thing, and usually in time to enjoy a generous share of the exotic sandwiches and ice-cold hock he always took on map-reading exercises in his one-man leather picnic case, fitted with crested, sterling silver flasks and boxes. Fascinating luxury. Any fool, he told her chummily, could be uncomfortable. The majority of women, he reckoned, were especially good at it.

Three times so far, since the beginning of the Short Course, they had munched and drunk and chatted whilst waiting at a prearranged rendezvous among the Camberley pines or on Bagshot Heath, taking it in turns to scan the horizon through Major Rankine-Burke's field glasses for signs of the errant Student Officers. Ten minutes was the average estimated official time of travel between the starting point and the rendezvous. It had been known to take till nightfall to round up Esme's colleagues.

Mortlake himself put it down to the feminine inability to use a compass or translate a contour line into a physical feature on the ground. Esme herself had a simpler explanation.

After the others had all crashed off into the undergrowth, it would only be a matter of time before Major Rankine-Burke betrayed his location with a whiff of Sobranie tobacco-smoke drifting on the afternoon air . . . a rattle of a Land Rover door as he got out his picnic equipment, or even a flash of the red bandanna handkerchief that he wore tucked sportively into his stable belt, making a pin-point of colour through the leaves.

"Perfectly valid methods," Mortlake tittered as Esme admitted all this to him. "We ought to send you to the SAS for a course in guerrilla warfare. Good old-fashioned initiative's a pretty precious commodity in the army. Getting rare. Want a wad? Smoked salmon today. God, those bloody track suits they issue you girls are awful."

He didn't add that Esme's slender limbs and easy carriage more or

37

less negated this sartorial disadvantage. A fellow couldn't afford to get
fruity with a WRAC girl he found himself alone with in a woodland
glade. The repercussions could be frightful. Pity. Esme Hansard was
what you might call clubbable. Jolly clever too. Worth an extra slice
or two of the pink stuff any day.

Their sylvan tête-à-têtes had largely anticipated the content of the
Leadership symposium. It was staged in the cadet mess ante-room
the following day. Esme had been looking forward to it. Here at last
was something worth talking about. Better than endless forms and
how to write a letter the army way. Staff Duties in the Field, they called
that. Or, in other words, combat writing skills. Terribly terse and totally
incomprehensible.

The symposium, however, began with a pleasingly constructed
paper from an invited lecturer from Staff College up the road. The
conclusions were hardly earth-shaking. Following the crowd was a
squaddie's job. Leading it was an officer's responsibility. Definitions
of Leadership were elusive, as successive generations of military
thinkers had shown. The magic ingredient, it seemed, remained
defiantly obscure.

The paper ended, comment was invited from the assembled Student
Officers and cadets. A fidgety silence ensued. Concerned for the
feelings of the lecturer who must be abashed by the poor response
he'd stimulated, Esme decided to rescue the symposium. It looked
like being a shameful flop.

"Was there anything in peculiarity of dress or manner," she had
quizzed, "that might signal possession of exceptional leadership
ability? Because," she added, "it must take some force of personality
to deviate from military norms . . ."

Mortlake Rankine-Burke smiled gratefully at her.

"I think Miss Hansard has made a valid point," he beamed.

Exterior accidents were *not* reliable indicators, stated Major
Fanshaw, WRAC, who commanded the Instruction Wing, hurriedly.
She glanced with distaste at Mortlake Rankine-Burke's irregular
accoutrements, signifying as they did in his case mere possession of
a private income and disinterest in promotion. Mortlake was
something of an embarrassment. Taken as a whole, the WRAC
College, Camberley was opposed to the spirit of nonconformism.

"Anyone else?" Major Fanshawe scanned the roomful of wary girls
in the hope of some bromide contribution. Throat clearing was all she
got. Planning to berate cadets and Student Officers alike for their
mulish feebleness at a later date, Major Fanshawe was about to
announce the symposium closed when she was forestalled by Esme.

"I can't remember who it was who said effective leadership always involves walking out of step," she said, "Perhaps it was me but . . ."

A gust of amusement met this self-denigrating wisecrack. She went on, ably supported by Rankine-Burke, to finesse several striking illustrations of her point from the Directing Staff, himself included. It was not the way OC Instruction Wing had intended things to go. Esme had hit a rich seam of subversive anecdote. Anarchic tales of triumphs based on flagrant disobedience to orders. The smile Major Fanshawe reserved for 'informal discussions' became progressively more frozen. The discussion, lively now, ran over time by forty minutes. Unheard of.

Esme attached no importance to this circumstance. She was in her element. A good student, she had been taught at university, was always relentless in pursuit of truth. And testing the tensile strength of accepted doctrine was a student's duty.

"Captain Mayhew's ready for you, ma'am," the orderly room sergeant greeted Esme portentously as she stepped indoors.

"Got her sleeves rolled up, has she?" Esme grinned, braced for the customary daily dose of censure. Personal criticism, Aunt Alice had warned, was to be expected in the early stages. So far, it had been plentiful.

"Nothing like that, ma'am, I'm sure," soothed the sergeant, glancing nervously at Esme's hair. "Just a little talk."

"Esme! Come and sit down," Philippa's graduated row of pearl-white teeth gleamed briefly between her precision-tinted lips as Esme was ushered in to her. "Would you like some coffee?"

"Oh, yes, please. Thank you very much. I would."

Unscheduled 'little talks' came with coffee . . . Timetabled 'interviews' never did. Both categories of encounter between individual Student Officers and members of the Directing Staff took place fairly frequently throughout the eight-week Direct Commissioning Course. And then there was the occasional 'word or two' thrown in. The shaping of an officer was a continuous business. Snip, snip.

But if some of the hair-raising tales told by the cadets were true, *they* were positively hacked. The silken severity which characterised the handling meted out to the Short Course officers was replaced in their case with crude hatchet jobs. Compulsory diets for the stolid . . . dated make-up lessons for the soap-and-water faced . . . An eight-month regimen of skin thickening personal reconstruction. They did a lot of floor polishing too, poor things. Cleaned their own shoes exactly as Aunt Alice had described. Incredible. Asked how they stood it by Esme and her friends, the cadets announced with lobotomised docility that they thought such treatment good for them.

Technically other ranks, and five months wiser in army ways, the cadets had been saluting the Short Course officers energetically since the day of their arrival. A compulsory courtesy from their point of view, it had been no kindness to Esme and her companions when, for two days more, they had shambled untidily around the pine-ringed enclave in civilian clothes, helpless to respond to respect they had not earned with anything more impressive than a nod or shy 'Good morning'.

"The army excels at making outsiders feel sub-human," Esme observed to her colleagues reassuringly, between one port of administrative call and the next. "I suppose it sharpens the appetite for inclusion. I imagine that's what's behind it."

She was overheard by Major Fanshawe who marked her down as a person who thought too much. It was awe, not analysis, that was required of newcomers.

Then came the temporary issue of other ranks' uniforms, rank badges, collar dogs and lessons in saluting and being saluted. There were rules and exceptions to the rules . . . as with irregular verbs or English spelling. Learning was by trial, error and reprimand.

Esme and the other five Short Course officers, however, lived in considerable style in the officers' mess, sharing everything with the Directing Staff . . . except an ante-room. The modern, purpose-built concrete, glass and cedar building provided separate drawing-rooms for instructors and instructed. By this means did the Directing Staff preserve a dignified aloofness from their pupils. And both groups could complain of the other in decent privacy.

So Esme, having eaten a good many meals at the same polished teak table as Philippa Mayhew, had some slight knowledge of her. With grass-green eyes and copper hair, she moved like a goddess in her uniform, the undisputed queen of Camberley. Her lightest utterance was given weight by the luxuriance of her person. She must be twenty-seven-or-eight, Esme judged. Boadicea in a Playtex Living Bra.

Liking her, Esme sensed the feeling was mutual. Familiarity, however, was not encouraged. The Directing Staff began to call the Student Officers by their first names on the fifteenth day in accordance with the guidelines laid down by the Commandant regarding social intercourse with the graduate intake. The students, on the other hand, continued to address the DS by their ranks and surnames.

At Camberley there were invisible chalk marks drawn everywhere. Most remained undiscovered until someone or other stepped over one of them. Invariably a 'little talk' would follow. Not a pleasant way to learn a lesson, possibly, but it was the Camberley way. A series of proficiently managed shocks left no external scar on the finished officer. Their existence, none the less, modified her behaviour permanently. That was the unexpressed intention anyway.

"Now," said Philippa, arching a russet eyebrow as she added a trickle of cream to Esme's coffee cup, "Why do you think I wanted to see you?"

"My drill?" Esme hazarded, playing for time, trying to predict from whence the expected attack would come. Philippa was congenial in a general way, but she was DS . . . hand in glove with authority. There were so many things one could do wrong, Esme mused, without the least consciousness of having transgressed at all.

But no, she was assured, it was not her drill. As an officer, she would never in the future form part of any squad. If necessary, an NCO would guide her steps with muttered imprecations from behind.

"Try again," said Philippa.

Guessing games were another Camberley gambit. Esme stifled an exasperated snort. Nobody ever came straight out with anything. Her hair? Well, she wasn't going to invite yet another suggestion that she should cut it . . .

It might be, as it had been once, a matter of having failed to salute a speck moving in the distance who turned out to be Colonel Camilla Crump. But no, the Commandant's dumpy silhouette was unmistakable to Esme now . . . after a full-scale interview.

"Or maybe the results of the Q Administration test . . ."

Esme glanced at her nails, a pusillanimous shade of pink, since a recent 'word or two'. The ginger colour she had thought harmonious with the lovat-green of No. 2 dress uniform had been disallowed. Not disliked . . . but considered too innovative. These detailed comments on officers' turn-out were not restricted to uniform. Plain clothes too must reflect a set of attitudes approved and framed by Camberley. Twin sets were highly thought of for wear on Wednesday evenings and at weekends . . . And tailored 'frawks', as the Commandant called those garments, for the rest of the week. The army recognised no boundary between private and professional life. A whole and homogeneous existence.

Luckily, Aunt Alice had given Esme a cheque to spend on three good 'frawks' and she was well provided in that area. Nor had she, like poor Joan Simmonds, any temptation to undertake domestic labour. Joan, a certificated teacher, had done VSO in Bechuanaland before joining and was used to roughing it. Carpeted for making her own bed, she was given a week to accustom herself to personal service. She must *not* pick up her dirty plate and hand it helpfully to the mess stewardess at meals.

"No," Philippa shook her head, so that a wing of her page-boy haircut blazed across her cheek, "not your test results. Although I'm

41

bound to say, Esme, I think it showed some discrimination to confine your essay on using words instead of numbers to identify army forms to a separate page. It enabled me to remove it before OC Instruction Wing saw it . . ."

"But I meant her to see it," Esme wailed. "I thought she'd be interested . . ."

"No, Esme. Field officers are never interested in suggestions from probationary Second Lieutenants. Even from graduates. Particularly from graduates. It's a law of nature. You must save up all these ideas of yours – and some of them are excellent – until you go to Staff College."

"How soon will I be able to go?" Esme pricked up her ears. It was at Staff College, she had already heard, that all the really interesting things were aired. Strategic warfare and tactics . . .

"Not until you're thirty or very nearly . . ."

"*Thirty!* My brain will die."

"Why should it die, Esme?"

"Because it won't improve with keeping. Brains don't, you know. Mathematicians do their best work before they're twenty-three . . ."

Caroline had told her that. Caroline who had been reproached for suggesting the mechanisation of the Army Record Office over dinner . . . 'shop' talk was unacceptable as conversational material in the mess . . . As anti-social as reading a book at breakfast time instead of the permitted newspapers. Pressing for the rationale behind that ruling, Esme had been told she must just accept it.

"That's the trouble with you graduates," dreary Deirdre had snarled when issuing the correction. "You always want a reason for everything."

Certainly Esme wanted explanations for every single thing. Caroline, on the other hand, said that there were none and expecting them was a waste of time. Caroline was so sensible she made Esme want to scream.

"Well, we're not here to talk about the keeping qualities of your brain," Philippa squashed Esme's scholastic ambitions hastily. Esme's brain, or what she did with it was exactly the problem, as it happened. OC Instruction Wing was keen to see less evidence of it in future. Esme was here to learn what she was taught . . . not upset the Directing Staff. A question here and there was one thing, instituting full-blown debates was another.

"You see, Esme," Philippa picked her way cautiously, watching storm clouds gather in the younger girl's grey eyes, "We all know you're highly capable . . . Quick to catch on to most things . . . and we enjoy your company in the mess but sometimes your approach is just a little too, er . . . cerebral. Do you see what I mean?"

"No," Esme frowned, "Not really. Why else would the army take to recruiting graduates unless it *wanted* cerebration . . ."

"Mmm," Philippa eyed Esme keenly. She didn't voice her private opinion that the policy-makers hadn't reckoned with the volatile nature of intelligence. Esme herself had said it. It wasn't a substance that remained inert in storage.

She was frank with Esme.

Doubtless Esme was used to the company of quick-witted people like herself but the army wasn't that kind of mental playground. Camberley was not a college in the way she understood the term . . . Not a place for proposing new ideas. Only a place for reinforcing old ones. A production line for the formation of officers along traditional lines. She must realise too, that whatever civilised appearance might be given to things, there was a limit to the amount of free discussion – even with graduates – that was allowable in an establishment like this. Yesterday's seminar had been a case in point. Esme had seized it and by the end it had got out of control.

"You mean," said Esme beadily, "there's a difference between training and education. One's restrictive and the other's permissive. I seem to have mixed them up."

"Exactly. As usual, you put it very well. And Esme, some of your jokes . . ."

"Jokes?" Esme questioned woodenly.

"Yes, they're a little near the bone. Let me give you an example. Do you remember the time you and I first met?"

"Yes. You helped me and Sergeant Smith with all my luggage. You were extremely kind . . ."

"But Esme, were *you*? Remember what I said to you when I left you alone to unpack in your room?"

"Well, yes," Esme was taken aback. "You said, 'We usually wear a dress for dinner,' I said, 'It must be a large one if we're all to cram into it' . . . It was only a *small* joke, if you can call it that. I'm a classicist. I can't help noticing grammatical . . . oddities."

Philippa laughed, a low, drily attractive gurgle. "You're improving. I bet at the time you'd have called it a grammatical *lapse*, wouldn't you?"

"Probably," admitted Esme. "But you laughed . . . So why . . ."

"Yes, I did laugh. Partly because it was funny to be kicked into touch by a brand-new Student Officer who hadn't been in the mess five minutes."

Angry and confused, Esme flushed. Philippa thought her bumptious. The last impression she had ever wished to give.

43

"I must have seemed appallingly rude. I'm sorry. I think perhaps I was a little nervous."

No you weren't, Philippa thought bitterly, hating the task of chipping away at Esme's confidence. Because that's what her brief amounted to. The only consolation was that it would have been so much worse if OC Instruction Wing had done the work herself instead of yielding to Philippa's persuasion to delegate this interview. Major Fanshawe's touch was too heavy for delicate material like Esme Hansard.

"We always seem to be picking on you, Esme," Philippa went on earnestly. "Please understand it's only because we all want you to succeed so much. The Commandant takes a particular interest in you . . . She was a great admirer of your aunt's . . ."

Disarmed, Esme smiled, a ravishing, sun-drenched smile that warmed her eyes to lilac-blue. Aunt Alice would be thrilled, in her craggy way, to know she wasn't quite forgotten. Of course, the Commandant wore a FANY flash . . . She was a member of that stillborn female mounted force that was the ancestor of the ATS and WRAC . . . Esme had touching faith in soldiers linked however tenuously to horses. Look at Major Rankine-Burke . . .

"Good," Philippa was relieved to see the 'all forgiven' signal. One that most of the DS had remarked upon at one time or another after a tricky passage with Miss Hansard. "I knew you'd take it well."

"You mean you'll pass on my agreement in principle to close down half my mind. All right, all right," she held up her hands in surrender. "No more red herrings. Only serious questions."

Philippa was ready to tear her hair out by the roots. Even Esme's gesture was faintly insubordinate. Second Lieutenants did not use their hands in speech. They kept them submissively folded on their laps if sitting . . . or if standing, by their sides. Esme would not come quietly. But the WRAC, the older girl considered cannily, would not lightly let her go. Looks and spirit were at a premium and the Corps' wastage rate was high. Even so, they might find they had bitten off more than they could chew with the Hansard child.

"C'mon, young cobber, let's go to lunch. Let's see if you can walk as far as the mess without upsetting anyone."

It was odd, Philippa reflected, rising to put on her hat, how Esme's name had been tacitly excluded from the 'shop' rule in the DS anteroom. She was like the weather. Her ups and downs affected everybody's mood. And her drill was a daily comedy which sent the entire administration staff thronging to the windows overlooking the parade ground.

Mortlake Rankine-Burke called her the 'two-year-old' . . . Which was not inapposite. Esme did resemble a filly, highly bred and highly

44

strung, packed with known potential and correspondingly hard to train. A challenge posed by quality.

"What does 'cobber' mean?" Esme was intrigued by the unfamiliar word.

Walking back to the mess, she learned that Philippa was Australian by birth and of Irish parentage. The fourth sister in a family of eight, she had come to England nine years ago to do a nannying job. But all along, it had been her intention to join the British army. During her first year in England, working in a Kensington house, she had concentrated on losing her ripe Queensland accent, acquiring instead her present Home Counties vowels . . . Learning the vocabulary and ways of the English people she wished to get along with.

"You should have heard me in the all-night Boots in Piccadilly Circus asking the counter girl for Durex . . . What you call Sellotape . . . She was convinced I was a prostitute."

A linguist herself, Esme was caught up in the mechanics of Philippa's metamorphosis. Hadn't the shape of her face changed with the shedding of all those diphthongs? How long had it taken? How often did she see her family?

"I went back last year," Philippa answered in a warmer tone than the memory warranted, "to my youngest sister's wedding. She's got a baby now . . . and another on the way."

There was no point in telling Esme that she had been tolerated rather than welcomed in her parents' noisy, overcrowded house . . . Drunkenly upbraided by her father for becoming a stuck up pommie bitch . . . And told by her mother that she was now permanently on the shelf. She should have married the cane plantation owner's son who'd been hot for her when she was seventeen. But oh no, Lady Muck had been too busy with her poxy school work . . . As for that poisonous, lying accusation of rape she'd made against him which had come close to losing Dad his manager's job . . . So what if young Norm had come on a bit strong? Was that a reason to chuck away her chances . . . What the heck did Philippa expect out of life?

What Philippa had been determined to get herself was a place in life, which, unlike her mother's, wasn't purchased at a price of endless, debilitating breeding. A room to call her own and independent status. Reason enough to reach for a commission in the army.

Men? What could any of them do for her but turn her into a domestic drudge? A lover or two were necessary to her, naturally. Philippa preferred them younger than herself, not over-bright and grateful for her condescension. No he-men. There were enough of those back home. She kept her choice arrangements well away from Camberley. Virginity or its close resemblance was a qualification for key promotion

45

in the WRAC. Married women were wasted women in WRAC eyes. They might survive a posting or two after the wedding, but that was usually that.

Esme, she determined, should probably be told this, or some of it. But not just now.

Combing her hair, side by side with Esme in the mess cloakroom, Philippa wondered what had impelled her to reveal as much detail as she had. Nobody else had drawn her on the subject of her pre-army history.

But Philippa found herself wanting to exchange a token of trust with Esme. She wore brighter armour than the rest. Thinner too. She had been well loved and it showed. Cherished as the apple of a forceful woman's eye, it was marked in the fearlessness of her speech and walk . . . Radiated from her shell-fine features spaced so happily in their shield-shaped frame. She would be easy meat for the envious. A red rag to a coarse old cow. The WRAC harboured quite a few of those.

"Anyway," she said, zipping comb and compact back into her uniform bag, "my stint as an Aussie au pair girl's not for publication. Between you and me, cobber. By the way, what do you think of your hairstyle?"

She surveyed Esme's reflection in the looking-glass critically. The ash-blond braids wound into school ma'amish earphones, Philippa suspected, was the latest in Esme's tongue-in-cheek quest for a uniform *coiffure* acceptable to Major Fanshawe. The effect, witty and unquestionably neat, conformed to written regulations. None of which would spare Esme yet another dressing down if OC Instruction Wing detected any hint of satire.

"What do I think of it?" Esme grimaced, noting how perfectly Philippa had grasped the elipse of English usage favoured by the WRAC. People here generally asked you what you thought of something when they meant they disapproved of it. "I think it suits me and works superbly with the hat. So naturally," she added slyly, "I'll change it."

"Good on you," Philippa patted Esme's shoulder, reverting to her native accents. "We'll have you with red patches on your collar yet. It's all an act, kid."

That voice was to be a sign of their newborn alliance. A private guarantee of friendship outside the superficial structure. A new loop woven into the intricate lacework of sponsorship and patronage which influences individual fortunes in the army.

"Going to the cadet mess party tonight?" Philippa sounded normal again as she pushed open the door into the hall.

"Got to, I suppose," Esme wrinkled her nose. "We all accepted the invitation. Spotty Sandhurst teenagers . . . Ugh!"

"Well, you never know,' Philippa responded lightly, parting from her in the hall. "Duty parties sometimes turn up trumps. And listen, don't give up, will you?"

The appeal was timely. Increasingly dismayed by the narrowness of the Camberley template, Esme had begun to despair of ever fitting into it. But perhaps, as the tenor of Philippa's 'little talk' hinted, it was only a case of turning sideways to slip, undiminished, through the cutter. Surely, it must be worth it.

"And this is Clive Carson," the teenaged President of the Cadet Mess Committee piped, reaching the end of her recitation of names. "Esme, Joan and Caroline are on the Short Course," she supplied by way of a conversational catalyst. "Commissioned. They've got degrees. White, red or *rosé*? Would you please excuse me?"

As easily as a flea, Esme thought crazily, emitting voiceless squeals.

Neither she nor the individual identified as Clive took a glass from the wabbling tray proffered by a WRAC stewardess. They waited immobile, gaze locked, for the group round them to disperse. Catatonic in this first, ages-long instant of mutual knowledge, their eyes ceased to blink. Valveless conduits conveying the essence of one to the other.

There were no terms negotiated by alternating movements of invitation and reserve . . . Neither smiles nor words. No awareness, either, of music, conversation or circulating canapés and drink. All common sensation was suspended. Time, temperature, taste and smell were meaningless on this transcendent plane of being.

Whoever Clive might be, an arc of crackling light looped between him and her, holding them apart and barring the path which lay between them. Irradiated by such elemental force, they scorched the emptying space around them.

As in a dream, he said to her, "Do you want to dance?"

"No, I don't think so." Esme's voice left her like a thought, without stirring vocal chords or resonating on her palate. Disembodied, like the rest of her.

"Stay there," he commanded quietly, as easily, it seemed to her, as he might direct a limb belonging to his body. He turned from her, and thrust his way into the crowd.

Sitting down to await his inevitable return, Esme felt gravity had lots its power over her. Sitting, standing, lying . . . every atom in her was inflated like a hydrogen balloon. Bombarded with energising particles streaming from a visionary presence. What objective reality could such a phenomenon have? It half occurred to Esme that his rays might be like those of a star defunct millenniums since . . . Mere description made no sense of him.

Clive Carson was about her own age, Esme called his image back . . . four inches taller or thereabouts. His eyes were brown . . . For a man, enormous. Lazy, mesmeric swamps . . .

She saw him coming back towards her, concentrated and contained with two glasses in his hands. He wore his clothes, she saw – a white barathea blazer, a white silk shirt opened to his chest with a long, dark-crimson scarf knotted carelessly about his neck – as a fortunate animal wears its fur. Certain that this perfect covering will renew itself in perpetuity and never be less than totally exclusive. Tailoring bespoke from nature . . . like his brown, waving hair, which sprang thickly from his temples.

Esme did not ask herself how she looked to him. She knew. Whatever she had seen in him, he had seen in her. And whatever that might be, it was beyond the reach of vocabulary.

"What's it like here?" He sat down beside her, his torso turned to shield her from the approach of any other person.

"A cross between a reformatory and a finishing school . . ."

Esme talked for quite a time describing Camberley, its ethos and curriculum, aware that his interest was not in what she said but the way she said it. He listened to the inflections in her voice intently, watching the way her mouth moved and the Gallic legacy which lingered in the accompanying slim, swift gestures of her hands. From time to time his pale, full-lipped mouth with its chisel-modelled edges curled, breaking into a smile like foam on a summer-time bathing beach . . . or retreated, a rapidly-receding tide.

"How old are you?"

"Twenty-one," Esme said. "How old are you?"

"Twenty-three," he answered. "Nearly twenty-four."

This struck neither of them as in the least absurd. In such matters as they had in hand, conventional chronology was critical.

Placing his forefinger on the back of her hand, Clive leaned close to her. An instinctive offer of his smell, allowing her to mark the emanation of healthy masculinity he exuded. Sebum, soap and something else, an olfactory signature that tagged him as her mate.

To him, her skin smelled of wet, wild bluebells. Untrodden territory.

"Who are you, exactly," Esme demanded, drawing away from him. "What are you doing here? You're too old to be at Sandhurst, aren't you?"

Looking down his long, straight nose, Clive flared his nostrils exhibiting delicate comtempt.

"I'm at Mons. It's near Aldershot," he said, leaving Esme no better off than previously. She had never heard of Mons.

Mons was another officer cadet training establishment, he told her. It specialised in inducting odds and sods . . . older cadets. People who, like her, had left universities with degrees, people who, like him, had dropped out of universities without degrees. Overseas or Commonwealth cadets whose governments paid the British government fat fees to train them . . . and other ranks who had attended the Regular Commissions Board and passed it. The Household Division units and cavalry of the line were beginning to prefer Mons to Sandhurst.

"Why's that?" Esme asked, succumbing pacifically to the repeated rhythmic passage of the back of Clive's hand up and down her forearm.

"I don't know," he shrugged. "More amusing people go there, I suppose."

"Yes, but why did you?"

Esme's question, urgent and staccato, left Clive unruffled. Polite overtures would have bored him. Her palpable excitement stirred him as nothing else had done for months. The sheen on her entranced him.

Drawing Esme to him, so that the point of her shoulder nestled into the hollow of his own, Clive began to talk to her. His voice, as near a whisper as full tone can be, rolled over continents of experience that she had never known.

Clive's father was a senior diplomat, now in Washington. His parents had been in Venezuela, however, when Clive had left Harrow and spent the next year as a trainee gaucho on that country's Foreign Minister's cattle ranch. Yes, he had enjoyed it, although one night encamped amongst the pampas grass an Indian had tried to knife him . . . an imagined quarrel about some girl in a shanty town's *cantina* . . .

Pausing here, with a glance at her, Clive quivered fastidiously, seemingly at the remembered imputation of sexual slumming. This drew a cluck of sympathetic indignation from Esme and, from him, a grunt of satisfaction.

Subsequently, Clive had left to go up to Oxford. But Balliol sent him down at the beginning of his second year . . . Why? For a number of reasons too boring to relate.

After that, he had gone to join some friends in Italy who were occupying an Umbrian country house belonging to the parents of some friends of theirs. The house was very large, the principal mansion on a great estate.

What he and his friends had done there, Clive seemed unable to describe with much clarity. They had watched the stones grow and drunk princely quantities of wine from the cellars of their absent but unwilling hosts . . . The inadvertent burning down of an unimportant nineteenth-century service wing of the house had, however, intensified their unpopularity with the Conde Domenico Monte Pietro. The Conde, overreacting, in Clive's opinion, to this partial and wholly beneficial amendment to his property . . . and himself a member of his country's Diplomatic Corps, had used those channels to contact Clive's father.

Exercising the only means of parental control at his disposal, Carson *père* had instructed Coutts Bank to discontinue his son's allowance. It was to be restored to him only when he had obtained a place at an officer cadet school and had been provisionally accepted into any regiment foolhardy enough to take him. Once Clive's father was satisfied that an earnest attempt at reform was being made, then he would use what influence he could with the Household Division. He had now done so. And Clive had attended and survived an interview with the Colonel of Queen Anne's Dragoon Guards, a regiment of Household Cavalry otherwise known as the Silvershods. In six weeks' time, Clive would pass out of Mons and join them.

The Colonel's only interest in Clive, or the only one he reported to Esme, had been his record as an amateur jockey over sticks. The regiment owned several steeplechasers.

This account of himself, Clive gave without special emphasis on one incident or another. His delivery, halting, hesitant and laconic, succeeded in making fluency seem spivvy by comparison. Whether by design or accident, he had adopted an existentialist style. No one occurrence was contingent on the last. Life was a series of unconnected events, mostly tiresome. Transient inconveniences. Praise and blame were equally valueless to him. Clive was hip.

Quite properly, at that juncture, he omitted to add that his future Colonel had referred in passing to his mother's close relationship to a premier Scottish Duke or that the additional private income promised him on commissioning would meet the Silvershods' exacting standards. Impecunious gentlemen weren't encouraged to apply to the Silvershods. They would not enjoy themselves.

"Do you ride?" He suddenly enquired of Esme.

"Yes," she said. "No good at anything else, actually. Could never hit, catch or kick a ball to save my life."

Permitting himself an expression of noiseless mirth, Clive regarded her appreciatively. He liked the sprightly rigour with which she spoke. No debby drawl. Unusual.

There was some more talk about the Silvershods. The black helmet plumes they wore on parade . . . The solid gold badges of rank the officers wore on their mess dress . . . The list of tailors and hatters approved by the Colonel for supply of plain clothes to his officers. Who was making Esme's uniforms? Huntsman, Clive conceded, was a sound selection. The Savile Row firm was on his Colonel's list . . .

"So everything's all right," Esme concluded his narrative for him.

"Except," he gravely pointed out, "I'm in the army."

"Won't you like it at all?"

Clive passed over this, commenting that he didn't intend to devote an excessive amount of time to military duties.

Not at all sure how he would avoid it, Esme said nothing. She was certain that a man of Clive's wide experience would know how to maximise his leisure.

Shifting slightly, he became absorbed in his shoes.

"Gucci," he sighed after a period of contemplation. "Quite good for ready-mades, I think. I didn't expect to meet someone like you here. Why did you join the army . . ."

Prepared to be evasive on that point – because lately, she had sometimes wondered – Esme found it unnecessary. Clive had decided that they would now dance. The floor cleared in the middle of the ante-room was thinly populated as most couples had moved out on to the adjoining terrace. The night was sultry, thick and humid. How long they had been talking, Esme couldn't calculate. Eternity had taken over.

They tried a few independent, individualistic steps to a Rolling Stones number, which was not a success.

"I feel completely unnatural doing this," he muttered, pulling Esme into his arms. They swayed for a moment, face to face until the four-inch gap between them closed to nothing and Esme's cheek lay alongside his.

Invaded by a luminous happiness, she couldn't quite understand why there should be an ache akin to grief behind her eyes or a pain sharpening between her legs. Before this, she had never known desire except as mental compatibility linked to optical approval.

"Why did you come here?" The question was torn from her. His only answer was to tighten his arms around her. "We're not doing anything in time to the music . . ." she added a moment later.

"I never do anything in time to the music," he murmured. "I really can't stand this any longer. Can we go to your room?"

"I don't know. It's in the officers' mess . . ."

"Oh yes, you're commissioned, aren't you? Allowed into the parlour . . ."

Esme was relieved. It was too soon to be alone with him, but too soon, also, to be parted from him. It was one o'clock, and the party, in accordance with Major Fanshawe's rules for cadet mess entertainments, was over.

51

"Are you ready?" A man, shorter than Clive with white-blond hair, sharp-nosed and hollow-cheeked, tapped him on the shoulder.

"In a minute." Clive detached himself gently from Esme and placed his arm around her waist, guiding her from the floor out into the noise of engines starting, headlights wheeling in the dark, 'goodnights' and so forth.

Most people, Esme saw, had already gone. The blond man followed and circled them, chivvying them along.

"That's Tiggy," Clive remarked indifferently. "A stateless person. Mongrel German . . ."

Impervious to these insults, Tiggy pranced along beside them until Clive's car, a ton of low-slung metal was reached, some way along the drive. Clive fished in his pocket for the keys, tossing them across the roof to the other man.

"Is that your parade ground?" He peered at the adjacent square, matt silver in the moonlight. "I can't imagine women marching."

Esme knew by now that any reply would only offend his notions of conversational symmetry. Not every statement of Clive's required a gloss. Very few, in fact. Ever sensitive to the verbal, Esme rightly perceived his pronouncements as a form of sculpture . . . To be placed upon a plinth and admired by a crowd of invited *cognoscenti*. So Esme smiled a dark, sardonic smile, the first of many.

"Is she coming with us?" the young Teuton enquired irrepressibly, "I'll get in the back . . ."

"No," Clive said shortly. And to Esme: "Will you be here tomorrow afternoon?"

The following day was Saturday and Esme saw no reason why she should be elsewhere than here. Shopping in Guildford with Caroline could be cancelled. She nodded. He got into the car, still holding her hand, got out again, cupped her face and kissed her fervently on the lips.

"I'll be here at two o'clock. In that ante-room . . . where we were. Sleep well."

Falling in love was as simple and irrevocable as that.

Returning to the officers' mess, Esme avoided the students' ante-room. There was a light on in there and a knot of girls were conducting a post-mortem over drinks obtained from the nightcap tray Sergeant Smith had left out for them. Talk, normally the stuff of life to Esme, was tonight impossible. Only thirteen hours separated her from reunion with Clive. Little enough time to realise her altered state. To study a new grammar of communication.

In her room upstairs, she loosened a lock of hair from her pony tail and stroked it across her nose repeatedly. From childhood, an indispensable aid to concentration. In infancy it had been tufts of plush from her teddy bear's canvas belly. Poor Rummie, he was almost bald now from Esme's early depredations.

The bear, given her by her Aunt Alice's old boss, Brigadier Drummond, when she was still a baby, had always accompanied Esme everywhere. Like the worn, folding leather frame which enshrined the faded wedding photograph of her parents. Daddy in his *képi* . . . Mummy in a foolish hat, holding a huge bouquet and wearing peep-toed shoes. Both of them so ethereally beautiful. Woodsprite lovers. Here yesterday, so history said . . . Gone today if history didn't lie.

Sometimes, examining this icon, Esme wished her parents had looked towards her instead of at each other. Silly, of course . . . They had known nothing about her then, and precious little afterwards. It was she who had always haunted them, not the other way about.

They would be free of her, Esme thought once she was in bed and her mind slipped its daytime moorings. Someone else had come to take their place. Someone rather like them, who faded in and out . . .

"Free ride in the offing?" Tiggy probed as the Aston Martin sped towards Aldershot.

"Shut up, Tigs," Clive said.

"Don't get emotional, Clivey, baby. That's not cool. Know who she is?"

"No, do you?"

Tiggy, bosom friend of Clive since their shared schooldays, was known for official purposes as Prince Heinrich Sebastian Strelitz-Vaarburg-Johannenloe. He possessed an encyclopaedic knowledge of European genealogies, fostered by his much-married mother.

"Esme Hansard? Not a clue. Looks as though she might be someone. No feathers round her fetlocks . . ."

"Maybe," Clive's attention wandered. "Take her out tomorrow?"

"Why not?" Tiggy agreed. "Tea. Nothing *louche* for little Esme. Take it from me, that baby still wears Chilprufe vests."

The assessment there was taken by both to be figurative. And entirely flattering.

Stopping the car outside a run-down house in Queen Anne's Gate, Clive switched off the engine.

"There's a guy in here who doesn't have much fun," he remarked. "Play I Spy with Tiggy. Shan't be long."

In the back seat, Tiggy hummed tunelessly. Esme looked at the house, to which Clive gained prompt admittance after pressing one of several bells. A number of flags flopped from a peeling pole, jutting from above the crumbling portico. Brass plates screwed to the pillars identified the place as a legation building shared by a cluster of small African nations.

"Tozo's one of Clivey's pets," Tiggy interrupted himself long enough to give a foretaste of what might now take place. "His pater's King somebody or other. Eats unwanted callers. That type. You'll like Tozo."

"Oh," said Esme. "Is he going to join the Silvershods?"

"No fear. Going to be Commander in Chief of his pater's army. You know the sort of thing . . . spear chuckers in beat up tanks. Tozo'll have a fruit salad of medal ribbons on his chest from day one . . . Won't last much longer either," Tiggy elaborated amiably, drawing a finger across his throat. "Lot of palace coups where he comes from."

The four of them had tea at the Ritz. Esme poured with dignity and application, the nucleus of an exotic group.

Tozo, raven-skinned and perfumed, lounged in the flowing white robes he wore for weekends in Queen Anne's Gate, crowned with a small embroidered pill box fastened to his woolly hair with a woman's jewelled hat pin. He waved a chocolate eclair expansively, taking bites alternating with puffs at the cigar wielded in the other hand. Tiggy nibbled cucumber sandwiches with exaggerated daintiness, sticking his little finger out when he raised his cup. It made Esme laugh which was just as well since Clive was contributing nothing to the conviviality of the party.

"My, that boy's so butch," Tiggy needled shrilly. "What do you think, Tozo dear? How many maidens did you say a bloke has to despoil to qualify as a brave in your outfit?"

Clive, gracefully semi-recumbent in the small, gilded elbow chair, smiled tolerantly, eyelids drooping. Esme pretended to an intense involvement with the hot water jug.

"Hush, my dear fellow," responded Tozo in his perfect, archaic English. "Not in front of ladies. My mother," he went on tangentially, licking cream from his fingers, "was an Ethiopian slave. Taken in battle, naturally."

Two women in hats turned round and stared.

"Is that the best kind?" Esme curvetted gamely into the conversation. Clive's silence made her nervous.

"They're the hardest to catch . . . Run like gazelle, fight like crocodile . . . You can't breed warriors from purchased women . . . Tell me, what's a nice gel like you doing in the army?"

Esme shrugged defensively. "One has to be somewhere, doing something, doesn't one? Anyway, just think, if I wasn't in the army, I should never have met the three of you."

"Ah," Tiggy interposed languidly, "but will your meeting us be to our mutual benefit, I wonder . . ."

Esme bristled. There were undertones she did not understand here. It was as if she had been subjected to some kind of initiation trial. Or warned off Clive?

Glancing in Clive's direction, she saw he had somehow magnetised the deferential attention of a waiter, who stood, head bowed in muttered conversation with him. The hiss of new currency notes changing hands concluded his transaction.

"I think I shall have a women's army," commented Tozo grandly. "Will you come and run it, Esme? My father will offer you a competitive salary . . ."

"We'll see you guys around," said Clive dismissively. He was suddenly energetic. Esme rose at his touch under her elbow, smiling down on Tiggy and Tozo, looking, as she hoped, graciously remote.

"I think," Tozo pressed his palm to his chest as he and Tiggy watched the departing pair, "that our friend has love in his heart."

"Yah," snapped Tiggy, "could be. Dry Martini?"

Outside Clive steered Esme through the Piccadilly traffic, abandoning her on the corner of Sackville Street to assist two elderly gentlemen who, halt and poor of sight, were tenderly attempting to usher each other across the thoroughfare. Watching him, Esme's heart was strained to bursting point with adoration. She had not even noticed the two old men herself.

Rejoining her, he said: "Come and look at something with me in this gallery and then I think we should have a little rest."

Curious as to how this repose would be achieved, Esme knew better than to ask. Clive's will and wisdom was like that of God. Too old, too sure to question.

5

"I didn't know you were a virgin," Clive politely panted, rolling off her lightly. He stroked the damp tendrils of hair away from Esme's temples. "Why didn't you tell me?"

"I thought it might put you off. Make you nervous . . ."

"Make me nervous!"

Clive's rare, rasping laugh filled the damask-lined cabin of a room. "Oh, you're marvellous! Make me nervous . . . But what about you? Didn't you . . . I mean, how did you . . . ."

"Choose you?"

Momentarily taken aback, Clive was still. He did not associate the power of choice with girls. He selected, they consented. Turning to prop himself up on his elbow, he studied Esme, appreciating the elegance of her make anew.

She was perfect. Every dimension an exquisitely phased progression from the former to the next. No contour of her bone or flesh surprised him but every one pleased him beyond expectation. Revealed, she was as advertised in her clothes. And yet in her inner weave, he detected a thrilling metal threat of wilfulness. She had intended to withhold knowledge of herself from him. Clive respected that in her. They would be good together.

"No, I mean, did I hurt you?"

"A bit," Esme admitted equably. "The first bit was fairly bad. But you were quite right not to mess about. That mistake's been made before. Square at the fence and then you go over, don't you?"

Clive laughed again.

"Cigarette?"

"What, in bed?"

"Of course," he handed her the packet, adjusting her pillows so that she could sit up, "Smoking's traditional after sex. A ritual."

"Well, I must do it then, mustn't I? I never got as far as the cigarette before, though I must say I've tried."

Stretching luxuriously beside her, blowing triumphant wreaths of smoke, Clive exulted. So now he knew for certain. Experienced women did not talk this way to men. She was as unconscious as a baby chatteringly chasing rubber ducks around her bath.

"What went wrong before?" He asked her, brushing his lips impulsively across her naked shoulder. Other men had seen her but had failed her as he had not.

"I never thought the geometry could work. You know. How could *that*, fit into *this*." Esme patted her pubis in prettily graphic illustration, a picture of content.

"And how do you feel now?" Clive thirsted, suddenly, for a compliment from her.

"Greatly relieved to know I'm normal, I can tell you. And happy. Now I know what it's all about. A flash of pain and then you go spinning away on a spaceship into stars . . . or lifted in an eagle's claws . . ."

"Oh, darling," Clive, enthralled, crushed out his cigarette and kissed her, "There will never be any more pain, I promise you."

Glowing, Esme treasured the endearment. It was the first time he had called her 'darling'. And she liked 'never' too. It suggested a 'for ever' flipside to the coin.

The telephone rang. It was Clive's elder brother who owned the tiny apartment in this Carlton Terrace attic. He had dialled the number by mistake and was displeased to get an answer. He presumed Clive was there with a woman and if so, would he see to it that the sheets were parcelled for the laundry and left with the caretaker in the basement. No bloody hairpins on the carpet, no cigarette butts in the ashtrays, no lipstick on the cups. Clive was to be out of there by the following evening when his brother would return from nursing a dismal Cornish constituency which was a bigger exercise in futility than hoping for responsible behaviour from Clive. He wondered sometimes why he ever let him have a key. And so on.

Clive gave Esme a softened précis of this conversation, remarking that his brother was a stuffed shirt who couldn't wait to be Prime Minister. So far, he'd lost his deposit once and now looked like being pipped at the post in a forthcoming by-election by a Liberal candidate. All very boring. Did Esme have any brothers and sisters? No? Then she was lucky. Was she hungry? They would have to go out as there was nothing to eat here.

"But can I walk?" Esme coquetted, playing the invalid a little. She *was* sore but found the sensation agreeable. There ought to be traces of so great a transition as she had been through.

"Let me look," Clive inspected the seat of Esme's complaint with gratifying medical minuteness. "I think," he said, "A warm bath for both of us and Vaseline for you. Brave girl."

They had a good deal of fun with Clive's brother's expensive unguents, poured out of cut crystal flasks with repoussé silver caps.

Evidently he was a great collector. His little *pied-à-terre* was like a section from a carefully preserved antique doll's house, crammed with old and precious things. Like the bed they'd made love in . . . A fruitwood boat-shaped thing cornered with ivory swan's head finials; spectators with chalcedony eyes. Esme had been sorry to learn it wasn't Clive's. She wished he'd told her. Would he . . . could he have a place like this of his own soon?

Longing to know the answer, Esme knew she couldn't ask. It saddened her to discover that the greatest physical intimacy did not, after all, confer the right to have curiosity satisfied.

"Good," Clive said, sniffing the scented steam rising from the bath, "A witches' brew of degeneracy. Get in. No, you go there. A gentleman always takes the tap end."

They ate in a dark, throbbing place near by, riotous with other lovers and loud-voiced gangs of imperious youth, The waiters' names all began with K, Esme noted vaguely, and they addressed their strident customers as 'squire'. Not Clive, however. They knew him but they treated him gingerly, avoiding Esme's glance like harem eunuchs in their master's presence.

Intoxicated by her new-found power, the power of a woman too valuable to look upon, Esme drank the dry Martini Clive ordered for her and wondered what to talk about. Clive himself seemed happy enough to clasp her foot beneath the table with his ankles and pout over the menu's many pages.

Quail's eggs? Did Esme like them? Oh, she had never had them. Goodness knew where they got them at this time of year, Clive said, but they had better have them. If they weren't up to scratch they could go back . . . Was Chablis all right with her? It was boring, Clive acknowledged, but he was too tired to be original. How did Esme feel? Was the racket of these awful people bothering her? Perhaps they should leave and go to the Savoy. Nice and quiet. Middle-aged and middle-classed, as he said.

But they didn't go and quite soon, Tiggy added himself to the thickening crowd of 'awful people', blowing in with a half dozen or so of guffawing companions, hung about with squawking, parrot-coloured girls. Sending them off to commandeer a table, Tiggy hung over the back of Clive's chair insinuatingly.

"Nice time, you two?"

"Perfectly nice," Esme replied primly. "Where's Tozo?"

"Doing a rain dance somewhere," Tiggy shrugged. "Clivey? Are you a happy, well adjusted boy this evening? Nothing you'd like to confess to Father Tigworthy? Get it off your manly little chest . . ."

"Clear off," said Clive genially. 'You can come round for a ride with us tomorrow if you want. Say nine o'clock at Jack's."

"Shan't," Tiggy screwed his face up in a pantomime of childish anger. "You two look too boring. So long."

"You mustn't mind Tiggy," Clive commented. "He can't help it."

"I don't mind him," Esme protested. "I like him. I just wish he'd like me, that's all."

"Oh, he does," Clive looked up at her. "That's why he's being such a bore. Can't make friends with girls . . ."

"Only through you," Esme cut across him.

"Sort of. Prefers to pay for women . . ."

"Perhaps he should see a psychiatrist . . ."

"Yah, maybe. He's a very funny guy. Funniest I've ever known. Don't let's talk about Tiggy any more. It's so boring."

Esme fell silent, frustrated but resigned. Clive had the knack of making his decisions final.

She didn't know that Clive had exposed more of himself to her than he did to most people. What she knew was that Clive loved Tiggy and that was all right with her. David and Jonathan were fine. She would have to win Tiggy to her side, that was all. With him would come all the rest. Other friends, other ties and eventually, permanence.

Later, when they were drinking Clive's brother's brandy, Esme asked what 'doing a rain dance' meant.

"It mean's Tozo's chucking up and weeping into a gents' lavatory pan somewhere. Always happens after his sixth dry Martini. Loves it but can't take the pace. We'll check him out tomorrow."

"You say American things sometimes," she told him.

"Got an American grandmother," he said. "Great old lady. Makes handbags out of people she doesn't like."

"Sounds like my Aunt Alice . . ."

"Yes?" Clive yawned tiredly. "Come on, let's go to bed. You going to wash your knickers and things? There's a dryer contraption somewhere."

Clive didn't want to talk about families yet. That was probably right, Esme thought. This was a time for forgetting everyone but themselves.

Even so, she felt herself being pulled inexorably into an enchanted circle.

In the morning he took her to a livery stable in a mews behind a street fringing Hyde Park. It was run by an ex-cavalry trooper, a Corporal of Horse, retired some years ago from the Silvershods.

"Jack," Clive silenced Esme's reminder that she could hardly ride dressed as she was, "always has some spare clobber hanging around."

Jack, a wizened, wily horse-coper, had some riding gear as promised. An old ladies' habit which he pulled from the bottom of an empty feed bin. Shaken out and dusted off, it looked feasible.

"That any good to you, ma'am?" he queried. "Breeks are a shade roomy, but if you could use a side-saddle . . ."

"I can," announced Esme to the little man's evident astonishment. Aunt Alice always hunted side-saddle.

After a few undisturbed moments in the tack room, Esme emerged with the habit's apron concealing the ill-fitting breeches. The jacket fitted well. The boots pinched intolerably but would be better when she mounted. A stock, borrowed from Jack himself, bowler and varnished bamboo stick completed Esme's makeshift equestrian outfit.

"Looks the goods, don't she, sir?" the liveryman leered slyly, leading out a spindle-fine grey for Esme. "She is a bit sharp is this one, ma'am, but she goes well under a side-saddle and she'll not have you off if you show her who's boss. Real ladies' mount. Jericho do for you, sir?"

Clive regarded Esme quizzically. She looked very well indeed.

For her part, Esme wouldn't meet his eye. This was a new moment of truth. A cavalryman's woman should show herself able when it came to mastering man's oldest symbol of authority and nobility. Watching the mare's diminutive hooves strike sparks on the cobbles, she experienced a moment's inexplicable self-doubt. The creature was crazy with her corn.

"The horse," Esme mumbled, fiercely rallying herself, "has not yet been born . . ."

"Will I put you up, ma'am?" Jack enquired, steadying the skittish mare. "She's called Habibi. Drop of Arab blood."

"More than a drop, I should say," Esme stuck her foot out for Jack, gathering the double reins without fuss or fumbling.

"Oops a daisy," chaffed Jack, rather rudely, as she alighted neatly in the saddle, "To the manner born, eh, sir?"

Whatever the response from Clive, now astride a big bay discharged-officer's charger, Esme ignored it proudly. To the manner born indeed, she growled inwardly, pulling in the girth. Of course she was born to it. Aunt Alice was a FANY. Really, people thought that just because you didn't live in London you were a complete

hobbledehoy. Or looked pained when you showed you weren't. Clive
had already pointed Harrods out to her as if she were a foreign tourist.
She'd rapped his knuckles for that.

"I come from Westmorland, you know, not another galaxy."

"Ready?" Clive touched his leather-covered cane to his cap in
response to Jack's two-fingered salute. "Back in an hour, Jack."

"Right you are, sir. No hurry. Those two aren't wanted before this
afternoon."

Frighteningly, Habibi shot across the Bayswater Road as if jet-
propelled, missing a lumbering bus by inches. Once safely on the turf,
Esme let her have her head, guessing she'd come back to hand if she
sensed her rider was unafraid. Clive, who never gave advice to anyone,
saw it would be both unnecessary and unwelcome. Esme, straight-
backed and brave, could definitely manage.

They overstayed their hour in the park by a considerable margin,
lost to any sense of time. Riding through the heat-hazed midsummer
Sunday morning with all the church bells ringing.

"Race?" Clive proposed when they had stood awhile beneath some
elm trees letting the horses crop the grass.

"No," Esme demurred. "I don't know this horse and she's not mine.
Canter."

So they cantered, rocking side by side, swishing through the long,
seeding grass. Esme could never have imagined passing into
womanhood so beautifully. Clive understood suddenly why all the
greatest works of art were calm. Remarkably unremarkable. But he
didn't mention this discovery. Talking should not be overdone. They
had talked enough. Esme inspired ideas. It didn't occur to him to share
them with her.

On their return, Jack treated Esme with more respect than hitherto
since she had brought herself and the mare back in two unbroken
pieces. He knew too many girls who rode for 'social reasons'. Miss
Hansard became a person of account in his crinkly, judgemental eyes.

"You've not lathered her then," he said, pulling off them saddle.

"No," said Esme. "Is she prone to lathering?"

"As a rule," said Jack laconically, eyeing Clive.

Not prone to lathering himself, Clive was greatly incommoded by
the size of his erection. They went back to Carlton Terrace and made
love for the fourth time.

"Get rough," Clive said hoarsely in the middle of it all. "Cut me up.
Use your nails."

"Honestly?"

"Honestly. Oh, Esme, *Esme!* . . ."

Afterwards they sorted through the contents of Clive's brother's wonderfully well-stocked medicine cabinet.

"That stuff," said Clive seizing upon gentian violet. "Look, it's got a brush. Put some on my back. Lots."

"Won't it sting?" Esme hesitated, dismayed at the damage her nails had done.

"Yes. I want it to. It's half the fun. Reminds me of having grazed knees when I was a little boy. Go on."

Clive flinched ecstatically until she'd finished. To avoid staining his hand-made poplin shirt, he put on a clean T-shirt from one of his brother's drawers.

"Never knew why he wore these things before," he remarked. "So damned Yankee. Must be more to Bro than meets the eye."

They went to see Tozo then. Ashen, he was not particularly disposed for company. Too courteous to eject his visitors, however, he entertained them to ham sandwiches in the legation's dreary reception-room. They were brought by a sad-eyed servant, who addressed Tozo as 'Excellency'. In cord trousers and a rather dirty sweater he didn't look too excellent, despite his gallant claims to feeling it.

He would have been delighted, he grizzled hospitably, recruiting all his forces, to have introduced Esme to the Head of Mission. Then they could have had a preliminary discussion about the Women's Army plan. The more he thought about it, the more he liked it. Modern. Unfortunately there was no one here but servants today. The mission chief had gone down to his bungalow in Surrey.

Clive looked very solemn. And Esme, taking her cue from him, managed to erase the wrinkles forming at the corners of her mouth. Clive, she thought, showed the better breeding. Not a flicker. Aunt Alice would approve of him.

"Well, Tozo," Clive rose, still unsmiling, "We're off. Want a lift back? I'm dropping Esme at her place first but then it's Mons. I've got my boots to do. Commandant's inspection tomorrow."

To Esme's well-concealed relief, Tozo declined the offer.

"Don't want to play the proverbial gooseberry, old boy."

He would get the legation limousine to bring him down. The black bastard who drove the thing was under exercised.

They all shook hands although Tozo and Clive would meet the following day in less salubrious circumstances. Mons was rough and tough. And a princeling or two cut no ice with training sergeants.

"Ever been in a bungalow before?" Clive cautiously enquired, manoeuvring the Aston out of Queen Anne's Gate.

Thinking a minute, Esme said that, actually, she didn't believe she had. Very strange, considering the world was full of them.

"I wonder what it's like," Clive said pensively.

63

Outside the mess at Camberley, he came round to her side and opened the car door for her. He hugged her long and hard, attracting covert interest from people passing in the glass-walled hall.

"I'll try and ring you tonight. Will you be in?"

"Of course."

"Who's that redhead watching us?"

Esme skewed round a little in his arms, and waved at Philippa, pleased to see her friend.

"She's called Philippa Mayhew. She's on the Directing Staff. Orderly Officer this weekend."

"I see. Is that your No. 1 dress? I like that bottle-green. She looks as though she's in the Rifle Brigade . . ."

"Well, she's not. She's in the WRAC."

"I can't see why anyone like that should want to be in the army." Clive was staring in open admiration.

Esme began to recognise remarks of that kind as a compliment of sorts.

"There are quite a few of us," she said.

"No," he said. "Not like her . . . or you. My Eleanor . . . my Esme of Aquitaine."

The reference to the medieval queen who rode at the head of her own troops to make war upon her royal husband delighted Esme.

"I'll be on exercise next week. In the Brecon Beacons. Going tomorrow evening. Will you write to me? I'll tell you the address tonight."

Thereafter Esme never felt the Camberley pin-pricks. Perhaps there were none. Women, after all, whatever their background or profession, understand that ultimately the vast majority of their kind achieve consequence through the calibre of the man they capture. True, Esme had not yet captured but she had captivated.

Clive's shining car was parked several evenings in the week outside the Camberley officers' mess. Before long Major Fanshawe herself, as President of the Mess Committee, invited Clive to wait for Esme in the Student Officers' ante-room. A singular concession. Love melts barriers, even in the army . . . or so it seemed to Esme. But it wasn't love that melted Major Fanshawe's heart. It was something more enduring.

Clive Carson might only be an officer cadet, a man who cleaned his own boots, called drill sergeants 'sir' and slept in a sleeping bag to keep his issue blankets pristine for interminable and otherwise unpassable kit inspections . . . But very soon he would be an officer of the Household Cavalry, closer to the monarch than any other kind of soldier save Guardees. A privileged species breathing a rarefied atmosphere of exclusivity and influence. In army eyes, a magnificent young person. The most junior cornet in the Silvershods was, in terms of worldly status, unimpeachable. And to a pretty girl on the make, worth two colonels in the Signals or Royal Corps of Transport any day.

But Esme was not on the make. She was high on a cloud of sexual exaltation, spiced with a trace of emotional anxiety. She knew no more about the ethos of Clive's chosen regiment than she knew about the place where she herself would go. Thus far she had gleaned a little information about the Silvershods but had not much with which to compare their glamour. Men, she took it for granted, always had extra things. What did it matter, since women could have the men?

"You'll get engaged to him," said Joan, "I know you will."

"What makes you think that?" Esme pounced, rapacious for additional evidence of the obvious. Like any woman in love, she read fortune forecasts in magazines. Studied entrails.

"Oh, come on. Haven't you seen the way he looks at you? When he comes here to collect you he bores straight through the likes of us. Tiggy's a scream, though."

It was true. When Tiggy accompanied Clive he put himself out to be amusing for the benefit of Esme's colleagues. They were not the kind of women who stirred him. A gaggle of dear old frumps he called them, unfairly.

"Tell me, Essikins, Darling Heart," he said to Esme one day, as they left the mess, "Do they all run up little dresses for themselves in the pitch dark? Awfully smart, considering."

"Horrible, horrible man," Esme reproached his vitriol gaily. "If you don't like my friends, stay away. They say the kindest things about you two even though all you do is tease them. Beasts."

"I am not a beast," Clive said, coldly factual. "I spoke to that Caroline person just now. She seemed quite sensible. She's interested in ballistics."

"Are you?" Esme asked, startled.

"No, but I pretended."

So successfully, in fact, that Caroline, normally detached, evinced some interest in the forwarding of Esme's love affair. There was more to Clive Carson, she confided, than she had previously believed. Despite his supercilious manner, he was really quite sincere and probably better equipped upstairs than he would like anyone to think.

"Will you be able to get a posting together, do you think?" Caroline asked Esme dubiously, her broad, intelligent brow slightly furrowed.

Esme neither knew nor cared. She lived only for the vibrant moment. She was dancing on a high wire, dazzlingly incautious. Beyond the reach of counsel.

"Are you sure about him," Philippa asked her one day, falling into step beside her. She had meant to say 'Are you sure *of* him,' which means something different. But her nerve had failed her. It was not Esme, after all, who boasted openly of her conquest, but others all around her.

A nimbus of congratulation crowned her. If she still had faults they were easily forgiven, whether for her own charm's sake or that of her romance. It was acted out beyond Camberley's perimeter fence, but it was not difficult to imagine how she spent her evenings and weekends or in what company. Esme had been to a cocktail party given at Claridge's by Tiggy's mother for her London friends and got her name into *Tatler*. It was Major Rankine-Burke who spotted it, bringing it into the students' ante-room for Esme to see.

Quite pleased, Esme said she'd only ever been in *Country Life* before, when she was fourteen and put in charge of the stop-watch for a dressage test. Aunt Alice had been one of the judges.

It was on the night of the Claridge's thrash, a Wednesday, that Tiggy, driving his own car for once, which happened to be a noisy Morgan, had raced it up and down the Camberley parade ground with Esme in the seat beside him and Clive crushed up morosely in the back. His car was off the road. It was two o'clock in the morning and all the messes were dark.

"Tiggy! Don't, *please!*" Esme shouted at him. "Stop it! They'll sack me in the morning . . ."

"Lovely, lovely, lovely," Tiggy carolled madly. "Esme's no longer in the army. Esme can come with us," he sang. "Essikins is *free!*" Then he started to sound the klaxon.

"Put a sock in it," Clive protested half-heartedly just as a light in the Commandant's flat snapped on. Esme groaned. Aunt Alice wasn't going to like this. Dismissal for unsuitable behaviour in the company of two far from sober *youths*. A terrible disgrace. The square at Camberley, as anywhere, was sacred. Holy ground.

The next morning nothing happened. No interview, no 'little talk', not even a 'word or two'. Esme, with an aching head, cringed in hourly expectation of a summons throughout Army Organisation, Pay and Q Administration. During drill, Miss Blenkinsop took the unusual step of making Esme right marker.

"You should know your way around the square *now*, Miss Hansard, shouldn't you ma'am?"

Esme felt mildly nauseous. This was typical Camberley torture. When would the good hot row come?

At lunch Colonel Crump varied her custom too, and joined her officers in the dining-room. Everyone rose respectfully at her presageful appearance.

66

"Do, do please sit down. Don't interrupt your lunch," she waved a scarlet-tipped hand imperially. "I thought I rather like the sound of Chump Chops Champvallon," she purred throatily. "A change, you know."

Chump Chops Champvallon was one of the most unappealing and frequently executed dishes in the Army Catering Manual.

The Directing Staff all smirked except Major Rankine-Burke who fell over himself to hold out a chair for the Commandant.

"No, Mortlake, thank you very much. You're so kind, but I do believe I'll sit here in this patch of sunshine."

Colonel Crump settled her queenly bulk opposite Esme, sending the Hussar scuttling to the sideboard to fetch her a glass of claret.

"And one for Miss Hansard too," she boomed, "in fact, why don't we all have a glass. My treat. Did you have an enjoyable time last night, Esme? Motor cars can be such fun, can't they? I remember when I was in 48 Ack-Ack Battery up in the Hebrides . . ."

FANY talk ensued.

That was Esme's ticking off. Grateful for this featherlight rebuke from so august a personage as Camilla Crump, Esme's wavering devotion to the army was renewed and strengthened. Justice had been combined with mercy and with such style. How could she ever think of leaving an organisation which embraced Clive, Colonel Crump and Philippa Mayhew?

A small sorrow acted as fixative to this tightening bond. Tozo died.

It happened on a Mons exercise which again took place in the Brecon Beacons. A mountainous waste in Wales, which from Clive's description sounded very much like the place Esme came from. Treacherous terrain at any time of year, the week of the exercise the weather had been filthy.

At the end of a long day's running, lying still in bogs and leopard-crawling in the driven, wind-chilled rain, Tozo had been found lethargic and mildly incoherent by his companion in a two-man tent when, at long last, bedtime came. The other man had made nothing of it at the time. He, too, was half-way round the twist with cold and misery. But Tozo, Commander-in-Chief-elect of his father's army, fell unconscious, not asleep. He died unnoticed, of exposure.

Even Clive's seemingly unalterable composure was briefly ruffled. The sight of Tozo's best boots, lovingly preserved in an Asprey's carrier bag and kept for parades only, on top of the tin locker in the barrack room the African had shared with Clive and Tiggy at Mons, moved Clive to murmur, "I can't believe I saw him in those things last week. He had the best boots in the company."

"You won't be going to Wongobongoland to lick the black mammies into shape, now, Esme," Tiggy added his lament.

"No, I won't, will I?" Esme sadly said, although she'd never considered it.

Tozo had been a gracious man. Nor could Esme forget that he had been bred out of a woman who ran like a gazelle and fought like a crocodile. They'd had something in common there.

Nor could Tozo's few friends honour him in death apart from signing the legation's scruffy visitor's book. His body was flown home almost furtively. The Foreign and Colonial Office did not like dead officer cadets.

Four days before Esme's course ended Joan Simmonds was advised by Major Fanshawe that her commission would never be confirmed. She might return to civilian life or join the ranks and try for a commission later. Humbler than any officer has a right to be, Joan chose the latter path.

That evening she confided in her erstwhile colleagues, with tears but without rancour, that Major Fanshawe said she had no style. No panache. A borderline case from the first, she hadn't developed the essential touch of swank.

Esme cancelled her date with Clive, knowing she must help sit out the last, despairing hours with Joan. Outsiders couldn't help with this. It was a strictly WRAC affair. Family business. There was a wake in the students' ante-room which went on until the small hours. Even Caroline got squiffy.

Reckoning up the bar chits next morning after Joan's lonely, ignominious removal to recruit-training, in a taxi, Sergeant Smith took the chits to Major Fanshawe. She said nothing, it was not her place. But OC Instruction Wing interpreted what she saw. With so much alcohol consumed, there must have been indiscretions. Any girlish vows of eternal friendship must be immediately forsworn. Philippa Mayhew had better deal with it.

After luncheon Philippa took her coffee with the students in their room and had a 'word or two'.

"I know this must seem very hard to you, but don't try to keep in touch with Joan. It wouldn't be kind in the long run, whatever you or she may feel now. Let her find her feet without harking back . . ."

Our world, thought Esme, is no longer her world. We stay in Elysium and she goes.

Scraping up enough exam marks for Esme, who had badly neglected her Army Organisation and Pay, was difficult, but it was done. Esme might not know how many companies to the Parachute Battalion, but it was a detail. She had more important things to offer. The sheer exhilaration that pulsed around her presence. The shine of her. A light to lead.

None the less, Caroline passed out top. She got horrifically high marks in every paper and had possessed from the very beginning an imposingly serious mien. She was the kind of girl who forms the ballast in every female society, always having a sharpened pencil or a spare collar stud to lend to scattier beings. She thought ahead, looked before she placed her long, well-shod feet. No one following after her would come to grief.

"I do wish," Colonel Crump brayed regretfully at the Directing Staff's final meeting, "we could have seen her be just the tiniest bit *naughty*. Still, I suppose we can't have everything from the same officer."

The course ended with a gala luncheon which parents were invited to attend.

The mess kitchens laboured mightily and brought forth virtually everything in aspic. Sergeant Smith produced the best the mess owned in the way of linen and silver. Mortlake Rankine-Burke, as wines member, attempted to simplify his task by ordaining that no one would drink anything unless it was champagne. Major Fanshawe overruled him, saying he must not denude the cellar. He must arrange a balanced cull of current stocks. Dreary Deirdre was flowers member and came up with rather nuptial-looking explosions of carnations.

There was no parade, no Sash of Honour – women officers were not entitled to swords in those days – no white horses. It was a quietish, but pleasant affair. The Student Officers were commissioned anyway and official ceremonial had no part to play in their departure from Camberley. Esme was very glad. No marching.

Aunt Alice arrived, chugging up the drive in the Land Rover. She descended, rumpled but majestic in an ankle-length pink slub-silk duster coat purchased in 1952 for a wedding. Her cartwheel hat of navy straw lay on the back seat, and on it Gimlet nestled.

"What does it matter if it keeps her happy," Alice brushed Esme's remonstrance aside. "Mmm, darling," she kissed her niece, "How well you're looking. I must say I do like your Number Ones." She referred to Esme's new, tailor-made officer-quality uniform which she was wearing for the first time. "Turn around. Yes, I think they've done a good job. First-rate cloth and just enough padding on the shoulder . . . You should put that chignon in a net . . ."

"Oh, Aunt *Alice*! Look, my tunic's lined with scarlet." Esme lifted the edge of her jacket, to display this delightful optional feature. "Isn't it gorgeous . . . I had it done in real silk . . ."

Of course, Clive had gravely recommended that. Superior comfort.

"Spiffing, darling. Ah, Camilla, my dear," Alice greeted her old friend the Commandant without hesitation although she hadn't seen her for twenty years, "How very nice to see you. My girl shaped up, has she?"

There followed one of those barfing sea-lion exchanges which typify women of that type and generation. Happy, Esme left her elders to their aperitif and wandered away to talk to Philippa, who from today she might call by her Christian name.

"Well, cobber," Philippa said of Esme's posting, announced the previous day, "I'm sorry you got Mill Hill. Not very exciting for you. The situation's difficult there. The OC lives out . . . Never mind, I expect you'll sail through everything . . . But don't suffer in silence. Keep me posted."

In ebullient spirits, Esme didn't catch the note of uncertainty, of concern in her friend's voice. And in any case, a detachment of the WRAC band, which had been bussed across from the depot, was playing brassily and breathily in the hall, 'The Lass of Richmond Hill'. The WRAC's own quick march. A tune to embolden a mouse, never mind a woman badged with a rampant lioness.

This was a wonderful day. And it would end in an evening spent with Clive. Aunt Alice was staying at the Nuffield Club in London tonight and would drive back to Westmorland independently next day. Esme had to get the Bean Can back there for two weeks' leave. Caroline and all the rest would leave this evening with their families.

They looked proud but bemused, those other families. Uneasily smiling fathers, mothers reassured by wine and flowers, but discomfited by daughters defined by uniforms. Not de-sexed exactly, but distanced . . . Stiffened with underlying buckram.

They weren't service people. But Mortlake's wicked cocktail brew soon made the party jolly. Super girls deserved a cracking send off. Still couldn't read a going map for toffee, of course, except Esme. Smashing kid.

When the port was passing round the table Colonel Crump rose to make a speech.

This was an informal get-together, she said, and she wouldn't keep them long. The five girls had had enough lectures lately. She wished only to remind them on this special day, that they, not rich grocers who had bought a handle to their names, were the inheritors of the knightly code. Did they realise that, were they only young men and not young women, they would be entitled to write 'esquire' after their names? The form might not exist for ladies, but the substance of chivalry did. Weaponry might alter, so might modes of transport, but the values of the mounted caste remained unchanged. A tradition to guard and cherish.

"Horses first, soldiers next and officers last. Or in other words, my dears, the privileges we officers enjoy are great, but the degree of self-sacrifice expected of every one of us is limitless. Best of luck and have a good leave, all of you."

It went straight to Esme's heart. Glancing in her aunt's direction, she saw Alice was struggling for mastery of her features.

Clive did not turn up.

The hour appointed, seven o'clock, passed. Esme waited in the empty students' ante-room with her heart sinking faster than the setting sun. She went to her room at nine, so that Sergeant Smith shouldn't report her continued presence to the other ante-room. Pity, and an invitation to join her seniors, would be unbearable.

Walking up and down, smoking cigarettes, one eye on the darkening drive outside the open curtains, Esme racked her brains. What could have happened? What possible misunderstanding had there been? She passed and re-passed her suitcases, stacked and ready for tomorrow.

Clive didn't even know her address at home. How could she leave without seeing him? Ringing him was useless. Mons was a vast, sprawling military slum of a place. There was only one telephone available to officer cadets and it was permanently engaged.

A moment later she zipped Rummie crossly into a bag. The teddy bear's inanimate compassion was bringing her close to tears. Her parents were already packed, thank God.

A knock on her door put an end to this agony around eleven o'clock.

"Oh, Esme! You *are* still here. I said I didn't think you could be . . ." Philippa looked astounded. "It's your chum on the line . . . In the mess secretary's office . . ."

Esme flew past her, thanking her on the run.

"Clive! What . . .?"

"No, it's me," Tiggy said. "I've had to queue for this bloody telephone for hours. Look, Clivey pulled off something amusing this morning and they've locked him up . . ."

Locked him up! Esme's mind spun. This was madness.

"Yah. He's in the slammer . . . the cooler. Whatever you want to say . . ."

The story had to come out quickly because Tiggy was allowed less than two minutes on that telephone. Clive had arranged a birthday compliment for an Irish drill sergeant. Selected members of the squad, parading routinely for him, had each discreetly deposited a bottle of Guinness behind his left leg, where it would be invisible from the front. On the command *Quick march!* the bottles had been left behind, forming the message 'Happy Birthday'.

71

"Neat job, wasn't it?" Tiggy pleaded for his friend.

The sergeant, touched as he had been, had scowlingly halted the squad and taken the names of all the Guinness men. They were placed under close arrest and marched away to the guardroom to undergo their inevitable period of confinement.

"Rules is rules, gentlemen."

They'd let the rest go after a few hours. But Clive as instigator was still under lock and key.

"Sorry, Darling Heart."

"Look, Tiggy . . ."

The pips went. Damn! Esme had not given her address. Still, she could send it on a postcard with the mess's outward mail tomorrow.

Awash with relief, Esme went in search of Philippa. She had to tell someone how ingenious her man had been and that he hadn't let her down. Not really. He hadn't meant to. A miscalculation. *Why had he been so bloody, bloody careless?*

What a pity it was that she hadn't known earlier about this prank. She and Aunt Alice could have been together this evening. As it was, Aunt Alice was probably a little hurt although she had refused to show it. All for nothing.

Esme cursed Clive in the same breath that she forgave him.

While she was on leave at Lowlough, restless in the first few days, she relaxed after the delivery of a parcel from Hamley's toy shop. It contained a rubber duck. Around its neck, a ticket swung with a scrawl of handwriting: 'To keep you company in your bath until I can. Love Clive.'

So odd of him. So typically disconnected. But wonderful too. No apology for wasting her last night at Camberley. Just the rubber duck.

Swimming the duck up and down her bath that night, with the sheep bleating on the fell, Esme wondered about Clive's commissioning ball. It had been proposed in passing that she should go as his partner. It was to be held at the Cavalry Club and be what Clive called 'pretty smart'. But nothing more had been said about it. Oh, well. Perhaps it was to be a family party. Only wives and daughters of the regiment. How stupendous of the Silvershods to give their newly commissioned cornets a ball . . .

Esme allowed herself no more thoughts along those lines. She had been trained from infancy never to regret invitations she had not received. It wasn't dignified.

6

"Miss Hansard, ma'am," the 2ic announced Esme formally.

She was wearing her No. 1 dress hat as this was the first meeting with her new OC and a salute was mandatory. No hat, no salute. Not like the American army. Esme smiled and saluted simultaneously. The proper thing to do, as this was by way of being a social interview. Longest way up, shortest way down.

Her greeting went unacknowledged, unnoticed too. Daphne Deveril was leafing through some papers on her desk.

"Thanks, Alice," the OC said without looking up. "Ring the unit hairdresser, will you, and say I'll be late for my appointment."

Captain Potter shut the door and left Esme standing there with no idea what to do next. Was she supposed to stand to attention and if so, for how long? Seconds went by, feeling like minutes.

"I'll be with you in a minute," the OC broke the silence at length. "Sit down. The chair in the corner. May as well be comfortable. You can take your hat off."

A gravelly voice . . . gin and Jaguar posh.

Uneasily, she sank, as indicated, into an armchair like the ones in the mess, covered this time in bilious-green tweed. Always G Plan. There was a low, laminated-wood coffee table beside the chair, with a glass ashtray on it. Esme put her hat down on the table, instantly disliking her seat. Daphne Deveril's eyes when she finally met them, would look into hers at an acute, downward angle. An unpleasant flutter in her stomach told her this might matter.

"Cigarette?"

Daphne pushed a pack of Gold Leaf across her desk without looking

73

up. Her arm, freckled and red, was squeezed tight by the sleeve band of her uniform blouse. Unpleasing.

"No, thank you," Esme lied in a voice consciously forced down below its usual register, "I don't smoke."

No comment was forthcoming at this. More paper shuffling. A black fountain pen in Major Deveril's pudgy hand scratched signatures on a number of pages. She opened a drawer and found a lighter, snapping the cap several times before she lit a cigarette for herself, face averted from Esme.

"Perhaps, ma'am," Esme ventured, "You'd prefer me to come back later . . ."

The sole response was a glare from two pale, bulging eyes magnified behind spectacles. They were rimless at the bottom and had light-blue, upswept frames at the top with sparkly bits. Once again, they were bent on the papers.

Miserable, apprehensive, Esme sat and waited. Philippa's last, parting remarks, which had seemed so odd at the time, came back to her. *Don't let anything faze you. And: It could go either way . . . You might get on very well . . .*

With an outward show of unconcern, Esme looked out of the window.

Some saplings planted on the edge of the parade ground shivered in the breeze. Beyond, ugly red-brick barrack blocks, festooned with iron fire escapes, cut off any more distant view. A squad of pale-faced Sappers was being marched up from the Postal Depot. Stable belts, olive drab denims, DMS boots, navy berets and coarse khaki shirts rolled up to the elbow. Tattoos on their forearms. They shuffled to an untidy halt, looking more like dejected prisoners of war than peacetime, volunteer soldiers.

In the corridor Alice Potter was talking to the RSM. Something or other was very amusing to judge by the laughter. Esme wished she knew what it was, so her mind would have something to grip on instead of darting about in this frenzy of fancied entrapment. She found herself searching her conscience. But she'd done nothing wrong . . . hadn't had time to . . . Oh God, was it going to be Camberley all over again?

"Now," said the OC, putting her papers aside ostentatiously, and drawing a file towards her, still without looking up, "let's talk about you. Sure you won't smoke?"

Shaking her head, Esme was able to see Daphne's face fully for the first time. Broad with a mottled, high-coloured complexion. The mouth, curveless as a letter-box, held a cigarette wedged in its corner. A plume of blue smoke rose steadily past a thick crown of dark, grey-threaded hair, styled like the Queen's.

"No, thank you, ma'am."

"Please yourself," Daphne took the cigarette from her mouth and gave Esme a long, critical look. "Don't you think its rather impertinent of you to suggest leaving my office?"

"I . . ."

"Don't you think an intelligent person would avoid telling a new boss that she didn't know how to arrange her time properly? Because I'll . . ."

"I'm sorry, ma'am," Esme interposed, "I really didn't intend to . . ."

"Never mind what you intended," Daphne thrust Esme's apology aside violently. "It's what you actually *did* we're discussing. And never, never interrupt me again. That's point one. I expect subalterns in my unit to keep their silly traps shut until they're invited to open them. Have you got that?"

"Yes, ma'am."

"Good. That's a start. And what's all this I hear about you going out last night?"

Bewildered, almost light-headed, Esme admitted that she and her two new subaltern mess-mates had gone out after dinner for a drink at a pub in Hampstead that had a garden. It had been a nice evening. She didn't add that they'd hoped to find something to eat which might compensate for the sparse quantity of food served at dinner or its virtually uneatable quality.

"There seemed no harm in going out for a while," Esme proceeded cautiously, "I knew you lived out, ma'am, and Captain Potter had gone to her room . . ."

"Did it not occur to you that I might just drop in after dinner to welcome you to the mess? Well, didn't it?"

"Nobody told me . . . Did you, ma'am? Come, I mean. If so, I'm most dreadfully sorry . . ."

"Whether I did or not is irrelevant. The point is that *you* did the wrong thing. And don't go blaming the others. Officers are expected to accept responsibility for their own actions . . ."

"But Major Deveril, ma'am," Esme rebelled at the injustice, "I really didn't know . . ."

"That's no excuse. And how many times do you have to be told something? What is it that I've already told you this morning that you've forgotten? Go on, tell me."

Esme bit her lip, swept with anger at being treated like a recalcitrant toddler. After an interior struggle, she spoke the expected, conciliatory words.

"Not to interrupt, ma'am."

"Exactly . . ."

In a daze Esme listened to a list of strictures on her behaviour and bearing which seemed to have little or nothing to do with her. She wore her hat incorrectly. But the way that she did so, dead horizontal, had been held up as an example at Camberley.

Her salute was a caricature of what is should be. Daphne, Esme remembered resentfully, had not even deigned to watch her salute.

For a person of her rank, she had far too much to say. She had not been allowed to say anything. Was it conceivable that Major Deveril could be referring to the conversation at dinner last night?

She had got on well with her opposite numbers commanding the other two platoons, Moira and Nancy . . . Had chatted politely over coffee with the older officers who worked in the Ministry of Defence and were accommodated at the 13 Company mess . . . Had discussed the ease with which central London could be reached on public transport or by car . . . But who would have told Daphne Deveril all this? Alice Potter? And if she had, what was wrong with it, anyhow? Religion, politics, sex and 'shop' were the forbidden topics. Not tube timetables.

Esme felt dizzy and cold. She mustn't cry. She never had at Camberley. Stupid to start now. Grown ups of twenty-one with degrees didn't start howling . . .

Daphne Deveril, as if reading her junior's thoughts, opened a drawer and produced a large box of Kleenex. She placed it on the edge of the desk nearest Esme with a complacent air of well-worn routine.

"I've heard a lot about you," Daphne said, removing her spectacles and narrowing her eyes. "And none of it," she slapped the palm of her hand on the file in front of her, "Not a word of it, let me tell you, fills me with optimism. Connections don't impress me. Nor does any silly degree. I doubt very much if you're suited to army life. At any rate, you'll have to prove yourself here. You've got a hundred women to administer. I expect you to know every one of them personally by the end of next week. Do you understand?"

"Perfectly, ma'am," Esme lifted her chin. How could she possibly know a hundred women that well in ten days? But to get out of this office and away from this woman was the main thing. She was mad.

What followed was a meandering description of Esme's platoon officer's job. It spat from the OC's slitted mouth like spread shot from a gun. Stinging but diffuse. Liaising with the Sapper employing officer . . . welfare and discipline. The importance of inspecting the WRAC girls' blocks . . . kit checks . . . organising sports . . . keeping an eye on her platoon sergeant. Sergeant Higgins who was idle and light-fingered.

"It's not Exercise First Flight, here, you know," Daphne sneered. "This is real life . . ."

Esme was to do the sergeants' mess accounts meticulously . . . Fudging the fruit machine figure was an old trick. Major Deveril wouldn't stand for it. Esme was personally responsible for several thousands of pounds of the sergeants' mess money. Woe betide her if she was found in possession of too little of it. Or there again, too much of it. The military audit board sat next month. Esme should be ready with her vouchers, single entry cash book and bank statements, all tied up and reconciled . . . to the last halfpenny.

She said something about the Sapper officers' mess which on this unit was separate. A dead and alive hole. If invited there, as she would be, Esme was to conduct herself in a manner becoming a WRAC officer. She was never to forget, sleeping or walking, on and off duty, she represented the Corps. Drunkenness or raffish behaviour would not be tolerated.

Esme felt the colour drain from her face. Drunkenness? Last night she'd had one tomato juice before dinner, a glass of wine with it and half a pint of shandy in the pub.

"Ma'am, I can assure you . . ." Esme began an indignant defence. She was not allowed to continue.

"I may as well tell you, Hansard, I don't like you but your future rests in my hands. If you perform your duties faultlessly, I shall recommend that your commission's confirmed in four months' time. But if you take my advice, you'll give it up as a bad job. I can write a report on you now saying you're unsuited . . ."

"No. No, thank you," Esme managed to say, controlling the waver in her voice. "I shall do my best and I think you'll be satisfied."

"Have it your own way," Daphne lit another cigarette. "I think you're making a mistake." She regarded Esme steadily for a moment or two.

"May I go now, ma'am?" Esme tried to flex her leg muscles. They were leaden with shock.

"I'm surprised you don't." The older woman blew a trio of smoke rings. "Any intelligent person would have realised this interview was over ages ago. What do you think?"

Esme got to the door somehow, replaced her hat, saluted and left. She was trembling. Someone she'd never met before hated her. What could the Camberley DS have written in that file?

When she reached her office there was a note on her desk. Clive had rung. He would ring back. Somewhere in London, Clive was thinking about her. She could bear almost anything as long as he did. Just this little scrap of paper had the power to calm her. The shivery, shaky feeling subsided.

"You're back, ma'am," Sergeant Higgins announced inconsequently, putting her head round the door. She was grossly fat with a greasy bun perched on top of her head. Her skin, too tight for the underlying bulges, made her features seem oddly oriental. She flapped some large pieces of paper. "Ration states, ma'am. Could you just pop your monica on them for us?"

Esme flinched. Masses and masses of figures to check. Seven days' worth by the look of it. Still, it would give her something to do. Something taxing but clean and emotionless.

"You can if you like, ma'am," Higgins said breezily. "I shouldn't bother if I were you. Last officer never did. Lance-Corporal Gallagher's dead reliable."

"I think I'd better, if you don't mind, Sarn't Higgins," Esme stretched out her hand.

"What's up? OC gunning for you?" Higgins cheeked, surrendering the ration states without further resistance.

Esme looked up at her coolly. If the slow flush dawning on the NCO's face was anything to go by, it was a sufficient reproof. Officers' business was private. A question of dignity.

"A gentleman rang for you, ma'am," Higgins went on more soberly. "I left a note. Did you find it?"

"Yes, yes, thank you."

"He your boyfriend, then?"

Higgins resurgent. She could be put down but not flattened. Esme smiled, glad of the human curiosity that prompted the question.

"Yes. Yes, he is." It felt good to say so. "Do you think I might have a cup of coffee?"

"Right away, ma'am."

Esme set herself to wade through the ration states. Every column tallied. The hundred or so names of course meant nothing. Most women were present and eating in the other ranks cookhouse according to the strokes. A handful were Sick, Sick at Home, Absent without Leave, or on Leave. She listed those absent for whatever reason, making a note to quiz Higgins about them. Every detail. She would need to absorb the histories of each girl in her care by the end of ten days. That's how long Major Deveril had given her . . . Simpler to start with the problem situations . . .

Remembering that Higgins was allegedly one of the problems, Esme checked her shoulder bag which had sat here on the window-sill throughout her encounter with the OC. She knew how much money she had in there. One five pound note and a ten bob one, a florin and a sixpence. They were still there. Of course they were. Higgins was probably as much a thief as she herself was a dipsomaniac.

Creating suspicion must be a part of Major Deveril's strategy. But what on earth did she want to achieve by it? A terrifying, disgusting woman.

Resting her chin on her hands, Esme willed the telephone to ring. Why was Clive always so vague. Why didn't he say *when* he'd ring back . . . or leave a number? It was always the same. He flashed in and out of her life like a humming bird, elusive and beautiful. Thinking of him made everything in her abdomen plead for his presence. Brought his smell wafting from whatever Olympian place he inhabited . . . Perhaps he wasn't in London . . .

"There you are." Nancy from 3 Platoon walked into the office with her hat on and courteously saluted. You always did that if you went into somebody else's room, Esme remembered. Even if the officer in question was of equivalent rank or junior.

"Coming for lunch? I waited to catch the bits after your interview with Daphne but in the end I had to go down to the depot, you were in there so long. What was she on about? Let's hang on for Moira."

The subalterns, Esme discovered, never walked about the unit singly when Daphne Deveril was around. There was safety in numbers.

"It's because you didn't cry," Moira, a raw-boned hockey player with a Vicar's wife's countenance, sagely opined, at the conclusion of Esme's account of what had transpired. "She expects you to cry. We all do. If a subbie doesn't bawl, she goes on till they do. The whole idea is to break you down and then build you up again."

Moira said it without a trace of resentment.

"In her own image?" Esme enquired sarcastically.

"You've got to remember," Nancy told her later in the powder-room, "Moira's a devout Christian . . ."

"You mean she's a devout fool," Esme snapped nervily. "I'm sorry. I didn't mean to be horrid. I've just had a very bad morning. My boyfriend rang and I missed it . . ."

Seeing she was now close to tears, Nancy put her arm round Esme's shoulders.

"Come on. Chin up. You're a heroine. Nobody's outfaced Daphne within living memory."

At lunch nobody except Daphne said anything. She dilated on the price of tomatoes and what George, her retired officer lover, thought of it. Esme was astonished. Was this conversation? Eventually she understood it. Daphne, who was thirty-six and looked fifty, was immensely proud of her illicit domesticity. The best way to purify drains came next. Drummer Boy Disinfectant versus Domestos.

Alice Potter supplied the minimal element of reciprocity by murmuring admiring agreement at intervals. Laughing sycophantically, whenever the OC made some banal joke or other.

Esme felt very sorry for Potter. Grateful to her too, for keeping Daphne happy.

The subalterns excused themselves before the pudding and slunk away to Nancy's room. She had a kettle there and some instant coffee. Cheese and biscuits as well. The less time spent in the dining- or ante-rooms before Daphne went home to her putrid love nest, the better.

"Bloody hell, Thewlis has been at my nail varnish again," Nancy inveighed against the little batwoman she and Esme shared. The only thing to be said for the kid was that she didn't work with the mailbags. Hence, she hadn't got scabies. The parasite was rife among the postal girls. Outbreak after outbreak. Poor things scratched themselves raw.

Esme started to say something whereupon Moira switched on a wireless and turned up the volume. Security.

"Your best plan this afternoon," Nancy advised, "is to stay well away from the office. Go down to the depot. Talk to the girls . . ."

"What about?" Esme asked.

"Oh, just ask them if they've got any problems. That's what we're here for. Under-employed, glorified social workers."

Moira poured the hot water into mugs and looked disapproving. *All* the women had problems if you were prepared to look for them. Deep problems.

"Well, yes. Never mind," Nancy waved that aside. "Just you keep moving, sweetie. You can put in some time jawing with Major Midgley who employs your girls . . . He's always good for a cup of buckshee coffee and a gas . . . When you run out there, push off to the pay office. Find something to witter about . . . Do the accommodation blocks with Higgins. I'll send her down to meet you . . . Just stay one step ahead of any telephone calls."

Esme learned that unless she kept out of range she was likely to be landed with an extra Orderly Officer duty. A punishment for nothing. The OC didn't need a reason. No comebacks. Any old pretext would do. New subbies generally got one as a welcoming present. Esme, having resisted the anticipated tearful submission to the OC's authority, might very well get two . . . or more.

"Don't worry," Moira said, "I'll listen out for your telephone and take any messages from your chap. Getting you out on your date tonight is the afternoon's mission."

Esme could have hugged them both. The army always threw up real friends when you needed them.

Two weeks later Esme lay dosing blissfully in Clive's arms in the dark. They were in Tiggy's mother's basement flat. It was handy for Jack's for one thing and Tiggy's mother was in Monte Carlo with her latest fiancé. A Spaniard this time. "Ma'll probably wear a mantilla on the beach from now on," Tiggy said. "Likes to get in character."

But Esme was not thinking of Tiggy. She turned to look at Clive's sleeping face where it rested, slaked and trustful on her shoulder. The long, little-boy lashes curled on his cheek, veiling his great brown, boggy eyes. His mouth was smudgily ruddy still from the bruising of love-making. It was open too, which made him look so sweetly defenceless. So unlike his waking self.

These were the times Esme loved. When Clive lay in her power like Samson in the toils of Delilah. Hers, completely and utterly, smelling of new sweat and spunk. She ponged quite a bit herself, she supposed. The marvellous thing was that neither of them minded. Nothing about each other's bodies could ever offend them. Clive's unsinkable torpedo in the lavatory that time in Knightsbridge . . . The fragment of fibrous menstrual tissue that had floated away from Esme in the bath when they borrowed that hideous little hovel in Fulham. In the tub with her as usual on that occasion, Clive had fished out the clot and examined it, saying how wonderful nature was.

And Esme liked to think while Clive slept, heavy and spent on her breast. About the things they had done in the evening . . . places and people. The words they had spoken. Esme analysed every syllable of Clive's sparing speeches for each possible shred of potential significance. She wished she shared the trick of saying so little and meaning so much. It was his face, she considered. Brooding and sunny by turns. The fugitive smile . . . beaming unexpected like sunlight in the midst of a rain shower . . . tucking itself away prudishly behind a cloud again, leaving shadow behind.

Drifting half in and half out of consciousness, when the door to the bedroom clicked open Esme came to herself almost immediately. A friendly weight sat itself down on the edge of the bed.

"Tiggy!"

"Esme? Darling Heart, is he awake?"

"No, Tiggy, what are you doing here?"

"Rehearsal parade at Windsor. We're clop, clopping along after the Queen's carriage when she has President Mumbojumbo here on a State Visit next week."

"Who's Mumbojumbo?" Esme asked, thinking, against her will, that her own short experience of the army was in stark contrast to that of the boys. Glittering helmets and cuirasses were a long way from scabies and Daphne.

"God knows," Tiggy said. "We call them all Mumbojumbo if they're black. Actually I've a feeling this one's greenish-yellow. Polynesian kind of fellow. Weighs thirty stone. Bit dicey with the carriage . . ."

81

They were speaking in whispers. Clive didn't wake. Esme, sitting up now, was uncovered to the waist. It didn't seem to matter. She was close to Tiggy because they were both close to Clive.

"Give him a thump. Always did sleep like a dead hippopotamus. We've got to get back to Kensington Barracks, pick up our gear and get over to Windsor. Rehearsal starts at seven. It's nearly five o'clock now."

Clive stirred and lay blinking for a moment on his back. Esme was annoyed with him. She had known nothing of this parade business. It was Saturday. They were supposed to have the whole day together. They were going riding, weren't they? Why hadn't he warned her? But she couldn't bring herself to admit there was any lack of confidence between them. Not in front of Tiggy. Half his security seemed to rest on their relationship these days.

"For God's sake, Tiggy," Clive groaned, "What time is it?"

He sprang out of bed and retired to the bathroom-cum-dressing-room to get into his clothes. Velvet jacket, soft silk shirt, droopy bow tie and evening-dress trousers. They had been at Annabel's the previous evening. He emerged in a moment, immaculate and vital, as if that evening of champagne, laughter and unforgettable glances were just beginning again.

"Bye, honey."

He kissed her on the mouth, gentle and passionless like an affectionate brother. It was one of the things she loved him for. Knowing what kiss for what moment. He never got it wrong.

"Go back to sleep. I'll ring you here later in the morning."

Just that. No timings, no plans, no explanations. The two men went to the door but Tiggy turned back.

"Want an apple, Essikins?" He produced one from his dinner-jacket pocket. A magician cheering a disappointed child. What on earth was he doing with an apple in his pocket, Esme wondered, taking it gratefully. She jammed it between her teeth to prevent herself crying out after the other half of herself.

There was no hope of sleep for her now. Bereft, Esme tossed and turned through the dawn. She didn't want to be in this flat without Clive. She felt like a trespasser.

It was a new variation on previous incidents of the kind. Clive telephoned her out of the blue at Mill Hill, gave her an address to find and report to. Then they went out, came back and made love. Usually morning came, tender but wordless, when they parted till the next time.

He never came to fetch her. Never took her to his mess. Sometimes they ran into friends of his and joined up with them. Sometimes they didn't. Wasn't it time, Esme fumed, that they came to some better arrangement? Said to the world that they were together in every way that counted and wanted to stay together. Recognised, official. Dammit, it wasn't as if the whole world didn't *know*.

Clinging crossly to the thought that Clive's bottom was really too big for perfection . . . probably that was what gave him his rock-steady seat on a horse . . . she was inspecting some cornflakes in the tiny kitchenette's cupboard when the telephone rang. Esme glanced at her watch. Half past nine. Tiggy's mother? She hoped not. This would all take some explaining.

"How are you this morning?" As always, Clive's voice disarmed her, reducing her to craven dissimulation. "Did you sleep?"

"Yes, very well," Esme lied.

He gave her the address of a house on the Chelsea Embankment, belonging to some people called Harmsworth. Could she get there by seven o'clock that evening?

Yes, yes, she could. Esme forgot all about the size of Clive's bottom.

Walking to the Bean Can which was parked on the opposite side of the square, she asked herself what she would wear. Were they going to a ball or a bistro? That was Clive all over. She should have asked. But she never did. There was something terribly deliberate about Clive's silences. An electric fence round his thoughts. Now she had the whole day to waste.

But he wanted her with him again. His desire pulled love from her as a baby's mouth sucks milk from its mother. Esme could never deny him.

The autumn months went by like this punctuated by Esme's attempts to define her job and take a hold on it.

She tried to set up some Adventure Training for her women but the regulations were impenetrable. Designed, apparently, to confuse and discourage. Taking the manual to Daphne for clarification, she left the OC's office no better informed. Daphne just droned on about the virtues of outdoor activities for postal workers, reminisced about her own experiences of camps, canoeing and rock-climbing excursions . . . and explained nothing at all.

Esme wrote a letter to a Captain Boddington-Snirk somewhere in Whitehall as he seemed to have something to do with it. He replied with a single line referring her to no less than four other manuals as amended by this and that subsequent direction . . . and letters which had passed in the past between one authority and another.

"You won't get anywhere," Nancy commented blandly, painting her nails, perched on the edge of Esme's desk. "Basically, if the OC's not interested you don't stand a chance. Actually, I doubt she understands the manual any better than you do."

"But if she doesn't know her job, how can I get to do mine?" Esme demanded.

It was a question that no one could answer. Esme took to reading the Manual of Military Law in the intervals between presiding at pay parades and orderly rooms, restricting the privileges of women hauled up before her on charges of drunkenness or disorder. The same ones, over and over again. "My lovely old lags," Esme called them. They made her laugh with their hangdog expressions and lame-brained excuses. They were bored and frustrated. Who wasn't?

"These women would be better off doing some commando training," Esme spoke to Alice Potter one day. "They really do *want* to be in the army and they could make terrifying troops."

"It's not feminine," Potter said firmly, toeing the WRAC party line.

"Nor are they," was Esme's rejoinder. "Why pretend any different? We should make the best use of what we've got."

Sergeant Higgins required her to do kit checks intermittently as women were always losing items of uniform, either that or using them as shoe dusters. One woman, a favourite target for this disciplinary exercise, hit on the idea of simplifying her life by sending all her underclothes home in a parcel. They were her personal property, she pointed out correctly, and not having them would spare her the trouble of washing them. Esme laughed.

She applied first to Alice Potter and then to Daphne for advice on the best way to handle this original thinker. Much talk of historic experience of personal hygiene and women, but no solution to the present conundrum.

Lacking official guidance, Esme sent Lance-Corporal Gallagher, her junior platoon NCO, out to re-equip the woman at Marks and Spencer's, funding the expedition herself. The RSM didn't like it but hadn't any better ideas. It was no good. Pleased with the newness and whiteness of her replacement trousseau the woman bundled it off home to Durham in case anyone stole it.

"Serves her right," Daphne sniggered to Alice who'd had the tale from the RSM who'd had it from Higgins, "for taking too much on herself."

Esme worried constantly about her commission's confirmation. If she wasn't gazetted, how would she break it to Aunt Alice? Resigning was one thing. Being chucked out was another.

Esme canvassed Philippa Mayhew's advice.

Struck by the bleakness of her tones on the telephone rather than anything she actually said, Philippa drove up in October and gave her protégée lunch at her club, the Duchess of Melrose's, in Beaufort Street. Very ladylike and discreet. A haven of civilisation and sanity. Chintz, flower arrangements and elderly waitresses in muslin aprons with ribbon-threaded caps.

Philippa was the only currently serving member of the WRAC to belong. The subscription was swingeing.

"An investment, young cobber," she said. "I get to talk to the boss ladies of the *other* services. And one or two of our members are married to top brass. A four-star general or two and some Army Board people. Casts a bit of a glow over my prospects and lets me out of crawling to menopausal majors."

It was in this category that Daphne fell, Philippa was convinced.

"All you have to do is sit tight. Believe me, the cavalry will come . . . How's your beaut feller, by the way?" She asked, reminded of the reality lurking behind her figure of speech.

"All right," Esme spooned up *crème brûlée*. "His troopers are providing the guard for Horse Guards this month. I must say I like this. We could have it in the mess. I told you I was messing member, didn't I? Nobody else wanted the job. The trouble is, with only eight mess members there's far too little extra messing money to manoeuvre with. You really have to use your imagination . . ."

But Philippa was not so readily put off.

"No wedding bells yet?"

"Give us a chance. He's got to settle into his regiment yet. And he's young, you know. Only two years older than me. Isn't there something about being twenty-five before a man can apply for marriage allowance?"

"Shouldn't think he'd need it," Philippa commented, signalling the waitress to take their coffee into the morning-room. "Met the folks yet? Anyway, we're not here to talk about him," she added quickly, hating to see Esme cast down. "Daphne's the thing. Carry on as you are and don't lose any sleep over her. If she tries blocking your commission, there's a lot of people will want to know why. You did *well* at Camberley, you know. Eccentrically maybe, but definitely well. No two ways about that.

"The root of your problem, I suspect, is that we were too frank with Daphers. Gave you too big a drum roll. She's jealous. That's all there is to it. She's never cut a dash in her life. You have, young cobber. Enjoy it."

Esme went away greatly comforted. Her confidence in prosecuting unit affairs increased from that moment.

Daphne, naturally, did not like her any the better for it. Particularly when Parsons, one of Esme's recidivist privates, was charged with stealing money from the military mails. A Court Martial offence and Parsons chose Esme for her defending officer.

Esme liked Parsons. She knew her, and not just from the rogues' gallery of photographs she kept in her office together with highly unparliamentary notes locked up in her safe. It was in that way that Esme parried Daphne's peremptory enquiries about her women. She knew their names, their faces and backgrounds. She knew their sisters' and brothers' names and a lot else besides. All learned by heart like irregular verbs. She bore the expense of photography personally and updated the notes and the gallery whenever a woman was posted in or out.

But there was more to Parsons than her gorilla-like figure, her acne and her shocking, rollicking service record of beer-soaked indiscipline. Her bed space, which stank of soiled underclothes and decaying morsels of clandestinely imported food, was adorned with garlands of Manchester United scarves and a socking great crucifix. There was something touching in that. Esme detected a thread of poetry in Parsons' soul. Anyway, the woman laughed at her jokes.

"Whether Parsons wants you or not is irrelevant," Daphne declared. 'Irrelevant' was one of her favourite words. "She's too simple to know how hopelessly inexperienced you are. She'd do much better to pick the 2ic or Moira. Then she'd be in a reasonably safe pair of hands."

"Better still, ma'am," Esme countered, "she should have a civilian solicitor. She's entitled according to my reading of the Queen's Regulations and I'm pretty sure she'd qualify for legal aid. The trouble is, that she won't. She insists on my defending her and I'm afraid ma'am, she has the last word on this."

Daphne Deveril's face exhibited every shade of purple in rapid succession. But Esme was right. She knew her military law and would stand by the letter of it. She'd had long hours of boredom to make herself master of section, sub-section, clause and subsidiary clause. An experienced officer she might not be, but she was a practised student. Dense matter, if coherent, did not dismay her.

Unfortunately, that was far from the end of the matter. Although an open and shut case in which Parsons was pleading guilty to the charges, Daphne would interfere. Esme, she decided, would need help in preparing her plea in mitigation. She couldn't possibly know what to put in and what to leave out. The result, Daphne insisted, would be time-wasting waffle.

Esme would have none of it. She stoutly claimed the right of privacy for her client in the shaping of such case as she had.

"Be it on your own head, Hansard," Daphne snarled venomously.

"If you make a bloody buffoon of yourself and Parsons is dismissed the service, we'll all know who to blame. I suppose you know that Parsons would sooner die than leave the army? But you're too vain to care about that, aren't you? No, you're hell-bent on boring the court to death."

Actually, Parsons had very little chance of being retained in the service. Not with the length of her conduct sheet. Her latest heinous offence would put the tin lid on it.

On the day of the Court Martial, the officer presiding, a Royal Artillery major, took up his position with two captains, all caparisoned in service dress complete with hats and Sam Brownes, behind the baize-covered trestle table, furnished with water carafes, pads and pencils. The rest of the room, cleared for the purpose, was filled with tubular steel chairs for voluntary onlookers, a table and two chairs for Esme and Parsons, and a similar one for Moira who was prosecuting.

The atmosphere was tense. Parsons was in the dock, and so in a sense was Esme. Marched in to hear the charges, Parsons stood rigidly to attention, bareheaded, before being dismissed to sit beside Esme.

"Will it be all right, ma'am?" Parsons half-whimpered, half-whispered, pale with awe at all the dry solemnity.

"I think so," Esme said. "Just relax." She sniffed. "Hmm . . . did you have a bath?"

"Yes, ma'am. Corporal Gallagher made me . . ."

"Never mind, Private Parsons," Esme tried to give the confidence she was far from feeling herself. "I bet you it turns out to be worth it."

Reassured, Parsons revealed a row of blueish-grey teeth.

Esme sat quietly through the prosecution evidence and admitted the facts on Parsons' behalf. She had taken fifteen pounds altogether in postal orders and cash. A very grave matter.

Finally it was her turn to address the court. Studying her hands to make sure they were steady before she began, Esme delivered the three short paragraphs of limpid prose she had honed, polished and committed to memory, with an unprecedented amount of nose-stroking. Poor Rummie had lost a tuft or two from his tummy. As Esme explained to him, the circumstances were exceptional.

"May it please the court . . ."

Parsons' mother, an indigent widow, was being pressed by a loan shark for payment of interest on a debt. Close to her mother and beside herself with worry about her, Parsons had taken the money to gain her some temporary relief from a bully's threats. Her action, completely out of character, had been prompted by despair. Of late, the enormity of what she had done had depressed Parsons' normally

87

robust spirits. To those who knew her, this change evidenced the deepest and most poignant remorse. As the court would clearly see from Parsons' long and rumbustious conduct sheet, she had never in the past committed any act of dishonesty. Her terrible folly, she well knew, had jeopardised her right to continue in the army . . . a life she loved and which had engaged her loyalty. And loyalty, as her offence would suggest, was a virtue for which Private Parsons had a measureless capacity. The court was entreated, therefore, to deal leniently with this unhappy but uncommonly good-hearted woman.

That was all.

Esme, whose voice had plashed like drops of thundery rain into the deep pool of silence around her, thanked the court for its patience and sat down. The silence lasted a while. The respectful hush that greets the end of a symphonic performance. Unabashed, Esme waited, her features as passionately serious as they had been from beginning to end.

The upshot was that Parsons was awarded a kindly admonition from the President of the Court and a stiffish fine, to be stopped over a period from her pay . . . but she was *not* dismissed the service.

Nor had the court been bored for one single instant by Esme's plea. On the contrary, it had been electrified.

"Ah," the President greeted her when she made her appearance in the ante-room before luncheon, "here comes our delightful advocate. What can I get you?" He turned to Daphne who was drinking gin and tonic, "Can I sign a chit in your mess, Major Deveril? I do think this girl deserves a drink, don't you? I'd certainly have wanted her on my side if I'd ever been in that kind of jam."

At lunch itself he paid her yet more attention, attending to Daphne's remarks with the mildest hint of impatience.

"Go carefully," warned Nancy, when they both went with Moira for the usual post-prandial conference in her room. "Celebrity's lethal round here."

And sure enough, that afternoon, in a fit of abstraction, or possibly understandable euphoria, Esme had the misfortune to stray over some grass forbidden to foot traffic. The infringement was witnessed by Daphne who chanced to be looking out of her office window at that moment.

"Alice," the OC yelled to her 2ic's office, "Give Miss Esme Hansard an extra Orderly Officer duty. She's getting too big for her boots."

Alone and unseen in her office, Alice Potter shrugged. She was used to these *non sequiturs* and her own confidential report hung in the balance. Daphne was a dangerous woman to cross.

"Right, ma'am," she called back. "Will do."

Sighing, Potter resumed checking the report before her for typographical errors. It was an off the record, unofficial catalogue of complaints against Esme Hansard, imputing to her a long list of obscure failings and faults. It was much the same thing as had been directed to ADWRAC Metropolitan District shortly after Esme arrived. This version was destined for higher realms still. WRAC1 in Lansdowne House. Quite pointless, since Esme's commission was to be confirmed. The lineage for the *London Gazette* had already been sent. Daphne's inconsistencies were nothing new.

Potter slumped back in her chair, mouth turned down in a despondent hoop. Would to God she had some gilded youth on a string like Esme Hansard. She'd marry him like a shot and get out.

"Come in here a moment, Esme, will you," she called, hearing the younger girl's steps in the entrance foyer.

"Well done for this morning," she said to her. "I'm afraid you've got an extra."

"What *for*?" Esme groaned.

"Does it matter?" Alice Potter ran her hands through her hair.

"Why doesn't somebody . . ."

Shaking her head frantically, Alice signed Esme to push the door closed.

"It's no good, you can't beat the system. Look, you might try applying for this."

"But what system *is* it?" Esme asked, barely glancing at the piece of paper she was handed.

Potter shrugged. "Take my advice. Apply for the course . . . subject to gazetting, naturally."

Esme did. The course in question was a Joint Services course of instruction in Photographic Interpretation. It sounded quite interesting, and unlike the Signals Courses, for which the Royal Signals was always trawling WRAC establishments, blessedly untechnical. It began in March. If she was accepted, Esme calculated, she would be out of Mill Hill in under twelve weeks. If she survived that long.

In fact she was shown the gazette entry concerning herself at the end of the first week in December.

"Relieved?" Alice said.

"Not particularly," Esme dissembled. Daphne should not have *that* satisfaction.

The path was clear now, to RAF Wyton.

Hearing what steps she had taken, Clive went on pulling leaves off his artichoke calmly.

89

"Where is this RAF Wyton place?" he said, wrinkling his Michelangelo nose.

"Huntingdonshire," Esme replied. "I know it's a long way but I just can't stay in that place any longer."

"I don't know any RAF people," Clive remarked simply as if this was an insuperable obstacle to Esme becoming acquainted with any herself. "I've never been to Huntingdonshire," he added, consigning that county to the list of desert places outside his sphere of knowledge.

"Not signed a visitors' book north of Bedfordshire, have you, darling?" Esme goaded him mildly.

"No, I haven't," Clive agreed. "Better not to, I think."

Esme enjoyed him in this mood. This frequent mood of petulant arrogance. His careful, selective ignorance of any world outside his own tickled her sense of the ridiculous. He was as funny as Tiggy, if not funnier. A subtler, more consistent comedian.

"Don't you want that?" he saw that Esme was slow with her artichoke, as she was doing most of the talking. "I'll finish it. Hand it over here.

"It doesn't matter anyway," he expanded, after some moments spent expertly denuding Esme's choke. "My regiment's going to Germany straight after Christmas. Here, this is the best bit. Open your mouth."

Esme chewed the *fond* dutifully. It could have been a bath plug for all the impact it made on her. Germany! How long had he known?

"I wish you were coming with us," Clive said gloomily. "You could type the colonel's letters or something."

Pleased to be wanted as one of the party, Esme wasn't going to tell Clive for the fifth or sixth time that WRAC officers didn't type anybody's letters. Too difficult to describe her actual duties, anyway. They were so peripheral . . . and too often led to deadlock or failure.

"Do you know," she said, "We had a questionnaire come round yesterday. The subalterns, that is. We had to fill in lots of boxes about our jobs. And one of them asked what the intellectual satisfactions were."

"What did you put?" Clive looked up with sudden interest.

"I put 'not applicable'."

"They won't like that," Clive snorted, approvingly.

Encouraged, Esme occupied the rest of the meal telling him about the annual sergeants' mess Games Night which had taken place on the previous evening. An occasion to which the officers were invited and compelled to attend.

"Oh, I know," Clive said equably. "Roulette and shove-ha'penny, and that sort of thing. We have something like it. I can't think why.

Everybody hates it. Completely unnatural."

"Well this certainly was. They wanted to dance with us. Apparently, it's normal there."

"What, women?" Clive looked astounded. "Women, dancing with women . . ."

"*Yes*. All in a sort of night-clubby gloom. They were slobbering over us. It was dreadful. This woman, Staff Sergeant Magwich, was hugging me to her huge bosom, and the more I tried to get away the more she . . ."

"What was your Commanding Officer or whatever's she's called doing?"

"Watching . . . grinning her head off. I sat down after the first time and tried to refuse to do it again. But she just poked at me and called me a spoil sport."

"Surreal."

"Oh, it was," Esme assured him, "I tell you, it was. I haven't done anything like that since I was little, at dancing classes . . ."

"She must be mad. Isn't it against Queen's Regulations or something?"

"I thought of that. But it doesn't mention *dancing*. Well, anyway, now you see the reason for Huntingdon."

"Wotcher, Darling Heart," Tiggy leaned over the back of her chair. "Got the nosebag on again, I see. Food's not bad here, is it?"

He had, Esme saw, a wondrous silver-maned creature on his arm, shimmering like a wicked serpent in a tube of virulent-green sequins. He did not introduce her but exchanged a few words with Clive before dropping a fraternal kiss on Esme's hair. "Well, hello and goodbye, young lovers. 'Tonight'," he began to sing absurdly, " 'I have a love of my own . . .' "

"Who was that?" Esme applied to Clive for the identity of the girl. "Is she one of . . ."

"No. She's a model," he muttered. "Tiggy says she's OK with an Elastoplast over her mouth. Doesn't charge in money."

"What does she charge in?" Esme was fascinated.

"Introductions," Clive told her succinctly. "Clive knows all sorts of greasy foreigners who'll never spot her accent."

"That's the foulest thing I ever heard," Esme glared.

"Isn't it just? Tigs sells himself too cheap."

Amoral and mercurial, Clive could always redirect the trend of Esme's thoughts.

"Why don't you find him a decent girlfriend?" she asked with asperity.

"I wish you wouldn't talk about him so much," Clive said with wonderful soulfulness. "I shan't be here much longer. I say, can we go?"

Later, "You won't go off with anyone else while I'm away, will you?" Clive said, running his tongue along the inside of her thighs as a preliminary to making love to her. "No aeroplane people. No female sergeants."

"No, of course not." Chuckling, Esme scratched his neck lightly with the tips of her nails. He whimpered pleasurably.

"You know, Esme, I . . ." Whatever he'd been going to say, he decided against it. Instead he said, "I'll write every day. It's going to be so boring without you."

7

As Philippa had foretold, the cavalry came to Lowlough Farm in the shape of a letter from AG16. The WRAC officers' postings branch. Esme was on Christmas leave at the time.

Not only was she accepted for the Photographic Interpretation course, at the end of her leave Esme was not to return to Mill Hill. Not even to pack. This would be done for her and the box sent on, care of military forwarding, to a completely new unit. The WRAC Battery attached to the Royal School of Artillery on Salisbury Plain . . . Major U. B. Spotteswoode, WRAC commanding. Larkhill, they called the place. It sounded quite pretty.

After that, she would report direct to RAF Wyton in March. Esme's spirits soared. The Mill Hill ordeal was over. It would be intolerable, anyway, without Clive. She felt a pang of regret, however, for Moira and Nancy, wishing them a speedy deliverance. One day they would all meet again to luxuriate in nostalgic recollections of misery.

The reasons for her rescue were immaterial to Esme. Probably they had nothing to do with her personally. It was simply that her particular mind cast was needed elsewhere. Mind training. At last, something to get her teeth into.

"Will I have to know anything about gunnery?" she asked Alice hopefully, roasting chestnuts before the sitting-room fire on Christmas Eve afternoon. "I don't see what use I can be in under three months . . ."

"Take it from me," Alice deflated her, "you won't have anything to do with it." And went on to tell her about ATS girls manning anti-aircraft gun emplacements during the war. Rapt, Esme listened with Gimlet curled up on her knee. Aunt Alice was always riveting when she talked about the war.

"Then they sent us all home," she concluded, brushing chestnut skins from her skirt, "to put our cocktail pinnies on. Shall we go to the midnight service or is there anything worthwhile on the telly?"

On the whole she found Esme reasonably buoyant. More so since the posting order had come. She was full of anecdote and passing references to someone called Clive.

Whenever she spoke of this youth, whoever he might be, Alice found herself struck by Esme's resemblance to Veronica in the days before her marriage. The face which had years ago stiffened into a mere photographic icon, sprang alive in her daughter's sporadic moments of vibrancy. Unnerving, because generally speaking, Esme had always looked more like her father.

There had been young men before, of course, Alice reminded herself, and without a doubt, there would be more. But there was a new vulnerability about the child, which disturbed Alice. That her niece was no longer virgin in heart she guessed, but the thought that her body was also encroached upon never occurred to her.

Had it done so, there would have been energetic enquiries of the youth and his parents regarding his future intentions. Alice, a magistrate, had come across the so-called sexual revolution and despised it. As for guardianship, the word meant what it said.

It was a matter of conscious policy with Esme not to say anything to Aunt Alice, about Daphne Deveril, for instance, that might rouse her formidable protective instincts. Intemperate letters would fly in every direction. Esme herself would be branded a trouble-maker with a heavy-handed guardian who threw her weight around. It had happened before. So her own occasional letters home from Mill Hill had been resolutely vivacious.

On Boxing Day Alice invariably made a cold collation from the substantial Christmas dinner leftovers and kept open house for her neighbours. They could come and go from twelve o'clock on.

Elderly for the most part, one or two stamped into the house wearing the Vale of Lune Harriers' hunt members' coat, having attended the meet down in Kirkby Lonsdale. Anything went.

Old Lady Makepeace wore wellingtons as she did for every daytime occasion including this one. She was rumoured to have put paid to an overbearing husband with a twelve-bore and was very much looked up to by local society. She was rich, although she kept her hens in the kitchen.

To Esme she said, "Know what? You're wasted in the army, gel. Ought to get married. Taken a fancy to anyone yet?"

Because the old woman was so artless, and because she missed Clive acutely and wanted to talk about him to anyone except Aunt Alice who would only probe and fuss, Esme confided she had. But he hadn't asked her yet. It was early days yet.

"Stuff and nonsense, gel," the old lady replied, helping herself liberally to breast of cold turkey. "Nobody worth having ever *asks* you. You got to run 'em to earth and then stop the hole."

"Isn't that unsporting?" Esme asked, laughing.

"T'aint sport, gettin' a man. It's business, that's what it is. Mark my words, stay in the army and men'll think you're peculiar. Bloody peculiar."

Stung, Esme turned away. Lady Makepeace was halfway to senility and hopelessly out of date anyway.

For the rest, it was mainly people like Commander Witherspoon saying things like, "Jolly good show. In the army, eh? Jolly good show."

No one, it seemed, took Esme's chosen profession the least seriously.

Larkhill was like going to a military department of heaven.

In factual terms, it was an outpost of the military empire marooned in the midst of Salisbury Plain. Devoted entirely to initiating Gunners at every stage of their careers into the ballistic mysteries of their complex art and testing new artillery weapons, the place, anything but pretty, was on a colossal scale . . . As was the mess.

Any feelings of diffidence Esme may have had were quickly dispelled.

"Oh yes, ma'am," said an ancient functionary in black jacket and striped trousers, in the cavernous, polish-scented hall. "It's Miss Hansard, isn't it? Leave your car keys with me and I'll get your baggage brought up to you. If you'll be so good as to wait, I'll just notify Miss Laurence you've arrived. She'll take you up to the WRAC quarters. Shall I send a cup of tea up after you now? And a bite to eat with it . . ."

Evidently, there was no shortage of staff here. The Gunners, clearly, looked after themselves. Not like the half-measures and shifts independent WRAC units were put to.

In less than five minutes Esme was shown to a room by a tall, decisive brunette called Paula whose job, she discovered, she would understudy during her time at Larkhill. She explained the ground rules appertaining to the WRAC part of the mess while they walked down corridors and up staircases.

"Men up here by invitation only," she stated, "but never between tea and dinner. We don't want them around when we've got rags in our hair or mudpacks on, do we? Beamish will valet your civilian clothes as well as your uniform if you slip her the odd quid. But watch her with woollies. She gets the water too hot and then wrings them like floor cloths. Stand over her or do it yourself.

"Oh, and she'll light your fire for you too, before you come home from the office if you tell her. All right? Good. I'll come for you at say, seven o'clock and take you down to the bar to meet some people. Tell you who's who and what's what. You don't want to be bothered with every Tom, Dick and Harry. All right?"

Very much so, Esme thought as the door closed. Her room contained all the usual army furniture, had two long dormer windows overlooking a wintry garden with low, humped pasture land beyond. A brief flurry of hail tapped the panes.

The best feature of all, however, was the tiny, hot coke fire in an Edwardian grate which cast its glow all over the slope-ceilinged room. On the desk a small silver specimen vase held a posy of slightly mud-splashed Christmas roses. Thoughtful of someone. A smartly monogrammed correspondence card lay propped against the flowers.

'Got here safely, I hope,' a bold, flourishing hand had written. 'Shan't dine in mess tonight as have prior engagement. PL will look after you. All your drinks on my chit. Have a nice evening and see you in the morning. Ursula Spotteswoode.'

How very, very kind of her. Esme's faith in the army was restored. She arranged her photograph frame on the bedside table and made Rummie comfortable on the bed. She felt completely at home.

The bar, not unlike the cocktail lounge in a smart hotel, boasted a service counter as long as a railway station platform. A score or two of men, busy with gin and tonic and gossip, swivelled their eyes in Esme's direction when she walked in with Paula, making a half-beat's pause in the hubbub of conversation.

Most were attired in conventional, dark lounge suits and a high percentage sported identical haircuts, Esme noticed. Longish, with aggressively straight side partings . . . the hair from the crown brushed in a curvacious wave over the left temple and tucked, like a girl's, behind the left ear. Here and there, flamboyant silk handkerchiefs sprouted from cuffs. Old-fashioned gold collar pins were popular too. One or two wore their blue patrols with the melancholy swagger that attends all officers on duty.

At any rate, they were a very different crew from the Postal Sappers with their suede shoes and Jack the Lad suits. Different from the *dégagé*, desperately understated young cavalrymen that Esme knew too. Anxious, on their sartorial showing, to be indistinguishable one from the other, they were all spawned, seemingly, from some sort of ideal Gunner matrix.

Since, up to now, only two young women had lived in the mess, Esme, clearly, would be in request. Equally clear was Paula's acknowledged position as master of ceremonies. The task of making any kind of social decision for herself was taken right off Esme's shoulders.

"Oh hello," she said offhandedly to a fresh-complexioned young man who sidled up to the low table where she sat holding court with Esme beside her. Ignoring the agonised look on his face, she chatted with him indifferently, looking straight over his shoulder.

"No, I'm not going to introduce you," she replied to his unspoken importuning. "She doesn't want to waste her energies on people like you. Shoo!"

He slunk away rejected, to the sound of masculine mockery on the further side of the room.

"Nice try, Ludo . . ."

"What was wrong with him?" Esme asked, amused but sorry for the boy.

As Paula crisply explained it, Ludicrous Ludo was a Young Officer, only recently emerged from Sandhurst and now undergoing a course of basic gunnery instruction. A dismal one-pipper and the lowest form of life at Larkhill. That included other ranks, who were very highly qualified and correspondingly paid. Majors were two a penny here and lieutenant-colonels scarcely less common. YOs were a bit of a nuisance.

"But I'm only a Second Lieutenant myself," Esme protested.

"You will find," Paula, who was a full Lieutenant, countered scientifically, "that in a place like this, you can add at least two ranks to your sex for purposes of practical status."

Of the few that Paula deemed qualified to be presented to Esme, a Major Ivor Llewellyn was one.

Compactly built, darkly good-looking . . . almost foreign-seeming, he paused by Paula's chair with the object of exchanging a word. Paula's superior air deserted her. Bridling with pleasure, frisking her legs, she engaged him in a longer discussion than it appeared to Esme he wanted. Something to do with some people she'd met at a wedding in Woolwich recently.

This was very different from the cool, imperious Paula of a moment ago. Esme was not quite sure where to look. Flicking her eyes back and forward . . . from the bar, to the windows, the door and back to Paula again, in the hope she'd soon be ready to relinquish her hold on the increasingly restive Major Llewellyn, she found her glance snagged on his more than once. A look of detached, unsmiling interest. Any shelter, she read his expression, in this blizzard of boredom.

97

Embarrassed for Paula, her sponsor in this place and only friend, so far, Esme felt herself redden. She was about to get up as if to go to the ladies' room when Paula finally ran out of steam. With a curt nod in Esme's direction, Major Llewellyn spun on his heel, just slowly enough to avoid the impression of rudeness.

"Ivor," Paula made a desperate bid to reclaim his attention. "You haven't met Esme. She's here on temporary detachment . . ."

He offered his hand with a perfunctory smile. "I hope we're making you comfortable . . ."

"Oh, thank you, yes," said Esme. "The mess is incredibly hot . . . warm. I shan't need my vest."

Good God, why had she mentioned anything as drear as a *vest* to this man? She didn't even wear vests . . .

If he noticed the slip, he gave no sign of it but talked of the Siberian weather that haunted the plain at this time of year. He hoped she would enjoy her time at Larkhill . . . Most WRAC officers did . . . The YOs, he was sure, would be enchanted . . . and devastated to learn she was leaving them so soon. And now, would she very kindly excuse him.

"See you later, Paula."

Esme's cheeks burned. YOs indeed! Excuse him? It was not *she* who had detained him.

"What a . . ." Esme never said it.

Paula pre-empted her with an enthusiastic account of the career of Major Ivor Llewellyn. He was thirty-two now, had been only twenty-eight when promoted Major . . . the youngest then in the whole Royal Regiment of Artillery . . . had already been to Staff College . . . The army's university of strategic studies, Paula loftily interpreted for Esme's benefit . . . Was now involved in highly secret work assessing the nuclear capability of the Soviet forces . . . would obviously command his own regiment one day, and from there on would be unstoppable. He was a career soldier.

'Oh', and 'really', was all Esme had managed to say by the time they walked into the dining-room.

"Of course, most women are scared stiff of him," she added, handing Esme a glossy damask napkin from a fresh pile on a table by the doorway. "They don't realise how lonely he is. He works under tremendous pressure . . . where shall we sit?"

Esme shrugged. The dining-room, too large for the usual single long table, had any number of these. There were chandeliers and massive paintings lining the walls. Pictures of men, horses and machines, pitched into hell.

"Wherever you think . . ."

"I suppose we'd better sit with Carol. She's the 2ic. Not exactly a ball of fire . . ."

They sat down, one on either side of Carol Bunyan who didn't seem overjoyed to have their company. After a grunt in response to Paula's introduction of Esme, she returned to her conversation, mostly one-sided, with an officer morosely drinking soup on the opposite side of the table. A retired widower, Esme later found out, who lived in the mess and whose two horses lived in the stables. Bunyan had designs on him, or so Paula said.

"What's this?" Esme indicated a silver-topped bottle of clear brown fluid with things floating in it.

"Chilli sherry," the retired officer supplied, seeming glad of a change of interlocutor. "You put it in your soup."

Esme did so when a plate of consommé was put down before her. Rather more than she should have done.

Taking a rest between flaming mouthfuls, Esme noticed to her additional mortification that at the other end of the table Ivor Llewellyn was seated, in earnest discussion with two pale, bespectacled men, whose imprecise turn-out suggested they were civilians. He seemed very determined not to look in her party's direction. Not that Esme wished him to. Now she saw the real reason why Paula had wanted to sit here. How perfectly awful.

Then the lights dimmed, flickered, recovered . . . and went out completely. A groan of pretended dismay greeted the blackout. After some little delay, mess servants came bearing great, many-branched silver candelabra, working their way between tables with the aid of torches.

Just as the first few candles on Esme's table were lit, she saw that Ivor's gaze had been fixed on her under cover of the relative darkness. He turned back to the boffin types immediately.

Obscurely relieved to find that he didn't think her quite such a nonentity after all, Esme devoted herself to lamb cutlets with Sauce Robert. Paula was welcome to Major Llewellyn. He was middle-aged and unmannerly. A bore. A swarthy, self-important little Welshman.

The power cut lasted three hours, promoting a blind-man's-buff camaraderie. Expected to behave like children, subalterns usually do. There were impromptu games of tag and sardines, to the delight of the mess staff, to whom the latest crop of YOs were akin to the newest generation of a very old family. Senior resident mess members got apple-pie beds. Esme herself helped to make one. Plenty of the mess's everyday port was drunk too. All infantile, inebriate, innocent fun.

Ivor, Esme noted, watched from the sidelines, stationed with other mature officers, in ante-room chairs, a decanter between them.

Tolerant but remote from the action. Difficult to imagine that Major Llewellyn had ever been young. What the YOs called a military shit . . .

Turning her lamp out that night, after watching the fag end of an old film in the Boudoir, as the WRAC officers' private sitting-room was jocularly dubbed, Esme wondered if there might be a letter from Clive in the morning. Every day meant every day from his first day in Germany. But possibly not *quite*, in Clive's case.

One had to make reasonable allowances.

"I suppose you know why you're here," Ursula Spotteswoode challenged her, as soon as Esme had removed her hat and sat down in front of the OC's desk.

A straight elbow chair this time. The right height to permit level eye contact. In spite of the booming voice of the giantess in front of her, Esme felt certain that here was someone who played fair.

"No, I don't, actually, ma'am. But I'm . . ."

"Because Daphne Deveril thinks you're a clot. That's why. Are you a clot?"

It wasn't a rhetorical question as the ensuing pause proved. Evidently Ursula expected an answer.

"I don't believe so, no, ma'am. May I thank you for your hospitality *in absentia*, last night?"

"Latin, eh? And no. No, you mayn't. Should've been there m'self. Couldn't. What did you make of the Christmas roses? Fair specimens, aren't they?"

Agreeing warmly on their quality, Esme found herself talking about gardening and her Aunt Alice's constant difficulty with keeping soil away from those winter-flowering blooms. Ursula was Gardens Member for the mess, it seemed. The planting here was typical. Suffered from lack of continuity . . . They seemed to go on for quite a long time about that.

"So you're not a clot in your own estimation," Ursula switched the subject again. "Hmm. Well, we'll see . . . Bunyan's a clot y'know. Tries hard and all that. Makes it worse, of course . . ."

Faintly shocked that Major Spotteswoode should criticise her own second in command so freely . . . a person who was, after all, Esme's superior officer, she covered her confusion by reaching for her shoulder bag. It sat beside her chair on the floor. A searing, excruciating pain tore through her.

"Ouch!" she snatched back her hand. The second joint of her middle finger was punctured. It began to ooze blood.

"Got to watch out for the family," Ursula trumpeted, unconcerned as Esme nursed her wound. "Bit sharp some of them. Bad people. *Bad!*"

She flung the rebuke in the general direction of what Esme had taken for a roughly circular, silky-haired rug. It turned out to be nine Pekinese dogs. Three generations. A matchless strain, according to Ursula. Chun Reds. Very rare.

"Be all right when they get to know you. Go a bit haywire if they think you're timorous."

Timorous? But it was no good, Esme divined, arguing with Major Ursula Spotteswoode. She was used to the type. It included Aunt Alice and quite a lot of her friends. Camilla Crump, for example. So she apologised for alarming Ursula's 'family' and said the bite was insignificant. Her own fault for being so stupid.

"So you should be," Ursula agreed, not really listening. Something was going on in the brain she kept under her bouffant, pale-lilac rinsed hair. It looked incongruous, capping her barbaric Aztec features.

"We're very proud of being Gunners, you know," she said. "Very proud."

Esme noted she wore the Gunner collar insignia as a brooch on her barrack dress sweater. The sweater was not of regulation pattern or colour. Not even near. It was a cream, cable knit Argyll, with the WRAC green epaulettes sewn on it. And her shirt, so far from being Moss Bros white poplin, collar detached, was green and brown check Viyella . . . collar firmly attached and not very happy with the WRAC braid tie which encircled it casually.

"Our women here," she went on, "Are very high calibre. Very brainy, some of them. Mind you, I've no idea what most of them do. Hush, hush, see. Lot of sums. Any good at sums? No. Nor me."

And yet Major Spotteswoode, for all her outrageous deviance, was impressive. Esme liked her at once.

Her theory of command was eccentric too, but seemed to work. Ursula rode her unit on a loose rein, maintaining perfect control. She placed great emphasis on the efficiency of NCOs and was disinclined to trouble her officers.

"Just a few little jobs," she would mutter in the mornings. "Nothing much to do. You youngsters had better get off and have lunch in Salisbury. Nothing worse than a lot of whey-faced subalterns hanging round. Nobody joins the army for the money. You're here to enjoy yourselves."

Pleasant as these excursions to Salisbury were, Esme preferred lunching in mess. Ursula made a great ceremony of this ordinary, workaday meal. She and her officers foregathered in the mess ladies' room, a spacious, mirrored apartment with dressing-tables and tablets of Roger & Gallet soap. When noses had been powdered and hands washed, an instinctive line of march formed up behind Ursula, almost as if there had been a command.

Next they processed down the corridor, across the hall and into the dining-room. No bar or ante-room . . . Ursula didn't drink spirits at lunchtime. Ursula first, with the dogs surging round her feet, Paula came after, being next in height if not in seniority, Carol Bunyan . . . and Esme, shortest and youngest, in the rearguards. Bags, by tacit agreement, were held fashion-model-wise, along the right forearm. And heads, for some reason, were held very high throughout this portentous parade. Male officers of whatever rank simply scampered out of the way.

The dogs fell out at the dining-room doors, forming their customary circular *laager*. A hazard to be negotiated by officers, staff and visitors alike. Complaint was unthinkable.

Esme loved the whole thing. Among masses of much more important people, Ursula had the knack of making her complement count. Leading them as she did, literally and spiritually. The mystique of command.

In under a week Ursula had come to a conclusion about Esme and whether or not she was deficient in sense. It arose out of an extraordinary discussion in the office Carol Bunyan shared with Paula and Esme. The matter turned on the acquisition of some flowering shrubs to soften the stark approach to the women's accommodation block. What, enquired Ursula, hands on hips, did everyone think?

Carol Bunyan put on her glasses, knitted her brow and began to speak. There was a plantation just off the Andover road, belonging to the park of a mansion, but out of sight of the house. There was a lodge in view, but as far as Carol knew, uninhabited. It might be practicable, with the use of a garden fork, to lift some self-seeded rhododendrons, wrap them in sacking and hide them in the boot of a car. The operation would be safer if carried out at dusk . . .

Catching a stray lock of hair with which to stroke her nose, Esme took her cue from Ursula who appeared to be giving this plan of action her serious consideration. Doing things the difficult way was characteristic of the army, anyway. Look at Adventure Training . . . Still, it would be rather unpleasant, Esme considered, to be scrubbing around a private woodland in the dark . . .

"And what does our one-pip wonder think?" Ursula spun round to her suddenly. "Any ideas, young Esme?"

"Would there be anything terribly wrong in just buying some plants in Salisbury marketplace?" She heard herself blurting. "I suppose it sounds naïve . . ."

"Not that stupid after all, are you?" Ursula observed triumphantly, throwing her 2ic a withering look. "You can spend twenty pounds. Battery funds'll run to it. You and Paula take the battery transport down after lunch . . . Or now if you want. Have a cream cake at Snell's. Bombardier'll drive you."

When Esme returned with a selection of azaleas and so forth, Ursula announced, *fortissimo*, that she had dictated a confidential letter to WRAC1, copy to AG16, stating that Esme possessed officer qualities in exceptional degree. The letter was to be placed on her documents. That would scotch Daphne Deveril's cretinous blatherings.

"Satisfied, Miss? I think you'll do. Don't want to spend your life down a bunker, do you?"

Here, Ursula referred to the Photographic Interpretation course which Esme was entered for. She warned that at its conclusion, Esme would spend all her working hours immured in some secret, underground location. Nobody knew where it was. And no WRAC officer who'd been sent there had ever re-emerged to give the game away. The Official Secrets Act had something to do with it, naturally, but Ursula, rightly or wrongly, hinted darkly at other forms of coercion. A word to the wise.

"Tell you what," she said, "I'll take up that letter m'self. Tell 'em you're not going. Stay here with us, eh? I'm doing you a favour, mind. It'll mean putting on their idea of a uniform."

At that moment, Esme would have died for her.

On such minuscule affairs as rhododendrons are the futures of army officers often decided.

Clive wrote eventually, after three weeks had passed by. Esme's insides turned somersaults at the sight of the envelope, embossed with the royal arms on the flap.

When she plucked it out of her pigeon-hole, the hall man on duty grinned at her unconcealed pleasure. A very nice young lady, was Miss Hansard. And cute, into the bargain. Kept the young gentlemen around here guessing, she did.

"That the one you've been waiting for, ma'am?"

"Oh, George . . . Yes, it is."

Clive made no excuses for his tardiness but had covered three sides of foolscap in neat, thin-nibbed writing. Esme sized that up at once, together with the unexciting salutation and valediction: 'My dear Esme', and 'Much love'. Same as ever, he gave nothing away. He had only ever called her darling once.

His prose style was threadbare, communicating events with the flatness of a boy writing from school to his sister about how many times he'd been beaten and how many Rugby goals his side has scored. Dull, but endearing:

> *They got us out of bed at sparrow fart last Friday.* Clive wrote dourly: *because some Staff Officer or other said the Russians were coming. Really boring because we all had hangovers thanks to a mess night. (Most of the ante-room furniture was in matchsticks and we've got to pay for it). Anyway, we all shoved off in our tanks thinking we were going to be heroes. We crawled halfway to the border when they tell us it's a joke. (False alarm.) You probably can't imagine what it's like turning a tank round to go home in the middle of two divisions all trying to do the same thing. We made two miles an hour and had to eat compo rations. The tinned smoked cheese is best ...*

There was more about a German farmer who'd wanted to hold up the column with a herd of cows. Tiggy had been roped in to deal with him in his electrifying German. One of Clive's troopers was allowed to dismount from the tank and stay behind to help the farmer milk his cattle by hand. It had all been amazingly boring.

How was Esme? He missed her a lot. Gunners were supposed to be frightful. Clive wouldn't know, never having met any. He'd seen some lately at Hohne Garrison Mess but, of course, hadn't talked to them. They looked boring. Tiggy was so bored he let off a thunder flash. The Colonel heard about it but was quite sympathetic. Tiggy knew someone with a house in Gstaad. They might push off there in the Aston for a few days next week and ski a bit. He wished Esme were coming. Could she please write back quickly.

That was it. And every word of it precious to Esme. Write to him quickly? No, she would not. She would make herself wait for a week. At *least*!

Later in the day, as all of Larkhill was shutting up shop and going home for tea, Ivor Llewellyn fell into step beside Ursula.

"Can't you tell that young officer to put her hat on?" He gestured at Esme who was walking on ahead with Paula.

"Don't be a fool," retorted Ursula. "You can see she's just had her hair done. Got a headpiece on her, has that one," she expanded. "You could do worse, Ivor."

"Not for me," he said shortly. "She gets far too much attention as it is."

"Llewellyn, you're a stick-in-the-mud."

After dinner that same evening in Hohne, Clive lay on his bed twirling a smoking Browning nine millimetre automatic in his hand. A side arm issued to officers during the scare. The armoury hadn't rounded them up yet. Clive wouldn't dream of being so officious as to hand his in voluntarily.

In the armchair beside him, Tiggy was slumped. The dartboard, recently affixed to the door, had fallen to the carpet with a thud. Both contemplated the scarred and splintered door without interest. There were a few clean perforations too, where the shots had gone wide. What was a door? Cheap, as barrack damages went.

"Another one?"

"No," Clive answered his friend, yawning. "I feel I need something."

"Got some grass in my room."

"No. Not that . . ."

"Toss yourself off then," Tiggy suggested, emptying the chamber of his gun peaceably. "Want a race?"

Clive ignored this proposition. Wanking was for schoolboys and no-hopers. A man such as he was should have no need to resort to such squalid compromises. Even in the wilderness that was NATO-occupied Germany.

"Ever been to the teachers' mess, Tigs?"

Clive was reluctantly interested to know what, if anything, these young women recruited on government contracts to teach soldiers' children had to offer. FME, most of them. Failed Marriage England, or so it was said. However, they were women and presumably willing to give officers in need relief at nugatory cost.

"Once," Tiggy admitted. "They're all right. Go around in quilted housecoats. Fluffy slippers. Cheap wine."

From which scant information, Clive inferred that Tiggy did not recommend this source of feminine comfort. His erection subsided slightly. Not sufficiently so, however, to dissuade him from further research.

"Do they expect to be taken out to dinner?"

"The officer quality ones do."

Clive's eyes snapped, suddenly alert. Tigs knew such a lot. "*Are* there any officer quality ones?"

Tiggy shrugged. "Not in Esme's league, no. You know how it is, they talk so much. It's always boring."

"I need Esme," Clive decided. "Scheduled flight from Frankfurt. Fastest possible route . . ."

"Expensive," Tiggy commented unnecessarily, appreciating that Clive couldn't wait to hitch a lift with the RAF. Uncool thing to do, anyway. "What will you say to the Adjutant?"

"Got to visit my tailor," Clive said unhesitatingly. "That pin-stripe he made me . . . Colonel doesn't like it."

"That should do," Tiggy approved. "My compliments to Darling Heart," he instructed blithely, as Clive left the room to go to the telephone.

He opened the drawer in Clive's night table. Blast! No little treats in there. Coke was hard to come by in Hohne. A very boring place. Better give Clive a shopping list.

"Good girl," Clive hugged her to him at the airport. "Got the Bean Can? Let's go then."

"Yes, but go where?" Esme asked, a little hurt that he hadn't made more of the fact that she'd got two days' leave at no notice at all. It seemed so unkind to Ursula who'd simply taken one look at her face and said, "Am I your gaoler? Off with you," and prevented Carol Bunyan from recording the time on her leave schedule. She really wanted to tell Clive about that.

"It's wonderful to be with you, again," Clive's voice strummed across her nerves, a knowing finger on harp strings. "Tiggy sends his love."

That was the real message. The secret signal . . . the guarantee of Clive's love. Esme took it for granted that when he mentioned Tiggy to her . . . drew her into the circle of that inalienable bond, he communicated the depth of his feeling for her.

She turned on to the M4, no longer caring where they were going. The mystery tour could have only one end. Fusion with Clive and the whole of his life. He started to direct her from the Hammersmith flyover. "Turn left . . . bear right . . . stay in this lane," and finally, "Park here." They were in Orme Square, outside Tiggy's mother's flat.

How infuriating of him not to have told her. But the dilation of his pupils and pallor of his skin told her what she needed to know most urgently. Nor did Esme miss the way his hand shook as he put the key in the lock.

Once inside the cramped lobby, he put his hands round her waist and said thickly: "Have you ever thought you might be able to do it in your clothes?"

Esme had never considered such a thing but had no time to say so. Clive covered her mouth with his own, emitting moans that shuddered upwards from the soles of his feet. He fumbled at his fly. Esme felt the rod spring hard against her. He pulled up the skirt of her tailored, gaberdine dress, tearing at her underclothes recklessly. He entered her violently, excitingly . . . bringing her crashing to the ground underneath him as his own knees gave way.

"I feel like a peasant," he said happily when it was all over. "A nice change."

"It's all right for you," Esme answered him in a voice she knew sounded sulky. "All you have to do is hook your front up and there you are, all proper again. I must look like a rape victim . . ."

"Poor you," Clive was instantly sympathetic. Appearances mattered to him too. He sat up and pulled Esme into his arms. Gently, dextrously, he removed all her clothes before going to fetch her a kimono from the Marquesa's wardrobe. She was married now. Gone down a notch, Clive pointed out.

"Put it on. We can have a bath soon. I've put the immersion heater on. This all right for afternoon tea? Or this?"

Clive had found a tin of caviare in the cupboard and one of lychees. They ate both, direct from the cans with a spoon, sprawling on the sofa in the sitting-room. The flavours went surprisingly well together, they agreed.

"Have you got some trousers or something," Clive asked, "Because we're going to see some rather strange people tonight. They're all right," he added, seeing her look of alarm, "It's just they take dressing down pretty seriously."

Before leaving the flat, Clive hung Esme's dress and his own suit on hangers, over a bath of boiling hot water. For the creases, he said. Then he washed her discarded stockings and pants, studiously domestic. She watched him, soaking up reserves of peace at the sight.

They lasted her a while, but not long enough to wholly offset the tedium of an evening spent in a large flat near Vauxhall Bridge. Not exactly their kind of stamping ground or their kind of people, or so Esme would have said, had she been asked.

The place, in a down-at-heel building, was a warren of small, carpetless rooms, painted in violent colours. Bull's blood, green and purple. Pervaded with the sickly scent of joss sticks and wailing sitar music, the walls were decorated with posters depicting Hindu deities. And the people of whom there seemed to be dozens, matched the decor.

Girls with bundles of Pre-Raphaelite hair trailed about in long, draggled skirts, barefooted or wearing laplander's boots. The men wore paint-plastered jeans and a great deal of crude silver jewellery. Someone was always talking to someone else on the telephone. About what, precisely, Esme had no idea. The language used was some kind of code. Gibberish.

One or two people spoke to Esme, asking her how she knew Clive. When she said it was because of the army, they stared, edging away. Clive himself abandoned her on a sofa with a peculiar orange drink, called tequila. He came in and out at intervals, stroked her and said he wouldn't be long.

He was long. Very long. From feeling awkward at first, in her silk shirt and Mary Quant slacks, Esme advanced to lassitude. Amid all the hurly-burly, she fell asleep on the sofa, waking once, when somebody shoved an omelette at her on a cracked plate. It tasted strange. Later she was sick in a malodorous lavatory.

How they got back to Orme Square Esme never knew until the morning. Apparently they'd taken a taxi. The Bean Can was still parked outside that block of flats. They'd have to take another taxi to go back and get it, Clive remarked easily.

"How do you feel?" He called from the bathroom.

"All right, I suppose." Esme was uncertain. She felt muzzy.

"Good. I'll go out and get some eggs."

Later they were back among the confusion of the night before. Or its daylight aftermath. Acrid smells, dirty plates and overflowing ashtrays.

"Hi, Esme," one or two people said. She settled herself to wait for Clive, wishing he hadn't insisted on calling on these people again. Surely they could just have collected the car without coming up here . . .

Flicking the pages of some incomprehensible underground magazine, it occurred to Esme some time later, that she hadn't seen Clive for an hour and a half. It was three o'clock in the afternoon. She was hungry. And lonely. She got up to look for him, relieved to encounter one of the more normal-looking men in the corridor. He wore his hair in a braid but was kind.

"Oh, I was looking for Clive. Have you seen him?"

"He's not here," the braided man replied. His eyes met Esme's with something she recognised as embarrassment. "Look, we're making some curry . . ."

Esme's body temperature plummeted. She fled.

8

Hurtling down the A3, Esme wanted assuagement badly. Every haemorrhaging artery of feeling shrieked for a tourniquet. Every tormented nerve craved morphine. A soothing masculine prostration to pacify her outraged feminine pride. If not from Clive himself, then from someone else. Someone must minister to her wounds.

Ivor Llewellyn should do it. Compensate her for Clive's desertion. Make up, a little, for the humiliating search through that Orme Square house for a neighbour with a key to Tiggy's mother's flat so she could pick up her suitcase . . . And banish the memory of the look on that neighbour's face. Amortise a wasted day of leave and the raised eyebrows that would follow.

Yes, Ivor should be taught to want her. Want her so madly he went down on his knees . . . She would teach *him* what it was to treat Esme Hansard lightly. That would never, never happen again.

Esme had no need to form these intentions into words. No wish to disentangle one emotion from another. No ability to distinguish between one sensate organ and the rest. Skin, skeleton, intestines were united in a blind, indiscriminate quest for solace at any price. She was hurt, more so than she had ever been in her life before and she would have surcease. The ointment of masculine homage on her wounds. Immediate and worthy healing. Ivor Llewellyn, none other. Not some calf-eyed YO.

To think about Clive hurt far too much. She had to think about somebody else. Had to re-make in herself what had been destroyed.

Reaching Larkhill, racing up the back stairs to her room, Esme flung herself down on her bed. She bit Rummie's ear hard, hard. There must be no tears. No grief for a man she had already forgotten. No puffiness round the eyes to warn off the man elected to ameliorate her suffering.

To get this comfort she would have to stalk it. Hunting was always good. A lust for action that took one's mind off things. That's why Aunt Alice did it.

Calmer, Esme considered her tactics, surveyed the territory. She would come at Ivor on his unguarded flank . . .

Dinner downstairs was almost over. Ursula ate early anyway and retired to her spacious field officer's quarters, preferring her own television set and fireside. Unless there was a special occasion she was rarely seen in the public rooms after nine. So from her, no trouble till the morning.

Paula's habits were unpredictable. It didn't matter. Any comtempt of hers would soon ripen to envy. Esme would show her the right way to manage Ivor Llewellyn . . . and then she could have him.

Ivor, she knew, often clicked a few billiard balls around after dinner before retiring to do some work in his rooms. Any time between ten and half past, he came down to the bar to sign a chit for a nightcap. Single malt whisky. There would be YOs aplenty there, showing off to each other. Most of the more senior men were married and lived out. It left Ivor without peers to hedge him in.

Suddenly she was enraged with Ivor too. Unreasonably, she asked herself resentfully why he was not already hers. Why should she have to chase a man like him? A second string. An also ran . . . But the best that could be had here.

Esme washed her hair, had a bath and went to work. Effective work it was too. Anger lends brilliance to eye and complexion. And at a certain stage of cold resolution, virtuosity to the hand wielding an eyeliner brush. Heliotrope. It looked good with the light-spangled rush of rain in her irises.

"Esme! We thought you were away . . ."

"Here, here! Sit here . . ."

Esme made a feint of merely signing a chit for a small measure of brandy and taking it out of the room. She saw Ivor was alone, as usual, exchanging desultory words with the bombardier bar tender.

"Oh no," a groan ensued. "Don't go . . ."

"Talk to me . . ."

"You're so mean with yourself . . ."

"Well," Esme relented, halfway to the door, "you know what you were telling me the other day about *jump* . . ." Ivor, she noted out of the corner of her eye, had raised his head at this, "and the calculations you use to make allowances for it . . ."

It really wasn't very difficult. The YOs were delighted to pass on

110

the elements of their lessons in gunnery. And Esme, like many who are not outstandingly numerate, was quite instinctive about geometry. It enabled her to keep the ensuing conversation going with the appearance of penetrating intelligence. 'Drop' she demonstrated herself with a balled piece of silver paper from a cigarette packet, propelled by an improvised peashooter. The higher the elevation, the steeper the drop, surely . . . 'Jump' varied the trajectory still further . . . but did it compensate? And would the same calculation do for a ball as a shell . . .?

Quite astonished at herself, and the use she could make of the vocabulary she'd acquired, Esme tied the YOs up in knots.

"Yes . . ."

"Ball's obsolete, anyway . . ."

"No, Ludo. You're telling her all wrong . . ."

"Be quiet . . ."

If Ivor had had any thoughts of drinking his second whisky in the bath, he abandoned them.

So this lissom pet of Ursula's was interested in gunnery, was she? She was lovely, he mused. Spoiled . . . too aware of herself. Look how she turned her gem of a profile this way and that . . . The little witch knew it was divine. Listen how she played on that voice of hers, pinging it around the room like tubular bells . . . All Esme Hansard had ever lacked, Ivor thought, were a few very good spankings early in life.

Nevertheless he could hardly sit here and let the YO thickos misinform her so woefully.

Ivor slid from his seat and walked into the trap. The YOs admitted defeat and withdrew. Nobody could argue with Llewellyn's antlers. Larkhill's stag of stags was nuzzling the choicest hind for miles around. His looks, his rank, his rumoured influence . . . entitled him.

Things are the same in civilian breeding contests, but rarely so cut and dried.

The next evening he took her out to dinner. It might have looked better to refuse the first time, but what with Ursula's overt concern at her early return to duty and Paula's covertly malicious curiosity, Esme was glad to have this trump to play early.

They went to the Walnut Tree, one of those places that pretends to be a country pub but charges Mayfair prices. At any rate, way above any YO's touch. Gunner subalterns do not, in general, have private incomes.

Ivor had booked. Following the proprietor as he piloted them through an archipelago of glossily polished, oaken tables, Esme received the daunting impression that her escort had put a great deal into planning their evening together. A table beside the blazing log fire had been reserved and long-aproned waiters were already poised there, holding out chairs.

Oh dear, there was no need for all this, Esme thought. She wasn't going to be worth it.

"Ivor, old chap!"

A brindle-haired gentleman with a matching moustache swung round from his chair, impeding their progress.

"Evening, sir," Ivor caught Esme by the elbow, drawing her arm through his own. "I hear you're off to SHAPE . . ."

There was a conversation between the two men then, which didn't interest Esme although she put herself to the trouble of looking polite. Very difficult when you were bored stiff. Brindle-hair's wife, however, a sharp-eyed matron of some forty-five summers in a cashmere twin set and two rows of yellowish pearls, treated Esme to an unblinking stare of appraisal. An awful old trout, Esme thought, keeping the noncommital curve on her lips.

"Esme," Ivor said in the end, "I'd like you to meet Brigadier Chumleigh-Walters and Mrs Chumleigh-Walters . . ."

"Pauline, to you," interposed the Brigadier's wife, meaning Ivor. And frostily, to Esme, "Have you known Ivor long . . ."

Intervening, the Brigadier said she wasn't to pester the pair. Doubtless they'd be needing their dinner.

"Remarkable figure . . ." Esme heard the Brigadier begin as she moved away. "Might do . . ."

She heard Pauline Chumleigh-Walters start to answer some inaudible remark of her husband's.

Gratified, Esme silently vowed that they were all in for a big disappointment. 'Might do', indeed.

"He and my father were at the Shop together," Ivor explained as a waiter spread a napkin on Esme's lap. He went on to describe the Brigadier's current and future appointments whilst scanning the wine list. Far too many initials and acronyms for Esme. Army language was so ungainly.

"What's the Shop?"

"It doesn't exist any more but it used to be the Officer Cadet School at Woolwich where they trained Gunner and Royal Engineer cadets . . ."

Interested, Esme gave him her undivided attention. The illustrious history of these two ancient Corps was worth hearing about from Ivor's lips. On this subject he was a vivid raconteur. And so his father had been in the army, had he? And his grandfather . . . Both had retired as majors to live on their memories and slender military pensions . . . Welsh? No, the family hadn't been seriously Welsh, now, for three

112

generations. They moved about with the army and tended to retire in the villages close to Wiltshire or Hampshire garrison towns . . . where all their friends were.

Esme kept Ivor going like this through the cream of sorrel soup, baked oysters and mulberry sorbet, all of which he strongly urged upon her. They drank Pouilly-Fumé . . . one of the smokiest years, and Nuits-Saint-Georges, both of which, as Esme knew, were very expensive. Poor old Ivor. He was going to regret this.

Then marinated strips of venison fillet came to be flambéed with much ado at their table . . . salad and juniper-flavoured potatoes. Food as good as any Clive had fed her. Mentally, Esme trampled on his resurgent image. *No, no no!*

"And what about you?" Ivor asked her when the waiters finally left them alone. "Where's the family home?"

There seemed no particular point in not telling him everything. It *was* a good story. Ivor deserved *something* in return for all this. And Clive had never . . . *Get out of me!* Silently, Esme screamed her exorcism. She focused desperately on the unwitting Ivor.

His opinion of her, already modified, underwent a transformation. Spoiled? Who, in view of the tale she so matter-of-factly unfolded, could do other than spoil her? He himself would buy her the moon. And kill with his bare hands any who attempted to harm her. Poor little orphan child . . . Ivor pulled himself together. He was getting disgustingly maudlin . . .

"I hope," she said laying her knife and fork together neatly at the end of the story and the venison, "That it doesn't all sound like boasting."

"Do you really mean to say," he returned, open-mouthed, "that you knew Drummond?"

"Yes," Esme scintillated, enjoying herself. "He gave me the teddy bear that's on my bed at the moment."

"But . . ." he could scarcely understand her insouciance. "Have you any idea how famous that man was?"

"What? For all the stuff he did in the war?"

"Well, yes. But he was one of the greatest amateur yachtsmen this country has ever known . . . Owned a sloop . . ."

"Really? I'm not interested in little boats so I wouldn't know," she squashed him, thinking it was time for a little wholesome teasing.

Ivor looked severe. 'Little boats' was overdoing it, wasn't it?

"And Vaughan . . . Do you know he's one of the most senior generals in the whole British army now? He'll probably be a field marshal before he retires . . ."

"Hmm. He sends Aunt Alice a Christmas card every year and she sends him one . . . He and his wife took me out from school once when I was about twelve, I think. We had a picnic . . ."

Surveying Ivor, Esme put her head on one side, pleased with her handiwork. By the look of him, Major Llewellyn was well and truly flabbergasted. He'd had his money's worth, after all.

"You don't seem very impressed with all the people you've known," he accused her, sounding aggrieved. Ivor would never have treated a useful connection casually.

"Well," Esme replied affably, "they're really only people who've known *me*, you see. It makes a difference."

Chagrined, Ivor stared at her for a moment. Was she as insanely arrogant as she sounded . . . or just staggeringly obtuse?

Spotting the discord in her remark, Esme decided not to unsay it. It had satirical content. She lowered her lashes.

Detecting the sparkle beneath them, Ivor asked her why she was laughing.

"Laughing? I'm not laughing. You didn't say anything funny, did you? You haven't a humorous reputation . . ."

For the rest of the evening she wound him up and spun him round like a top. Dizzy, dazzled, Ivor began to sense she was playing with him. He felt like a hapless ball of wool caught between a kitten's paws. The claws pricked, almost to pain.

Ivor saw her to the foot of her staircase.

"Won't you come up," she invited half-heartedly, because she was tired, over-full of rich food and wine, and a little bored with making game of him. "I think we've got a bottle of something in the Boudoir."

"No," he said. "It's late. Work in the morning . . . and I've got to think of your reputation . . . whatever you may think of mine," he added ruefully, remembering her gibe.

"I didn't think anyone thought of things like that any more," Esme mocked him, hollowly. Ivor, of course, was of a different generation . . ."

"Well, I think about it," he answered her gruffly. "Goodnight, Esme." And he marched away.

Not, however, for long. He was back again for more of the same three more evenings that very week. And always the entertainment was costly.

Esme took what comfort she could from her new conquest. Ivor liked talking about the army, and she didn't mind it. They even had an acquaintance in common. He had met Philippa Mayhew when she'd been in charge of the WRAC contingent down at Shoeburyness where the Gunners had an independent battery. A prototype battleaxe, Ivor thought her, for all her beauty.

114

"Not to me, she isn't," Esme said simply. "Pretty cosy, in fact."

Ivor looked whipped, exasperated and proudly affectionate all at once. And Esme grew ever more skilful at producing these myriad effects. Anything to blank out the look, the feel, the sound . . . the smell of Clive.

Dreams, on the other hand, were outside her control. Sad dreams, bad dreams, terrible nightmares. The sad ones were worst. When Clive spoke to her, and she woke with the answer alive on her lips. But he was never there. Then tears would leak silently from the corners of Esme's eyes, while her jaws, clamped together, denied any voice to the mourning inside.

Unhealing, the raw wound of separation throbbed on as memories of the day she sustained it lost some of their sharpness. Examined, the sequence of events might have meant something different . . . If she never found out, Esme felt, her life would have an irreparable rent in it. A misfortune to be accepted, hidden and forgotten. Like Clive's rubber duck which she had tried to throw away once. But she couldn't. She had rescued it from her waste-paper basket and put it behind her shoes at the back of her wardrobe. Not weakness, no. The duck, after all, hadn't dumped her among a pack of strangers.

Every day after breakfast, in spite of herself, when she put her hat and gloves on in the hall, in preparation for the walk to the office, her eyes lingered longingly on her pigeon-hole. Nothing came except a letter from Aunt Alice and a belated bill from Hillard's Couture for her mess dress.

In the office, Paula was understandably brusque with her. Esme began to regret seriously that she had no real work to exert her. Something, none the less, came her way.

A servicewoman who worked on a classified project appeared several times before Paula on orders. Charged with wetting her bed, urinating on duty and collapsing incapable on several occasions. Common at Mill Hill, such offences were rare at Larkhill. Virtually unknown.

There being only one office available for these low-level court rooms, Esme and Carol vacated it during the hearings. But it didn't prevent Esme seeing the girl marched out on each occasion, or hear her being lectured by the battery sergeant-major. Every time, the girl just stood there miserably quaking, as if she hardly knew what was happening to her. Bayliss was her name.

It wasn't as if the unit medical officer's opinion hadn't been sought. He said Bayliss drank too much beer. So often, they did, though usually in the lower grades of employment.

One day, seeing the girl shamble out of the battery offices, Esme said, "Paula, don't punish Bayliss again."

This was really too much for Paula who'd had it up to her chin strap with Esme Hansard and the way she monopolised Ivor. Stiffly, she advised Esme to mind her own business. She was only supernumerary here. So far, AG16 had given no ruling about a permanent job for her.

"But haven't you noticed," Esme ignored the rebuff, "the shape of her head's changed. And if you don't tell Ursula, I will."

"Don't be absurd. How can the shape of her head change?"

Esme walked into Ursula's office without knocking. The consternation she caused there and elsewhere, justified the omission.

Within twenty-four hours Bayliss was diagnosed as having a massive cerebral tumour. Her life was in danger. The nearest military hospital had no facilities. Bayliss was rushed to a London hospital for nervous diseases. Esme went with her, forgetting for once that she never wished to set foot in the capital again.

It was Esme who, through the night, sat and waited in uniform, enduring the curious stares of housemen, surgeons and nurses while the theatre team operated. It was Esme who supported the parents when they arrived, a bewildered, poverty-stricken couple from Newcastle. It was Esme who had to tell them that although Bayliss would live, she would never again work at any but the simplest, repetitive tasks. And certainly not in the army. She would be discharged. No disability pension, unfortunately. The tumour had not arisen out of any aspect of Bayliss's occupation. But there were service charities which could help and would be informed . . .

With nothing but bad news to give them, Esme was almost unmanned by the pathetic gratitude of those parents. At least she had given them clear information and spoken with kindness of their daughter.

Such a bright, popular girl, she had been, Esme improvised, never having known Bayliss healthy. Her curly chestnut hair would grow back again, hiding the livid scar in her poor, pale, bristly pate.

When she had done all she could, harrowed and exhausted, Esme was too tired to think much about the staff car Larkhill sent to collect her. It was a fair bit of pomp for a second lieutenant and Ursula had scorched telephone wires to provide it. But no thanks were expected. A life had been saved, not to mention the army's blushes.

When the sentries saluted her routinely as her car passed through Larkhill's gate, Esme reflected that it was the first time she'd actually deserved it. And only by chance. Not Paula's fault. She had a thousand things to think of before the shape of a private's head. These things were all luck. If only she'd spotted Bayliss earlier . . .

Esme went straight to bed and dreamed of nothing and nobody.

116

In the morning a bouquet of three dozen red roses lay encased in Cellophane on the hall table. Esme glanced at it in passing, assuming some senior officer had had it delivered to the mess to take home to his wife for an anniversary present. Something like that. Her pigeon-hole was empty again.

"These are for you, ma'am," the hall man said, indicating the roses.

Nonplussed at first, Esme gazed vacantly at him. Then she grasped what he'd said. For her . . . for *her*! Her heart was turning cartwheels of celebration. Thumping joyously, as she undid the miniature envelope enclosing the card . . .

With all my admiration, from Ivor.

The day went dark on her. Why could not Ivor be Clive? The roses which could have meant everything might as well have been dish-mops.

Dully, she went through the motions of going to the silver room and selecting a vase from the number the silver man showed her. It was listed in the book. Assayed in London in the year 1889. Twenty-two troy ounces. Presented by Captain Evelyn Hardacre, RHA on retiring. Esme signed for it.

"That's the way, ma'am," the custodian of the mess silver approved, closing the book.

"Nice to have these bits and bobs used in a personal way, isn't it? No good for the great rooms, of course . . ."

Esme gave him a watery smile and left a message to have Beamish put the flowers in a bucket of water until later. She supposed she would have to arrange them.

In the office Esme got a warm reception, even from Paula. It was hard to find a quiet moment to ring Ivor and thank him for the roses without hurting her feelings. Esme's campaign had gone sour on her.

"Look, Esme, I want to talk to you," Ivor managed to corner her that lunchtime in the mess. "Seriously," he added levelly. Esme had the sinking feeling that always went with Aunt Alice's overdraft interviews. This was going to be much, much worse, she was certain.

"Oh yes," Esme said hopping frenetically from foot to foot, "you must come up and see your flowers in the Boudoir after dinner. It would be too selfish of me not to share them . . ."

"Good," he said firmly. "Paula and Carol are going to the cinema in Salisbury tonight. Nine o'clock then."

How had he managed that, Esme wondered bitterly. Bribed them? Or got Ursula to put them up to it.

Waiting for him, Esme turned all the electric lights on to create as repellent an ambience as possible. The roses stood there in their vase like some appalling referee. She was going to take them into her own

117

room, after all, when she heard Ivor's foot on the stairs. He was whistling under his breath. Very businesslike.

He got straight to the point.

"Now, Esme, I haven't pawed you about like a YO would but you must know how I feel about you. I want to know how you feel about me."

"Feel about you?" Esme prevaricated, standing behind the sofa.

"Yes. And you'd better come out from behind that thing. I'm not going to eat you. Come and sit down, you're making me nervous."

Haltingly, Esme told Ivor that she didn't have any particular feelings for him. How could she after so short a time? She liked him, of course . . .

"Is there anyone else?" Ivor cut across her bluntly.

"No . . . yes. I don't know. In a way. Possibly. Not at the moment."

"I see," he replied. "It's really rather a pity that I didn't . . ."

Oh God, no. He wasn't going to talk about money was he? The fortune he'd spent . . . Esme put her hands over her ears. But he pulled them away, the first time he'd touched her in any way intimately . . . And he didn't talk about money.

"I just wish I'd known about this from the beginning. I'll admit, I'm disappointed. I've made rather a fool of myself, haven't I?"

Thinking she could hardly sat that it was she who'd made a fool of him, Esme was silent. She wanted Ivor Llewellyn at her feet, and to her dismay, she had got him. The injured pride in his voice was unmistakable. The wretchedness on his face reproached her as harsh words could not have done. She knew how it felt. How terrible that men should be as vulnerable as she was.

"Well, that's all there is to it," he said finally. "Nothing to be done, then. There's some work I must finish before the morning so I'll say good night and leave you in peace. I had hoped . . . Well, never mind."

He went, leaving Esme curled up in a foetal ball of guilt and unhappiness on the sofa. She stayed there, unaware of the time passing, only roused by the sound of Carol and Paula returning.

"Oh, isn't he here?" Paula said, pushing the Boudoir door open. "We brought some . . ."

There was a bottle of champagne in her hand. Very good of her, all things considered.

Esme rushed past them, out of the room. They'd thought he'd been going to propose. Well, he had, but he was not the man she wanted to hear a proposal from. Ivor was miles too old to even think of like that. Obscene. He was like a walking suit of armour. He clanked with correctness. So boring. Unconsciously she echoed Clive's idiom in her head. How could he ever have thought . . .

This time, Esme did sob on her bed. She had got everything wrong. Ghastly old Makepeace was right. People worth having never asked you. You had to ask them . . . and then stop the hole, as she said. No good if you'd let the fox run away from the set . . . How could she have made such a mess of things?

A day or two later Ursula called Esme into her office.

"I'm afraid I've got some news you won't like. You'd better sit down." Shakily, wondering what was coming, Esme did so.

"I don't understand it," Ursula looked grim, "I've argued against it . . . Because you seem to me to have the makings of a first-rate regimental officer . . . But AG16 insist on you going on this course at RAF Wyton. There's nothing further I can do or say to prevent it."

"I understand, ma'am," Esme said bleakly. "Thank you, anyway, for trying."

"One thing I want you to be quite clear about," Ursula linked her mannish hands on the desk, "is that this has absolutely *nothing* to do with Ivor Llewellyn, although I'm fond of the man. I'm sorry, you know. I thought you two might make a go of things . . . But I never interfere in the personal lives of my officers. It's out of my hands. Is that clear?"

"Yes, ma'am. I'm sorry too."

"Well, I shall miss you," Ursula gave her an old-fashioned look. "But I imagine this comes as a relief in the circumstances."

In her very last week at Larkhill, a period spent dodging Ivor half the time and trying to behave normally the other half, miraculously, as it seemed to her, Esme received a letter from Clive. Such a very thin letter. She kept it in her bag until evening, dreading to know what was inside:

> *Dear Esme, you can rip this letter up if you want to. But I wanted to tell you how ashamed I am of what I did. I can't explain it. I just felt so disorientated. I miss you so much. I know I don't deserve a reply, but if you do write back you don't know how relieved I'll be. Hohne is still boring. Tiggy sends his love. Yours ever, Clive.*

Any normal woman would have torn the letter into a thousand pieces but Esme was not normal. She was in love. Any woman in possession of her senses would have asked herself what she was supposed to make of 'disorientated'. But Esme was out of her mind.

Esme's brain presented the familiar symptoms. Faith founded on a meanly written line or two. An uprush of optimism anchored to air.

Clive, she told herself, never did say much. She understood him.

119

It was all in the gaps. Always had been.

She left Larkhill, having taken leave of all who had mattered to her there, including Ivor and certain of the mess servants, with an absence of regret they were sad to see. She drove out of the gates believing that the only permanence that could ever matter to her was Clive.

In any case, in the army, save for itself as an abstract, there is no abiding home anywhere. Affections are everything.

9

RAF Wyton sobered Esme up fast.

From first crossing the threshold of the officers' mess, she knew she would hate it. This was alien territory. Everything, from her sketchy welcome to the look of the furniture, lacked solidity.

Perhaps, she was to say later, men who fly make little of their home on the ground. It would explain why their terrestrial nests were shoddy, shiftless, expendable structures, like this one.

Esme waited alone in the foyer, marvelling at its emptiness. Since there was nobody there, she did what she could to tidy her hair with a handbag mirror and comb. It was windy outside. Wasn't it anyone's business to be here?

After a self-conscious interval spent looking at unvarnished paintings of aeroplanes, a man in air force uniform passed her and would have kept going if Esme had not appealed to him. Oh yes, OK, he would fetch someone.

A mess servant manifested himself after some further delay, admitting he knew of Miss Hansard and that she was expected. There was a room allocated. He took her and her luggage to it. No mention of any officer having been detailed to receive her and show her the social ropes of the place. No talk of tea or the whereabouts of the ante-room.

It couldn't be like this, really, of course, Esme cheered herself, surveying the comfortless cube she was left in. First impressions were often untrustworthy. Someone would come.

Unpacking her possessions and taking stock of the room, Esme saw that it had a loudspeaker positioned over the door. A reminder of

121

wartime . . . She hoped nobody was thinking of scrambling *her.*

Still so new to Her Majesty's Land Forces, Esme was already accustomed to the leisurely courtesy with which messages . . . commands even, are conveyed between army officers in stately relays and always with compliments. The idea of being barked at by a machine set her teeth on edge. Fortunately, the thing seemed to be disconnected. It should, she thought, have been taken away altogether. Very slack.

The clumsy, yellow-varnished furniture which crowded the inelegantly proportioned space was disagreeable. So was the harsh, striped counterpane on the bed. Rummie looked very put out. The steel-framed windows gave a view of an airfield. Not a tree to be seen. Only a few miserable, wind-starved shrubs and stationary aircraft in the middle ground stood between this building and a flat, featureless horizon. Engines shrieked and moaned an accompaniment to the sound of the blustering wind.

Finding a lavatory on her own initiative, but no bath, Esme began to think of changing for dinner. When was dinner? Where was the dining-room? It was half past six already and she had been alone in this place for nearly two hours.

No wonder Clive didn't know any air force people. They certainly gave themselves rarity value. She could write him an amusing letter about it . . . In a day or two when she'd collected more material. Silence didn't go very far.

In the midst of these doleful reflections, to Esme's relief, the sound of feminine laughter met her ears. Oh, good. The WRAF officers were coming at last. They walked straight past her door, however, and Esme opened it herself just in time to see a group of three chattering girls in blue uniforms disappearing into a room down the corridor.

"Excuse me," she said in a firm and confident tone, "Could you tell me what time dinner is, please?" This surely would restore them to a sense of their obligations as established mess members.

Esme could not have been more wrong. There was an uncomfortable pause, while two of the girls stared at her, apparently astonished to be thus accosted by a stranger. There was no compunction on their faces at all. The third girl, already out of sight in the room, called out that she thought it was at seven o'clock. *Thought!*

Getting the location of the dining-room out of them was like extracting directions from a committee of supercilious mutes. Silly little squeaks and contradictory gestures. And then they shut the door, making it clear they wanted nothing more to do with her. Nobody, it seemed, was going to offer her a drink, accompany her to dinner or introduce her to anyone.

Furious, homesick for Larkhill . . . even for Mill Hill, Esme brushed her hair, tied her ribbon with aggressive precision and walked downstairs to obtain some kind of recognition for herself. There was no tradition of civilised behaviour here. Maintaining the army's standards single-handed was going to be difficult. But maintain them she would. Mustering her courage with violent effort, Esme asked herself what a handful of RAF hobbledehoys amounted to compared with a firing squad? By God, these people would soon know whose daughter she was. Or feel it, at any rate.

"Good evening," Esme stood poised inside the swing doors of the dining-room. "My name is Esme Hansard. I am a WRAC subaltern posted to RAF Wyton to join the Joint Services Photographic Interpretation Course. How do you do?"

Nobody answered. A number of puzzled male faces raised themselves from their plates and regarded Esme with expressions of mild offence. Like cows interrupted in chewing the cud. It was a hideous moment. Nor was there any convivial long table of the sort endorsed by the army. On the contrary, there were a number of small square ones, laid for four and covered with seersucker-cotton table-cloths. Like a respectable transport café.

Meeting her hostile reception with an elaborately graceful inclination of the head, Esme approached a table where two men were sitting.

"Do you think I might join you, or are these two places reserved for someone?"

One of them shrugged and indicated his permission with a wave of his knife. They returned to their conversation, excluding Esme. How she got through the meal she never knew.

Later, picking up some roneoed instructions about the course schedule from the hall, a man in a sports jacket passed her, stopped and walked back to her.

"Hullo," he said, looking her up and down, "You doing anything tonight?"

"No," Esme replied economically.

"Want to go to a disco?"

"I'm afraid I never go out with people I don't know," she said frigidly.

Plainly affronted, he shrugged and walked away with his hands in his pockets.

Much later Esme was to learn from one of the WRAF officers that he was a pilot and she had been a fool to snub him. Pilots were the glamour boys around here.

"I don't care if he's Batman," she flashed on that occasion. "He's not the sort of person I notice."

But the first night she spent completely alone, drafting letters to Clive and tearing them up. Finding the balance between forgiving and lecturing was going to take time.

"Seven o'clock, ma'am."

Crash! Something landed on the bedside table. Esme opened her eyes in time to see the retreating figure of a burly mess steward. There was a thick-pottery workman's mug of tea beside her. A good pint, there must be. Turgid orange stuff. Ugh! And really, a *man*. Didn't the WRAF run to batwomen?

And a quarter past eight was a barbarous time to find oneself traipsing over miles of tarmac to the place where the course was held. Driving around the base in private cars was forbidden. An air force officer, holding on to his hat, led her group at a break-neck pace. Esme was the only woman. She had to trot to keep up.

The rest were air force personnel past active flying duties, a naval petty officer and two strangely reserved army NCOs in the Intelligence Corps. Sergeants, they had eyes only for each other. Most were married and lived out. The Int. Corps pair were putting up at a local pub, lucky things. God knew if it was above board or not. In all, there were about fifteen of them.

At least when they got to the classroom designated, the Directing Staff turned out to be all army people. An elderly major, a pasty-looking captain and a lieutenant colonel wearing various regimental insignia. The Colonel had an interestingly far away look in his eyes. Lovely, lovely brown jobs. Esme feasted her eyes on them. Finally, some proper people to deal with.

"Good morning to you all, gentlemen . . . and er, lady," began the Major, smiling. "My name is Bigge. Welcome to the Joint Services establishment here . . ."

An explanation of the course, its scope and content followed. The object of the Photographic Interpretation facility for which they were all about to be trained, was to provide early information to the Defence Chiefs of all three services, regarding any changes to enemy economic and military installations. Anything from the number of fighter planes on a particular airfield to the development of new industries heretofore unheard of in the region under surveillance . . . Or missiles arming a merchant vessel.

The method employed was to mount special cameras at various angles on the fuselages of reconnaissance planes, usually in pairs so that the minute differences between the images recorded could then be studied in stereoscope . . . A piece of optical equipment which unified two adjacent images and gave them three-dimensional character. Hence an otherwise meaningless disc might acquire the identity of an oil storage tank, interpreted in relation to the mapped terrain and associated objects . . . And on an infra-red image, certain heat shadows might represent a squadron of bombers already dispatched to menace NATO countries.

The stereoscope was useful, of course, said the Major, brandishing a double-lensed, four-legged thing, but in time they would all learn to rely on their natural vision.

"This is vital work, gentlemen, for which women," he said, beaming straight at Esme with the bridge of his nose, "have a particular talent. Tending as they do . . . no offence, my dear," he shot another unfocused smile at Esme, "to have less knowledge than we chaps about military and industrial hardware, the ladies are rarely misled by preconceived notions about what *should* be there. Their deductions are not only often inventive but amazingly accurate . . ."

His far-away senior nudged him and spoke a few rapid words in Major Bigge's ear, careful it seemed, to avoid looking at anyone else in the room.

While this private confabulation lasted, Bigge stood stock-still, his poached-egg eyes continuing to look in unswervingly divergent directions. It would be a day or two before Esme realised that he was a human stereoscope.

So far, so good, anyway. This was something worth doing, Esme thought. She could make a real contribution here to the defence of the realm. Isn't that what she really joined for in the first place?

No wonder they wanted her here despite her attempt to cry off. Hadn't she just been told the reason? A woman's eyes, linked to her unprejudiced reason were an invaluable, specialised weapon in the war against Soviet tyranny. She was needed here. The WRAC, wiser than she was, had known it all along. Esme squared her shoulders.

"And now, gentlemen, I'll pass you on to my colleague here, who'll quickly run through the trigonometric aspects of the work . . . Sergeant," he broke off, "would you be so good as to just hand out these logarithm and cosine tables . . . You all have a slide rule on your desks, I take it?"

There was no slide rule or anything like it on Esme's desk. Tentatively, she raised her hand. Oh, crumbs. Sums! Terribly big, grown up sums. Not so good. Not good at all . . .

"Ah yes, Miss Hansard," the Bigge addressed her directly, "I wonder if you'd be so kind as to follow the Colonel and myself through here for a moment? We'd just like a word. A little query on your Positive Vetting, that's all . . ."

Positive Vetting? There had been no Positive Vetting in her case. Ursula had remarked in some surprise at the failure of sinister SIB men in shiny-blue suits to come and interview Esme. Their brief, she said, was to pry into your private life and weigh up whether or not you could be blackmailed.

There had been an oversight, Esme presumed. The SIB men were probably here now. They would find nothing to worry about, she determined. Clive was not a married man or one of those commercial attachés in the Russian embassy . . . of which Camberley had warned.

It was nothing like that.

Placing a chair for her, Major Bigge hummed and hawed. He didn't introduce the Lieutenant-Colonel, who sat on the edge of a table, slapping his leg with a swagger cane and examining his impeccable, conker-brown shoe.

"Now, Esme . . . May I call you that?" Bigge leaned, arms folded, against the window-sill. "You have got 'A' level maths, haven't you?"

"I certainly haven't," Esme laughed. "I didn't even take it."

"Oh, well, yes. I see. But you do have 'O' level, don't you?"

"Maths? No, I'm sorry, Major Bigge," Esme looked from him to the anonymous officer whose face stayed averted, "I don't. But you know all that. It's on my documents, isn't it?"

"Oh, quite, quite. Absolutely. On your documents . . . hmm." He seemed at a loss for a moment. Esme kept quiet, alert to peculiar vibrations in the room.

"Well," Bigge struggled on manfully, with a wild, swirling glance at his unhelpful companion, "that's not an insuperable problem, I don't think . . . Tell you what, we'll fix up some extra coaching for you in the mess. How about that? Bring you up to speed, eh? Captain Clarkson will tutor you. I'm sure he'll look on it as a pleasure. Oh, and we'll have to get a PV done on you. No nasty little secrets in your case, I'm sure. Well, er . . ."

He laughed awkwardly and it became obvious to Esme that the interview was over. Rising to leave, she saw the Colonel purse his lips in what looked like a moue of regret. An expression uninterpretable to her then.

As she closed the door behind her she heard him say, "No good, I'm afraid. Once seen, never forgotten. Pity." There was a low-voiced mumble from Bigge in reply.

Walking back to the classroom, Esme took it for granted they were talking about something else. The Colonel's stray remark didn't fit in with her maths coaching . . . How difficult was all that going to be?

Too difficult, as it turned out. Two to three weeks went by during which Esme made some spirited contributions in class as to the geometric strategies to be employed over discovering unknown measurements.

"You're a little genius, aren't you?" Captain Clarkson said to her once when nobody else in the room could devise a method that would yield a stubborn value. "Now do it."

"Oh, I can't do the actual thing," Esme scoffed.

"Come on, sir," barracked the naval petty officer in support of her. "That's not white woman's work."

Clarkson smiled resignedly and asked somebody else. He knew Esme couldn't do it. Their sessions in the mess had made that clear to him very quickly. Esme was charming, highly intelligent, willing too . . . but she just didn't have a mathematical brain. In so many ways she was better than all the rest. Her spatial perceptions were excellent . . . her creativity almost breathtaking . . . but when it came to the nitty-gritty of number she dug her toes in. Couldn't or wouldn't remember the formulas.

"How do you go about getting off this course?" Esme asked an air force colleague, battling against the relentless wind on the way back to the mess one Friday teatime. He was a nice, down to earth wing commander. Grandfatherly type.

"Esme, love, nobody gets off this course," he bellowed to be heard above the gale. "Not unless they go stone blind. The security classification's sky-high. They'll never let you go. They'll just keep putting you through the course over and over again until you get the hang of it. Coming to Happy Hour?"

Standing in the seedy bar, ankle deep in spilled beer, at an hour when decent army officers were having afternoon tea round their ante-room fires, Esme vowed they would let *her* go. There was no knowing to what lengths she might go to escape this infinity of rudeness, rowdiness, and logarithms. She was Dame Alice Winstanley's niece. One of history's great escapers. Esme owed her very existence to that.

"How's it going?" A distinguished-looking man with many rings round his uniform cuffs managed to make himself heard above the cacophony of drunken pilots' whoops. "Coping?"

"Hardly." Esme chatted to him a while as best she was able until with a weary smile he excused himself. Poor man looked as if he had all the cares of the world on his shoulders. It didn't strike Esme that she might be one of them.

"Don't you know who that was?" One of the WRAF officers who had been standing near bustled up.

"No. Who was he?"

127

According to the WRAF girl he was an air vice-marshall . . . or an air commodore or something. Important, anyway. These titles just rolled off Esme's eardrums like the sounds of a language she did not understand.

"You should have called him sir," bossed the girl.

"Your ranks are none of my business," Esme's temper flared. "I call male officers of my own service by their rank or their rank and their name if I know it. And I haven't the faintest intention of changing. People introduce themselves properly to me or they don't. I still haven't had the dubious pleasure of learning your name."

Over the lonely weekend, Esme had plenty of time to review her position. Something came back to her. That lieutenant-colonel . . . the far-away one. She had never seen him again after the first day. And his one and only overheard comment, which had seemed unconnected with her own affairs at the time, now sprang up in her memory, hitting her with the force of its meaning. *'No good . . . Once seen never forgotten.'*

So that was it. They had never wanted her for Photographic Interpretation at all. They had known, or someone had, that she was completely unqualified. What they had been after was a recruit to the secret services. M . . . something or other. And they had wanted to look her over in an environment where she wouldn't suspect . . . But that Colonel man had thought her personal appearance too striking to blend with a crowd.

Stupid, stupid man. Didn't he realise that one put one's best foot forward on the first day of anything? Lipstick, eye make-up . . . the lot. Studying herself in her mirror, Esme thought she might have blended very well into any background. Her hair was this indeterminate ashy colour . . . Anyway, it could be dyed. Her eyes reflected whatever light there was going. She didn't have to wear high-heeled court shoes . . . She could plaster her hair down flat and dreary as well as the next woman . . .

It all fitted. The Positive Vetting people didn't come because they'd been into her background minutely already. They knew all about her. But not nearly as much as she knew about herself. How very foolish of them not to have taken her into their confidence . . . Asked her advice . . .

Esme was still very young.

Too late, anyway. Spilt milk. She knew she would never have a second chance with those people, whoever they were. The rejection was final. That was acceptable, but the cover up wasn't.

Never forgotten, indeed. Well, she would be if she let them bury her alive in that bunker place. She was quite useless anyway. It was up to her, Esme Hansard, to get them all off the hook. If she failed, she might never see Clive again.

Stone blind, the old winco had said. How could she possibly manage that? Esme sat a long time, stroking her nose with her hair. No inspiration enlightened her.

Early the following week, however, a blinding flash illumined her path. In Major Bigge's Tuesday afternoon class.

"Now gentlemen . . . and lady," he cajoled them, "You'll be glad to hear we're going to do something new . . ."

He distributed maps to his pupils together with a new kind of optical instrument which looked like a jeweller's loupe. He gave them a reference and told them all to put the loupe on the square. And then, they were to apply their leading eyes to the lens.

"Now, Esme. You first . . . What can you see?"

Esme saw that the lens was calibrated into a scale. One to ten. The moment had come.

"It's all little eights," she looked up with a smile which suggested she was pleased to have got something right.

Major Bigge's face was a picture. If anything, his eyes went wider of centre than usual. He seemed quite excited. Kept rocking back on his heels, puffing and chortling.

"Oh dear," he cackled cheerily. "Oh dear, oh dear, oh dear!"

Esme was off that base within an hour or two. No more than the time it took, in fact, to impress upon her the extreme delicacy of much she had seen and heard whilst at Wyton . . . And to warn the WRAC to expect the speedy return of sub-standard goods.

Before she left, she was taken to the office of the many-ringed officer who had spoken to her at the last Happy Hour. At her appearance, he rose from behind his huge desk, extended his hands and grinned broadly.

"I need hardly say how sorry we all are about this," he said expansively. "It has been a great pleasure to know you . . . I understand from Major Bigge that a defect in your eyesight makes it impossible for you to carry on . . ."

"Quite impossible, I'm sorry to say," Esme chirruped back at him. "Every time I look at a figure now, it's an eight."

Many-rings shook her hand with great warmth. He would have been very glad to have Esme on his personal staff. A quick, lateral thinker. But she belonged to the army.

I loved your letter. Clive wrote from Hohne to Lowlough, where Esme was on indefinite leave: *I showed it to Tiggy. He says you ought to write a book or something. Where are they sending you now? I bet you've got them all in an uproar. I hope it's London next time. I'm longing to see you. We've got to do this boring NATO exercise first but I'm going to be sent on a tank gunnery course at Bovington afterwards. It's in Dorset. Please write another long letter. I shall be watching my pigeon-hole. All my fondest love, Clive.*

Esme folded the blue sheet of paper and put it back in its envelope, satisfied. A racy, pacy edited account of her sojourn at Wyton had served her purpose better than a screed of reproaches. Never shout at a runaway dog if you want it to come back, Aunt Alice had said often enough.

And now Clive was coming home to England again. A tingling anticipation irradiated Esme. At the back of her mind she deplored this in herself. Shrank, just a little, from adventures that would certainly expose her to heartbreak and more disappointment. But who, being young, reflects on the torments of gout before reaching for the next glass of wine? Esme did not.

As for the army, it had a compelling, episodic charm. Enough to keep her guessing what would come out of the bran tub next. Two booby prizes and a sugar plum so far. Nearly a year now, and so much had happened. Most of it a waste of her talents and time. And yet, through it all, Clive was shot, a shimmer of colour revealed afresh whenever the folds of her life were shaken out again.

10

"She fancies you, ma'am. That's what it is."

Esme gazed at the Company Sergeant-Major in disbelieving horror. She was stout and slow on her feet. The Royal Army Ordnance Ammunition Requisition and Distribution Depot at Mereworth Barracks in Ludgershall was her last posting before retirement.

She was, of course, vastly experienced. A powerful factor in the OC's flattering decision to leave Esme in charge of the company whilst she herself went away for months on a pre-Staff College course at Warminster. Esme would have ADWRAC at District Headquarters to call on in a major crisis . . . and the CSM for day to day things.

There were no other subalterns, the unit strength being relatively small. The Technical Storewomen, trained and employed here, moreover, exhibited the same level of refinement as the Postal girls. Esme was thoroughly at home with unwanted pregnancies, wet mattresses and tooth and nail, hair-ripping fights. She knew the procedures inside out.

"I'd rather you made a pig's ear of things than some 'just add an egg' acting captain," the OC had said prior to departure. It was the nearest she ever got to a compliment. Esme had taken it, however, in the spirit in which it had been meant. A warm commendation. One that arose largely out of Esme's respectful insistence that the OC should send three of the four identical paisley print dresses she'd bought for off duty wear in Warminster back to the shop.

"I know you have your mind on higher things, ma'am," Esme had tactfully deposed when asked her opinion of this purchase, "But if you

131

wear the same dress to dinner every night, people will think you've only got one."

"Think so?" The OC looked crestfallen. "Why should they think that?"

At pains to differentiate, for the OC's benefit, between an order for half a dozen uniform shirts and the selection of garments for social appearances, Esme had come up with the illuminating suggestion that the OC was suffering from the Moss Bros mentality. Good-naturedly, the OC had reported this striking diagnosis to ADWRAC . . . who was more than ever convinced that Esme could administer the company alone.

At this precise moment, however, she felt completely out of control. Exposed to unknown forces. Good God! How could she be *fancied* by the orderly room corporal? Such a thing was too grotesque to contemplate . . .

"Do please have a seat, Sarn't-Major," Esme said, after a pause. Next to sitting down herself, as she already was, viewing somebody else's collapse into solid support seemed the best that could be had in the way of first aid.

The last thing Esme had expected to result from her appeal to the CSM to restrain Clegg's frequent, prolonged and unnecessary incursions into her office, was a sensational announcement of this personal nature. Certainly formulas like, "Thank you, Corporal Clegg," and more directly, "That will be all, Corporal," were water off a duck's back to Clegg. But surely the woman was merely garrulous . . . a bit of a bore.

"I think we'd better have some tea," said Esme faintly.

"Pot of tea in Miss Hansard's office," the CSM barked the order through the door to the orderly room. "And look sharp about it. Not you, Clegg," she growled, "Not you . . . Private Findlater, you get my medicine. Look lively now. Miss Hansard hasn't got all day."

The CSM, mused Esme, not for the first time, sounded very much like Aunt Alice's shepherd chivvying his trio of wall-eyed Border collies.

Tea came in a moment, delivered by the orderly room private with Sarn't-Major's flask wedged between the sugar bowl and milk jug. Any mention the CSM made of her 'medicine', was generally taken to indicate her portable supply of white rum.

"Now, ma'am," the CSM lifted the teapot, "Half and half?"

That query referred only to the proportion of tea to rum. Milk was added to give the mixture a respectable tint.

"At least half and half, Sarn't-Major," Esme responded with feeling.

"Permission to smoke, ma'am?"

132

Nodding, as the CSM drew a leather cigarette case from a pouch in her uniform's lining, Esme ground a teaspoon round in her cup, mouth turned down in disgust.

"Drink up, ma'am, you're as white as a sheet," the CSM urged chirpily. A slack afternoon was looking brighter by the minute. Poor Miss Hansard was in a rare old taking. Not got the experience, that was her trouble. Sharp as a tack about some things . . . slow on the uptake about others.

Esme drank. How could she . . . should she react to being ogled by a woman? A *corporal* . . . The thing was perverse. Broke every taboo. That business at the Mill Hill sergeants' Games Night had been nasty enough . . . Revolting, childish and somehow pathetic . . .

But this was different in texture. Clegg was young . . . Rather attractive in a lean, hard-limbed, athletic way. She had presence too. A harassing, suffocating dominance which filled Esme's office too often during the day. Quite inappropriate. So Sarn't-Major had dealt with her.

"I said to her, 'Corporal Clegg, you don't like Miss Hansard do you? No, you don't. Because unlike Miss Langley, she won't have nothing to do with you. You just leave Miss Hansard alone,' I says to her. 'She's not your sort. She's a proper officer. Knows her place. Time you learned yours, Clegg, if you want to hold on to those stripes' . . ."

The CSM was settled into her groove for as long as Esme would let her run on. A respite to get over her sense of flesh-crawling outrage and look at the whole of the picture. Sarn't-Major seemed quite unaware of the wider implications of all this . . . if it were true. But with her mental processes revived by the spirit, Esme began to realise that every word of it was detestable fact.

Had she but known it at the time, she had seen it all for herself.

It had been that day during the first week in the officers' mess here, when she had gone to the room which would eventually be hers. At that time it was still occupied by the subaltern who was handing the Mereworth Barracks job over to her. Helena Langley.

Esme had knocked on her door at half past six in the evening. Knocked twice, she remembered. She was impatient to reappraise the effect of an expensive new dress. Difficult, without the use of the cheval grass in Helena's room. These were provided for WRAC officers but not for the men. For the moment, Esme had been allocated a room furnished for male occupation and had, therefore, no way of admiring more than her face in the hand basin mirror. Not unless she stood on a chair to get an uninteresting view of her midriff. Esme had already tried it.

Responding sluggishly to the knock, Helena, wrapped in a

133

transparent nylon négligée unbecoming to her Rubenesque curves, had listened to her replacement's request in poker-faced silence. Esme recalled the scene as having been awkward in the extreme. Most odd. Anyone would have thought there was something vain in wanting to look in a decent mirror . . . Langley had been very peculiar.

"All right," she had inched open the door inhospitably, "You can come in, but don't look at the bed."

Look at the bed? Esme had not come to look at the bed. So of course, she immediately did so. The bedclothes, all in a muddle, lay half on the carpet. The half that remained on the bed swathed a figure. A shock of short, dark-blonde hair lay on the pillow.

Esme went away, much more annoyed than embarrassed, imagining that she had seen Helena's boyfriend. Who he might be, she had no idea. She knew next to nothing then about her WRAC colleague, or indeed the rest of the mess members. But why make such a performance about it? It served Helena right for flouting the convention that forbade men in WRAC officers' quarters between tea and dinner. Jolly inconsiderate.

And as for her dress, she had thought, storming away down the corridor, from what little she could remember of her image reflected in the glass, it should go some way to melting the indifference of these Rug and Oil Company subalterns, whose appreciation up to now fell a long way short of Esme's expectations. Her reception here had been correct but cool, which puzzled her. Had she, Esme wondered, peering worriedly into he mirror, *faded*? Passed her peak at twenty-two . . .

With Clive such a long way away, she badly wanted friends near at hand. Needed the companionable ease which is supposed to exist between brother officers sharing a home. It wasn't as though, Esme had ruminated then, she hadn't done her best to be low key and sisterly in her deportment. Flirting was bad form when you didn't intend to deliver. The whole Ivor débâcle had taught her that lesson once and for all.

And yet, when she was near, ante-room and dinner-time conversation at Mereworth had always sounded tinny. No remark of substance was ever made to Esme. Wistfully, she had regarded the clusters of young men playing Bridge or Backgammon after dinner . . . fondling their dogs . . . plotting excursions and pranks which didn't include her. But she had been rather a success at Larkhill . . . accepted as part of the family. Here, she was made to feel like an interloper. It had been very depressing.

But all that was months ago, and since then everything had been a lot better. It had come about gradually.

Esme hadn't recognised the completeness of the thaw until, one afternoon in the ante-room, she had sent a cup of scalding tea flying into the fork of a subaltern's trousers.

"Christ! That's what happens when you let a woman into your life," he gasped. "Bloody peeling balls . . . Oh, God, Esme, I'm sorry to swear . . ."

The progress of his injury, treated with Aunt Alice's comfrey ointment panacea, was earnestly discussed at every meal from thereon, once senior people were out of the way. Esme knew she was loved now, although it had taken time . . .

"Sarn't-Major," Esme arrested the CSM's scandal-mongering flow. "I saw Clegg in Miss Langley's bed. I didn't know who it was then, but I shall have to do something now."

"Oh no, ma'am! There's no call for that!" Consternation elongated the CSM's features. "I've read Clegg 'er fortune good and proper. She won't get in your way no more." She shook her grizzled head vigorously, "NFA, I say. No further action. S'not worth the trouble, ma'am. Really it isn't."

"What do you mean, Sarn't-Major? Of course we have to take action. Lesbian relationships are against stated Corps policy. Failing to report on this would be a dereliction of duty. Clegg's posting order came in yesterday. She's going to the depot on promotion to sergeant to train brand-new recruits. You know that as well as I do. As for Miss Langley," Esme's mouth was screwed up in distaste, "*where* did she go?"

Back-tracking fast, the CSM urged Esme to drop the whole matter. Simply leave it alone. She seemed extraordinarily agitated. Were she here, the CSM averred, the OC would do nothing. Very soon Clegg would cease to be this unit's problem. Why stir anything up?

The answers that Esme could think of involved words like duty, legality and responsibility . . . And what about the potential pressures a person like Clegg could bring to bear on lowly recruits, unequipped to resist it? It was all so blindingly obvious. Basic Camberley stuff. Not the sort of thing of which a very junior officer ought to have to remind a senior NCO.

"Don't do it, ma'am. Forget it. It won't do no good, I'm warning you . . ." The CSM was practically pleading.

Esme, brought up to look on any senior NCO as a young officer's most reliable mentor, promised to give the situation more thought. There must be some justification for the CSM's distress. What was behind it, Esme was unable to see.

The internal telephone rang.

"Esme Hansard speaking . . ."

"There's Mr Porteous called in to see you, ma'am. Are you free?"

135

"Mmm. Yes. Send him in. The CSM and I are about finished now."

The CSM rose picking up the tray. "I'll leave you to get on then, ma'am," she said heavily. "Now, don't you be hasty."

"Not hasty, Sarn't-Major, no. I'll tell you what I decide. Come in, Martin."

Martin Porteous, accompanied by his two brainless English setters, held the door open for the CSM gallantly, before saluting Esme and plonking himself down in the seat just vacated.

"Any tea going?"

There was, of course, or coffee if he preferred it. Clegg brought in the specified brew with a lascivious smile at Esme. She shuddered, wondering what made Clegg think she was out of discipline's reach. How dared she set foot in here again. What was the CSM thinking of? Dignity demanded an impassive reaction.

"Close the door behind you, Corporal Clegg, please. And don't disturb me again."

"Anything fresh?" enquired Porteous hopefully. He was one of several subalterns who now regularly called on Esme during the working day. Hours could be filled with unit gossip or the *Daily Telegraph* crossword puzzle.

"Yes," Esme said sharply. "That," she pointed at the door, "has been sleeping with Helena Langley in my bed, the bed *I* sleep in . . ."

"Sorry, Little Bear, that's stale. We all knew about Goldilocks. Why did you think we were so chary of you when you came?"

Esme leaned her elbows on the desk and clamped her hands over her mouth, fearing for a moment that she might actually vomit. Tears of revulsion and rage came to her eyes.

"Hey, what's up, sweetheart?" Anxious, Porteous got up and put a hand on Esme's shoulder. She shook it off.

"Do you mean to tell me that you thought . . . That you all thought . . ."

"Well, you never know with the WRAC, do you? Could be one way, could be the other."

"Why didn't you just *tell* me?"

"How on earth could we? We'd no idea who *you* were knocking off then. How were we to know you had a bloke at Bovington all along. I mean, it's a bit much, having other ranks infesting the mess . . ."

"You don't have to tell me." To her amazement and shame, Esme found herself dissolving into messy tears. The effects of delayed shock. "I just thought I must have got terribly plain."

"Never that, sweetie." Porteous was dismayed. He produced a large, clean handkerchief and spitting on it fussily, removed mascara stains from Esme's cheeks. Young men, Esme discovered, could be very motherly.

The rest of the day was devoted to restoring and reassuring Esme. They nudged up against her like a school of porpoises comforting a wounded fellow. A process observed by the mess servants . . .

"Right, mate," said the civilian steward to the Sergeant cook on his shift, "I'll have a quid on it with you. It'll be two teas for Mr Porteous's room in the morning."

"More like the lot of them in together," sniffed the cook. "Dead kinky is officers. Look how many of them sleeps with their dogs. Perverted bastards prefers 'em to wimmin."

At about ten o'clock the subalterns, including Esme, all piled into the largest car available and motored up to London. In time to play three or four hours' worth of illegal Black Jack in the tawdrily-appointed, upper back room of a strip club, where Martin – his subscription paid by group contributions – was a member. A dull game, Black Jack, but played with method and concentration it paid the monthly mess bills, which was more than a subaltern's pay did.

At four in the morning the club closed. Martin and his group were ushered out past the dustbins at the rear of the premises.

"You come back not too soon," invited the Asiatic proprietor equivocally. The winnings of Mr Porteous and his guests were modest but consistent.

It didn't matter. The Mereworth Barracks syndicate had invested in a number of memberships. Gold Tooth T'ung was due for a rest.

They walked, huddled close about Esme, two with arms linked through hers in the dark Soho alleys on the way back to the car.

"Feeling better now?" one of them asked her.

"Twenty pounds better," she giggled. "I don't think poor Mr T'ung's awfully keen on me."

Tiggy Johannenloe was leaving a call girl's flat as she spoke. It was only the distinctive notes of her voice that made him glance at her party as he slid behind the wheel of his Morgan. Spotting Esme, he supposed he'd better tell Clive that Darling Heart had acquired other interests.

Sad. But it might, he considered, be the best thing all round in the long run.

Despite the return of her exterior poise, Esme felt her retrospective humiliation very keenly. Everything inside her recoiled, gathering into a spring of retributive energy.

If this sort of thing wasn't weeded out root and branch, the reputation of the Corps would suffer. It had suffered already and she'd borne the brunt of it. Been ostracised for weeks. Others, younger and weaker than she was, might fare worse.

Fortified by grapefruit, Weetabix, bacon and eggs and toast, all consumed in the customary breakfast time silence, Esme arrived in her office a full half hour before her usual time.

"Good morning, ma'am," the orderly room staff straggled to their feet, visibly disconcerted. Unpredictability in officers was not, from their point of view, a lovable quality. Clegg kept her eyes stonily fixed on her typewriter.

"Good morning, everyone. Is the CSM in yet? Tell her I should like to see her in fifteen minutes' time."

Esme rather regretted that. What difference would fifteen meaningless minutes make to anything except to get Sarn't-Major's back up? But this was to be an 'interview without coffee'. Fairer to warn Sarn't-Major.

In the meantime Esme was forced to resist the impulse to loosen a lock of hair from her daytime chignon. In uniform, nowadays, nose-stroking was no longer an option. Tiresome.

When the CSM trudged in on the dot of ten to nine, she was stiffly uncooperative. A circumstance for which Esme had herself to blame. It wasn't easy, managing people over thirty years older than you were yourself. Still, it was part of the job.

"Won't you sit down, Sarn't-Major," Esme placated, "I want to understand what you meant yesterday . . ."

She had nothing to add to her advice of the previous day. She would give no reason for it beyond the assertion that in over twenty years of soldiering she'd never known any good come of voluntarily disclosing unsolicited information. She'd always kept her nose clean . . . walked her shoes nice and straight . . . and yes, if Miss Hansard put it that way, passed the buck. It was safest.

"But you know best, ma'am," the CSM sniped from behind a wall of steely reserve as the interview terminated, "You're the officer."

Left alone in her office, Esme straightened her shoulders. Regardless of the CSM's attitude, there came a time when every officer had to cut loose from sergeant-majorly apron strings.

She dialled ADWRAC's number at District Headquarters direct. ADWRAC, said the Chief Clerk there, was on leave for a fortnight as stated in the District Orders, a copy of which Miss Hansard should have received. Could anyone else help?

Balked of early guidance from somebody she trusted, Esme looked up the Manual of Military Law. The procedure in cases like this was clear-cut. What advice could anyone give her except to carry it out? It would be unpleasant but could not be shirked. Clegg should be marched in to hear the charges against her like any other malefactor. Esme intended to remand her for trial by Court Martial. As acting OC that fell within her powers. Afterwards it would be in other hands. The buck would be passed all right . . . by the book.

To make amends for her earlier frigidity, Esme went herself to the CSM's office to tell her this news. The older woman, pale at the best of times, went the colour of parchment.

"You don't know what you'll be starting, ma'am."

"Wasn't that a touch impulsive?" Ivor put the glass he'd been carrying to his mouth back on the table. "No wonder Sarn't-Major's upset. Poor old bird. Twenty-five years without anyone rocking the boat and along comes little Miss Blue Eyes and capsizes it."

"My eyes are grey," said Esme, aggravated. Wasn't anyone on her side?

"Hmm," returned Ivor absently.

Esme quite enjoyed it when he said 'Hmm'. Girls at school said their fathers fell back on 'Hmm' a lot. A single syllable that tended to promote a feeling of humdrum security. A minor point in Ivor's favour. There were times when Esme wanted to lean on someone . . . and this was one of them. But Ivor was proving a broken reed tonight. Not at all responsive.

This was the third time Ivor had taken her out to the Walnut Tree in recent months. They had an agreement. No strings. And with that, for the moment, he was content. Esme was geographically accessible, good company . . . a decorative companion for dinner whenever he felt like a change from the mess.

She no longer flirted with him, he noticed, nor seemed ill at ease with him either. She had other friends. Apart from that bare fact, he knew nothing about her emotional life. She wasn't confiding in that way, thank heaven. To be looked on as an avuncular figure was just about bearable . . . to be treated to a gushing recital of another man's attractions would not be value for money.

Whatever hopes still simmered in Ivor, he was careful to keep them on a very low light. Esme's rejection had certainly hurt him. Worse, it had surprised him. He was a man who had planned his life's route and had not so far found any gates closed against him. Since the early, reckless, YO days he'd been sparing of attentions to women. They took up time, made demands, and always they had diamond rings flashing in their eyes.

An ambitious man could not afford to get saddled too early with a wife, in the army. Especially if he had no income other than his pay. Even with the marriage allowance and married quarters, both partners were pinched. Battered cars and wives appearing at Ladies' Guest Nights in frocks that had been seen a dozen times before . . . houses that were too small to accommodate children without squalor. Ivor had seen it all before as his contemporaries, one by one, had succumbed to the trials of under-funded, peripatetic domesticity.

And too often a girl, married purely for her nubile freshness, failed to develop any 'Colonel's lady' quality. His mother had possessed that kind of unflappable grace but unfortunately his father had lacked the drive which could win her the position she deserved. Too soft.

Ivor was not ashamed of these thoughts. Why should he be? He intended to go all the way . . . and any partner would have to match his speed. Esme, he thought, had the right racing lines. She'd probably go the distance without being carried. Ivor was going too fast to take passengers.

What Esme was telling him now underscored his view of her. She had acted with firmness and promptitude. Been unafraid to accept the burden of command. But she was boxing out of her league on this one. She had overrated her strength. A good fault.

"Well, what would you have done?" Esme demanded.

"With a Gunner? Exactly the same as you," he said to her. "But Esme dear, the WRAC is different."

"I don't see how you make that out," she objected, "apart from the obvious things."

Ivor told her, while she ground her way industriously through a plateful of jugged hare and red cabbage.

Lesbianism, he said, was endemic in the WRAC. An integral part of its structure. Camberley might pay lip service to the spirit of prohibition but couldn't afford to go overboard with strict application of the letter. They made an effort to keep it away from the junior ranks, yes, in the hope that the thing would finally wither for want of new blood. But any head-on confrontation with the problem would simply empty the WRAC sergeants' messes . . . and break the Corps' backbone.

"So basically, you think I'm being prim and missish?" Offended, Esme masticated tensely. It was support she wanted . . . endorsement, not a lecture. "Anyway, where did you get hold of all this, Ivor?"

"I've been in the army twelve years, Esme . . . And the Gunners have always had a good working relationship with your people . . ."

No service, he went on, could be run without a hard core of stalwart NCOs. The WRAC couldn't survive a witch hunt . . . It would be disbanded amid public recriminations and questions in parliament. The entire army, which had good reason to be grateful for women's past services, would wish it had never touched them with the end of an RSM's pace stick.

"Well, why didn't Sarn't-Major tell me all that? I gave her ample opportunity to put a case to me . . . I would have listened. There was the Mill Hill thing . . ."

"Esme, if she were half as articulate as you, your wretched Sarn't-Major would be on the General Staff . . . running the WRAC, not rubbing along as CSM of an attached company out in the sticks. On top of that, do you realise how many *officers* of your Corps are involved?"

"I know one," Esme's lip curled. "Helena Langley."

"She's expendable. But would you really like to see someone like Ursula Spotteswoode disgraced . . . Stripped of her rank, without a job and her pension lost?"

"Ursula?" The catch in Esme's throat caused her to choke. She didn't seem able to stop. Ivor seized a pitcher of water from a neighbouring table and made her gulp a tumblerful.

"Better?"

"Yes. Ursula?"

"Yes, Ursula." Ivor surveyed Esme sympathetically. It was really too bad the way these girls were launched into a world they didn't understand without a map. "You liked Ursula, didn't you? Just about everyone does. She's a bloody good officer, wouldn't you agree?"

"Yes, I would," Esme replied quietly, chastened and a little frightened. She would never do anything to hurt Ursula.

"Oh, you needn't worry. Ursula's girlfriend died eighteen months ago. She was a quartermaster who'd been retired with multiple sclerosis. Ursula took a cottage in a village round here, lived out and nursed her friend till she died in her arms. Then she moved back into the mess. Her posting down here's already been extended three times."

Esme's appetite had deserted her. "How do you know about all this, Ivor?"

"Everybody knows except kiddywinks like you. But actually, Ursula got rather pissed one night and told me the whole story. In the end I had to put her to bed," Ivor's mouth twisted wryly. "That's what you might name exceptional bravery beyond the call of duty. Anyway, there's no one I have more respect for."

"No, nor me. What will happen?" Esme waved the dessert menu away.

"The shit will hit the fan . . . But this time, I think they'll let it drop to the ground without sploshing you. Everyone's allowed one mistake."

"But I didn't *make* a mistake! What's the good of telling me the rules if they don't tell me they're not supposed to be kept?"

"That's something we all have to learn for ourselves. Do you want coffee here or in the bar?"

"Here," Esme said glumly, trying to imagine the dapper Ivor getting Ursula into her night clothes. Did he really do that?

They started to talk about Caroline Clough who'd taken over Paula's job at Larkhill. Paula had gone to Rheindalen. How was Caroline getting on? Ivor was warm in her praises. Caroline had voluntarily subjected herself to the technical training of every girl employed on the unit . . . and naturally, done it in a fraction of the official time. Caroline, with her background in applied mathematics, would have made a very able Gunner . . . had she only been a man. Ivor foresaw rapid promotion for Caroline. Or a place at Shrivenham to do a further degree at the army's expense. One or the other.

On top of that Caroline had taken up playing fives. A fast-moving game requiring stamina and an above average feel for ballistics. It was interesting to note, Ivor said, that Caroline's interests were complementary. She was someone who meant to make her mark.

"She thinks there ought to be stricter rules about WRAC fitness levels. More officer involvement in team sports. You must admit, Esme, some of your lot are bloody slack . . ."

Esme was no longer listening. She visualised herself at the wedding of Ivor and Caroline. Bound to happen. Caroline, who could never be a real Gunner, would settle in time for being a Gunner's wife. A sensible solution which would suit them both. It would be a marriage made in heaven, she was sure.

A similar, if less roseate thought struck Ivor simultaneously. Caroline would make a very practical partner. At the prospect of courting her, however, his imagination faltered. The difference between running on soft sand and driving an E-Type Jaguar . . .

Crushing the comparison, Ivor sent for the bill and took Esme back to Mereworth Barracks soon after. No, he wouldn't come in.

"I've got some figures to analyse before hitting the sack," he sounded clipped. He pecked her on the cheek. "Good to see you. Take care."

Noting that he didn't volunteer himself as a sounding board for any further developments in the Clegg business, Esme smothered a tremor of disappointment. The noble isolation of command had its drawbacks.

Nor was it Esme's orderly room corporal that preoccupied Ivor as he drove past the Mereworth Barracks guard room. Thoughts and wishes, teeming in his unwilling brain, mocked his every effort to subdue them. But speed was a tried and tested way to rid the mind of persistent nuisances.

Accelerating his souped up MG to close on a hundred miles an hour on the Salisbury road, Ivor was dazzled by the undipped headlights of another vehicle careering towards him in the opposite direction. Hogging the crown of the road . . . Ivor wrenched his wheel blindly to avoid collision. Locking his knees and elbows, he braced for impact.

Nothing. No prang. Sweat poured down Ivor's back as he glanced in the rear-view mirror where the other car's tail lights were blazing a vermilion trail. An Aston Martin? Too dark to be sure. Couldn't get the number. Shit! Ivor would have had that lout's nuts sliced up and fried for breakfast.

Martin Porteous let Clive in when he rang the mess doorbell. The steward had gone off duty.

"I think . . ." Clive smiled his elusive, between-April-showers smile, "I mean, does Esme Hansard live here?"

Martin felt the charm of the man beat out at him like a wave of heat from a sun-baked rock.

"Shut up, you two!" he admonished the mindlessly barking setters. "She signed out for dinner. But I'll go and see if she's back, if you like . . . She may have gone to bed."

"Thank you so much."

The steady look in Clive's eye informed Martin that Esme in bed would fit this chap's agenda perfectly. The Bovington connection. Had to be. A typical cavalry type. Disarming dithers sheathing a will of tungsten steel.

"What are you doing here!" Esme greeted Clive, standing in the middle of the corridor draped in a bath towel, her hair carelessly piled up and moisture pearling on her skin. She was radiant with pleasure. This was the very first time since Camberley that Clive had ever come to her.

He didn't answer her question. Clive didn't go in for confessing to his motives. Enfolding her with possessive roughness in his arms, he said, "Where were you this evening? I rang you but you weren't in."

"No," Esme traced the whorls of his ear with the tip of her tongue, "I went out to dinner."

"Who with?"

"A Gunner I met at Larkhill."

"A Gunner," Clive repeated, his upper lip curling up. "Is that who you were with last night in London?" He increased the pressure of his grip on her slightly. "Tiggy saw you."

For a moment, Esme was at a loss to know what he meant. Her and Ivor in London? Tiggy . . . She hadn't seen Tiggy for weeks . . .

"Oh! Do you mean at Gold Tooth T'ung's in Frith Place? I didn't know Tiggy ever went there . . . I didn't see him. The subalterns here and I play Black Jack there sometimes."

In and amongst establishing that there was nobody else in this part of the mess, that he could have a bath and that Esme would have another one with him, Clive was able to reassure himself that no trespass on his territory had been perpetrated. He didn't like to think of himself drinking at a common well. The suspicion that Esme might have compromised his exclusive rights had impelled him along ninety inconvenient miles. Loss of cool. It was not what Clive expected of himself.

Lying up to his chin in hot water with his heels on Esme's shoulders, while she massaged his pectorals with her toes, Clive grumbled. Jealous? Of course he wasn't jealous. Jealousy was a low-grade emotion. Where was Esme's flying saucer thing? They could play frisbees with it before putting it in.

"Oh, Esme! God! Esme . . ." Clive climaxed forty minutes later. "That is so *good* . . ." He waited for the last ripples to subside before withdrawing. A long, lingering *finale*, merging into velvet blackness.

He slept an hour and then touched her between the legs, to the side of her clitoris, not directly on. She hated that . . . the secondary pressure was enough. Was she awake? Could she do it again?

"No, darling. Not now. I need a rest."

She could always do it. Again and again. Esme could have an orgasm all on her own just thinking of Clive. But she didn't tell him so. If Clive wanted more, he would have to come back for it. A trace of angst about her other friendships had done him . . . and her, a power of good. So far unfamiliar with it, Esme perceived in his jealousy a useful gadget, packed with unexplored potential.

The pillow talk was about a WRAC captain on the permanent staff at Bovington. Clive hadn't a clue what she actually did there. Probably something vague like administration . . . whatever that meant. She was 'all right'.

"By which I suppose you mean you've only ever seen her at a distance and not found her outstandingly offensive from that vantage point."

Snickering, Clive admitted that was near enough the truth. His amusement was tinged deliciously with fear. It gave him a jolt when Esme read his thoughts . . . Like someone bursting out of a cupboard in a darkened room. Exciting. Something other women could not do . . . Would never be allowed to.

Woken later by Esme's unreliable alarm clock, Clive dressed quickly. Twenty to seven already.

"How do I get out of this place?"

144

Esme didn't know. They should have asked Martin last night. There was bound to be a system. But the front door, and all the downstairs public rooms here were locked by whoever was last to go to bed . . . The PMC had made the rule . . .

"Doesn't matter," Clive kissed her quickly. "Want to go to polo at Hurlingham a week on Saturday?"

"This is beautiful," Esme stroked his pale-yellow sweater admiringly.

"It's cashmere," Clive said. "It's better."

"Isn't everything about you better?" Esme twitted him. It was wiser that Clive shouldn't know how sincerely she believed in his betterness. But Clive, being what he was, was pretty sure of it.

Downstairs, a kitchen porter coming on the early shift was bowled over by Clive's civility in helping himself to a fried egg sandwich before allowing himself to be shown out by the scullery door.

Still in bed, Esme waited for her tea. What would Clive have said if he'd known the history of this bed? But he wasn't the kind of person to whom one told one's troubles. He didn't carry other people's parcels in or out of uniform.

The charges raised against Clegg were quashed. Lack of evidence . . . no witnesses, maintained ADWRAC. Esme's incisive depositions to the contrary were ruthlessly suppressed. The WRAC and the Judge Advocate-General's department between them had decided what was in the best interests of the service. And that was that.

There was to be one concession. Clegg would be discharged forthwith under an Adjutant General's Administrative Instruction which covered the case. In fact it was the only way of doing it. Esme's error was as much procedural as it was political but ADWRAC saw this as an insignificant, easily correctable detail. Almost forgivable beside her failure to intuit the unwritten rules of the Corps.

"But my authority at Mereworth has been completely undermined," Esme pressed her point unwisely.

"You should have thought of that before," snapped the woman seated at the far end of the room. The distance placed between the senior officer's desk and the junior interviewee's chair was an established climatic indicator.

"It was precisely my authority, ma'am, and that of every officer and NCO in the Corps, that I was thinking of when . . ."

"I don't think there's any future in going on with this," the other cut in quickly. "Best not to say anything you may regret. Put it behind you. It's finished with. Everyone's allowed one mistake. In future *ask* . . . and never put anything like that in writing."

145

The interview was over. Jaw clenched, Esme rose. Her stomach churned. She felt utterly belittled. She had done nothing, absolutely nothing to deserve this treatment . . . What kind of fool did they think she was?

"I do hope you're not going to leave here with any sense of bitterness . . ."

"I shall consider my position, ma'am," said Esme tightly. "Redress of Grievance is an avenue I may choose."

"Then you'll be a bigger fool than any of us took you for," ADWRAC spat with venom. "You'd better leave. Perhaps your OC'll be able to penetrate that thick skull of yours . . ."

Saluting, Esme left the room and the building without a sideways glance. Inside she boiled with rage. The WRAC was a law unto itself . . . or was lawless. Justice was a long way down its list of priorities . . . Why were they so keen to alienate rather than include . . . These people couldn't handle a mangy mongrel let alone Esme Hansard. She would have done anything she could to meet them halfway . . .

ADWRAC sank back into her chair. She felt drained. All these university people were the same. They were much too independent for their rank . . . were generally unmanageable. Discontented young women who seemed to think they should climb the ladder faster than the rest. When they joined, they were too old to mould . . . Once they were in, they were still too young for the level of involvement they expected. Hopelessly crude. Frankly a disaster.

She lifted the telephone and dialled AG16 direct. This was a delicate matter. They had better come up with something good before the Hansard girl opened another can of worms.

"This is ADWRAC Wessex District speaking . . . I'd like to speak to Colonel . . . Oh. I see. Well, yes, thank you, Chief. I'll speak to Major Mayhew, if she's there. Philippa! Congratulations on the promotion. Look, I've just had Esme Hansard here . . ."

Outside, a Parachute Batallion band was playing. A popular tune recently in the hit parade . . . Esme's mood began to lift in the way that every soldier's does . . . And her feet, itching like the hooves of cavalry mounts when they heard the drums. Impossible not to feel that strange ache around the heart . . .

"Eyees, *right!*"

A passing squad of red-bereted men snapped their heads around in Esme's direction. The NCO in charge of them saluted her, his flattened hand vibrating like a violin string. An ordinary compliment, but just then, balm to Esme's lacerated pride.

"Eyes front, Sarn't," Esme returned the salute smiling. She knew she could not resign. Would not even, probably, seek Redress of Grievance.

There were bad moments, plenty of them. But the army could throw stardust in disaffected eyes. An alchemy worked with bits of coloured cloth, the flash of light on metal . . . the cheesy smell of soldiery . . . the thump of boots and rhythm.

The day at Hurlingham shone brightly. The Silvershods met an Argentinian team in preparation for a trophy match at Windsor later in the season.

The weather, hot, was made for Esme's new, sleeveless cream tussore dress. It had been purchased with most of her Black Jack winnings from Harvey Nichols. An extravagance that would necessitate playing again before the end of the month. Well worth the trouble to see the disturbance in Clive's eyes.

Another girl, Roxanne Campbell, sat on a rug with Esme while Clive played alternating chukkas. Roxanne, minimally chinned and with an upper lip so short her mouth was permanently open, wore her shimmering brown hair in a waist-length cape, tossing it back every thirty seconds for no particular reason. She had a coronet on the 'saddle' flap of her Gucci handbag.

"You're Tiggy's friend, aren't you?" she said.

Assenting, Esme didn't see how she could deny it, although it was not the way she would have thought of describing herself when she was here alone with Clive.

"Clive says you're in the army," Roxanne waited to speak again until Clive himself, standing dashingly in his stirrups, thundered past, close by them. "You look quite normal to me. Just like anybody else . . ."

"That," replied Esme evenly, "is probably because I am."

"Must be jolly queer though. What do you do all day?"

"If you're really interested, I'll tell you. But it's quite complicated . . ."

"Oh, *please* don't bother," Roxanne entreated. "Loathe anything complicated."

"What do you do?" Esme asked, relieved not to have to scratch up a reason for her existence. The only thing she did continuously was wear the uniform and wait for something to happen . . . Something that might occasionally need doing. She felt the distance between herself and her civilian contemporaries now as an unbridgeable chasm of misunderstanding. The army had a way of cutting you off from everything else that was going on.

"I do lunches. Directors' lunches. For people in the City," Roxanne said. "Mainly for friends, of course. So it's tremendous fun."

"It must be," Esme responded as zestfully as she could. Lately she had felt an unaccountable desire to buy her own food and cook it. Wash up . . . *not* wash up . . . run out of things. Have working relationships with corner shops. "Did you do some sort of training?"

"I went to Atholl Crescent. You know, in Edinburgh."

Esme did know and would, given the chance, have developed the Edinburgh theme, it being the only ground they seemed to have in common.

"Mummy made me do it after I came back from Switzerland. Clive says you went to university. You must be awfully bright. I'm terribly dim . . ."

A vibration in her voice informed Esme that Roxanne felt threatened. Wished to convey, moreover, that academic achievement was a vulgar excess.

"Not too dim to run a business, anyway."

"Is Tiggy bringing you to my sister's dance next week?"

Esme was spared the necessity of answering this strange enquiry by a flying clod of turf, which landed, happily, in Roxanne's lap, not her own.

"Oh how *bloody*, bloody boring!" The earth, dry, had made a large dusty patch in the middle of Roxanne's pale suede mini-skirt. Fearfully exercised by this catastrophe, she said she would have to go home and change.

"See you sometime," she said.

Esme was happy to be left to watch the satin-coated, close-coupled horses with their semaphoring ears wincing each time a stick swished close to their legs.

When Clive came off the field, he flung himself down beside Esme and asked how she had liked Roxanne.

"Not bad for a hamster, is she?"

Laughing, Esme said that's exactly how she looked. A pretty, sniffy little rodent. She was a kind of cousin of Clive's.

A large crowd of Silvershods and Argentinians with their girlfriends went to eat in a new place on the King's Road that evening. Esme had to take the Bean Can because Clive had let the Aston run out of petrol.

It was a warm summer evening and the street was lined with cars. Not much room was left, even for Esme's tiny vehicle.

"Park there," Clive said suddenly as they were crawling past a seemingly endless line of open topped convertibles, parked nose to bumper. Seeing a long space just before a zebra crossing, Esme dodged into it.

She made nothing of the zig-zag lines . . . If they'd had any significance, Clive would have said so. She was distracted, anyway, by the crowds of laughing young people overflowing from the pubs on to the pavements, wanting to be among them. There was pop music spilling from open windows and a classical guitarist playing hauntingly near by. A smell of grilling meat and window-box geraniums.

When they left the restaurant three hours later the Bean Can wasn't there. Esme searched with Clive up and down the street. She had left it just there, hadn't she? After so much wine and talk, it was difficult to know whether she was coming or going. Clive wasn't very helpful.

"It's got to be here somewhere," he said. "We'll come back in the morning . . ."

Invited by one of the Argentinian players to return with him to his Knightsbridge flat, they gave up the search. Esme was very tired. So tired, that the South American offered her the immediate use of his spare bedroom. He and Clive would drink a nightcap and see what they could find out about her car.

The Bean Can, it turned out, had been confiscated. Towed away to a police pound in Chiswick. A reality Clive revealed when he woke up beside her at noon the following day, a Sunday.

The South American had driven out to Hertfordshire to lunch with people that he knew there . . . And Clive would have to get busy finding some petrol for the Aston, which he'd left outside Tiggy's mother's flat. He was giving Tiggy a lift back to Bovington . . . They wanted to start by half past two as an early night was definitely called for. If Esme got a taxi to Chiswick, she might be back in time to have a bite with them . . . Unlikely though. So they'd better say goodbye. Clive would ring her at Mereworth Barracks this evening.

It cost Esme ten pounds to repossess her car. With the taxi fare it made serious inroads into her narrow cash reserves.

Clive, she guessed, must know about this charge. But he couldn't realise, Esme told herself, that, to her, ten pounds was not a trifling sum. With so much money himself, he never thought about it.

The Chiswick pound was a dismal place. Rows and rows of imprisoned cars waiting forlornly to be ransomed by their owners. She heartily wished she hadn't had to come here on her own. The money didn't really matter that much.

Fighting down a Cinderella feeling, Esme drove out of London back to Ludgershall and Mereworth Barracks. She had to grapple too, with a hateful suspicion that Clive had known all about those zig-zags on the King's Road. Had put her car, her convenience, and her pocket all at risk quite consciously. Had been too mean to stump up for the fine.

But none of it fitted in with other things. The way his sleeping body fitted like a silk-lined purse around her own . . . the looks that were better than pet names or endearments. His quick, domestic peck when

149

he left her in the mornings. The touch on her arm that shot her through with effervescence.

The OC came back, her course being over, and listened grimly to Esme's version of the Clegg affair.

"Well, I suppose I'll live it down eventually," she said. "You realise you've probably scuppered my chances of promotion for a while. And as for Sarn't-Major, she's sweating on her pension."

It was forcibly impressed on Esme that it was customary to reward long-serving NCOs with promotion to the next rank simultaneously with retirement to enable them to draw that rank's higher pension rate. But the golden handshake wasn't automatic. A last minute cock-up of this sort would tend to tighten purse-strings.

"Her own fault," the OC was philosophic. "She should have kept her mouth shut. Never could resist a good gossip, couldn't Sarn't-Major. Bloody Clegg. Well, let this be a lesson to you, Esme. The army expects muck to be swept underneath the carpet, not out of the bloody door. What do you think you are? A bloody housewife?"

"Just as long as the carpet looks nice and clean," Esme countered rashly.

"Just so. You're getting the idea. Learn that and you'll have learned all you'll ever need to know about the army."

"I'm not sorry," Esme said contritely, "that I did what I did. I still think I was right. But I *am* sorry if you and Sarn't-Major will lose anything by it . . ."

"Stow it, dear. OC's job, isn't it? Carrying the can. Get some coffee in here and some of Sarn't-Major's medicine. I'll forgive you, thousands wouldn't."

"How do we ever put the house in order?" Esme was perplexed, when later the three of them sat drinking the half and half mixture companionably in the OC's office.

"Tell her, Sarn't-Major."

"Ma'am, we don't. The army's a right old muddle and it won't ever change."

Sorry to see her go, the Royal Army Ordnance Corps officers dined Esme out of the mess with the full panoply of regimental band, whole hundredweights of ornamental silver, mess wellingtons and monkey-jackets.

Even the Brigadier attended as a guest. He'd been greatly amused at Esme's ploy of driving her potty little Hillman on to the parade ground in order to get as close as possible to her squad of women on a rainy day's inspection. He might have been apoplectic at the *lèse majesté* . . . and with reason. But all he had said was, "There's a young woman with a field marshall's baton in her knapsack. Don't care to get wet for any damned silly old tradition, do she? Like her style."

And, as the Colonel said, in his brief address before rough mess games were permitted to commence, "Esme's OC tells me that there's no safer place for her than the corridors of power. So, gentlemen, let us drink to Esme. Good luck to her . . . and us."

Then everyone under thirty-five removed their spurs in preparation for beating each other senseless in the friendliest possible manner.

Hampered like the OC by her uniform gold brocade, Esme watched these adopted brothers play with shining eyes. She would miss them. Unlikely to see any of them again, she pressed them to her memory. Sadly, one could not marry everyone. At that moment Esme dearly wished it otherwise.

11

"I know you'll find simply heaps to do," the Brigadier protruded her top rung of teeth professionally, "a clever girl like you. This is a tremendous opportunity for you to show us what you're made of. So we'll expect to see a very busy little bee, won't we?"

"Yes, ma'am, I'm sure it'll all be slightly above my head." Dextrously, Esme balanced confidence with modesty. "But naturally I'll try."

"Oh *good*," the Director of the WRAC shot her snow-white cuffs, determinedly enthusiastic, "I knew you would."

The Lioness of lionesses, as Esme privately dubbed her, was embowered in an office at the top of Lansdowne House. Encrusted with feminine knick-knackery, it overlooked Berkeley Square. A perfect spot for formulating policy and shopping.

From Esme's own point of view the location was ideal. Clive had now embarked on a two-year stint at the Silvershods' depot in Windsor. From there he could reach central London in less than half an hour. Except on Thursdays, the Silvershods' compulsory dining-in night when the officers wore dinner-jackets and bedroom slippers. Wine was drunk from bumpers made out of dead chargers' hollowed-out, silver-mounted hooves. He described other rites ranging between the obscene and the idolatrous, with relish. A mummified phallus, allegedly once attached to a Grand Master of the Knights of Malta, featured in one of these ceremonies. Excuses were not accepted nor were outsiders ever invited.

"What fun for you all," Esme responded equably. "I wish we had some jolly secrets. It serves us right, I suppose. Women are much too

153

frightened of appearing childish. Do you think we could find a bit of Boadicea to play with?"

Clive, who had indignantly inhaled an excessive amount of air at this impious comparison, was careful to expel it slowly lest anything as common as a sigh escape him.

Coincidentally, if less interestingly, Ivor had command of an élite training battery at the Gunners' depot in Woolwich. He had sent her a very efficient-looking, privately printed change of address card to tell her so.

"How about the theatre and Quaglino's for supper next week?" he had written on the back. Decent of him. You could count on Ivor for a clear-cut programme of events. No disappointments and no surprises.

Philippa's club was only a step away, and Philippa herself had a flat in Stanmore near her place of duty at AG16, from which position of influence she had pulled strings to temporarily attach Esme at the Directorate. An unprecedented privilege, Colonel AG16 had impressed upon Esme, for one so junior. The Brigadier had reiterated the point at tedious length this morning.

Esme's request for living out allowance, argued on the basis that Mill Hill, where she was currently accommodated, was twelve tube stops distant, met point-blank refusal. Any dilution of the army's influence at this early stage of her career would not, she was smilingly informed, be to her benefit. That smile was final.

This was a major fly in the ointment. Although Daphne Deveril had been posted to Germany some months ago, she had left a strain of malediction behind her which her mild successor seemed powerless to banish.

What she could do to assist the Brigadier or her staff, Esme had not been told. Or not precisely. She was to look, learn and listen when she was permitted . . . remain constantly alert for every little chance to be of service.

Alertness – in practice an agonising tension – was highly valued by the WRAC, supposedly because it added an air of purpose to idleness. It certainly, Esme had found, produced fatigue without achievement.

But here, at the nerve centre of the Corps, Esme would, according to the Brigadier, be rushed off her feet . . . Quickly immersed in a plethora of matters so complex and diverse as to test the keenest brain. She would be thrown in at the deep end . . . generally kept out of mischief.

Whereupon Esme instantly understood that she was not so much an outstanding officer to be employed above her station as a loose cannon to be bolted to the quarterdeck. Rehabilitated after the Clegg fiasco.

154

Either way, Philippa was to be most heartily thanked for saving her from the depot. Esme's one visit there during Camberley days had horrified her. Women shouting, women marching in huge numbers, women crying in smaller numbers . . . But for Philippa, that would have been her fate. The depot was the usual 'punishment' posting for headstrong subalterns. There or 13 Company at Mill Hill.

As the door swung closed behind Esme amid the ushering Chief Clerk's hushed admonishments, the Director removed a file from her pending tray. It concerned the employment of WRAC personnel by other arms throughout the army. The list of established posts, alas, was dwindling. The impetus of the palmy wartime days when women were welcomed eagerly to relieve a desk-bound man to active, front line duty was fading. It was in the area of officer employment that the problem was most acute. Even posts where the Corps' tenure had seemed secure were openly challenged now despite the sacred cow status the women's services enjoyed.

The latest addition to this file, which the Brigadier perused with reddened cheeks, was a memorandum from some understrapper of the Chief Engineer's located in this very building many floors below:

The last three WRAC officers posted to fill the Staff Captain 'A' appointment at the Royal Engineers Brigade Headquarters at Goole upon Hull have functioned below the standard expected of RE officers fulfilling equivalent responsibilities, established the first paragraph baldly.

The Corps of Royal Engineers concludes that the Women's Royal Army Corps is unable to supply officers of the requisite calibre.

It is intended, therefore, Paragraph 3 announced: *that in accordance with a timetable which will allow the officer currently in post to complete the conventional two year tour of duty, to disestablish this post as a WRAC preserve, thereby enabling RE officers to benefit by the critical experience which the appointment offers.*

Clearly it was a matter that would require earnest meditation. To that end, the Brigadier opened a desk drawer and took out her needlepoint. She completed the shading on a tent-stitch rose petal whilst weighing up the battalions she could muster to outface the demonic forces at work in the Chief Engineer's office. One could not, she concluded, making a large, woolly knot on the reverse of the canvas, give in to this sort of thing.

True, Goole had been a trouble spot in recent years. A succession of seemingly reliable girls had been sent there and proved, according

155

to their confidential reports, to be resounding failures. Particularly the last one but one. A very messy affair that had been. A run of shockingly bad luck. Nonetheless the appointment up in Goole was vital. Something would have to be done to stem the tide before the murmurs that the WRAC had no role beyond that of self-administration gained currency in Treasury circles. Perhaps the graduate intake would help halt the process of erosion . . . Miss Hansard, for example. Ursula Spotteswoode thought highly of her, for what that was worth. So did Camilla Crump. An opinion to be taken seriously.

Unaware of these conjectures and how they might ultimately affect her, Esme was led to a utilitarian, brown leather-topped table and uninviting wooden chair. This was to be her place, facing the wall in an office she shared with a couple of middle-aged majors.

She had, she thought wryly to herself, been put well and truly in the corner.

"I wonder," said one of the older officers after Esme had sat obediently unoccupied for fifteen minutes, "if you would like to water the pot plants?"

"I should think," Esme responded with good-humoured candour, "that I'm well enough qualified for that."

"You mustn't," reproached the other officer forbearingly, busy totalling figures with an adding machine, "expect to run before you can walk. And don't you usually address field officers as 'ma'am'?"

"Usually, ma'am," Esme agreed with strictest accuracy. Philippa had forbidden this respectful address after Esme's first congratulatory ma'aming of her.

"Don't you dare," she grimaced. "Parades only and I shall steer very clear of any parade featuring you."

In the afternoon, after a solitary bowl of soup in Selfridges, Esme was given a trayful of files. Low priority stuff, so the G Major said. Most of it was long overdue for attention and would have to be dealt with some time. If there was anything there that Esme could understand or progress, she was by all means to do so. Delighted with this *carte blanche*, Esme attacked the stack of manila folders with gusto.

The second file on the pile yielded something of immediate interest. She re-read it several times. The nub of the matter turned on a memorandum from the Directorate of Infantry. In a nutshell, would it not, in view of a projected future fall in the birth-rate, make sense to recruit women directly into regiments? When Esme thought of her first command of female ruffians, it struck her as a pertinent question. One that had received no kind of acknowledgement let alone reply after a lapse of several months.

"What about this?" Esme showed the file to the weary drawn-faced

156

officer who'd given her the pile. "Shouldn't we reply?"

"I don't think so." The G Major, who was heavily engaged in drafting a feline reply to the Goole memorandum, blew her nose. "Unless in evasive terms. Yes, do that and then we can put the file away. The less rubbish hanging round, the better. Anyway, home time for you."

A commuter now, at five o'clock Esme joined the outfall of pin-striped, bowler-hatted military toilers. They funnelled, floor by floor, into the mirror-glass and mahogany-panelled lift to spill into the foyer and scatter.

A few men looked at Esme in the lift but none spoke. They could not place her. Without the mutually introductory minutiae of uniform to read, soldierly camaraderie dissipates. Esme saw she would have to make a concerted effort to find friends among her male counterparts. Some of them were youngish. Not much older than Ivor, anyway.

The 'old ladies' of WRAC1 seemed socially unpromising by comparison. Lunch? They never had lunch. Far too busy. They ate sandwiches at their desks. Men? They had no personal acquaintance among the other Directorates in the building. Too snowed under with work for that kind of thing. And usually, they added virtuously, they worked late.

Esme did not intend to imitate them. Rattling back to Mill Hill on the tube, she considered the Directorate of Infantry's query. It had lunch potential.

The following evening Philippa met Esme at her club with the object of giving her an early supper there before a gory, warry film showing in Leicester Square.

"Just the thing, cobber, after a day of dust and files."

"I've found a very undusty file," Esme remarked cheerfully and told her about the infantry's thought-provoking proposal.

"It's a joke," Philippa said as she signed the bill presented by the club's gaunt head parlourmaid. "Just something to stir up your old ladies, as you call them. A tease. It must be. What do they think they want women *for*?"

"I don't know but I think I'll roll up in person just around half past twelve tomorrow and ask them."

"Don't go giving my Corps away. Remember it's my future command you're playing ducks and drakes with."

"Honestly?"

"Somebody has to do it. May as well be me."

"Don't you *want* to get married, ever?"

Marriage, Philippa shuddered, held no charms for her. She'd seen it at the sharp end. The hearts and flowers bit was very soon over.

157

"My mother could wind up with over seventy grandchildren as it is. I'm not going to help make up the numbers or become any man's batwoman. Where's your Mr Carson, by the way?"

The question flowed naturally from thoughts of domesticity. Are not all live bachelors mere husbands on the hoof?

"At Windsor. I'm seeing him tomorrow."

The flatness in Esme's tone was not lost on Philippa Mayhew. She knew something about Clive Carson too, that she could not bring herself to tell her junior. Something so painfully obvious that, standing too close, Esme had failed to see it. For a few weeks, two years ago, it had almost seemed as if it might not matter. But after all, it did.

Esme was like a child, Philippa considered, playing on a railway line. Too absorbed or too ignorant to read the signals. The only possible words of warning were an insult. Perhaps her attention could be caught another way.

"We've got someone working with the Silvershods in Windsor at the moment. She's their education officer. She comes under the Education Corps for postings, so we had nothing to do with it."

"Lucky, lucky thing," Esme said enviously.

"Mmm. I'm surprised your Mr Carson hasn't mentioned her. Lindy Evans. I think she might be quite lonely, you know. Why don't you ring her up some time. You may have things in common."

"She won't be lonely with the Silvershods. They're fantastic company."

"Major Mayhew's taxi," the bemedalled commissionaire spun into the lobby through the revolving door, bringing the smoky crispness of the autumn evening with him. "Madam?"

"Thank you, Archie. Have you met my fellow officer, Miss Hansard?"

"A pleasure, ma'am, I'm sure," the commissionaire produced the relaxed salute of the honourably retired, long-serving soldier. A Royal Signals Warrant Officer until recently, Hansard was a name that rang bells in his retentive memory. Hadn't he been the duty sparks on the dramatic day of the Nightjar rescue, all those years ago? It would be a turn up for the books if Major Mayhew's bonny young friend were the famous Nightjar baby. In the army, was she? Well, the service ran in families.

Unconscious of the fact that she had inadvertently brushed Esme up against her own history, Philippa reverted to her earlier topic as Archie closed the taxi door on them.

"Give Lindy a ring. You might find her keener to come up and have a giggle around Knightsbridge with you than you'd think. These all-male units have their drawbacks."

"All right. I'll do it if you want me to. But I'm sure she'll think I'm muscling in."

It occurred to Esme that Clive had been wrong about those Thursday dining in nights at the Silvershods' mess. Lindy must know what went on.

Philippa had done the best she could. Found a way of getting the unsayable said at the appropriate level. Everyone knew what was happening to Lindy Evans but nobody with the power to stop it would lift a finger. To Esme's old ladies, a post was a post at any price these days. The WRAC was a military staff agency and business was bad.

Next day, the nation woke to an unusually titillating scandal. For the indifferent masses a morning treat . . . A smudge too, on the larger army picture, which, without her knowledge, touched in the focal detail in Esme's personal landscape.

First into breakfast at Mill Hill that day, Esme dickered over the table where the newspapers were laid out as usual. Choice depended not on predilection, but on which of the journals displayed were actually subject to anarchic claims laid by senior mess members.

Common property, Esme soliloquised philosophically, is more common to some than others . . . There seemed to be an inordinate amount of giggling in the kitchen.

"Oh ma'am, ma'am," a stewardess catapulted through the kitchen's swing doors into the dining-room, "Have you seen it?" Her eyes blazed with excitement. The chafing dish she carried threatened to debouch its contents on the carpet.

"Seen what, Private Renwick?" Esme turned quickly from contemplation of the newspapers. "Mind the dish!"

"Right behind you, ma'am . . . It's there! Front page . . . and in the middle . . . She's an officer, ma'am . . . Look, ma'am, look!"

Esme looked. The cause of Private Renwick's feverishness was displayed on the front page of a shoddy tabloid. It was a paper to which most officers' messes subscribed despite its incontinent type. Fervently monarchist and richly Tory in flavour, most days it carried a grainy front page likeness of the Queen. Today there was a lurid variation.

Staring at it, Esme half expected the lewdness to transmogrify into something more sedate. What she saw must be a dysfunction of her own eyesight . . . Perhaps she *had* seen all those little eights at Wyton. Stubbornly, however, the appalling apparition remained steady on the page.

"Do you know her, ma'am? Do you?" Renwick, disencumbered of

159

her dish, was all but leaning over Esme's shoulder. "She's got two pips up, ma'am."

And indeed, the creature in the picture wore a full lieutenant's rank badges, like Esme's, on her shoulder. But an officer of the WRAC? Impossible. It must be a dressed up night-club starlet. A half-naked, publicity-seeking model . . .

If only the officer in question had been truly naked, the sense of besmirchment might not have been so overwhelming. Or this surge of unhappy hilarity so unwelcome.

"Will there be a Court Martial, ma'am? I mean, in a paper, ma'am, and in that state! Corporal Maggs says it's Miss 'Epworth who was at t' depot when she was there . . . D'you know 'er, ma'am?"

"No," Esme replied, grinding laughter down. "Bring me some toast, please. Nothing else. Tell them to make less noise in the kitchen, would you?"

Taking the paper slowly to the breakfast table, Esme began, incredulously, to read. And to examine the pictures more closely. There was no mistake. It wasn't just a journalistic stunt. This was a real officer. Name, personal number, unit and everything were given. And Esme did know her. It was the girl who as a cadet, had first introduced Clive to her at Camberley. A freckled-faced nonentity.

'White, red or *rosé*?' It was her. Indubitably *her*.

There she was in a vulgarly provocative cheesecake pose, her skirt hitched up to reveal frill-edged black suspenders. Her No.2 dress tunic was unbuttoned, her shirt, pulled out from the skirt band, was open too. Her large, melon-shaped breasts jutted insolently, uncovered and unrestrained. And on her head, the No.1 dress hat was perched at a rakish angle. The inside pages were as bad or worse.

This was Miss Hepworth's snook-cocking response, the copy claimed, to reprimands intended to deter her from flaunting her affair with a Royal Marines sergeant. The relationship, Esme saw, reading between the lines, had not been forbidden. Only for reasons of good order and discipline, the couple were not to be seen together, in or out of uniform, within a twenty-mile radius of the garrison areas where either of them worked.

None of that seemed unreasonable to Esme. Nor to the other 13 Company subalterns when they, in due course, foregathered in the dining-room. Even so, rebellion was sweet. Anything that put the 'grown ups' in a flurry. What a fool Hepworth was! Of course, it was disgusting of her. With the whole army to choose from . . . Supposing he *was* the sexiest thing on two legs . . . God, just look at Hepworth's boobs . . .

The exclamations quietened as the 'grown ups' walked into breakfast.

Trouble in the family might be stimulating, but intelligent children know better than to openly enjoy it. In the presence of their elders, the subalterns chorused their dutiful disapproval. Words of vituperation covered whoops of strangled laughter.

Abustle, when Esme got there, the Directorate was already preparing for a siege. A charge of collective self importance vibrated up and down the corridors. People kept slipping like conspirators into the Brigadier's sanctum. Slithering out again through a slit in the door with lists and martyred faces. It tempted Esme to ask if she should boil up a cauldron of oil or two. But no one was in the mood for levity.

The switchboard had instructions to put nobody through unless they were on a panel hastily convened by the Brigadier and her senior staff. The Minister's Civil Service sidekick, members of the Army Board, ADWRAC Metropolitan District, other ADWRACs, Colonel AG16, Colonel Crump and the depot's commandant. Former directors of the Corps and the general commanding Metropolitan District. No personal calls at all and absolutely nobody purporting to represent a newspaper. A statement would be issued presently after the appropriate consultations.

A laughing-stock, the Corps drew tattered shreds of dignity around itself. Would the Palace take a view? The Corps' royal patron should be informed.

"I have the honour to inform you, Ma'am," the Chief Clerk took down at the Brigadier's dictation . . . What next? Scarcely, 'One of your officers has bared her breasts?' How about, 'has acted in a manner unbecoming an Officer and a Lady' . . .?

The Chief Clerk, chewing the end of her shorthand pen, embraced that form of words for a preliminary draft.

Not privy to this knotty piece of literary composition, Esme asked herself how Aunt Alice would react, if and when she heard the news. She had never worn the WRAC uniform herself, but . . .

"You'd better get on with whatever you're doing quietly," Esme was advised unnecessarily by a passing staff officer. "What do you think of all this?"

"I think if we make too much of it, it may get worse."

"You could be right," replied that officer thoughtfully in passing.

Esme's plans to oblige Philippa by ringing Lindy Evans at the Silvershods' depot, originally against her instinct, were put aside. She couldn't make private calls today. She was to meet Clive at his brother's flat this evening at six o'clock. If he changed his mind, as he often did, it would be too bad. He couldn't get through to her. How long would this ridiculous fuss go on? What on earth would they do with Hepworth?

The same question was directed to Esme when she took her sketched-out list of queries and suggestions down to the Infantry's Directorate.

"Ah," pounced the youthful acting Majors A and G, "new blood! Any mothballs to declare?"

"No, but not much authority either. Or only by default. Do you want to talk about this idea or yours?" Esme wagged the file at them.

"To you sweetheart, we'll talk till the cows come home, won't we, Andrew?"

"Or at least until the six thirty to Walton-on-Thames goes," agreed the other affably. He was married.

"So what did you think of our Amazonian brainwave, then?"

But it was not a day for files and memorandums. It was a day for pie and peas and pints of lager in a Shepherd's Market pub, along with a certain amount of ribaldry over the WRAC's answer to Jayne Mansfield.

"But you can see my old ladies' point, can't you?" Esme felt in duty bound to restore decorum. "How would you feel if it was your uniform . . . or you employed her?"

"Oh, we should have shot her," Andrew, the married one, said jovially, turning for endorsement to the other. "Wouldn't we, Bob?"

"Or asked for her resignation before it ever had a chance of happening. Do you want another of those, Esme? Or do you want a short?"

"Neither, thank you. I shall be asleep all afternoon. Do they have some coffee?"

The Colonel of the Silvershods took his coffee standing in the ante-room, regarding its appointments with leisurely satisfaction. A comfortable mixture of war booty and G Plan stuff, with a heavy preponderance of plunder from the Peninsular Wars.

That had been a good time for the regiment. No carpets from that campaign, but a fortune in chandeliers, pier glasses, console tables, paintings, tapestries, gold plate and inlaid cabinets. The Spanish government wanted their Velasquez back. An impertinent suggestion which the regiment had rejected out of hand. Loot was loot. An impeccable root of title.

The Adjutant, whom the Colonel now engaged in conversation, agreed with him. As everyone would agree with him in a moment, when he spoke his mind regarding another matter. A lamentable necessity.

162

Officer Quality

"And you'll attend to the loose ends, won't you?"

The Colonel turned away from the Adjutant to greet his Chaplain. A man selected for his complete understanding that Silvershod souls were not as other souls. He received no mess bill and, in return, revered the wealth and pedigree of the men who supported him in luxury. It came naturally.

The ante-room filled up as other officers came in from the dining-room in dribs and drabs. They helped themselves to coffee and stood about in groups. None may sit whilst the Colonel stood. Or leave the room without permission whilst he remained in it.

Clive lounged against the marble chimney-piece with Tiggy, expecting some sort of announcement. Probably about the order of dress for the regiment's boxing match against the Grenadiers. The Colonel usually came up with something exquisitely arcane. It would be that or some other detail of protocol.

"Gentlemen," the Colonel cleared his throat, lifting his voice above the mild hubbub of desultory small talk. "I think you know my views. What we saw of Grub Street's antics this morning in no way alters them. An unpleasant episode for those affected by it, but we are not affected . . . nor ever will be. That is all."

"Amen. So be it," appended Tiggy sarcastically beneath his breath.

"What's he talking about?" A newly joined cornet hissed, looking anxiously from Clive to Tiggy.

"Haven't the foggiest," Clive lifted one shoulder an expressive centimetre.

Tiggy eyed his friend coolly. Clive's options, he knew, were very few.

"Would visits of condolence to Miss Evans be in order, Colonel?" some wag proposed. "Take her a black bra or something . . . Seems to be a shortage . . ."

"Miss Evans?"

The Colonel looked on his education officer as the regimental governess. Somebody who endeavoured to raise the abysmal level of literacy among the troopers. She *was* an officer . . . of a sort.

Not the sort he cared to have in his mess, however. The footing of spurious equality such an association would imply might give rise to embarrassing complications involving a susceptible cornet. An ambitious girl, presented with such opportunities as would not normally come her way could play havoc with a foolish young man's future . . . Impair the regiment's reputation.

Consequently Miss Evans was very well served at lunchtime with a tray carried to her in the Education Centre. The extra messing charge was waived, of course. Where she lived or how, the Colonel neither

163

knew nor cared. The Education Corps people had said they would take care of all that. They understood that the Silvershods were a special case . . . Were confident that the WRAC would not presume to differ.

Tone must be maintained . . . to enable the Silvershods to pick and choose its officers from those already picked and chosen. And, indeed, its troopers. The men could be such terrible snobs.

The Chaplain and the Medical Officer, on the other hand, hardly represented the same threat to the regiment's integrity. They were put in breeches and thereby tacitly labelled Silvershod retainers. Professional 'gentlemen' knew, or could be taught their place. Women had a way of breaking bounds.

"There will be no need," the Colonel replied loftily to the wag's unpleasant flippancy, "to trouble Miss Evans with our sympathy. Bad behaviour is something we do not notice in the Silvershods. Carry on, gentlemen."

With a speaking glance at his Adjutant, the Colonel quitted the ante-room, bound for the stables. An outbreak of coughing there worried him much more than any imaginary discomfort of Miss Evans'.

In fact Lindy Evans had endured a morning of relentless barracking from the troopers, who knew quite well that she was unprotected by the corporate authority represented by the officers' mess.

"'Ere, ma'am, does the Rack 'ave any regulation bust size for officers . . ."

"Cor, ma'am, is she a friend of yours? 'Er with the big bristols . . ."

Sending the worst offenders to Sergeant-Major had been only marginally effective. He had put the miscreants on charges saying that rudeness to women was unsoldierly. Not in the best traditions of the Silvershods. And, he had added as an afterthought, disrespect of an officer, *any* officer, was an abomination.

"But, sir, she's not a proper officer, is she? Because if she is, 'ow come she don't go in the officers' mess, then?"

"Mind your own business, Trooper. March him out, Corporal. Open arrest."

Lindy had not wanted any of the delicious lunch which still lay beside her on a schoolroom desk, untouched under its silver-plated covers. She was very lonely here, isolated and unacknowledged.

On the other side of the square a mess servant handed Clive mail from the second post on a silver salver. Invitations mostly. Roxanne Campbell's parents were giving a dinner party for somebody else's out of season country dance . . .

"Excuse me, sir," the mess servant hovered. "Adjutant's compliments, sir. In his office sir, in fifteen minutes."

Inwardly Clive swore. The Adjutant was the Colonel's hatchet man by definition. What did that bandy-legged prat want at this hour? Three o'clock was the time for the office, not before. Letter signing was done between three and four . . .

By half past two, Clive, who had always cultivated a blankness of mind regarding his future plans, was well instructed in the broad alternatives. With immediate effect Clive was to avoid any tainted contacts conducive to unfortunate misunderstandings. He ought to know better. The WRAC was utterly beyond the pale. Until this morning's exhibition of a very plebeian pair of udders, the Colonel had been prepared to blink at Clive's personal preference for low company. From today, however, the regiment's unwritten rules would be rigidly enforced.

If Carson couldn't content himself with wholesome tarts or buggery, he ought to marry to his own and the regiment's advantage. And if he must have a mistress he should choose one who *looked* like a mistress. Not one who passed for a lady. The regiment was entitled to know where it was working.

"Confusion being the enemy of racial purity," contributed Clive pleasantly.

"As you say," the Adjutant snapped. "The Colonel will accept your word. Should you dishonour it, then we shall assume you wish to part company with the regiment. Have I your undertaking?"

"Yes," said Clive standing rather loosely to attention.

"Yes, *what*?" the Adjutant bridled.

"Yes, Jeremy," amended Clive, clicking his heels, this being the custom of the regiment in the course of formal dealings of this kind.

"Good. I was sure you'd be sensible about this."

Inspecting his horse lines immediately after this encounter, Clive was forced to recognise the fork in the road. He had come upon it inconveniently soon. He resented having it pointed out to him.

"Watch out, Corp," a trooper muttered, whisking a soiled tail-bandage out of sight, "Mr Carson's got black dog on 'im."

"Moody sod," the Corporal of Horse cursed softly. And then more loudly, "Afternoon, sir. You're early. We've only No. 2045 coughing in 'ere and 'e's had 'is drench. Bit off 'is feed . . ."

Walking down the line of nickering horses, brooding over each artistically aligned wisp of straw, each sand-burnished, emblazoned bucket, Clive discovered he was seriously annoyed. He was supposed to see Esme tonight. Should he go or not? Leaving the stables with a word of approbation he was still undecided.

"I shouldn't," Tiggy advised, unasked. "No heroics. Not unless, of course, you intend making the supreme sacrifice . . . Break it off on the telephone like the average bastard. Follow up with a heartbreaking

165

letter for Darling Heart to treasure. Uncle Tiggy's charm school drafts these on behalf of backward students for a small consideration. I've always found a monastic vocation goes down terribly well with girls . . . Leaves them with their *amour propre* intact, you see. I myself have entered no fewer than five Trappist establishments the length and breadth of the former Habsburg Empire . . ."

"Shut up, Tigs."

Clive went up to London.

"Can you cook?"

"Well, yes, a bit," Esme said. "Scrambled eggs . . . baked beans on toast, that sort of thing."

Clive opened his brother's refrigerator in search of raw materials. This really was a bore. Appearing in his usual haunts with Esme on his arm, however, would prove a bigger bore if certain of his less reliable brother officers were also lurking there. Everybody knew what she did for a living.

"I thought it might be quite cosy to stay in and watch television tonight," he said. "A change."

They ate scrambled eggs and watched the television, curled up on the boat-shaped bed. In the crook of Clive's arm, Esme was as content as she had ever been in his company.

Inevitably her mind was busy. Wondering what this unexpected relaxation of Clive's usual manic activity portended. A change of mood, perhaps. A settling of intentions. A trial of domesticity. There was something about him this evening, something in his warmth and weight, that communicated an imminent desire for speech. How and when would he begin to say the things she wanted at last to hear?

Esme loved him still, with the same single-heartedness she had known in those first weeks at Camberley. But the will to love, strong as ever, contended fiercely with a debilitating lack of nourishment. She was too familiar now with his ecstatic, climactic cries. They meant something only in the moment of utterance. She longed for words with lasting meaning. Meaning that could be carried and cherished, that didn't flare like a match and die.

He was her first real love, and therefore he must be her last. She had given him her maidenhood in all its constituent parts. She had served him unreservedly with all her sympathies. He owed her satisfaction. Nor could he be lying here, with her, like this and be thinking of withholding it.

The news came on. Labour politicians talking. Clive leaned forward and turned it down.

"Couldn't you leave the army?"

Esme regarded him searchingly. As much as anyone could know the workings of Clive's impenetrable mind, she believed she did. This question of his was loaded. Was this the edge of his proposal? A cryptic message slid under a doorway?

"I'd have to resign. It would take a few months. Less on marriage . . ."

"But supposing you wanted to do something else. How long would it take?"

"Seven months, I think. Why?" Esme looked away, hiding her disappointment.

"It would be useful, wouldn't it, if you had a flat or shared one. We'd always have somewhere to go. And then you'd always be in London . . . Not posted away continually."

"You're not always in London."

"No, but mostly."

"Why don't *you* get a flat?"

"Allowance won't stretch to it. You know it's expensive in the Silvershods. I don't get my proper money until I'm thirty. But you could work."

"I do work," Esme was floored by this effrontery. Too staggered to remind herself or him that 'work' meant going through the military motions. Anyway, what could he mean by all of this?

"Yes, but at some civilian job."

"What, for instance?"

Dismayed by the haphazard tendency of the conversation, Esme played back the shots. The game was not going her way, but a rally kept the final outcome open.

"Can't you type?"

"That's what they asked me when I went to see a female employment agency once when I was at 13 Company with that terrible woman, Deveril. I said I had a degree in Classics and was currently serving as an officer of the WRAC. They didn't know what it meant until I told them. When I did they looked at me as if I was something unspeakable that the cat'd dragged in. Then they asked me if I could type. Of course, I had to tell them that I couldn't. No typing, no job, they said."

"But why can't you type? All girls type."

"Well, I don't," Esme said with asperity. "Any more than you do."

"You could get a job in a shop," Clive said. "Harrods. Or a boutique. Lots of girls do."

"I don't want to be a shop assistant. Would you?"

"It's hopeless, then."

"What's hopeless?" Esme was completely puzzled. More puzzled

167

than she was hurt by this strangely off-centre interrogation.

"Nothing." Clive was unwilling to reveal his hand. "It just means you'll keep going off somewhere. So boring. I don't like it when you're not here."

They made love then, Esme submitting to Clive's advances querulously. Her body took light from his more sluggishly than usual. Her orgasm came with his, but fell short of conflagration.

"What's the matter, honey?" Clive reared up on his hands, frowning down at her with concern. Visible concern that revived Esme's spirits.

"Nothing. I'm tired, that's all. We had a fuss at the Directorate today. Did you see it? In the papers."

"Oh, that. My Corporal of Horse said something. Silly girl."

"Yes. She introduced us, do you remember?"

"No," Clive said, because he had no recollection of the girl at all.

"Incidentally, you must know someone called Lindy Evans. She's your education officer . . ."

"No," Clive's instinct for self-preservation asserted itself. "I think there's somebody who comes in a couple of afternoons a week or something like that. She doesn't seem to want anything to do with us. Never comes in the mess."

"How dull of her," Esme said. So much for Lindy Evans and the amount they had in common. "Can we go riding at Jack's this weekend?"

"Sorry." Again, Clive thought at lightning speed. Jack maintained his contact with the regiment. Not secure. "I'm riding in a race on Saturday. Limerick. Shan't get back till Tuesday. Next Friday. We can go to this amazing Chinese nosher in Bermondsey. All the Chinese Embassy people go there . . . You have to take your own wine."

"No good," Esme cut across him. "I'm going out."

"Oh. Who with?"

"Ivor Llewellyn. Royal Horse Artillery. I used to go out with him a bit at Larkhill. You know, I told you."

"What's he sniffing round for?"

"My hand in marriage, actually," Esme speared his complacency. It was near enough the truth.

"Right of the line," Clive commented promptly. She was rejoiced to see the sharpness in his eyes.

"On parade, with guns. Yes."

Clive was only momentarily disconcerted by this curio of precedence. Hardly even that. The RHA were ordinary, penniless men benefiting by an extraordinary royal decree. Occasional moments of empty glory. Nothing to threaten the day-to-day pre-eminence of the Household Calvary and Guards. Even so, he processed the implications swiftly. Officers of the RHA were hand-picked from the Gunner regiments. Supposedly outstanding . . . in their lustreless Gunner way. What rules did *they* have about women, he wondered. What definitions.

"Will you marry him?"

"I don't think so. He's a military shit. Years older than me, anyway. He looks Spanish. Quite good-looking . . ."

"When can I see you again?"

With reasonable discretion, Clive figured, he could continue marking time . . . making up his mind.

"Don't girls go to dancing classes any more?" Ivor winced. It was the third time the sharply-pointed toe of Esme's bronze kid shoe had jabbed his shin.

She was very lovely though, in this stone-coloured filmy, georgette thing. He liked this extremity of understatement that stressed the translucency of her skin, left the eye fresh for her fine-boned structure and tumbled coils of shining, pale-beige hair. She was thinner, he noticed. It suited her.

"Ballroom dancing isn't a thing people my age do much," Esme said, unintentionally deflating. "I had lessons in the school holidays when I was about fourteenish. So did all the people who went to schools round us. And when we started going to dances we just kind of developed a compromise between the waltz and quickstep. Two forward and one to the side. Two back and one to the other side. You're not doing it properly."

"There could be two opinions about that," said Ivor, drily. "Stand on my feet."

"What?"

"Go on."

"I'll hurt you."

"No you won't. Not more than you have been doing. That's right."

"Super," Esme approved the new method of locomotion a moment later. "Sure I'm not hurting you?"

"Not a bit," Ivor swept her up and down Quaglino's little dance floor. He was a good dancer, expert but not flashy. All Esme needed, he mused, breathing in the clean perfume of her shampoo, was some tuition. This way of enjoying her body suited him. It involved no adolescent lunging. "How do you like this place?"

"I'm fascinated to be here," Esme said. "I didn't know it really existed, you see. It's in *The Girls of Slender Means*."

Ivor, unfamiliar with that recently published novel, questioned her. Esme, he acknowledged, was pretty clued up on this kind of thing.

169

She'd been interesting about the Noël Coward revival they'd just seen. Enthusiastic about what she called the play's skeletal symmetry. He hadn't known that plays had skeletons.

"So you see," Esme went on with reference to her present surroundings, "in the book, everything happened when Aunt Alice was young. So this place is a bit of an archaeological find."

"Just like me, I suppose."

There was a trace of pathos in Ivor's tone, but Esme felt his cheek bulge so that it touched her own. He must be smiling over her shoulder. A scratchy cheek. But a good, broad, dry hand in the small of her back.

Drawing away from him a little, she examined him. There were two or three threads of bright silver in his black hair. A crop of short, black bristles in his nostrils. He really was very dark. One of those men whose chins blued over after an hour or two. Not at all greasy, though. Having said that, Esme thought, Ivor's masculinity was in very strong solution. He had a way of making her feel . . . Oh, she didn't know. Sort of . . . *frilly*. A strange, uncomfortable sensation. Male maturity was difficult to accommodate, somehow. She wasn't used to it, she supposed. Not in close-up.

"What now," he said. "Looking for signs of decay? Or are we talking about downright putrefaction?"

"No," Esme smiled quickly. "I was thinking how handsome you are."

Knowing that statement extended no invitation, was spoken with the inconsequence of a girl flattering an uncle, Ivor smiled himself. A child she was not, and yet she could assume this mantle of unbreachable purity at will. And always did with him, since those first two extraordinary evenings at Larkhill. Then she had set out to ensnare him, he realised, with the merciless efficiency of a hardened female predator. Played him like a fish, landed him and let him go. Unfortunately . . . or fortunately, perhaps, he felt, she'd left a fragment of the hook in his lip.

"Come and sit down," he said to her. "Your eight and a half stones are beginning to tell on my metatarsals. Let's have some more champagne and you can tell me what you've been doing."

Esme had been doing quite a lot. She was busy with revisions to the Corps' official history in readiness for a new edition. She was in charge of plumbing and decorating a special loo for the Princess Royal in preparation for her annual attendance at the Directorate's conference.

"I have to get the lavatory smashed up afterwards whether she's used it or not. Don't you think that's an unbelievable waste of money?"

"It's usual," Ivor replied smoothly. Career officers never questioned royal protocol whatever they might privately think of it.

"That doesn't make it right," Esme persisted severely.

"Possibly not," Ivor agreed guardedly. He wasn't to be drawn on this one.

Esme had represented WRAC1 at a meeting of the Corps' Benevolent Fund at the Duke of York's Barracks. She had been asked her opinion of a grant of five pounds to an indigent ex-servicewoman who stood in need of a winter coat. Esme had persuaded her co-committee members to raise the grant to eight pounds to buy a better coat, which would last longer and obviate the need to repeat the disbursement from the fund's shockingly lean resources too soon.

"Very good," said Ivor, sincerely interested. His mother had been a great committee woman in her day. There was always something useful in the welfare line for women to do in the army.

It didn't strike Ivor that his mother had not actually been *in* the army. As far as he was concerned – and indeed his father was – she had been. Army wives were camp followers. Under military law when abroad. Officers' wives were . . . well, they stood in the same relation to the other ranks' wives as the officers themselves did to the men. Unofficially. The WRAC was an excellent preparation for all of that. One day, Esme's experience would be useful to her husband. Himself, perhaps?

Ivor deprecated his own stray thought. Premature, if not positively self-indulgent. Esme, he gathered, from a brief word with Philippa Mayhew, whom he had bumped into on the endless, grey linoleum corridors at Stanmore, was infatuated with a cavalry officer. Not cavalry of the line, either. Household Division. A Silvershod. Was she a snob, he wondered. He would not have thought so. Rather the reverse. A sexual snob, possibly. And who could wonder? Nature itself would push a female like her towards a high-priced stud. Regardless of actual suitability . . . A genetic imperative. As to availability . . . Even Troy had fallen.

'Infatuated', or had it been 'besotted', Mayhew had said. What *was* it all about? Had she seen him first and then seen something better? Someone who might open the stiffest doors to her? Not just the army doors. Not just a major's modest quarter on the married patch with other majors' wives for friends . . . Not a home that was moved from place to place in boxes. Not even a CO's residence. Did she want more than army men could give . . . and could she get it? Best of luck to her if she could, Ivor mortified his twinge of jealousy.

"And when you come to think about it," Esme was speaking now of her pet project, "From what I've seen, the WRAC exists to administer itself. The girls . . . our service women, you know, have proper jobs.

Some of them quite high-powered but we just seem to hang around and ask them if they've got any personal problems. We get in everybody's way. Theirs, their employing officers' . . . So most of the time, we're just loafing. At the hairdresser's or doing 'personal administration'."

"Egyptian PT?" Ivor chuckled. The army had all sorts of euphemisms for daytime sleeping.

"Yes, or having a nice time in Boots or W. H. Smith's or something . . ."

"Some officers have proper jobs, you know."

"Sure," Esme agreed. "Women in the Royal Army Medical Corps, or nursing sisters in the QA . . . They're *not* WRAC. They're badged with other Corps. Precisely the point I'm making, isn't it?"

"There're some WRAC officers doing real Signals jobs and Education people . . ."

"A few. So why not make them real members of the Royal Signals?"

Ivor could advance no case that would satisfy Esme. She'd got the bit between her teeth. All sorts of wild ideas. Why not basic weapon training for women? Women commandos . . . very loyal if trusted and absolutely vicious. She was sure her Aunt Alice had shot somebody once, although she always skirted round the story. And her mother could run, jump, climb and abseil as well as any man . . .

"Short sprints, probably," Ivor conceded. "But Esme, dear, you must remember, your mother and your aunt were very exceptional people living in very exceptional times."

"Well," she relapsed against the red plush banquette, "I'm peddling this idea all round the Directorates, including yours, and some of them like it. They like it quite a lot. Remember, the *Infantry* started this. At the very least we could do all their staff work and leave them to get on with training. Let the girls shoot for rivalry's sake . . . or self-esteem, or self-defence. I know they want to do it."

"Consider this," Ivor said sternly, catching at her flying hand. "No man would object to fighting at a brave woman's side. But can you imagine how he would feel if he met one as an enemy? To a real man, a woman's body is sacrosanct. *That's* why I'm not keen on this and why I think that whilst it's an amusing toy for you at the moment, you'll never get anywhere with it. If we use women, so will an opposing force. And the better men will lose."

Silenced, Esme regarded him with new respect. Ivor's was the only cogent argument she'd heard or was ever to hear against women bearing arms. It was irrefutable. But still, there were all the other things . . .

172

"How's your love life?" Ivor was tired of the debate.

"My love life? What do you know about my love life?" The wind was out of Esme's sails.

"What a little bird told me. The greater, red-crested vulture, actually. Your Major Mayhew." Ivor still found Philippa antipathetic. Of course she was too tall to be attractive. Played on her height in a rather irritating manner.

"Philippa? Philippa's at Stanmore."

"So was I the other day. I went up for one of these 'career planning' chats with my postings branch. It's when they bribe you to do this with the promise that you'll get the other afterwards."

"Do they keep their promises, though . . ."

"Don't change the subject. How are you and your Silvershod getting on?"

"Just fine," said Esme, rather pleased to be the subject of discussion between the Majors Llewellyn, RHA and Mayhew, WRAC. Good heavens, they were both quite important. Didn't they have better things to talk about than a subaltern's affairs?

The five-piece band, game greybeards with their old-fashioned combination of piano, drums, saxophone, double bass and trumpet, started up again. Plinkety-plonk nostalgia.

"Come on, let's dance again. I won't stand on your toes this time. You can teach me."

Four months passed in this way, including Christmas leave.

Exploring south of the river or the East End with Clive . . . or staying in. Tiggy had supper with them once. A shift of gear there, but no acceleration.

And in-between-whiles, Ivor, attentive, generous and sometimes a shade dictatorial. He took her out to dinner at the Connaught twice, and ruined it, rather, by talking about the Staff List all evening. Oh, yes and medium range missiles.

There was Philippa. Her flatlet in Stanmore was of a Japanese simplicity. Deliberate, Philippa said. She hated clutter and had cleared the landlord's out. White walls, white venetian blinds. One large pan, one small pan. Parsley in a terracotta pot on the kitchen window-sill. Ratty carpets up and out, floorboards sanded, sealed and meticulously swept. Tea in a caddy, coffee in a jar. No packets. Bags of hot water though, and a ceaseless round of laundry.

Philippa wasn't entitled to a batwoman in this job. Not if she lived out. She spent a lot of her off-duty time in rubber gloves. When she visited, Esme took her shoes off at the door without being asked.

Esme found enough to occupy her at the Directorate, becoming, after the initial stiffness, popular with the 'old ladies'. She kept them abreast of the younger end's attitude, they said. She told them that the girls would like the proposed new No. 2 dress skirt pattern but the officers wouldn't. And that the mess dress was a dowdy shape. It needed changing. Even Aunt Alice wouldn't have touched it. That square neck! Modifications were at the committee stage already, but not the ones Esme wanted.

"It's all right for you," the Brigadier said indulgently, "at your sylph-like stage of life. But we've got to cater for the fuller figure too, you know."

Esme gave up. It would be desperately unkind to point out that they shouldn't *have* fuller figures. The men weren't allowed to.

She rode at Jack's, alone these days unless he went out with her himself. Habibi was always made available to her.

"To tell you the truth, ma'am, I'm going to have to let her go. She's not up to a man's weight and she's bit too much of a handful for most of my lady clients."

"Oh, Jack!" Esme was anguished to think of the little horse falling into ignorant, unsympathetic hands.

"Don't you worry, ma'am. I'll see she gets a good home. Why don't you take her yourself? I'd give you a fair deal on the livery."

Esme said sadly she could not afford it. But Habibi was eleven years old. Halfway through her life, at least. Her price would be low enough to attract an unscrupulous dealer. And she didn't trust Jack, really. He'd send the mare to auction. The rent on his stables was probably very high and he needed to make a profit to survive. He wouldn't be sentimental.

"How about Mr Carson?" Jack wheedled. "Plenty money, hasn't he? Still seeing him, aren't you? Let him give you a nice present, eh?"

Esme stared frostily at him, issuing a silent reproof. Ladies did not accept valuable presents from men, unless they were engaged. One of Aunt Alice's cardinal rules of conduct. She and Clive were *not* engaged. A situation which might be rectified but not, tragically, in time to save Habibi.

The mare's future was settled, however, quite quickly after the Brigadier at WRAC1 was shown a memorandum from the Royal Corps of Transport's Directorate. The general responsible for the army's transport was somewhat struck by the suggestions made by a Lieutenant Hansard. Or so his aide deposed. Could the matter now be advanced to a higher level of responsibility for further talks?

What suggestions? What had Esme been up to? When the nature of Esme's wide-ranging 'preliminary discussions' was discovered, there was a splutter of amusement on the top floor of Lansdowne

House. The little wretch. The Devil would find work for idle hands to do . . .

It was judged that Esme had been of quite sufficient service at WRAC1. She had better be posted on before she tried her hand at amalgamations. Good God alive, whatever next?

The Brigadier rang Colonel AG16 and amid disabling gusts of laughter, called for Esme's rapid removal before she disbanded the Corps single-handed. She had been a breath of springtime but playtime here was over.

Catterick, decided Philippa, just before she was called in to discuss Esme's next move with Colonel AG16. There was an Assistant Adjutant's post falling vacant with a Signals regiment. The very thing for Esme.

Fresh air and a mass of young men, some of whom she would doubtless find agreeable. Not too far from her home, either. She would be better out of London. Away from whatever necromancy Clive Carson was practising on her. If he followed Esme to the far north of Yorkshire, Philippa would gladly eat her No. 1 dress hat . . . and her beret.

Esme got a splendid confidential report from WRAC1. Leadership capability? The Brigadier hesitated over the boxes momentarily. *Excellent*, she ticked. Could hardly be less since she'd been quietly leading half the British army by the nose. Dreadful child. Unfortunately there was no set of boxes for 'subversive capacity'.

They would all miss her. Miss her quick, light step in the corridors. Her tendency to bang doors . . . her pretty, somehow exciting voice. The way her hands flew like humming birds when she was keyed up about something. Her damned impudence too. It came out of a daughterly confidence in those she had come to know.

Saying goodbye to her, the Brigadier said:

"Well, Esme. I hope you'll give us 'old ladies' a good chit. We do our creaking best, you know."

Esme flushed a little, smiled and felt a lump enlarging in her throat. They *had* all been good to her. Concerning half a dozen others, including Lindy Evans, who had been callously abandoned to a less congenial fate, she remained in ignorance.

Aunt Alice was delighted at the prospect of having Esme so much nearer, for a while at least.

"That's marvellous, darling. And well done about your confidential."

Then, only because Aunt Alice was always interested in horsy things, she told her about Habibi. Could Aunt Alice think of a way to get her a good, permanent home? Any of her contacts, for example . . .

"You must have her," Aunt Alice said immediately. "I always meant to give you a horse for a commissioning present but Camilla Crump told me there were no stables at Mill Hill. And then you were never settled anywhere suitable for long . . . There's masses of stabling at Catterick, I happen to know. It used to be assumed, you realise, that every officer would either privately own a horse or be entitled to a charger . . ."

Rapture was hardly too great a word to describe Esme's feelings. Her own horse! And Habibi too, her equine soul-mate. Something of her own. Habibi safe! But what about transporting the mare north? It would cost a fortune and on top of the purchase price . . .

"You leave all that to me, Miss," Aunt Alice said. "A present is a present. You're a staff officer nowadays, so you go and arrange your mare's travel warrant, movement order and so on. Buy the tack if you can, if you think it's good enough. Bills to me."

Dame Alice Winstanley put the telephone down and went straight outside to her Land Rover. There was another stand of spruce further up the valley, on a small parcel of land she'd acquired when Esme was about six . . . for just this sort of thing. The timber wasn't ready for harvesting just yet . . . but she could borrow on it. You needed money to launch a girl. And for that particular girl and any horse, Alice would have carved her heart out.

"Oh," said Clive. "Signals? What kind of people are they?"

"You know very well," Esme clipped. "Every time you go on an exercise, you have one. In fact you've probably got one living in your mess right now."

Clive pouted. He had to give her best on that. Esme was getting awfully *up* on army things.

"I don't know why you have to go all the way up there," he groused. "It's such a . . ."

"Bore," Esme finished for him. "You can always come and see me."

Clive did not reply to that.

Esme gave eighty guineas for Habibi after some hard bargaining. Jack gave her the last guinea back for luck, as horsemen should and did, in those days.

"Thanks, Jack." Esme took the coins and wished with all her might that Clive might give her something too. The only thing she could accept from him in exchange for those things which, she knew, she must soon refuse him.

12

Esme was a year at Catterick. A time that fled by in a golden haze of attractively companioned leisure.

No one unconnected with the army, visiting Catterick Camp in the sixth decade of this century, would have guessed that its grisly gulags of contemporaneous concrete, Victorian brickwork and wartime Nissen huts housed a community largely bent on pleasure. Or so it seemed to Esme.

The south of England, native heath of the majority of army officers, was too far away to be visited every weekend. So the garrison, marooned on its unlovely moorland site, was forced to recreate itself with the materials that lay close to hand. Sports, both of the field and team variety, dogs, gossip, fornication, cards and horses.

Cultural diversions were in short supply and not much wanted. "Happy as pigs in shit," summarised the popular CO of the dominant Brigade of Signals, reporting on his command's morale.

Horses coming first, of course, in the scheme of proper officerdom, Esme chose the Garrison Saddle Club as the most eligible of several possible billets for her mare. Well managed and well staffed, it was located close to the enormous but homely mess she shared with all the Signals Brigade officers including several women. The latter were in a ratio of approximately one to ten.

The mess boasted a small lake jumping with fat trout, an untidy kitchen garden and as much indoor space as would permit a pack of libidinous youngsters to live in harmony with the 'crusties', as resident field officers were called here. In the public rooms the 'crusties' had their favourite chairs and little singularities.

But if these were affectionately humoured, there was reciprocity. The subalterns might wear out as many mattresses as they cared to as long as it was understood that *Punch* was to be circulated in strict rank order, that *The Times* was reserved as a senior person's eye mask for napping in the ante-room . . . And that the Paymaster's baleful Staffordshire bull terrier had first claim on the hearthrug in winter, and his favourite, south-facing window seat in summer. Junior dogs, of which there were a score, must fit in where they could.

Teatime was a bedlam of dog fights, dogs peeing, dogs being cuddled. Owners' breeding propositions, for themselves and their canine friends. Major Mulliner, WRAC's dogs, however, a trio of Yorkshire terriers, went off promptly at five to six to have their minds broadened by the news. Then their topknot ribbons were changed for dinner.

Liberality was rife.

'Dead gentlemen,' a wit had appended to the list of mess rules pinned up behind Esme's bedroom door, '*must* be removed from the ante-room before ten on the morning following cessation of vital signs.'

Not altogether a joke, as it happened. The previous year an elderly quartermaster had expired peacefully behind *The Times* one evening after dinner. His moribund condition had not been spotted till the dogs, whining, alerted his fellow mess-members to the situation by afternoon tea next day. Earlier, the servants had considerately dusted round him.

It was February, so the coal scuttle in Esme's room was replenished assiduously throughout the day and would be until 1 May. Then she would have to make do with the central heating, which just might, after high-level deliberations, be turned off in June.

"Not cosseting," defended the President of the Mess Committee sturdily to a civilian accountant. "Merely a matter of ensuring the personal efficiency of our officers. No one can tie a fly with chilblains on their fingers."

The PMC also fulfilled the modest duties of water bailiff. Anyone caught with spinning tackle in the vicinity of the lake would be horsewhipped. He taught Esme the elements of casting. Fishing, he maintained, was the best antidote to the stress and strife of army life.

Attached for duty to a regiment that undertook the basic military training of Signalmen recruits and which had nothing whatever to do with operational communications *per se*, Esme soon tumbled to the by now predictable conclusion that she had no specific tasks. Or rather, she had one. The composition of the Orderly Officer roster, which caused a vast amount of trouble.

"Don't you realise," a disgruntled captain burst into the office Esme shared with the Adjutant, "that I'm not available on Monday. It's my mother-in-law's birthday. I thought it was your job to know this kind of thing."

The Adjutant, a shy intellectual – quite out of place at Depot Sigs – deprecated the captain's bellicose manner, mildly.

"I say, Sidebottom. Well, I mean to say, I *say!*"

"*Siddybertome!*" corrected the discommoded captain, crossly.

Temperately, Esme explained that the portion of Part I Orders for which she was responsible was issued purely as a basis for discussion. Everyone had their life to live and some, doubtless, had mothers-in-law to pacify.

The Adjutant, over whose supposedly lordly signature the orders were put out, nodded in agreement. Captain *Siddybertome* could swop duties with the Colonel's dog for all he cared. And for God's sake, could voices please not be raised in this office. The regiment was enough of a bloody bear garden as it was. Far too much shouting and stamping going on. Just listen, he shuddered, at that man on the parade ground now. Sarn't-Major Lennox was a menace.

"Dismally inept rhyme," he apologised to Esme. The Adjutant was composing a verse chronicle of the Arnhem parachute landings. It took up most of his time.

The Colonel, on the other hand, was a pleasant-faced man of forty-five whose chief preoccupations were, in order of priority: the delinquency of his labrador; the fitness of the regimental rugby team; the depression of his wife and the paucity of attendance at voluntary church parades.

Both the wife and the labrador had seen psychiatrists according to their several needs. Occupational therapy (upholstery classes) had been prescribed for the one and tranquillisers for the other. Very logical, enthused the Colonel, since Amber was always ripping or chewing up upholstery . . . which cost a fortune in dilapidations on march out. Perhaps, he mused aloud to Esme when she took his customary elevenses to him one day – a glass of madeira and a slice of madeira cake – Gloria could learn to re-cover G Plan furniture so as to deceive even the hawk-eyed Barracks men . . .

It was a funny thing, he confided, that lately, even the keeny-meanies who used to make up a bit of a quorum for the Chaplain to sermonise on Sunday mornings down at the Garrison Church had fallen away. Gone over temporarily to Rome, he griped. The new General was a Catholic. Career officers, he added savagely, had no ruddy *conscience*.

Had Esme lots to do this morning? No? Hmm. Tricky finding things for girls to do. What about Esme taking on the Garrison Church flowers? Now, there was an idea. Better than burly staff sergeants stuffing ratty daffodils in jam jars . . . And she could slip up to the small

179

arms ranges and classify on pistols. Illegal, of course, but fun. She'd be bound to hit something some time. Everybody did. A feather in the regiment's cap, too, if *their* WRAC Ack Adj could fire a gun.

Esme did it all.

Became a better marksman than anyone could have foreseen . . . Not bad for someone with officially defective eyesight . . . Improved the rather basic standard of floral decoration down at the Garrison Church . . . Lunched with lonely Gloria.

Her children had grown up and flown the nest. And now she didn't need it, she had this huge, empty house to contend with. She couldn't even put her feet up. By half past eight every morning the place was swarming with the army-provided domestic staff her husband's command suddenly entitled her to. So she had to be up and dressed, looking Colonel's ladyish. Had to entertain flocks of boring people whether she wanted to or not. Had to run the Wives' Club, got pushed around by the majors' wives, oh so respectfully. Got roped into other things by the Brigadier's wife, got terrorised by the General's wife. *Her* husband was late of the Coldstream Guards, so of course she thought herself practically divine.

"Oh, Esme, all I want is a house of my very, very own. It needn't be big. Just mine."

Esme, with the callousness of youth, privately thought Gloria something of a drip. But listening to the Colonel's wife a couple of hours a week rendered the CO a real service. Every morning following their regular girls' date, he told her that Gloria had 'bucked up no end'.

It was from this and other things that Esme intuited the essence of her job. It was to be a friend to all. Stand between the subalterns and the Colonel's wrath . . . when wrath they had deserved. Stand between the Adjutant and the Colonel when the Adjutant wouldn't or couldn't play Rugby. Defend Amber, the Colonel's dog, from the RSM. That magnifico was a touch too handy with his pace stick if bitten. Listen to lovelorn subalterns pouring out their drunken hearts. Listen to some long, inarticulate story of a terrified recruit's which nobody else had patience for. Condense same and interpret to his exasperated troop commander. Allocate firing ranges to screaming squadron commanders when the Adjutant, offended by the racket, couldn't hear himself think, let alone consider making a decision. Loyally and enthusiastically attend every single dinner night in full fig. Sit next to the General's Lancer ADC and make him feel Catterick wasn't such a desert after all. Do her party piece and take snuff from the regiment's silver-mounted goat's head. Not a sneeze. Draft the orders for the Junior Signalmen's waterborne exercise in Scotland. Christen it Exercise Rubber Duck. Keep clear of the ducklings when they all came home full of their adventure and assorted parasites.

"If we get them in your hair, ma'am," the RSM stood rigidly to attention, "it could affect morale."

"Beneficially, I should have thought, RSM," Esme quipped sweetly. "Fleas for one, fleas for all . . . and conversely."

"That's as may be, ma'am," snapped the RSM, not being a man who exchanged badinage with women, Miss Hansard included. "And could you please refrain from obliging your cavalry muckers up the road by taking their prisoners? Guard room's overflowing. Can't have the whole regiment on guard duty, ma'am. We're in the army here, not the fucking prison service . . . Begging your pardon, ma'am."

Esme did blush a little over this. She fulfilled many of the Adjutant's duties now, he being stuck on the thirty-third stanza of his epic . . . But more than half the time she was flying blind. Making decisions on the basis of no knowledge. Still, the law of averages worked out pretty well in her favour.

So very many things. All small but they added up to something. The point was encapsulated by the Colonel one day.

"What's she called, Esme?" He had encountered her riding on some disused ranges when he was going for a solitary Rugby-training run. He panted to a halt, patting the grey's neck when Esme reined in to give her boss the time of day.

"Habibi, Colonel."

"Mean anything? Sounds Arabic or something . . ."

"It is," Esme replied. "It means 'darling of the tribe'."

"Coincidence," he grunted, towelling his neck. "Well, must push on. Enjoy your ride. Coming to us for dinner tonight, aren't you?"

Obtuse, for once, Esme missed the complimentary reference to her mascot status in the regiment. Not essential exactly, but a luxury they'd got used to.

Contented, engaged in a sustaining love affair with the regiment in its entirety, Esme noticed herself drifting away from Clive. Attenuated cords of yearning thinned and frayed as time went by. He never wrote. The last she'd heard of him was a Christmas card he sent to Lowlough. A reproduction of the Silvershods' drum horse's official portrait. 'How's the frozen north?' he'd scribbled hurriedly. 'Love, Clive.' Not even a single X for a kiss came with it.

It was a shock to hear his voice, however, on the telephone one day, proposing a skiing trip to the Dolomites at Easter. He missed her, he said. Esme's heart thumped as she agreed. How could she do this to herself? But she had done it. And then it came to nothing. Clive had slipped a disc and couldn't go.

Cheated, feeling foolish with two brand-new ski suits she might never use hanging in her wardrobe, Esme was forced to tell Aunt Alice that her Easter plans were cancelled. She would be coming home to Lowlough, after all. Why had she ever squandered so much time on Clive? Belief in this slipped disc of his fluctuated like the intermittent current transmitted by a failing electric circuit. The flickering light of faith extinguished by the gloom of disillusion.

She knew she must forget him. Close her affections' valves against him and open them to others.

There were others too, standing in the wings. Friendships that, although named platonic by herself, might with the warmth of encouragement, ripen.

"Oh, why doesn't my Colonel like me, Esme?" groaned a captain in the Duke of Wellington's on a night when the Signals Brigade entertained the garrison's other regimental officers to the rustic pleasures of a halfway decent local pop group, amateur cabaret acts, buffet supper and limitless alcohol.

"Could it have anything to do with your eyeshadow, Cedric?" she asked him, peering closely at his liquid, sapphire eyes.

"You don't think so, do you?" he replied, as if this were a novel solution. "That fellow's riddled with prejudice. I *like* cosmetics. My chaps do too."

"I'll bet," responded Esme. "I expect they're all in love with you."

"Good thing if they are," observed Cedric sagely. "Got to get 'em to follow one somehow. Go the extra mile for *mes beaux yeux*, y'know, 'cos I don't have any brains to offer."

Esme thought differently and was rather fond of him. His undoubted homo-erotic allure didn't detract from his considerable patrimony of manliness. The garrison's nubile daughters were all gone on Cedric.

Towards what would be the end of Esme's tour of duty at Catterick, she was volunteered for a Christian Leadership course. One of the regular programme of such affairs run by the Royal Army Chaplains' Department at their headquarters at Bagshot Park in Surrey.

"But why me?" Esme protested to the Adjutant. "It sounds horrific, being worked over by a posse of parsons for a week. It isn't as though I'm all that wicked . . ."

"Sorry, Esme. Colonel's orders, you've got to go. We can't spare anyone else. We've got the exercise on Warcop ranges that week and you'll be the only officer who's free."

Esme sulked partly out of genuine resentment and partly as a matter of form. The army insisted it was a Christian army, whilst confining the overall concept to 'straight bats', 'sheet anchors', and other items of virile religious imagery. It wouldn't do to display any keenness for what amounted to a virtual retreat. What on earth was Christian

Leadership, exactly? It sounded pretty squishy.

"Not a clue," the Adjutant confessed. "Would you find *force* and *coarse* disedifying?"

Arnhem was meant to be read aloud, of course, but slim volume publication was unavoidable, which made visual agreements as critical as auditory ones . . . The Adjutant cursed the day he'd ever planned his work around heroic couplets.

A fortnight later the regiment packed itself into a convoy of four-ton lorries and headed north for Warcop ranges. Esme, grumbling, turned the Bean Can south, bound for the chaplains' lair at Bagshot.

His Aston Martin was sitting on the carriage sweep when Esme got there.

Shaken by the sight as a recently reformed smoker's resolve is threatened by the unexpected offer of a cigarette, she stalled the Bean Can. Pent up with a kind of terror, her heart contracted. Pulse and respiration faltered, accelerating then, to stimulate the slowing brain and circulation.

Not Clive's, Esme decided, restarting her Hillman's engine. Another like it but not Clive's. British racing-green sports saloons of the marque were not ubiquitous but neither were they unique . . . Between them, the officers of Her Majesty's Land Forces accounted for a high percentage of the fast cars on the roads . . . The registration number meant nothing to her. She could never remember her own.

Parking, opening the boot and wondering whether to lift the luggage out now or leave it for a factotum, if any, Esme felt her spirit divide. Reproduce by binary fission. There were two of her now, singing a duet in clashing keys. Warring intents and impulses making a painful discord. She had to be here and couldn't leave. It wasn't him, in any case. How could it be? Clive would never allow a thing like this to happen to him. This was a duty not a voluntary house party . . . Would he be pleased to see her? How embarrassing would it be? Silly questions. Wasted speculations. It wasn't him.

Clive, attired in the palest khaki service dress, so pale it was all but cream, lounged indolently on a brown leather sofa in the great hall, drinking a cup of tea. Upon him was concentrated the appreciative attention of two senior chaplains, who stood with their backs to the massive, mock Tudor fireplace, rocking avuncularly from heel to toe.

"Ah," said one, breaking off whatever it was he'd been saying to Clive, "It's Miss Hansard, isn't it? Our only lady. Come and have some tea. You must be needing it. How was your journey? Tea's over there. Help yourself."

Numbly, Esme walked away to the side table. She mechanically poured herself a cup, keeping her knees stiff against their tendency to melt. Thick, ugly pottery, the chaplains had. Like their monstrous house, an overblown hunting lodge of the Victorian era, encrusted with roguish pseudo-medieval detail. Everything from Early English to late Perpendicular. Incongruities of pitch pine, wrought-iron and plaster.

A nasty, modern Axminster carpet with a sickly, swirling pattern covered the floor. The clumps of brown chairs, she noticed for the first time, were dotted with other people. Dim, colourless people, hunched up tensely, talking in near whispers on the fringes of the gallery-encircled hall. Officers in uniform and plain clothes, fanatic-eyed Scripture Union types, dying, by the look of them, to get down to business. Their faces swam in and out of focus nightmarishly. She knew none of them.

Esme walked back to the fireside group. Again there was an interruption to the conversation there.

"Now, let me introduce you," the senior chaplain smiled urbanely, "I don't know if . . ."

"Hi, Esme," Clive patted the seat beside him. "Sorry, can't get up." He indicated a stick, hooked over the sofa's arm. "Back's gone again."

"Oh," the senior chaplain looked rather put out. "Do you two know each other?"

"Old friends," said Clive. "Nice surprise." He managed one of those Clivish gestures of dismissal. A twitch of a shoulder muscle as emphatic as it was imperceptible. It conveyed that Clive was through with chaplains' chatter.

"I'll leave you to catch up, then," the uniformed cleric huffed, herding his colleague away to mingle with an influx of arrivals.

"That's better," Clive approved. "You'll be able to feel the fire now," he added.

Sitting down beside him, Esme smiled, instantly engulfed by his radiant charism.

"You were pretty rude to them," she reproached. "It's not done with vicars."

"Oh, I don't know," he said, "They were getting bored with me, I think. Keeping them from their duties. They've got to rot these other people up." He looked over his shoulder, grimacing with pain.

"But why are you here?"

That story was soon told. Clive's spinal trouble was genuine all right. A recurrent problem for several months now. He had been due to ride a horse for his regiment in a race at Sandown Park when he doubled up again a week ago. Scratched from the race and fit for little else, he'd been volunteered by the Silvershods for the Bagshot duty. The

184

chaplains had insisted on having a victim from the Household Division and would accept no substitute.

Clive was a rotten correspondent, Esme thought. But she should not have doubted his word as she had. Was he in pain?

"Not much. Just stiff. What are you doing here? Not your style, is it? Christian Leadership . . . What is it, anyway?"

"God knows. Well, I suppose if he doesn't we're in for a fascinating time. I'm a pressed man too. My lot scurried off to Warcop and left me to face the music."

"God," Clive invoked piously, "I wonder when they'll let us have a drink round here. This lot of creeps look to me as if they volunteered themselves. We'd better stick very close together. The whole thing makes me nervous. I wish we had Tigs to keep us company."

Esme, warm in her agreement, found she longed for Tiggy. Between her and Clive he was the missing link. The one whose Delphic speeches came close to precipitating explanations. He might have told, as Clive would not, what had transpired in all these silent months.

And yet Clive accomplished it all so easily. Made the present moment scintillate, bulldozing the past's rubble into a land fill pit.

"Well," he said. "Celebration time tonight. We could go up to London."

"Not till after nine o'clock, we couldn't. Look at this," Esme seized a piece of paper lying on a coffee table. "Evening prayers in the chapel," she read, "At nine o'clock."

"Hush, hush, who dares . . . This Christopher Robin isn't going straight to bed after saying his prayers." Clive took the paper from her. "We'll have till dawn for making merry . . . Dinner, seven till eight . . . Oh, God. Then we have a lecture on 'War and Christian Doctrine'. They can wash me in the blood of the lamb as thoroughly as they like. I'm going to dry myself off on the town . . . with Alice."

Clive and Esme, practised at the business, made themselves fantastic. Obedient to the letter of the course curriculum but rebellious against its spirit.

The mornings were devoted to lectures and excruciating discussion groups. The Soldier's Emotional and Spiritual Needs . . . The Role of Prayer in a Soldier's Life. For their syndicate, Clive presided over thumb-twiddling, sporadic comment and stared in cool amazement when one specky enthusiast attempted to develop a theme.

"Can't have this," he hissed at Esme. "Man's beginning to speak in tongues. Create a diversion, can't you?"

"What do you suggest . . . hand-springs? Haven't you got a thunder flash?"

Clive, who was never without these aids to sociability, finessed one from his trouser pocket and discreetly detonated it. A loud report, a sheet of light and clouds of smoke filled the library. Mess servants came running in followed by dog-collared Directing Staff. The confusion put them on till nearly lunchtime, when Clive, fearing an inconvenient general evacuation, owned up.

"Awfully sorry, sir. I didn't know I had one. It must have just rolled out of my pocket accidentally. May I buy you a gin and tonic?"

The clergyman, who wore a Brigadier's rank badges in black, regarded the young cavalryman with sorrow. He looked then at the beautiful Miss Hansard who stood wide-eyed and innocent beside him. A pair of saboteurs, of course. With stonily uncontrite hearts. What a pity. Hardest of all to reach, they were the sort the Church really needed. Where people like them led, others would follow if only out of curiosity.

They felt trapped, of course, the clergyman correctly and charitably concluded. He drank three gins, one above his allowance, and inwardly turned the other cheek. He'd had quite a morning.

The afternoons were free, either for walking in the extensive wooded grounds, reading, sleeping or something the course programme hopefully described as 'quiet contemplation'. Clive saw these hours as being ideal for love-making. Esme thwarted him.

"But why not? You always did before."

"Yes, but not now. I don't feel like it. Are you coming for a walk or not? We can go slowly if you want."

He walked with her every afternoon but one, when he went with Esme to her room, lay down on the bed with her and slept whilst she read. When he woke, he stroked her face and kissed her.

"Why won't you, honey?" He looked sad and bewildered.

"I just won't, that's all." Esme stuck to her resolve. "Anyway, your back. Wouldn't look too good if they had to call an ambulance in here, would it?"

Clive's infirmity apart, denying him wasn't difficult. She loved him but there could be no kind of joy in being used by him.

At dinner each evening, alone among the men, Clive placed an order with the steward for some wine for himself and Esme. It caused a degree of consternation. There was wine, a little, in the cellar. But none was held in readiness for everyday consumption. Dinner was conducted in an atmosphere of hurry and austerity at Bagshot. Wine drinking, let alone the committed way Clive and Esme went about it, was not anticipated on Christian Leadership courses. The senior chaplain gave up saying grace because of the wilful couple who were never ready.

On the last night they attended chapel demurely, both in a form of casual evening dress. Esme rustled deliciously in taffeta and Clive sang 'Onward Christian Soldiers' in a decidedly superior tenor. They were, mused the officiating chaplain as he gave the blessing, completely incorrigible. Pagan as Jupiter and Aphrodite. A couple who reserved their worship for each other.

Clive was sick of the old places and wanted to go somewhere different. Quaglino's was Esme's suggestion.

"How do you know about this place?" Clive looked round the old-fashioned night-club. There was no one here he knew. The place, popular with his parents' generation, had only a faded cachet nowadays. Very camp.

"Two ways." Esme told him about Muriel Sparks's book and about Ivor's hospitality.

"Is he still around?" Clive eased himself behind the reserved table he'd liberated with a substantial bank note.

"No. I haven't seen him for a long time. He was only ever a friend, you know."

"Hungry? Or just champagne? I could shuffle round a bit if you wanted to dance."

"How do you do it?" Esme asked him.

"Er . . . Two forward and one to the side, I think . . . And then two back and one to the other side. The usual."

"Quite," said Esme. "Ivor can't understand how we make any progress like that."

"*Come Dancing* fan, is he? I don't suppose anybody much comes here these days, do they?" he said, perusing the wine list.

"I come here," Esme countered firmly. "And I am someone."

Clive glanced up at her. She was, he thought, astonishingly like himself. No one, male or female, more so. He was very glad he'd seen her.

As the course broke up the following day, just when Esme was about to get into her car and drive away, he said, "I suppose if I had a thousand pounds you'd like a ring."

"I would, yes." Esme's words were hoarse, barely audible. Why now, when they had no more time left . . .?

"Just be a brave girl, a little longer." Clive kissed her and told her to drive with care.

Too stunned to analyse his words, Esme drove rather weavingly down the drive. In the rear-view mirror she could see him watching her, standing by the Aston. It was the worst and most wonderful of all their partings. What had he meant? Why hadn't she asked him? She couldn't think.

Twenty miles or so on her road, Esme realised she was

187

hallucinating. Black culverts of fatigue drained a flash flood of adrenalin.

In the darkness of tunnels underneath the railways, she saw fast-moving trucks looming towards her. She swerved to avoid them before understanding there had been nothing there. Several times her eyelids fell. Brief moments of glorious sleep. She wondered if it would be safe to drive along these straight parts of the road with her eyes closed . . . Nothing seemed to happen. She could calculate the frequency of the bends. The sun was low, flashing between the branches and few remaining leaves . . . She felt so very tired. Another towering lorry . . .

Eventually she pulled into a lay-by and went to sleep for an hour and forty minutes. When she woke, a policeman was rapping on the window. His patrol car, doors open, was drawn up beside hers, slewed halfway across the road. Dusk was falling and his blue light revolved against the sunset's gold-fringed pink and mauve.

"Are you all right, Miss? Someone reported you being here . . . Thought you might have collapsed. Where're you going, Miss?"

*   *   *

Suggest interview this officer halfway through tour of duty, Daphne Deveril read Philippa's marginal note with appetite: . . . *Seems happy at Depot Sigs but duties not commensurate with abilities. Post as Staff Captain 'A' if willing? Experienced subaltern now. Should do well overseas. Potential vacancy to fill in Dekheila. Present incumbent engaged to be married. Col AG16 in broad agreement.*

So much for Philippa Mayhew and her machinations. Let her be content with advising the King of Jordan on his women's army project. Philippa was in Ammam and she, Daphne, was in Stanmore. That being the case, Daphne had lost no time in making an alternative suggestion to Colonel AG16 regarding Hansard's future.

The Sappers in Goole had put a stay of execution on the disestablishment of the WRAC Staff Captain 'A' post at the School of Combat Engineering. For the Corps, it was make or break time there. And Esme Hansard, with all this much-vaunted ability and experience of hers, could surely do her bit and help retain the post.

Madam, Daphne privately thought, had been a deal too happy lately. They'd made a fuss of her at WRAC1 . . . A ridiculous indulgence . . . And now she was getting a grossly inflated sense of her own importance up in Catterick. There was a glowing confidential report on file. Hansard might be able to pull the wool over the eyes of men, but not over Daphne Deveril's. Time to put a stop to it.

"I'm not sure," Colonel AG16 responded to her new aide's suggestion. "We quite liked the idea of Cyprus for Esme . . . She'll find Goole very isolated, won't she? She has a rather gregarious temperament . . . But if she wants a challenge and the situation's explained to her . . . On a 'need to know' basis, naturally.

"Philippa thought Caroline Clough might handle the Sapper situation . . . But put it to Esme, if you like. She can always stay at Catterick if she finds the Goole prospect too daunting. Or the Cyprus post . . . Of course, she does have a way with her . . . It might carry more weight with the Sappers than anything else. Men can be so stupid."

It was all Daphne Deveril needed. Never mind Miss Esme bloody Hansard's preferences. No need to tell her she had a choice. Just tell her what was expected of her. A taste of reality would do her good. Easily arranged with that prig Mayhew out of the way.

Esme was warned for an interview at Stanmore on a day Colonel AG16 would be away. There was never any risk she would learn more than Major Deveril chose to tell her.

"So you see," Daphne leaned forward across the desk, smiling wolfishly, "You're being offered an exceptional challenge. We're counting on you. Major Mayhew has confidence in you, and so does the Colonel. You'll need to keep your wits about you. But then, you're very good at that, aren't you, Esme? So this time we'll really see what you're made of, won't we? If the Corps retains this post it'll be to your credit. If we lose it . . . Well, you'll make sure that doesn't happen, won't you?"

Daphne Deveril took three solid hours to say it. She said it over and over again in slightly different words, taking off her sparkly upswept glasses and putting them on again. She thumped her fist on the desk several times. Neither tea nor coffee was served.

Sitting opposite her in an armless chair, Esme swayed with a combination of confusion, boredom and exhaustion. It was a long rail journey back to Darlington station where she'd left her car. Thanks to this harangue of Daphne's Esme had already missed several trains. And there'd be half an hour or more on the tube first, before she could start back north. How much longer?

She didn't want to leave Catterick but it meant promotion. Acting Captain's rank with pay. If you ever refused a posting, she'd been told they got their revenge by doing something awful to you. Hadn't Ivor said something of the kind? A vision of Mill Hill dissuaded Esme from any show of hesitation. The WRAC depot . . . Anything was better than that.

189

"Will they have accommodation for my horse?" Esme asked, as much to vary the noise as anything. Daphne simply never, never stopped talking.

"Your affair," Daphne glowered, annoyed at the interruption. It was typical of Hansard to show off about her possessions. "You'll have to write to the Brigade Major. You'll find it's the least of your problems . . ."

And off she went again. By the time Esme reeled out of Major Deveril's presence, she no longer cared anything about the Sapper dissatisfaction with WRAC officers. For the first time she knew what it was like to be tired to the point of tears. Ready to lie down in the Chief Clerk's office and scream and scream and scream.

Goole, she decided, haring up the platform at King's Cross, would be all right. Why should it be any different, basically, from Catterick? Men who build bridges under fire would be fundamentally alike to those who laid telephone wires under similar conditions. No harder to get along with. As for her new job, it must be more interesting than the Orderly Officer roster. So it was a headquarters and not a regiment. So what?

Daphne's windstorm of words whirled on in her brain, falling leaves in an autumn gale. There was, however, one crumb of solid comfort to be caught at. Philippa had recommended this move. Daphne had definitely implied that. Several times.

News of Esme's imminent departure from Catterick impacted on Depot Sigs like a corporate experience of *coitus interruptus*. Saddened by the sadness, she hardily pointed out that no one was irreplaceable in the army.

"No," grumped the Colonel, "But they may be inimitable. You'll be a hard act to follow, dear. Gloria'll miss you."

Even the RSM expressed regrets. "Just when I've got you trained in guard room management, ma'am."

Esme's last days at Catterick were marked by an immensity of kindness. Goole augured less invitingly.

The Brigade Major, name of Glossop, sent a curt line or two in reply to Esme's query regarding Habibi's reception. Coldfleet Barracks afforded no stable accommodation, he said. He had no personal knowledge of any private livery stables. The country, in any case, was intensively farmed and unsuitable for equestrian activities.

Not a word about looking forward to meeting Esme, never mind Habibi.

"I'll have her at home," Aunt Alice came, as ever, to the rescue. "Let's see if we can get her put in foal. Goole won't last for ever and you might end up with a nice youngster to bring on."

"Well, you've been a toff, ma'am," commented the sergeant of the Royal Veterinary Corps who managed the Garrison Saddle Club stables, when Habibi, making as much patrician fuss as possible was led up the ramp of the box which was to carry her to Lowlough.

It was a heart-warming, humbling tribute. Dogs and NCOs always know the score with people. To be dubbed an officer and a gentleman was precious stuff to Esme. Anyone could be a lady.

At Esme's dining out, the usual lavish combination of formality and rumbustiousness, the Colonel said much the same thing, proposing a toast to 'our brother officer'.

"Doesn't he mean 'sister officer'?" a civilian guest of someone's muttered in his neighbour's ear.

"No," the officer replied. "He means exactly what he says." Civilians never quite got the nuances.

The band played 'The Lass of Richmond Hill', and Esme had to stand up while everyone else banged the table. Tradition.

Less traditional was Esme's gown. She didn't wear her mess dress, having had something made in oyster-coloured satin. Quite simple, with a neatly fitted, round-necked, three-quarter-sleeved bodice, a gold buckle belt and long A-line skirt descending to her instep.

"Why are you wearing that tonight?" the PMC nosed. "Major Mulliner wouldn't like it."

"You'll see," Esme smiled broadly. "And Major Mulliner isn't here to be my duenna, is she?"

It turned out that the skirt of Esme's dress was removable, beneath it was a matching one, divided this time. Liberated by this garment, Esme was able to accept the Adjutant's invitation to ride on his shoulders and swing an ante-room cushion at the head of any challenger. It made racing water-filled contraceptives down the staircase easier too.

"I wish Gloria could see this," the Colonel said, highly satisfied. "Careful, now," he shouted. "The trick is not to burst it on the home run . . . Gently does it, Esme!"

Esme went home on leave to Lowlough, where Aunt Alice had assembled a stack of stud prospectuses to look at. Finding a husband for Habibi was an absorbing occupation. Would she make a good mother?

"Not she," Alice snorted. "I can see myself bottle feeding any foal we're lucky enough to get. Flighty piece, your Habibi."

A day or two before Esme was detailed to report to Goole, a postcard came from Cyprus. Clive and Tiggy were there, keeping the peace, allegedly, in pale-blue UN berets. You had to watch out for land mines,

191

said Clive. And some very peculiar people. The picture was of Kyrenia Harbour with the Dome Hotel in the background. It was where the British army showed off their stiff upper lips to each other and the locals. Killing.

Be a brave girl a little longer . . . Esme deduced she would be in a position to announce her engagement to Clive when he returned from Cyprus. That, clearly, was what he had meant. A worm of mistrust, however, prevented her saying anything to Aunt Alice. Stealth and patience.

Esme had wanted Clive so long, it scarcely occurred to her that she wanted him any less now than she had always done. It had been up and down, but it was going to come right. She would have enjoyed it more, of course, if it had come right earlier. The shine of newness couldn't last for ever. But it was necessary, to Alice Winstanley's niece and Veronica Winstanley's daughter, to complete the exercise.

13

"If you don't let me go by Wednesday lunchtime," announced Esme's predecessor in the Goole job, "I shan't tell you any more. So make the best of me."

"But Sophie, that's blackmail," Esme was shocked. A week's handover of the duties in any post was customary. Particularly in a staff appointment. Something the incoming officer had a right to expect in all but situations of emergency.

"Call it what you like," Captain Sophie Brafferton replied, unsticking a poster from the wall of her sitting-room and tightly rolling it. "Either I get out of this place on Wednesday or you put up with sharing the YOs' loos for another three days for nothing. I shan't say another word. It's up to you. Take your pick. Pass me that pile of books, will you?"

Sophie was packing her possessions into cardboard MFO boxes with frenzied speed. Hurling in clothing, photograph albums, records and record player, patchwork cushions and a typewriter with scant regard for order. Denuding the apartment in the mess, which would be Esme's when she'd gone, of any trace of her occupation.

Except, of course, her revolting colour scheme. Sophie had chosen a shade of pea-green for the large, high ceilinged sitting-room, Parma violet in the equally large adjoining bedroom and mustard for the bathroom. The carpet was brown, as were the curtains. Done when redecoration fell due three months ago, Esme would be stuck with the results for the whole of her stay in Goole.

There was one comfort. The huge, tall windows gave a view of the eerie landscape outside. Discarding her previous, approximate notions of flatness had been the first minor trauma of Esme's arrival here.

Nothing could ever be as flat as these gigantic, hedgeless fields. A carpet of cabbages spread its limitless, level span until it met the sky beyond the invisible river. There was nothing to show where the Humber flowed through its deep, mud-banked channel until a ship's superstructure came gliding wraith-like through the cabbages. A strange mirage in a dull, green desert.

Coldfleet Barracks stood a few miles down-river of the Port of Goole with its docks, derricks and great freight vessels plying the Scandinavian and Baltic trades. The Humber's tributary streams and wide drainage canals made it an ideal trial area for experimental pontoon bridges. And the soft black, silty earth challenged the ingenuity of military road builders as dryer, firmer land could never do.

All this Esme had learned from her new boss, Major Birtwhistle, that morning. It hadn't been part of her official briefing, but Esme was interested in these things. Believed it essential to understand her small cog's part in the overall working of Sapper machinery.

Birtwhistle had kept saying things like: "Yes, well, that's not important to you. So let's get on with talking about the Staff Captain 'A' 's chores, shall we?"

Those could be summed up in a word or two. Ceremonial and Discipline. In practice convening Courts Martial, assembling the paperwork and advising the staff on military law. Reasonably meaty and up Esme's street.

Under ceremonial came the management and deployment of the Royal Engineers' bewildering number of bands. There was a thick manual of regulations and its constant amendments to digest in connection with this. The concert orchestra, apparently, was especially sensitive. What on earth a military unit was doing with violins, cellos, oboes and so forth, Esme could not think.

"More civilised for dinner nights," Birtwhistle clarified. "Don't want trombones oompah, oompahing down our ears. All right for drowning out what passes for conversation in infantry messes, but it wouldn't do here."

The bands were accommodated in specially built modern premises a few miles away. Esme was to visit them when rehearsals made it convenient.

"And then, of course," remarked Birtwhistle, clicking the top of his biro, a thing he did constantly, "there's the social side of life. We have members of the General Staff and important civilian engineers coming here for conferences from all over the world. You'll be responsible for issuing invitations, transport and accommodation. Making things go smoothly and all that kind of thing. There's no nine to fivery here, I'm afraid. Absolute hive of activity."

194

And yet the place seemed cocooned in quietude. As if the busyness was working against the grain of time. Human voices rang louder to overcome a clamour of ghosts. An impression, merely.

The barracks themselves, contemporaneous with the battle of Waterloo, had been built originally to house Marines in case the French navy had ever attacked the Yorkshire coast. Once that defensive strategy had been abandoned, the Royal Engineers took Coldfleet over.

The buildings, handsome in their well-kept military plainness, made a continuous terrace, boxing in the parade ground's square. The permitted circuitous walkway was marked off with pairs of small bronze cannon. Neat pyramids of round shot stood beside them. A plaque set in the paving stones commemorated the hanging of a soldier on the square in 1887. After bending to read it, Esme could feel all the horror of that occasion . . . The roll of the drums . . . A regiment drawn up in ranks to witness the ritual extinction of their fellow. Discipline.

To the north lay the headquarters building, rather cramped for modern use . . . To the west, NCOs' tenements and the old quartermaster's store. To the east, the old armoury, soldiers' accommodation and cookhouse; and to the south, the officers' mess with various senior officers' residences behind porticoed doorways.

Here and there statues of Sapper heroes gazed out from their plinths, contemplating their superseded achievements. General Gordon, on the highest plinth of all, was riding his camel just below the level of Esme's office window. There was bird dirt on his tarboosh.

Coldfleet had been considered a model barracks in its day. Inward-looking, self-sufficient, an imposing fortress beside the muddy little hamlet from which the establishment took its name. Interested in its antiquity, Esme found the place vaguely oppressive and was glad of these great outward-facing windows pierced at the time of the Boer War.

"It's the only thing I'll miss," Sophie straightened for a moment to clip back a wisp of hair. "These rooms. At least they look a bit more cheerful now. You've got me to thank for that. Barracks would have painted the place magnolia again if I'd left it to them."

"I don't have a choice, then, do I? About the handover, I mean." Esme found herself quite unable to utter the expected compliments on Sophie's taste.

More important now, in any case, was the effectiveness of her handover. She could report Sophie's strong-arm tactics to the Anglia ADWRAC, of course. But it would be a bad beginning. It would make her look whingeing and weak.

And it would be a great relief too, to have a bathroom to herself.

The facilities nearest her bedroom were unusable. A row of urinals, three school-type cubicles and two baths, casually screened with tongue and groove boarding to waist level with bubble glass rising to eyebrow height.

Not particularly modest, Esme had felt unable to share these communal ablutions with a crowd of young men she didn't know. It left the female lavatories in the headquarters building and a basement powder-room in the mess intended for use on ladies' guest nights. Rare occasions at Coldfleet, if the smell of damp down there was anything to go by.

"Sorry," the mess secretary, a white-mustachioed, retired officer had said testily in response to Esme's quiet request that she be moved. "That's the best we can do. Accommodating a conference of senior officers at the moment, you know. Been pushed to fit you in as it is."

After this, the Brigadier's indifferently expressed hope that she was comfortable, when Esme had her arrival interview with him, sounded hollow. How could she be comfortable if, when going to bed, she had reason to fear any call of nature? The fear itself had been enough to stimulate a nervous irritation of the bladder occasioning Esme two sleepless nights without relief.

"Sophie, what's wrong with this place?" Esme asked suddenly, wanting very much to change the adversarial tone of their present conversation. "You seem so desperate to get away . . ."

"Nothing's wrong with it . . ." Sophie stopped at the sound of scratching on the door. "That's Lotus. Can you let her in?"

Opening the door which led on to the landing, Esme admitted Sophie's limping Burmese cat.

"Poor, darling, beautiful little Lotus," Esme crooned. Any creature with four legs and fur was sure of an outpouring of sentiment from her. "Why *is* she so shy of me?" The cat squirmed away from Esme's outstretched, caressing hand.

"You'd be shy," Sophie scooped the cat up, "If you had a YO's size ten brogue printed on your thigh bone. She was kicked," she elaborated, seeing the look of total incomprehension on Esme's face. "The vet said she was lucky to keep her leg. Smashed to a powder. We had a splint on it for months."

Esme rose slowly from a stoop. "But it was an accident, surely. He couldn't have meant to . . ."

"Accident, my foot," Sophie cradled the cat close to her cheek. "I saw him do it."

Esme asked more. The wheres and whys of the incident. All right, so this was a mess where officers' animals were not permitted in the ante-room. But everyone must make allowances for feline vagaries.

196

Nobody could go around hurting other people's pets and get away with it . . . Presumably Sophie had informed Major Glossop. The Brigade Major was responsible for the YOs' discipline . . . He must have taken the culprit apart . . .

Sophie laughed harshly. "I'll tell you what Glossop said, if you like."

"Well? What did he say?"

"He said 'Boys will be boys', for one thing. And then he said I couldn't expect to keep a moggie in a masculine environment. Anyway, the bastard who did it's gone now, thank God."

Speechless, Esme could think of nothing more to say except, "Can I use your loo?"

"Yes, go on."

Washing herself all over at the basin in her own room shortly afterwards, prior to changing for dinner, Esme's teeth chattered. Whether from cold or some other cause she didn't know. The radiator was hot when she felt it. There was no fire of any kind in here although there was a wall-mounted electric one in Sophie's sitting-room. That would be something once the other girl had gone. And as for keeping her at Coldfleet a second longer than was necessary, from very compassion, Esme had no wish to do so.

No wonder she looked so worn and bitter. Was she only a year older than Esme was herself? Whip-thin with dark circles round her eyes, she looked a whole decade wearier. Who wouldn't be short-tempered and surly after an episode like that? But Sophie couldn't have explained properly to Major Glossop what had really happened.

Mad, married and Methodist . . . That was the army description of Sappers, Aunt Alice said. They could be as mad and married as anyone else, Esme thought. But since when was cruelty to animals and unchivalry to women any part of Methodism's doctrine?

It was in this state of confused indignation that Esme ate her dinner beside Sophie in the mess's large, vaulted dining-room. A headquarters mess, like Larkhill's the public rooms were impressive rather than comfortable. Gordon's portrait in many guises – he seemed to have been addicted to dressing up – adorned the walls along with those of other Sapper worthies and pictures of their bridges by Terence Cuneo. High activity scenes with explosions. The usual assortment of royal icons too. Was it matt varnish on the modern paintings or none?

Sophie didn't seem inclined to discuss the pictures and the YOs weren't inclined to discuss anything at all with two girls. At the common table they adjusted their bodies in such a way to exclude them. Theirs was not a conversation, anyway, to which Esme could contribute. All about something called hard core. Shop, anyway. Not done at the best of times. Before strangers who couldn't understand the talk, offensive.

"Don't they ever talk to you?" Esme enquired covertly of Sophie.

"Who wants to talk to them?" was Sophie's waspish answer.

Understandable, Esme realised, considering what she'd been through with her cat. But still, there would have to be some improvements to domestic manners here. A fresh start made.

After dinner, which had not been good, disgraceful really, for so large a mess, Esme sat with Sophie in an alcove of the ante-room drinking coffee. There were two fireplaces in the room but only one of these were lit. The YOs were hogging it and made no welcoming gesture when the girls walked in. Had she been alone, Esme thought, she would have simply moved into their midst and shamed them into bringing a chair for her. But until Sophie went, she was to be deferred to in matters of social behaviour as with office procedures. She was owed that fundamental politeness.

So Esme sat, irritated by the loud-mouthed, actually rather self-conscious sounds of male hilarity. This was what came of the Brigade Major being married and living out. Ivor would have had these boys' guts for garters. And where were all these senior officers of whom the mess secretary had spoken so emphatically? Invited out to dinner, she supposed, by other married officers of their rank living in quarters.

Sophie did confirm this. Dinner was notorious here. All the money was spent at lunchtime when senior people were around to congratulate the mess secretary on the splendour of his catering arrangements. The resident members received small consideration. Too junior to count.

"I see," said Esme, thinking that here was another defect which stood in need of remedy. "When are they dining you out, by the way? They've really only got tomorrow . . . Or did they do it last week?"

"Dining me out?" Sophie regarded her companion with a mixture of sour amusement and pity. "You must be joking."

Esme was chilled to the marrow. She became conscious of a large presence casting a shadow over the low sofa where she and Sophie sat.

"Yes?" Sophie rapped. "What do you want?"

Esme smiled up at the young man, not wishing him to think that their own relationship need be shaped by past events. What was done was done. A line should be drawn across the page. His eyes slid sheepishly away from hers.

A hulking youth of twenty or so, he wore blue patrols, Esme noticed. Therefore, he was Officer of the Day. Deputed by his friends, no doubt, to carry some conciliatory message . . . Suggest a friendlier way of spending the evening than this unmannerly segregation.

He was indeed the elected spokesman of his group. His message, however, was so hostile, that Esme could not at first take meaning from his words.

"'Evening, Sophie," he began. "We just thought we ought to let your friend know that we don't want to mix."

Struck dumb by this appalling speech, Esme paled.

Sophie, on the other hand, was up and at him like a terrier.

"*Mix?*" She spat at him. "What makes you think Captain Hansard is interested in a lot of wet behind the ears Second Lieutenants? You're pathetic. Get lost, Williamson. And stay lost. Don't come near us again. How *dare* you?"

"What did he mean?" Esme said faintly. "I don't understand . . ."

"Never mind. Just ignore them. They're not worth worrying about."

"But how can I not worry about them?" Esme sagged back against the sofa. She felt as if she'd been struck. "I've got to live with them . . ."

"No you haven't," Sophie said, "Apart from eating. You've got your own sitting-room or will have. Get yourself a television. There's a hire company in Goole. I'll give you the number . . ."

"Look, Sophie, I've tried to ask you . . . What *is* wrong here . . . What's behind all this?"

"I told you. Nothing. Just mind your back and be self-reliant. You need hobbies here. Take up patchwork or something."

Esme went to bed early after visiting the basement powder-room. She wished to be rid of Sophie not only for her own sake and that of her Burmese cat, but in order to cleanse the legacy of dislike she was leaving behind her.

In her room, among the packing cases, Sophie Brafferton watched television and drank brandy from a private supply. For two pins she'd have told Esme Hansard what lay in store for her here. But Daphne Deveril had hinted that any sign of alarm from Miss Hansard . . . and Sophie would not go to Cyprus. Esme, Major Deveril had said, was to be allowed to make her own mind up. Not to be encouraged to prejudge the issue.

"You must bear in mind," Daphne had said, "The fact of your own very poor confidential report is bound to warp your outlook somewhat. Not that we blame you entirely but . . . The way I propose to put it to Colonel AG16 is that Cyprus will cheer you up." Daphne, grotesquely intimate, had winked here. "I think I can swing it. Whatever it takes to put you back on your feet. So when it comes to your replacement at Coldfleet . . . Least said, soonest mended, eh?"

Sophie wasn't going to risk Cyprus. She deserved it. Esme must take care of herself.

* * *

"There is no mail for you this morning, madam," boomed Pertwee, the civilian major-domo the Sappers employed for the mess. His resonant voice, produced from the depths of his barrel chest, made the hall chandelier tinkle faintly.

Esme turned away from her pigeon-hole sharply. She felt rather than saw the glimmer of triumph on Pertwee's spade-shaped face. She hated him. Loathed his dyed-red beard, his soft white, shovel hands. Detested the short white jacket he wore in the daytime, which caught up on his buttocks . . . disliked the pompous tail coat and wasp-striped vest he strutted in after six.

Most of all she had learned to fear the spiteful pleasure he took in humiliating her. Letters were the only thing that kept her going here. On the days none came, Pertwee took it upon himself to draw the attention of the resident mess members to her disappointment. Nor did he lose any opportunity of ignoring Esme's requests or comments when there were those of a YO to attend to first. He was not a soldier, unfortunately, and could not be called peremptorily to account. He came under the mess secretary, who always defended him.

"Oh, Pertwee's allowed some latitude, y'know," that retired officer proclaimed, stroking his white mustachios with synthetic joviality. "Good old Pertwee's an institution. Thirty years' service and never a day's work missed. That's loyalty. Got to wink at his funny little ways, haven't we?"

For months this had been the story of Esme's life. She asked for nothing over and above the minimum that was due to her sex and rank. Common humanity would have been enough. Perhaps that was the more ambitious aspiration of the two.

Sometimes Esme wondered if it was her specifically that Pertwee disliked or if it was women in general . . . or women officers as a class. She would never find out. There was no other WRAC officer for many miles around. Esme hardly saw women at all apart from her civilian batwoman. A decent, hard-working docker's wife, Mrs Dodds took Esme's clothes to and from the dry cleaners' in Goole on the bus. A treasure.

Unable, despite repeated efforts, to establish genuine empathy either with her mess-mates or the officers with whom she worked, Esme was isolated. It was the violent loneliness of exposure she experienced. Not the ennui of solitude.

Work, of which there was less than had first appeared, was little compensation. Those elements of it which were intrinsically interesting or made a break from routine were taken away. Like the time when the question of an officer's dress arose. The man in question was due to ride in an equestrian event, with a member of the royal family as a fellow-contestant. Belonging to a detached, independent unit of the brigade, he'd applied to the headquarters for guidance on uniform . . . or been directed to do so.

Esme, keen to solve a personal problem of protocol for variety's sake, had been ready to look up the precedents and make a satisfactory decision in keeping with modern conditions.

"No," said Major Birtwhistle, "I think this is outside your remit, Esme. It's one of the problems of having a WRAC Staff Captain 'A' in this job. They're not in a position to have an opinion on this kind of thing."

"But it's my job to have an opinion," urged Esme, referring to the empowering legislative instrument. "And I'm interested in clothes and I'm interested in riding . . . I *want* to have an opinion."

"Sorry," Birtwhistle smiled one of those resigned smiles of his, with which he so cleverly passed the blame for Esme's discontents up the chain of command, "Brigadier's orders. The 'G' Staff are to deal with this. Sappers, you see."

They turned to her quickly enough when taken by surprise.

The arrival of a distinguished-looking Dublin journalist at the barracks caused a mild sensation. He was a deserter, he said, surrendering formally to the guard commander. He'd skipped off a troopship a dozen years back rather than fight in Korea. In the intervening years he'd made a respectable career for himself as a newspaper man. To go any further he must work now in London where he would live in constant fear of arrest. Rather than that, he was giving himself up, expected trial by Court Martial and to serve his time in Colchester military prison. Then he could get on with his life. So the day's duty staff officer summarised.

"He's there in a cell, cool as a cucumber."

"What's he doing?" Esme probed.

"Drinking a mug of tea and fiddling with his typewriter. Likes to keep busy, he says."

Major Birtwhistle bustled officiously out of the office to inform the Brigadier before anyone else could.

In the meantime Esme consulted the Army Act regarding deserters and also the Queen's Regulations. Fiddling with his typewriter? Of course he was. He'd have all the time in the world to compose some copy which would make the army look both silly and vindictive. Korea was all so long ago. A journalist was probably looking forward to gaol with relish. Detain him there, and what a revenge he would wreak. Half of Esme envied him.

She found a paragraph that would let the army off the hook. She didn't expect to find anything of the sort but she did. A complete 'get out' clause designed for just such a situation as this.

A clerk came in and told her the Brigadier wanted to see her. The absence of compliments was, by now, familiar rather than striking. Perhaps it was just the Sapper way.

"Ah, yes. Come in, Esme. You're our legal expert, aren't you? What view do you take of all this? Jolly perplexing isn't it? It'll be good experience for you to look up the law for us on this."

The Brigadier's reedy, rustling voice went on, telling Esme what volumes to consult. Clearly disturbed, he walked up and down the room with his majors and full colonels ranged in a semi-circle around his desk. Looking at them, Esme guessed that nobody knew what to do. It was amusing to think that she, the person who couldn't even decide on an officer's riding dress, was their last resort.

"You do see, Esme, don't you, that this person is in a position to do us serious harm? We'd have Fleet Street down on us like a ton of bricks . . ."

He developed this point at length until Esme thought she was going to get varicose veins standing there, listening to him. Finally he dismissed her to go away and come up with the answer.

"With respect, Brigadier, I have it already," Esme said, delighted to be of substantial assistance at last. "Yes, there's a regulation which gives us *carte blanche* to let a man of this type in these exact circumstances go. A deserter surrendering himself after a passage of years during which he has become a prominent citizen or person of influence."

She quoted him the authority down to the very last sub-sub-sub-section.

A few faces brightened, others looked baffled. A jaw or two dropped. The Brigadier's reaction was delayed before he exploded. The career officers around him, chameleons by nature, took a prudent pace backward, composing their features to echo their chief's arm-flailing rage.

"It's a blatant miscarriage of justice!" he spluttered. "Criminal . . . Why should a mean little scribbler go free when better men are serving sentences for the same crime in Colchester?"

Around him, his staff with the exception of Esme murmured assent. Esme whitened with anger. Her own grandfather had been what this man called a 'mean little scribbler'. And as to whether there were better men in Colchester, no one, save God alone, knew.

"Well?" he screeched at her, his face contorted with unreasoning fury. "You don't say anything. Don't you think it's unjust? Unfair? How can you stand there . . . Just *stand* there . . ." He had become inarticulate. Apoplectic. The diatribe went on for minutes.

Feeling herself tremble, Esme controlled the spasm. She wasn't so much daunted by the capering Brigadier, but by the blast of freezing condemnation that came from the others in the room. She had no supporters here. Eventually the Brigadier's voice failed him. He coughed.

"Well?" he said again.

"Brigadier, again with respect, I am here to advise you on the law, not on justice. Justice is beyond my scope. I hope, gentlemen, that you will excuse me now."

"I don't suppose we can expect a woman to understand a soldier's feelings, sir."

The sneer came just as Esme's hand touched the door handle. She hesitated for a fraction of a second but withdrew. A fiery exposition of Aunt Alice's and her mother's sacrifices would achieve nothing worthwhile.

Esme's advice was taken two days later but its soundness was never acknowledged.

"We let that greasy little reporter friend of yours go, you know," Birtwhistle dug her in the ribs with his elbow at luncheon on the day of his release.

"It was the best thing," Esme responded warily. She had never even set eyes on the prisoner, let alone befriended him.

"Best for who?"

"*Whom*," Esme snapped. Her policy of passive resistance was wearing thin.

Somehow, every success metamorphosed mysteriously into failure. She was blamed for damage to a priceless piece of table silver the Brigadier had wanted to borrow for a great annual gathering of NATO generals and their aides. The Royal Engineers' Museum at Chatham had refused the loan. Birtwhistle, whose idea the whole thing had been in the first place, asked Esme how he could wrest the piece out of the museum despite the refusal.

"Ask again," Esme said, bored. There was no shortage of Coldfleet silver to put on show. "Tell them what arrangements we'll make for its safety."

The museum relented and the complicated battle scene, cast in silver, adorned the table. When the port was passed round and the traditional ban on handling such ornaments beforehand was lifted, a guest touched an intricate piece of the cast which promptly detached.

"This is your fault," Birtwhistle accused her next day in the office they shared. "A direct result of your bad judgement. The Brigadier may order you to pay Garrard's repair bill."

"If he does," Esme observed grittily, "the order will probably be illegal."

The same week at dinner, a YO told Esme he liked it when she wore her hair down, which she only occasionally did.

"Yes," he said, "It covers up that lantern jaw of yours."

Deeply cut, Esme blinked back tears. Then she flashed out at him: "You're no bloody oil painting yourself!"

This was dreadful. Esme hated herself for descending to fishwifing. But now, it seemed, she didn't even look right.

There was the warrant officer who, passing Esme at a distance of no more than five yards on three separate occasions, failed to salute her. She could not ignore it for ever. It was a calculated insult, not a mistake. Regulations were quite clear too. She must reprove him or face reprimand herself. Esme had never once heard of so senior a man putting a young officer in such a position.

"Excuse me," Esme hoped against hope that her voice didn't sound as much of a squeak as she feared, "I'm afraid you cannot have seen me . . ."

The warrant officer, old enough to be her father, turned with leisurely insolence and put up a slack salute. No apology. This was worse. But how did one go about getting a warrant officer Class 1 arrested and marched to the guard room? It could only be done by his equals . . . This sort of thing didn't normally happen . . . She had to leave it.

A general in Germany who kept up a cordial telephone dialogue with Esme complained many times that Sapper units of his command had no band. Dinner nights for the officers were dreary without one . . . And parades were pathetic affairs lacking martial music. Esme heartily agreed with him. Absurd that operational units in front line positions should go without this basic commodity whilst she had bands and to spare, eating their heads off, earning large fees for private engagements. Sanctioned moonlighting, forbidden to every other category of soldier.

"General," she said, "They keep telling me here that the bands are my pigeon. Believe me, I'd post you a band, lock stock and barrel, this afternoon if it were really up to me. But at the end of the day I can only recommend and advise. I keeping sending the Brigadier memorandums explaining your needs, but I get no reply."

"He doesn't reply to my bloody letters either," snarled the General. "Well, keep the pressure up, Esme. We could do with more people like you in that sleepy hollow at Coldfleet."

The storm broke soon afterwards. The General wrote again to Esme's Brigadier in the strongest possible language. Every example of the Brigadier's intransigent neglect was laid out in detail. Copy to the Chiefs of the General Staff, copy to the Minister of Defence. How much further, stormed the General in writing, was he going to be forced to take this? Because, if necessary, he would go as far as Her Majesty.

"You stupid girl!" raved the Brigadier at Esme. "What the dickens do you think you've been up to? You haven't the remotest conception of the trouble this will cause me . . . no more than you have of your job. Your supposed to *advise* me!"

"I have done, Brigadier," Esme returned dully. "I told you the General was restive . . . Anxious to make progress on the matter . . ."

"Too late now. Don't let it happen again."

Fighting an instinctive wish to insulate herself from the indifference and aggression which surrounded her, Esme began to have daily struggles with herself of a quite physical nature.

In the evenings now, when she had changed, she would stand at her sitting-room door, willing herself to open it. She must, she told herself, eat in the dining-room. If she started buying snacky things in Goole to consume in her rooms, she would be beaten. A deep breath, turn the door handle, and put one foot in front of the other. It was easier said than done. She did it, however.

Crossing the parade ground in the mornings after breakfast became an advance through enemy territory. As she passed each cannon, Esme felt herself flinch. Her footsteps swerved, refusing to obey her command to keep straight ahead. She realised what it was one day. For some reason she kept thinking that those old, dead cannon were going to fire at her. Smash her to pieces. Utterly crazy. She must pull herself together. Think what she was doing and not daydream.

She would sit for ages on the loo, squeezing out urine, drop by reluctant drop. Cystitis, said the MO, although there was no burning sensation. In fact it was no such thing. It was acute retention of purely nervous origin. Esme bashed on with the bicarbonate of soda prescription, continuing to pass water with extreme difficulty. Most days and most nights she endured severe abdominal pressure. Women got these things, the MO said breezily. Esme should try to drink more water.

Letters, then, were a torch beam in a dark cellar of gathering depression.

Habibi, reported Aunt Alice with uncharacteristic exuberance, was at last in the club. To a good, strong, sensible stallion renowned for the equable temperament of his progeny. The stud fees had been reasonable and Esme wasn't to think of chipping in for half of them. Was Esme all right? Her letters had been rather few lately. Madly busy social life, Alice supposed. Maiden aunts must expect to take a back seat.

Esme knew she shouldn't deceive her aunt about what was happening at Coldfleet. No longer cared what sort of Cain she would raise when she heard. But her troubles now were too great to share. Just bearing them took all of her strength.

Philippa wrote. She was getting on well but slowly in Jordan. The King was a dear. Sandhurst trained, of course. The ladies who interested themselves in the future of the Jordanian women's force, however, were charming but dilatory. Where was Esme now? Quite likely in Cyprus. However, she was sending this letter to AG16 for onward transmission through the usual system. If, by any chance, Esme was still in the UK, perhaps they could meet for a mutual update when Philippa came on a flying visit to Loan Services at Lansdowne House in early December. She would be staying at the Melrose Club and would love to see Esme on any or all of the dates on the back of this sheet.

Nothing from Clive.

Astoundingly, none the less, Tiggy wrote, also through AG16. He was laid up with a badly sprained ankle and was bored out of his mind. He'd already written to everyone else he could think of and hoped Esme didn't mind him banging on at her like this. No need to reply. Buzzing around in armoured cars was quite fun. Faster than proper tanks. He'd got the ankle skiing in the Troodos mountains. Not enough snow. The UN was supposed to be impartial over this Enosis business in Cyprus but the Brits liked the Turks. The kind of guys Tiggy himself would emulate, should he ever feel the urge to grow up. Real men. Always had some spare hash too, if you knew how to handle them. There was a bit of a frost last month when Tiggy's sergeant got out of the AC for a slash and stepped on a stray mine. Tiggy was in such a panic, he leapt out of the vehicle to help the man, grabbed hold of him, ran down the track with him, thought he'd acquired the strength of ten men . . . until he realised he'd only got half of the guy. Gone from the waist down. Some mine. Filthy. Anyway, Tiggy was sorry this was such muddled trash. Nothing like the corking stuff Esme came up with. 'Seeya,' closed Tiggy.

As good, almost, as a letter from Clive. The Silvershods must be due for Germany again soon, she thought. What would it be like living in a married quarter in Hohne?

Esme had lost touch with Ivor.

The day Tiggy's letter arrived, things came to a head at Coldfleet.

At dinner that night there were, as usual, only the YOs and Esme dining in. They were waited on by a civilian mess steward who served them several times in the week. Dick, he was called. Dick was a rheumy-eyed old soldier, dirty, and invariably the worse for wear with drink. Disrespectful and inefficient, he was tolerated by the Sappers. Like Pertwee, he was looked on as a family pet. And he could be very funny. Esme bore him no great animosity despite his occasional befuddled familiarities.

"Hands up for soup." He shambled as always through the swinging baize door from the kitchen. 'Hands up for soup' was a new one. Priceless.

Tonight Dick looked more disreputable than ever. His dress was disordered and a trail of spittle leaked from the corner of his mouth. He'd forgotten to put his false teeth in. The other servant who was supposed to assist him was off sick.

The meal wore on, with Dick blundering, swearing, and sticking his grimy thumb in every dish he offered. Esme had never known his speech so slurred before. As the senior officer present she felt she really ought to order him out of the room. But he was a civilian and she had no rights here. The YOs seemed to be enjoying Dick's performance. Cheering every time he bungled or spilled something.

"Pudding, ma'am?" he hiccuped. His breath smelled fearsome and Esme leaned away from him.

"What is there?" she asked, nose wrinkled in distaste.

"Ssh'nothin' " he replied, swaying. "Unless you want this."

Esme stared at him, puzzled. Even more confused by the YOs' yelps and roars. They were banging their fists on the table . . . And then she saw.

Dick was exposing himself to her. Waggling a horrid little tongue of pink flesh at her. It poked out of his repellent trousers, and he was massaging it.

"Attaboy!"

"Stiffen it up, damn you . . . Ten*shun*!"

"Dick, dick, dick, dick . . ." The chant, once established, seemed unlikely to stop.

Go or stay, Esme could not escape this nightmare with dignity. Feeling sick and rather drunk herself, she went, walking slowly down the length of the dining-room, the chant ringing in her ears.

Pertwee, who could have no conceivable business there, stood leering in the ante-room.

"Just attending to the fire, madam," he lied unctuously.

Esme's dreams that night were of Tiggy's sergeant. She thought she was drowning in blood. Waking, she found her sheets were sopping with sweat. A passing ship sounded its fog horn.

* * *

207

The Brigade Major tried evading Esme all of the next morning but she kept at his clerks until he capitulated and saw her. As she laid her complaint before him, he leaned back in his chair, balancing it on its two hind legs. He seemed to be making efforts to prevent a smirk forming on his lips.

"Don't be a spoil sport, Esme," he drawled at her. "You know what old Dick's like . . ."

"Dick was not responsible. He was plied with drink and incited to . . ."

"Oh, come on. The YOs look on you as fair game, Esme. You won't get anywhere in this man's army if you're going to throw these spinsterish fits . . ."

"Major Glossop," Esme cut across him, "Let me assure you, I'm not making this complaint as a woman, I'm making it as an officer. I have a legitimate . . ."

"Sorry, Esme. Glad to chat about it some other time but I have a meeting with the Brig in half a sec . . ."

Esme saluted and left. She went straight back to her own office and made a note of the date of her conversation with the Brigade Major in her HMSO desk diary. At lunchtime she bought a notebook from the village shop and made a similar, more comprehensive note. It might be important to get the whole conversation down whilst it was still so clear in her memory. She couldn't say why, but her antennae were beginning to discern the emergence of a pattern. A pattern linked to a central motif which was still missing.

She didn't have far to search. By chance only, Birtwhistle had the Chief Clerk dump a pile of files on Esme's desk that very afternoon.

"Weed them, will you," he said. "The security classification means an officer has to do it. Take all the spare bumf out and chuck it. All we need to keep is an outline record of the action on each file. No confirmations of meetings or acknowledgements of letters . . . get rid of anything which isn't vital to an understanding of the history."

Esme was quick. She had weeded files before. With her clear, incisive mind at work the pile reduced by half in just over an hour. Then she came on it. A file with no title. What's more it had already been ruthlessly weeded. Only two or three cryptically-worded documents remained. Not cryptic enough, however, to delude Esme's sensitised intuition.

The correspondence referred to a WRAC officer. One who had been Staff Captain here at Coldfleet when Esme was still at Camberley. She was dead. Death by misadventure, a Brigade memorandum to General Headquarters reported the coroner's verdict. On the next page, oblique reference was made to the girl's personal effects. It made Esme certain that the officer's private papers, found in her rooms after her death, had been tampered with. 'Cleared up' was the phrase.

There was one other letter which seemed to refer to a report from a medical officer. His report was absent from the file but as distilled by the Sapper signatory to this document, the MO denied ever having prescribed anything but a 'virtual placebo' to the deceased officer in the last month of her life. She had been having boyfriend trouble, the letter said patronisingly. A mild despondency . . . not a clinical depression.

Suicide. Esme was certain of it. These Sappers had been exonerating themselves and each other. Hushing it up. Editing the evidence. Selecting the possessions which were sent back to the deceased girl's next of kin. No notes, no diaries . . . no embarrassing or incriminating attempts at self-expression.

Birtwhistle was clicking the end of his biro. Esme kept her head down. Should she confront him with the file? Mention the officer's name without warning? No. He would only say he knew nothing about it . . . That he hadn't been here then . . . And that it was only an accident . . . Esme didn't know how she had done it or where. But the conviction was immovable. These people, or their predecessors in post, had harassed this girl as they were harassing her. Had harassed Sophie Brafferton. They'd overdone it once, and hounded their victim to her death.

"How're you getting on?" Birtwhistle broke the silence suddenly.

"Quite well, I think," Esme said. "By the way, I shall want two days leave in the first week in December."

"Up to you," Birtwhistle resumed his biro-clicking.

"Daphne's a pig," Philippa stood with Esme at the edge of the pond in Green Park. "Just a frustrated old bag who torments other people because her weedy RO won't marry her . . . And believe me, I did *not* recommend you for the Sapper job. As if I would . . ."

"I know. But she should have told me," Esme said, shivering. The day, damp and raw, was already darkening. Water fowl gave scattered, sleepy quacks as lights gleamed, blotchily pale in the mist. "Warned me . . . Told me something at least . . ."

"Yes, she should," Philippa agreed. "But according to you, she did. She told you that the Sappers were dissatisfied and that . . ."

"You know what I mean. She should have told me nobody could ever win there."

"The Corps have never accepted that. A post is a post."

"You mean every time an officer kills herself, we'll calmly replace her with more cannon fodder?"

209

"Esme, nobody knows what happened. It may have been suicide as you say ..."

"What do we know?"

"Not very much. Certainly I don't. There was some very muted talk at the time. Come on, we'll walk back. Tea, cobber. You look as though you need a decent meal."

"Yes, but tell me."

Esme, Philippa saw, was not going to let it drop. She could believe everything she'd heard from her about her treatment at Coldfleet. Three officers in a row with damning confidential reports? Not technically adverse but way below average. That in itself is suspicious. Sophie Brafferton had probably got one as well. That made four. But this suicide bee in Esme's bonnet was an extreme reaction and far more dangerous to her than anyone else.

"Didn't the Anglia ADWRAC come and see you?" she asked. "She's supposed to make an inspection."

"She came," Esme admitted. "And they never left me alone with her. I don't think it would have been any good if they had. She didn't seem like the kind of person who wanted to hear anything but gush. She perched on the edge of my desk, swinging her legs at Birtwhistle and saying how awfully interesting my job must be. She was looking at him, not me."

"Mmm." Philippa could see the lady just now. A full colonel, alone of her rank she'd kept her figure and china-doll, pink and white prettyness. She didn't like trouble. She only liked men. Preferably knighted, widowed generals. She was saving her well-preserved charms for one of them. She was going to be Lady Somebody or die in the attempt.

There were many things about the Corps which Philippa sincerely deplored. Within two or three years of espousing it, she had seen what was wrong with the WRAC and had made it her life's mission to reform it. She belonged to that inspired, tiny minority of women who see their way straight. She had set her course, beating through the prevailing contrary winds, shortening sail and adjusting her trim to survive.

Esme didn't share her disciplined agility. She was a freedom fighter. An idealist. And frankly, Philippa smiled to herself, not the safest companion for a career officer. On the other hand, she mused, Esme was a luxury she could afford. Must afford. Lose sight of what Esme Hansard stood for, and command of the Corps would be nothing but sawdust.

"All I can tell you," she responded to Esme's insistence, "is that at the inquest rumour had it that the witnesses gave conflicting evidence. She wound up under a bus in Goole. Some said it was a one way street and she looked the wrong way. Others said she deliberately threw herself under the wheels. The Sapper officer who attended said she was a normal, happy girl, doing a job she enjoyed, who was fully involved in mess life. Not surprisingly," Philippa said with that dry gurgle which Esme could interpret, "the parents were very happy to believe it."

"Did they write her a confidential report at any stage?"

"She'd been there over a year, so yes . . . Actually, I saw it when I was AG16."

"What was it like?"

"Mediocre," Philippa understated the case.

"There you are then!" Esme exclaimed as they approached the club's granite steps. Archie was stamping his feet with the cold, jiggling his medals.

"Good walk, ladies?"

Spreading toast with the club's excellent, spicy damson jam in the morning-room twenty minutes later, Esme returned to her deductions regarding the veracity of the coroner's verdict. Philippa, who could see a little way into the future, was very anxious to distract her attention.

"Oh, Esme, I must tell you! Guess who I saw at Brize Norton?"

At once, Phillipa could have bitten her tongue out. Brize Norton was a military airfield. Difficult to change now what she had been going to say.

"Who?"

"Um . . . Some UN people coming back. I thought I recognised . . . But really, I . . ."

It was too late. Esme was gone, swept out of the room in a whirlwind of euphoria. Could she use the members' telephone to ring Windsor? Nothing, Philippa realised, putting down her plate, would stop her.

"Hello! Hello . . . Is that the officers' mess at the Silvershods' depot?"

"Queen Anne's Dragoon Guards, yes," intoned the servant who answered. "How may I help you?"

"I'd like to speak to Lieutenant Carson, please."

"A moment, please, madam. I will see if Mr Carson is at home . . . And your name, please, madam, if I may . . ."

Esme waited for a long time, biting her lip with impatience. Why so long?

"Madam?" the servant came back on the line. "Mr Carson is not in the mess at the moment."

"Oh," a wave of disappointment drenched Esme. But at least he was back. "In that case," she said, "Could I please speak to Lieutenant Johannenloe."

211

"One moment, madam," the servant submitted imperturbably. "I will see if His Serene Highness is available."

A much longer wait this time. Finally, Esme heard Tiggy's voice.

"Hello," he said tonelessly. "Esme? Look, I'm afraid Clive's going to be rather tied up for quite a few weeks . . . I don't think it's a good idea for you to try and contact him just now . . ."

Esme's viscera turned over. It just didn't sound like Tiggy. His voice, but not his way of speaking . . .

"Tiggy? Is that you? Are you all right? Your ankle . . . is it better . . .?"

"Yes. Much better, thank you. And you? Are you well?"

"Yes, I am. But . . ."

"Look, I'm sorry. I have to go now. Goodbye."

A rattle, and the telephone went dead. Clutching the receiver, Esme listened to its mechanical purring.

"If you have finished, madam," the club's switchboard operator said politely, "please be kind enough to replace the receiver. Thank you so much."

Reappearing in the morning-room like a somnambulist, Esme was unable to speak. In her flour-white face, her lips had turned blue.

Philippa guided her back to a chair. Why weren't girls like Esme told the truth at the outset? Before they joined and were trapped in a rigid category? Because the truth was nowhere inscribed and never admitted.

"Esme, I have to tell you this now. I don't know what has happened but Clive Carson will never marry you. He will never be allowed to marry you. Officers of the Silvershods may not escort WRAC officers, may not become engaged to them and may not, in any circumstances, marry them. I didn't know how to tell you . . . I hope that . . ."

Esme just stared.

"To put it bluntly," Philippa ground out desperately, uncertain how much, if anything, Esme was taking in, "we're not socially acceptable to them. No exceptions have ever been made for individuals . . . Do you understand what I'm saying?"

Seemingly, Esme did not.

"I'm afraid they're not the only ones. Other regiments have similar rules . . . It depends somewhat on the colonel . . . They don't advertise it but . . . In the Silvershods, it's written in indelible ink . . ."

"*Where?*" Esme's eyes ignited. Her lips were drawn back from her teeth in a rictus of suffering. "He can show me himself."

Philippa could do nothing to dissuade her. Heedless, she sat down at a desk and wrote a note on the Melrose Club's stationery. Archie summoned a taxi for her but she did not get in it. The driver was to carry the note to Windsor and leave it at the Silvershods' guard room.

212

If Clive did not come to her by eight o'clock that evening, she would go to him. And if he was not there, she would go every day till he was. She didn't care how far she lowered the tone.

"I'm not sure I should let you use my club for this purpose," Philippa tried a last-ditch appeal to Esme's sense of propriety.

"Of course not," Esme conceded. "How thoughtlessly rude of me. I'll just have to get another taxi and go to Windsor myself, after all."

"No," Philippa said sharply. "Don't do that. Whatever you do, don't do that."

Esme had snatched the right to a showdown on ground of her own choosing. She was Veronica Winstanley's daughter.

14

Without Tiggy's powerful persuasion, underwritten by a stout offer to stand beside his friend, Clive would never have come.

"For Christ's sake," Tiggy remonstrated, "Let Darling Heart have her say for old time's sake. She's earned it. Consolation prize. Come on, I'll drive, seeing you're in such a bloody funk."

Whatever ignominy there might be in dancing to Esme's tune, he argued, it was better than that which would accrue if she made a scene in Windsor. Essikins was not, in Tiggy's estimation, a girl who threatened idly. And Clive had more riding on damage containment now, than the three additional years of active service he'd just signed on for. Much more.

The meeting took place in a cluttered administrator's office overlooking the members' car park to the rear of the Melrose Club. Esme stood with her back to the cold, uncurtained window, facing her visitors across piles of ledgers, correspondence trays and bill spikes. Six feet lay between them and six thousand light years of distance.

Throughout the interview Clive kept his head down, knuckles whitening on the back of a typist's chair. It was Tiggy who met Esme's ice-fire glare. Stood for the high-velocity impact of everything she said. How ill she looked.

"What did you mean, Clive? *'If I had a thousand pounds I suppose you'd like a ring'*."

"It was just something to say," Clive mumbled without looking up. "We'd had a good time."

"That's a reason for manipulating me . . . for monopolising me, is it? Do you *understand*, I have never been penetrated by any other man?"

Clive shrivelled visibly, hunching his head between his shoulders. Tiggy blenched beneath his tan. Old Essikins had a punchy way with words. Really terrifying.

"If you'd left the army . . ." Clive began.

"Oh, yes. Did you know that?" Esme snapped instantly at Tiggy. "He wanted me to resign my commission and be a shop assistant. Is that because your regiment prefers shop assistants to commissioned officers? Is it?"

"Don't be such a snob," Clive grated with unconscious irony.

"You're right. I'm too big a snob to go slumming like you do, Mr Carson."

Tiggy closed his eyes. His hair, bleached quite colourless by the sun, was strangely ageing with his darkened skin. Clive's lips moved helplessly.

"It might interest you to know . . ." Esme stopped in time. Trotting out her pedigree would be unseemly. Aunt Alice's name must not be dragged into this. They only understood one kind of nobility, these people. A kind that was not of heart or mind.

"Get out, both of you. I've finished with you. You're scum. Go away. Leave me *now*."

Sensing their hesitation, born of shock, Esme turned her back and looked at the window's complete opacity. Darkness and condensation. She heard their shuffling exit.

"Esme, I . . ." It was Tiggy who spoke.

"No. I have nothing to say to you. Never speak or write to me again. Leave me alone. Please go."

In the small square hall, with its refined furniture, Persian carpets and parquet flooring, Clive said, "Is she a member here? Quite smart."

Tiggy pitied his friend's venality. Disgust, however, could not tempt him from his loyalty. They had shared too much.

Alone, Esme turned to see the empty space where Clive had been and grieved tearlessly over the utter squalor of this ending. Numbed by ugliness.

"Are you sure you're fit to drive?" Philippa asked the following morning. "I could ring the Sappers and tell them that you're ill . . ."

"But I'm not, am I?" Esme's voice was clipped. She had managed one mouthful of scrambled egg, so far. She hadn't had much appetite for months. "I have to go back to Coldfleet. I'm curious to know what they think they're going to do to me."

"Wouldn't it be much cleverer simply never to go back. I could arrange that, you know," Philippa regarded Esme across the breakfast table.

She was strung so tight she might do anything. Philippa feared she was likely to work her own destruction if the M1 didn't kill her first.

"I could go absent without leave, I suppose," Esme said. "But that would put Aunt Alice in a hell of a position . . ."

By a split-hair's width, Philippa divined, she was still teetering on the edge of rationality.

"No, just listen, Esme. Whether you know it or not, you are very far from well. If I take you to an MO, here in London . . . Say at Milbanke Military Hospital, they'll probably take you in, at least for a night or two. Nervous prostration would cover it. *Then* they can give you at least six weeks' sick leave, which gives me time to work on Colonel Crump, who will then have time to work on WRAC1. The Brigadier will then approach Colonel AG16 with suggestions about a new posting for you. Very carefully vetted, this time. Look, cobber, you need a rest."

Esme was implacable. A rest? Her Christmas leave wasn't far off. After yesterday, she didn't want any time to think. It probably sounded very dramatic, but the way things seemed to her, she had one thing left in life. The chance to stop the Sappers before they murdered someone else. It was time the whole world knew about them. No more conspiracies and cover ups . . . No more connivance . . .

"How do you think you're going to do that, Esme? Army Goliaths don't even get nicked by little army Davids, you know. Escape them now and you'll at least have deprived them of . . ."

Philippa checked herself. Everything she said was giving Esme more ammunition. Ammunition that would be turned against her.

"I could order you, you know."

"If you do," Esme replied smoothly, "I shall obey you. But I shall write enough unsolicited reports to clog the whole of Whitehall. Somebody, somewhere will listen to me. I can wind up in waste-paper bins the length and breadth of London. But waste-paper bins get emptied. It'll take one eye, one second to absorb one single line of what I have to say . . ."

"Blackmail," Philippa interrupted.

"I know. But, please. I want to do this. Let me draw their fire . . . If I stop to lick my wounds now, I know I shall go mad."

Clive-inflicted wounds, Philippa concluded. She felt partially responsible for that. The English and their snobbery. The most rarefied of all their blood sports. Esme, she noticed, was not going to mention Clive directly. All she wanted was a counter-irritant. Two agonies, in her arithmetic, added up to none. Instead, a grey diffuseness of non-specific pain.

"All right," Philippa gave way, "But don't take any risks. Do you play chess?"

"Not very well. Why?"

"Because here are the possible end-games. The best you can hope for is stalemate . . ."

Esme returned to Goole by way of the Great North Road. It was slower than the M1 but ran closer to the Humber and gave more frequent opportunities for stopping.

"Make allowances for yourself," Philippa bossed. "Don't drive that car of yours too fast, and not for more than an hour and a half without a rest. Your concentration won't be top notch. Be careful and best of luck. You can get me through Loan Services . . . I'll tell them. I'll be back again after Christmas and if you want me before I fly on Friday, ring the club. And remember, if things get out of hand, you just go *sick*."

Philippa waved Esme out of the car park before getting busy on the telephone. No use ringing Stanmore. AG branches never gave officers' current postings away. A protection against importunate creditors and lovers. But in theory, Ivor should still be at Woolwich. And whilst there was little love lost between her and him, he might be grateful for a watching brief on the Coldfleet cauldron. Ivor, Philippa calculated, was not a man who changed his mind in a hurry over anything.

"Llewellyn," Ivor answered his office telephone with military concision.

"It's Philippa Mayhew, Ivor."

"Yes? What can I do for you, Philippa," he said brusquely. "You're lucky to catch me, actually. I'm leaving here next week. Lecturing at Staff College. Strategic studies wing . . ."

"Do you remember Esme Hansard?"

"Vividly," said Ivor. The colour of his tone suggested that Esme still had no real competitors with him. "I see that boyfriend of hers got himself engaged."

Philippa's circulation ebbed. "Oh yes?"

"Yes. In this morning's *Times*. Didn't you see it?"

Philippa had read no newspapers that morning. She had been far too preoccupied.

"Got it here somewhere. Yes. To a Lady Roxanne Campbell. Her father owns six thousand acres of prime land in Scotland and some more in Dorset."

With any luck at all, Esme would miss this news. As long as she didn't buy a newspaper on her way up to Yorkshire. She would arrive late at Coldfleet and probably go straight to bed . . .

"Well, I've just seen Esme and she didn't mention it. If she knows I don't think she cares. She's at the Royal School of Combat Engineering at the moment. It's very dull for her . . ."

"You do like to organise things, don't you, Mayhew?"

"Yes, I do."

"OK," Ivor said. "If I feel like giving my spark plugs a good blow through, I'll see what I can do. Won't be for a week or two though, yet. That it?"

"That's it. I'd be grateful, Ivor."

"Fond of her, aren't you?"

"So are you, I think."

She'd got him by the short and curlies there, Ivor admitted as much to himself as he put the telephone down. But he was very busy.

For Esme the next few days were bleak. A stark re-birth. A coming into this world with nothing, as the Book of Common Prayer's funeral service put it. But babies slept well, and Esme didn't. Hers was the unkindest of all bereavements. When the one mourned is not dead. She saw the Carson – Campbell engagement announcement in the *Telegraph*. It had appeared a day later there. Happily ever after with the hamster . . .

Clive had been courting Roxanne that day at Hurlingham. She saw it all. Was staggered by her own stupidity. Four years as Clive Carson's plaything . . . When had he stopped loving her and started using her? Had he *ever* loved her? That too had to be addressed. And Tiggy, whom she had thought her friend . . .

It came as a welcome if grisly diversion, on the same Friday morning that Philippa flew back to Jordan, to receive her confidential report. Marked 'A' for Adverse. The Sappers had done their worst. Interesting to see that many of the qualities specifically listed on the special form were dismissed as 'not tested'. The burden of the Sapper tale, told ostensibly by Major Birtwhistle as reporting officer, fell into the spaces allowed for random comment.

"All you have to do is initial it," Birtwhistle said, clicking his biro rapidly. "It only signifies you've seen it. Not that you necessarily agree with it."

"So I've often been told," Esme said. "But I don't believe it. What do you mean I don't 'enjoy the social side of my duties'? When have you ever known me try to get out of a dinner night or turn an invitation down?"

"Well, never." Birtwhistle looked blank. "But, I mean, you're always grumbling about writing invitations out, aren't you?"

"Of course. It's a clerk's job. Anyway, before I do anything with this, I want a copy made."

"What for?" Birtwhistle asked, suspiciously. The biro, a cheap plastic one, snapped. "Blast!"

"To show my guardian. Dame Alice Winstanley, late of the FANY and the ATS. DSO, MC with bar, Croix de Guerre . . . Retired, of course. She'll be interested in this."

Esme waved the report as she got up and made towards the door.

Why *not* say it, she thought angrily. The Sappers had dipped their spoon in the soup now. A taste of the noodles would do no harm at all. An appetiser. They could have the chunks of beef tomorrow.

"You're not allowed a copy," Birtwhistle said quickly, still boggling over Esme's revelation. Who was this superannuated old pike? Did she have any pull? Did she exist? Better play it safe. The Brigadier wanted the Staff Captain 'A' situation stitched up this time. A nugget of gold for his own confidential. And a smaller one for Birtwhistle's.

"Where does it say I'm not allowed a copy?" Esme asked innocently. "Tell me where the regulation is . . ."

"All right. But you're not to take it out of the headquarters . . ."

"I'm allowed twenty-four hours with this, Major Birtwhistle, and you know it. If I take a photocopy, I won't need it, will I? You can have the thing right back."

"No need to get aggressive."

"No. No need at all. Sorry. Back in a minute."

Esme photocopied the report in the orderly room. She initialled the original and added, "Seen. Not agreed."

"You can't do that," Birtwhistle objected when Esme laid the report back on his desk. "Initials only. It'll have to be typed again."

"However often you have it typed, Major Birtwhistle," Esme said evenly, "I shall do as I have already done. Either that or you'll have to make what use of it you can without my initials."

Stumped, Birtwhistle went off up the corridor to tell the Brigadier. Then he came back again. The fencing went on all morning but Esme kept her copy. She put it in her handbag and made good use of it that afternoon on a visit to the band unit.

"Well, hello there," the Director of Music greeted her. He liked her personally although he'd no wish to lose a third of his command to Germany. "Come for something to sooth the savage breast? Spot of Strauss . . . Or is that a block posting order you've got there?"

Esme smiled at him. All she wanted was the use of an office and a civilian typist.

"Be my guest, dear. Liberty hall. Brought the war to the enemy, have you? Want some coffee?"

220

"You're not the enemy. And I should love some coffee."

"With milk and sugar . . . or just the typist?"

Esme drank it black while she drafted her appeal.

'An overweening concern for her own well being' they'd accused her of. And by contrast, 'A marked lack of enthusiasm for the objectives of the Royal School of Combat Engineering.'

Wonderful. Esme's mind was clear and bright. Sharp as a day of sparkling frost.

She began to write. 'It has been difficult for me,' she said, 'to identify closely with the affairs of an organisation which has so crassly . . .' No, 'crassly' wouldn't do. Too emotive, 'so conspicuously neglected my personal welfare . . .'

She treated the Army Board to selected highlights of her time at Coldfleet Barracks. Not too much. Only things which had impinged upon her personally. Her desk diary was helpful in working out dates and times. Not too many of those, however. The thing mustn't look overly premeditated. She favoured incidents which had been widely witnessed . . . They wouldn't all tell the same story. There would be discrepancies. The occurrence with Dick, the mess waiter, was all the stronger for being compressed into a line. The subsequent dialogue with Major Glossop was reported in full. Complete with quotation marks.

At the end, she had one and three-quarter pages of neat typescript in one-and-a-half-line spacing. Nice, broad margins. The average military mind, Esme had discovered, had a short attention span. Safer to plan on the Army Board being composed of military minds. The regulations provided a tribunal for this appeal but didn't describe the nature of the judges.

One thing Esme did know was that her accusers were allowed a second bite of the legal cherry. They could appeal against *her* appeal . . . and she wasn't entitled to see what they said. But they'd have a hard time wriggling out of this. The best of it was they wouldn't be ready for it. The precious weapon of surprise. Philippa had told her that appeals were very rare. Most people simply sat down under an adverse confidential report. Kept still. Playing dead was considered the best chance of surviving an official mauling.

"Ah, Mrs Dodds," the Brigade Major bared his teeth in a smile that rose too slowly to his eyes. He hadn't reckoned on bumping into Esme's batwoman. A nuisance. "Better afternoon we're having, aren't we?"

"We are, sir. Yes," Mrs Dodds squared up to him sturdily. "Right wet it was this morning. Can I help you, sir?"

"Um . . . Yes. That is, I think I can help myself. Captain Hansard's out this afternoon and I believe she may have a document in her sitting-room that we need in the headquarters . . . We have to deal with it right away, you see . . . So I'll just bob in and check if it's on her desk . . ."

"Sorry, sir." Mrs Dodds smelled a rat. Nasty man, Major Glossop was. Heartless eyes. Whatever was on Captain Hansard's desk it weren't his business. Not in the mess. Mrs Dodds had worked eight years at Coldfleet and she'd always looked after her WRAC ladies properly. Including the poor dead lady. Right down she'd been . . . Any road, Captain Hansard was her favourite up to now. Always so grateful for anything you did for her. Real appreciative. Good tips, an' all.

She said it again for good measure: "Sorry, sir."

"Er . . . What do you mean?" Glossop wished the woman would go about her business. Not stand there blocking his path like this.

"Miss Hansard's room's locked, sir."

"Locked? Isn't that very unusual? Surely you have the key. Or Pertwee . . . Or the mess secretary."

"Mr Pertwee's having his nap, sir." Mrs Dodds folded her work-roughened hands across her stomach stolidly. "And t' mess secretary's gone to the bank in Goole to get the wages."

Major Glossop was in a tizzy, Mrs Dodds deducted. Up to no good. "I finish cleaning an' that in Captain Hansard's rooms at lunchtime, sir, and then I generally give her the key. Afternoons I does her ironing, like, in t' batting room."

A complete fabrication. Esme's room was unlocked as it always was. But Mrs Dodds did not like the Brigade Major. Sufficient reason, in her book, to prevent his shenanigans. She remembered the way that Headquarters lot had come swarming all over the deceased lady's things. It hadn't been their place to deal with the effects. It had been hers. Going into a lady's room . . . Not this time. Over Mrs Dodds's tiny but indomitable body.

Glossop retreated. Waking Pertwee was, of course, unthinkable. Pertwee had had the overseeing, as he himself expressed it, of men who were generals now. And generals were afraid of him. Glossop certainly was.

"It's all right," Esme soothed her batwoman when returning to the mess at teatime. "I know what Major Glossop was after and I'll give it all to him tomorrow morning. But thank you, Mrs Dodds. Thank you very much indeed. I'm sorry you were troubled."

So Glossop was scared witless about his own hide, was he? Either that or he'd been instructed to recover the copy of her confidential. More clearing up of private paperwork.

A whole six hours had passed in which Esme had not thought once of Clive. She noticed that herself. When there were naked blades around you couldn't afford a divided mind.

The next day developed yet more eccentrically.

"This," said Esme to Major Glossop, "is my appeal against Major Birtwhistle's confidential report on me. I give it to you, I think . . . That's right, isn't it? For you to pass to the Brigadier. From him it goes direct to the Army Board. I've sent three silent copies already to Anglia ADWRAC, WRAC1 and AG16. I thought it would save you some trouble."

It would also prevent the Sappers from losing her appeal in the system. That was far too easily done.

The expression on the Brigade Major's face, as she slid the typescript on to the top of his in-tray, was such as to give Esme the deepest satisfaction. The opening barrage in the second round had stunned this representative of the opposition. His arrogant mouth hung slack.

"Yes. Yes, thank you, Esme. Er . . . I'll see he gets it."

"Thank you so much," Esme sighed with pleasure. "I was sure you would."

Within fifteen minutes there was not a staff officer above the rank of captain to be seen about the headquarters. The Colonels AQ and G with their ancillary majors were closeted with the Brigadier. The orderly rooms were quiet, as was the G office where two downtrodden Sapper captains worked. Rumours flying. But not a sound issued from the Brigadier's office. The old building's partition walls were thick . . . And the council of war was probably being conducted in low, shocked voices.

Esme hoped so. She sat back in her chair and contemplated the back of General Gordon's head outside her office window. Gordon, the Bible-thumping pervert hero of the Royal Engineers.

Esme's heart was thumping too, a little. Where did any of them go from here? There were some exigencies of war you couldn't anticipate. What would they come up with? Infuriatingly, she would never know. The rules handicapped the weak to give advantage to the strong. Great odds against which to pit her wits. She would be parrying their return strokes, blindfold, now.

Not quite.

Returning to the headquarters after lunch, a meal during which Esme had received an extraordinary number of watery smiles and nervous glances from her seniors . . . even kindly words, she found a piece of paper in her in-tray which was unfamiliar. A scrap only, from a cheap jotter with a scrawl of red biro on it. Numbered points, written in evident haste, sloping markedly from left to right.

Reading it, Esme's eyes sparkled with gratitude. Here were the Sappers' proposed defences. A tissue of poor, pathetic lies. Dilutions, evasions and flat denials. And somebody had done her the anonymous kindness of plucking this panicky, perfidious fragment from a waste-paper basket. If this formed the basis of the rebuttals the Sappers were going to lay beside Esme's appeal, then the Army Board would recognise a contrast in the quality of the juxtaposed material.

Knowledge might not amount to power in the present case. But the existence of an unknown sympathiser was cheering in itself.

"Chin up, Esme," muttered a tubby little G captain when he scuttled past her in the corridor that afternoon. He was married, and never talked about anything except the progress of his current home-made brew of beer. He was probably Methodist too.

The army had given Esme no friends at Coldfleet. Instead it sent an angel. Two, with Mrs Dodds.

The contest was hard-fought and cunning. It was Alice Winstanley, astonishingly cool in the face of all the forces ranged against her niece, who gave encouragement and good counsel. Their quiet Christmas together was perhaps the best they ever had. Appropriate, since it was to be the last which took the old, familiar shape.

Esme railed tearfully against the Sapper savagery which gave her the New Year duty, cutting her time at home by half. She was the only unmarried officer on the staff. The others lived in married quarters in or around the barracks. Esme, whose home was counties distant, would be quite alone in the mess for a week. Alone too, with heavy responsibilities.

The mess would be to all intents and purposes closed. No food. The kitchen staff had to have their leave. Esme was to be given a subsistence allowance and had been told to feed herself at caffs in Goole. There was no restaurant of any substance there. Too bad. Breakfast? Esme was an officer. She must use her initiative, mustn't she?

No Mrs Dodds. She, of course, must have her holiday. And so no laundry, no bed-making, no early morning tea, no cleaning . . . no nothing. Oh, the heating would be on. A man would come in to refuel the boiler. The acme of generosity.

No Pertwee. Esme wouldn't miss him. But security would fall to her along with his gargantuan bunch of keys.

No bar, no newspapers. Esme must take thought for her own needs, mustn't she? Procure oil for her own lamp, as Birtwhistle advised sententiously, like the wise virgin she unquestionably was. He betrayed himself into a back-handed compliment with that witticism.

All this was highly irregular, Alice said, mooching up and down the home paddock with her niece. Verging on illegality. In wartime such a withdrawal of basic care would never have been permitted. Not for officers on straight regimental or headquarters duties. Being an SOE joe was a different matter . . . But the domestic privations were not the end of it. Esme had been left in charge of flood control. If the river rose, menacing property or life, she would be responsible.

"They wouldn't even let me look at the orders. For some reason they're *secret*. Can you believe that? They're locked up in a safe and I was supposed to memorise the combination."

"And did you?" Alice appraised the two horses. Taken in at night during the winter, they were out in the daytime, snuggled up in New Zealand rugs.

"You know what I'm like with figures. They forbade me to write it down but I had to. I feel so guilty."

"Don't. What do you think of your mare?"

"She's very fat," Esme said dubiously.

"Fat? Of course she's fat," Alice scorned. "So would you be. In fine fettle though, ain't she? Linseed oil and vitamins. Can't beat it."

There was some talk of equine obstetrics before Esme returned to what troubled her most deeply.

"But, Aunt Alice, even if I ever get into that bloody safe, it'll be full to bursting with papers and I won't know which the flood control orders *are*. It will take me for ever to sort it out. By that time people could be drowning."

"Statistically, it's not very likely. It's the Humber, not the Indus . . . Gimlet! Come *here*! Upset that mare and I'll make you into slippers."

After an exhibition of meaningless oral violence between woman and dog, Alice said, "Darling, you're missing the point of this. What the Sappers want is for you to say, 'I've had enough. Damn their duty. I'm not going back.' And they're counting on *me*, to overestimate my influence with the powers that be and egg you on. Then you'll be AWOL. A serious, chargeable offence which will make their rebuttal of your appeal look better than it is."

"Aunt Alice, you are so clever."

"No, darling. Just experienced. Now, I'm not going to make you go back. In some ways I'd sooner that you didn't . . . It won't take me two farts of Oberon's backside to sort out the Sappers, the Army Board, the Chiefs of Staff . . . and the WRAC by way of a savoury . . ."

Dear, dear Aunt Alice. She was never coarse unless she was very, very angry. Esme would scarcely have put it past her to call her tormentors out, one by one, and duel them all to death with sabres. How dare they give her niece an adverse confidential? A stain upon the family honour which would have to be expunged. Esme could read her thoughts. They coincided with her own.

"There's Sick at Home," Alice temporised, "We could do that. I must say you look very peaky. But I hate the idea of those people writing you off as a weakling . . . Or imagining for one moment we're running scared . . ."

"I'm going back. Win or lose, I have to finish this."

"*Good*! I thought you'd want to," Alice beamed. "We Winstanleys like to see things through. There's the 22 rifle in the back kitchen. Do you want to take it?"

"Oh, for heaven's sake, Aunt Alice. I don't need a blunderbuss. I've got you, haven't I? That's enough."

Alice fished a handkerchief from her pocket and wiped her eyes, dismissing the fleeting thought that her niece might be in any real physical danger as ridiculous.

"Bloody windy. Let's go in."

Everything after that went as usual. Both Esme and her aunt attended the meet on Boxing Day, leaving Mrs Fairbairn in charge of receiving early buffet lunchers. There was no scent, so the concourse of horses, hounds and humans in Kirkby Lonsdale's square boiled down to a mounted cocktail party.

Asking if Habibi was fit to stand so long, Alice said she was fit to run all day. A gross exaggeration, but the company would do her good. She must get sick of Oberon's provincial prosings. She was a society lady, was Habibi. Alice's approach to stable management was holistic.

Esme delighted her aunt by perching side-saddle on her mare. A very pretty sight, she said. Anything else, retorted Esme, would mean doing the splits.

Lady Makepeace was out this year on her vicious, kicking cob, rather proud of its red-bandaged tail.

"'Ware, 'ware . . . Give me a wide berth there, Esme, m'dear. Cornered that fellow of yours yet, have you? My, you're being a time about it . . ."

Esme gave her best, bright-blue-yonder smile and turned her own and Habibi's head.

"I got me another that's better than t'other," she fluted lightly over her shoulder.

Esme's wound was deep and festering. But the story of herself and Clive would crucify Aunt Alice. Therefore she must never hear it.

"In the army, eh?" Commander Witherspoon, who attended each

year on foot, edged through the spectating crowd. "Jolly good." The fourth year he'd said it.

Habibi, who'd never seen hounds before in her life, permitted herself to be sniffed by one. Tolerable.

"Oh, Ivor," Esme caught eagerly at the telephone-filtered sound of this familiar voice in the echoing quiet of the headquarters building, "Would you really come? Oh no, you can't," she relinquished the anticipated relief of seeing him. "Your parents must want you at home and . . ."

"My parents are over sixty, Esme. They go to bed at ten o'clock. Funnily enough they look on me as being quite young. In need of entertainment. It'll be a great relief to them not to have to go through the motions of seeing the New Year in."

"It would be marvellous. But, Ivor, I've nowhere for you to stay. The mess is all shut up apart from my room . . . You'd have to go to an hotel in Hull . . ."

He overcame every objection. Ivor would bring a sleeping bag. He'd doss down anywhere. He was at a loose end. So was she. But he was free to travel and she was stuck. He was looking forward to giving his new Mustang a workout. He would be with her long before the New Year struck. They'd do something to celebrate, come what may.

Mustang? What was that? Was Ivor bringing an American horse? She must have misunderstood him. Anyway, she must offer something in the way of hospitality. Drive into Goole and find an off-licence which sold champagne. She must, although she hardly dared. It was still raining. Down and down it came. Esme had prayed so hard against that rain.

"Looks bad, ma'am," the duty clerk came in with a cup of coffee for her.

"I know and I need to go into Goole for an hour . . ."

"Go on then, ma'am. Nothing's keeping you. If the dykes burst I'll stick a finger in them till you get back. Remember, if there's any flooding on the roads, put your foot down and drive straight through it. Bring me a packet of fags, ma'am will you? Craven 'A'. Bloody Naafi's shut."

Esme shrugged into her officer's riding mac, drank the coffee standing and ran off, exhilarated at the prospect of unexpected company. If only the rain would stop. She daren't leave the barracks for any length of time unless it did. Whatever would they do for food tonight? Esme'd had no dinner last night either. She could buy some cold things, she decided and filch some crockery from the dining-room . . .

227

Ivor, when he arrived six hours later in a roar of three thousand cubic centimetres, laughed the idea of cold food off. Flood warning or no flood warning, on New Year's Eve they were going out to dinner. Esme was a bag of bones. What had she been doing with herself?

"You should have seen me before Christmas," Esme said, not too ashamed of her emaciation, "Aunt Alice said I was a scarecrow. I'm *much* better now. But honestly, Ivor, I have to stay by the telephone. They switch it through to the mess after four o'clock."

"Well, *they* can switch it through to wherever we have dinner. Who gives the warning? The police?"

Esme realised she didn't know. Hadn't been told. Ivor took charge of everything. He rang the police who confirmed it was they who gave the duty staff officer at Coldfleet the flood warning.

"What's the best place in Goole to eat?"

"Well, sir," the desk sergeant at Goole's police station could be heard scratching his head. "I s'pose t' Copenhagen Hotel's the best. All t' masters go there and first mates when they're in port . . . I reckon it'll be a bit rough tonight . . ."

"Right," said Ivor crisply. "I want you to do me the most tremendous favour, Sergeant. Book me a table there, for, say, nine o'clock. Don't take no for an answer. I shall be there from then on and will ring you when I leave. So if there's any trouble you'll know where to get me. It's Major Llewellyn speaking, by the way. Royal Horse Artillery."

"Aye aye, sir," the policeman said, breathless with the pace of Ivor's imperious commands.

"Wow," said Esme. "How d'you do it, Ivor?"

"Never give 'em time to think. By the time he's woken up to the fact that I'm in no position to give him orders, he'll have carried them out."

So it proved. The Copenhagen was old-fashioned. An East Yorkshire version of a Wild West saloon with rooms. The public bar was noisy.

In the dining-room, brightly lit, bulbous-legged Victorian tables spread with well-worn, well-washed white damask table-cloths were laid with weighty, plated cutlery. Man-sized knives and forks. Nothing namby-pamby here. Pictures of steamships of various Goole-based lines marched along the walls. The waiters, many with seamanlike tattoos, knew their customers. As the police sergeant had said, Merchant Navy men, owners, and the occasional freight consignor in Goole to see his cargo safe on board or accompany it.

He had been wrong, however, about the atmosphere in here. This dining-room was the resort of serious men. There was a qualified jollity in the air and apart from Esme only two or three women present.

"Bad tonight, sir," the head waiter said, handing the menu to Ivor alone. This was not a town in which women made decisions for themselves. "No gale warning, though. Got a cargo loading, have you sir?"

"Right," said Ivor, ignoring the man's curiosity, "What are we having, Esme? There's soup of the day, grapefruit juice or prawn cocktail. Then we can have roast beef, roast lamb, roast duck or grilled York ham. Sounds all right. Oh, steamed hake, as well. What's the soup?"

"Mulligatawny, sir."

The ordering was concluded with dispatch. Vegetables? They came with everything. The wine list was short and utilitarian. Harvey's Reserve claret to start with.

"Ivor, I mustn't drink too much," Esme quailed at his forward-planning for champagne, cognac and more champagne.

"Rubbish. Mark of a true officer, to be able to cope with an emergency having taken drink."

Esme laughed delightedly. After four years or more in the army, she knew how true that was. It was nice to see Ivor again. He reminded her what the real army was like. The Sappers were a different, duller sub-species.

Perhaps, Ivor thought, he was hamming it up tonight. But he sensed his chance and he might not get another one.

"So," he said, woofting into a bowl of soup big enough to wash in, "let's hear it. What's been going on?"

Esme didn't trouble to ask how he knew anything was amiss. There were a thousand clues. And it boosted her flagging self-esteem to have a friend who would come so far for her. Someone who could take her and everything else in hand. There was a lot to be said for Ivor's military shittiness now it was working on her side. A shield to hide behind, however briefly. Ivor, a substantive major in the RHA, could take Birtwhistle on any day. She told him about everything except Clive.

"Brave, clever girl," Ivor stretched out his hand across the table when her narrative was done. She put hers in his quite naturally. Too thin to look as lovely as she had done when he first knew her, she moved him more than ever previously. She'd been through hell and kept her nerve. Fighting a close-quarters action against overwhelming forces.

"You know it's hopeless, don't you? That adverse confidential report of yours will stand."

"How can it, Ivor? They'll know I'm telling the truth."

"All the more reason to bury it. You know what truth does? It upsets the hierarchic apple-cart. Let a sprog like you walk off the field of

229

honour with the laurels and the whole of army discipline caves in."

"Philippa said it would be a stalemate," Esme acknowledged flatly. "I hoped to do a bit better than that for my aunt's sake as much as anything. This whole mess of mine must be terrible for her."

Esme reflected with shame that, of recent years, she'd taken Aunt Alice a lot too much for granted. Dropped her flat whenever Clive had whistled. And Ivor too. She had used him from the very start. First to glue her shattered pride together and then to fill the gaps . . . the long gaps left by Clive. Self-knowledge was supposed to be desirable. No one had ever said, to Esme's recollection, how unpleasant it was.

"Stalemate?" Ivor snorted. "That's optimistic. Take it from me, you'll be given an unofficial reprimand, lose your acting rank . . . posted somewhere dull and put on six months' probation."

"Back to square one, only this time under a cloud," Esme said. "Associating with me can't be all that good for your career . . ."

The head waiter intervened. It would be midnight shortly. The bar extension expired at half past. What would sir like. The Copenhagen carried two champagnes. Ivor ordered the costlier one.

He turned back to her and seeming to take a deep breath said, "Esme, I'm pretty well established. I don't need to worry too much about who my friends are. I don't have any close ones, anyway. Too busy. But what I need is a wife. Chuck the army and marry me. I'll be a lieutenant-colonel soon, with any luck. One day you'll be a general's lady."

There was a moment's silence in which the mounting rowdiness in the public bar increased and decreased in volume as the door across the lobby swung to and fro.

"Let me take you away from all this . . ." Esme snickered vaguely.

"Precisely. Get out from under. The army doesn't suit you. Not like this. As my wife it will be your setting, not your master. The army's a hundred warring tribes. But you and I could be a team . . ."

"But, Ivor, do you love me?"

"Oh, yes. I'm sorry, I should have said so. Didn't you know?"

"I suppose I did," Esme murmured to herself but stopped herself from saying that it hadn't seemed important. A sideshow.

"I was a stupid fool to rush at you like I did. Good God, you hadn't known me above eight weeks. And you were very young."

"True," said Esme. At twenty-five she felt like a sybil. A woman acquainted with a dozen sorrows. "But aren't I too young for you?"

"Hardly," Ivor said glancing down at his watch. "Half your own age plus five years . . . That's the right age for a wife, my father says. You're three years over the limit, actually."

"Oh *am* I?" Esme felt a healthy spurt of indignation.

230

"But not too old for a colonel's wife. Come on. It's midnight by my watch. Are we toasting our engagement or are we not?"

"Let's drink to thinking about it, Ivor."

That toast was never drunk. Ivor was wanted on the telephone. It was the desk sergeant down at the police station.

"I don't think we'll be troubling you tonight, sir. Rain eased off an hour ago. Forecast's fair. There's just one thing. I've got a Captain Hansard down here . . ."

"Same thing," Ivor said. "We're together. Happy New Year to you, Sergeant."

"And to you, sir."

Back at the table, Ivor said: "What a frost. I was going to knock that bloody lock off with a fire-axe. Your leaving present to the Sappers. Right, let's drink to plans. You can think while I plan."

Esme liked this harmless compromise. Could she really dodge the cloud and shelter under an arch of swords . . . as Ivor's bride?

15

As far as they could, as far as they dared, the 'old ladies' came through for Esme.

Contacts on the Army Board gave them access to an 'off the record' account of what took place when that ponderous body sat. General Vaughan, recently retired from the active list, had immediately declared his interest as a friend of the family when the Hansard item appeared on the agenda. His scrupulous withdrawal roused his colleagues from torpidity, prodding attention for the matter.

By the end of the brief ensuing discussion there was consensus. Miss Hansard had disclosed a basketful of dirty linen which required immediate if discreet investigation. Her appeal was considered highly competent. A stinging indictment lent credibility by its sobriety of expression. She must have had a most unpleasant time of it. Credit was due to her for having kept her head and used restraint. Credit, however, which was judiciously withheld.

"Agreeable as it might be," said the chairman to the other gentlemen surrounding a board-room table overlooking Whitehall, "to champion Miss Hansard, we mustn't be sentimental. The stability of the monolith outweighs the claims of justice to an individual."

It hardly needed saying.

"Adverse Confidential Report confirmed . . . Six months' probation. All agreed?"

No dissenting voice was heard.

Hints of this; private gratitude cloaked with official reprobation, were given to Esme when she waited on ADWRAC Metropolitan District at Horse Guards. Whatever could be done with china tea and Crabtree and Evelyn's special lemon biscuits to reassure her that six months' posting to Mill Hill as a platoon commander once again amounted to a formality, was done. The occasion was almost frivolous.

"Silly men," trilled ADWRAC, holding up Esme's report between finger and thumb. "If I were you, I should look at this . . . like this!" and she tore the document across. Two halves, which Esme knew would be Sellotaped together again by the Chief Clerk once her back was turned. Still, they were trying to cheer her up, which was a slightly better result than Ivor had betted on.

"Anyway, my dear, don't I hear something about wedding bells in the air for you?"

"Do you, ma'am?" Esme returned pleasantly. "How nice of people to chatter about one so. Actually my only personal concern at the moment is reinstatement and a good report. If you have nothing further now, ma'am, I shall go and resume my position as the prisoner of Mill Hill. Thank you for my tea."

Bravely, ADWRAC Metropolitan District paraded all her teeth. She had been warned about Esme Hansard's acerbic sense of humour . . . savouring as it did, unnervingly, of mint. Had she made some kind of joke? Difficult to tell.

Esme left by way of the arched courtyard on the Whitehall side, returning the mounted guards' salute mechanically. Harmless Life Guards, not Silvershods, thank God. The sight of those black plumes worked on her like rheumatism.

Nursing the increasingly decrepit Bean Can northwards up the Finchley Road, Esme asked herself for the thousandth time if being in love were a prerequisite of honest marriage. Supposing you wished you loved someone and decided to act as if you did . . . Would that be as good? At least, from his point of view.

Was there any truth in Ivor's recent, most alarming avowal that he could love enough for two? He'd kept adding these dollops of treacle lately to the plain pudding of his wooing. But Esme had no emotional sweet tooth. It was her own fault, she supposed, for making him try too hard.

And there again, what would it be like, lying each night for the rest of her life beside Ivor's body? This 'grown up' body, which contained ten more years of history than hers. Marked, perhaps, with eight more years of wear than Clive's. She had caught a fleeting glimpse of him that night at Coldfleet when he'd slept in her sitting-room. Ivor without his tie and top shirt-button undone had revealed a worrying escape of curling chest hair . . . The feel of him, skin on skin, would take some getting used to. Would he be circumcised like Clive? Would it matter if he wasn't? Who knew

234

the answer to this kind of thing? Certainly not Aunt Alice.

Esme had always imagined marriage as a kind of sibling companionship with a sexual dimension. A face to face relationship with a masculine mirror image. Ivor's version would be different.

As the weeks went by at Mill Hill Esme evolved a mental symbol of herself and Ivor. Two figures in silhouette, standing side by side, one a head taller than the other. The way things should be, many people said. The leader and the follower. The protector and the nurturer. The active protagonist and the loyal encourager. The hairy and the hairless. Ridiculous to be afraid of him because of that.

"You're under no pressure to decide whatsoever," Ivor insisted with never-failing good humour during his weekly outings with her. "Take all the time you need."

Sitting through plays, films and cabaret acts, Esme fidgeted, feeling pressurised by his patience. Half consciously she was waiting to fall in love, regarding herself in pained exasperation every Sunday evening, when once again it hadn't happened.

"What a gorgeous bloke he is," sighed a subaltern over a bouquet of spring flowers which Ivor had sent in what looked like a spontaneous outburst of ardour. "You must have a will of iron to keep him waiting."

"No, I think it's cowardice," Esme candidly replied and made her decision then.

Instinct had led her wrong before. This time, there would seem to be wisdom in trying common sense.

He gave her an Edwardian ring which had been his maternal grandmother's. A fine diamond solitaire with unusual ruby baguette shoulders.

"You don't have to have it, darling," he said anxiously, making lavish use of this endearment now, "but it's more valuable than anything I could afford to buy you."

"It's beautiful, Ivor," Esme put everything she could into her thank you kiss. Ivor always smelled of aftershave these days, and his mouth of antiseptic mouthwash. Like a boy scout, always prepared. Ready with polite and proper smells. A falsification of himself, a disguise that Esme could neither name nor penetrate.

Emerging from the kiss, working the ring around her finger, she said: "It's lovely to think this is a family thing. It makes me feel I belong already. Look, it fits . . . It must be meant for me. So generous of your mother to let me have it."

"If you hadn't wanted it, she'd only have sold it," Ivor said with unpoetic candour.

"But how could she when it belonged to her own mother?"

235

"My parents don't care very much for possessions, you'll discover," Ivor told her. "When they overspend their pension they just root through the house and find something to sell for ready cash. Mother's fur coat went years ago along with my grandfather's gold cigarette case and Hardy fishing-rods. They're running out of stuff."

Improvidence with their own resources, however, didn't prevent the senior Llewellyns from assuming rights over Alice Winstanley's.

"Well, well," whinnied Major Llewellyn senior, straddle-legged before the gas fire in the sitting-room of the semi-detached house outside Andover. "This is all very pleasant . . . and well done, my dear," he raised his glass of gin and French at Esme, "for bringing down this lone stag of ours at last. Ha ha! What? High time he was married. But . . . er, hadn't we better get down to practicalities . . ."

Fuming at the suggestion that she had somehow trapped Ivor, Esme saw the old man's eye swivel towards his wife.

"Lunch on its way, is it, Margie?"

"Oh yes, yes. Of course," she fluttered, rising. "Esme, dear, let us girls go off and dish up together while the boys talk, shall we?"

A guest in the house of her future parents-in-law, Esme was tolerant. But while Margie wittered about the new flocked wallpaper in the sitting-room, difficulties of managing with a daily woman just two half days a week and the highlights of Ivor's babyhood, she vowed things would be run differently in her house. Old Major Llewellyn might order *his* wife out of the room when it suited him, but Ivor would not do the same to her.

"Casserole of pork with Bramleys and potatoes, dear," Margie Llewellyn described the dish she bent to remove from the electric oven. "Ivor's favourite. I'll give you the recipe, before you go."

"How very kind," Esme murmured aridly. "Oh, and by the way," she added in more emollient tones, "I do love my ring. Thank you for letting me have it. I'm so proud of it."

"Oh, yes," Margie removed her oven gloves, eyeing the jewel on Esme's finger with something like regret. "Ivor was terribly keen that you should have it. I felt sure you'd prefer something modern . . ."

Involuntarily protective, Esme hid her hand behind her back. Should she offer to return the ring? She found she couldn't. It was hers now. Given to her fair and square. And the effort of acceptance had been made.

"Now," Ivor's father said some moments later in the small dining-room, "We've had a good old pow-wow, Ivor and I . . . Ha ha! We've decided the best place to have the wedding is at Woolwich. How's that? Eh? What?"

He said a great deal more in favour of that venue. The convenience of the guests . . . the magnificence of the mess . . . the long-standing family connection . . . the commodiousness of the garrison church . . . The only proper setting for a Gunner wedding.

"I thought it was *my* wedding," Esme interrupted, putting down her fork with a deliberate clink. Ivor's face, foreshortened as he leaned over his plate, communicated nothing.

"Of course it is, dear," Margie Llewellyn did her best to lubricate the moment. "Don't be so bossy, Edward." And then, turning again to Esme, "My husband's only trying to think of what will be best for everyone . . ."

"I'm sure he means to," Esme replied with a glacial smile. "But as hostess at my wedding, I think it's for Aunt Alice to decide what is best for *her* . . . and me."

"Well, that goes without saying, naturally," Ivor's father gobbled in his throat, his thin, dewlapped cheeks suddenly patched with red and white, "The casting vote rests with Dame Alice. But I'm sure she'll see reason . . . Ivor, pour some more wine. Let's try and get this girl of yours to relax . . . We're all family here, m'dear, eh? What?"

Esme concealed a grimace at her prospective father-in-law's toe-curling artificiality.

"You're marrying into the Gunners, Esme, dear," Ivor's mother urged. "That's something to be proud of . . ."

"I was quite proud enough to be marrying Ivor," Esme swept discord disarmingly from the table, "Never mind the Gunners."

Ivor beamed, slyly triumphant as his parents were caught in the chicane of Esme's charm. He knew she would never let him down. His father was a martinet but already she'd learned how to humour him. Just like his mother.

The conversation pursued other, less contentious routes until the cheese was on the table. It was then that Esme innocently remarked that she hoped wherever she and Ivor were posted after the wedding, whether he got command or not, that there would be stabling to enable a reunion with her mare.

"I don't think Aunt Alice will want her parted from her foal just yet, so that'll mean the two of them. Grazing will be critical . . ."

"I say, Ivor, old boy," Edward Llewellyn cut across her, falsely jovial, "All this is going to cost you a pretty penny, isn't it?"

"I know just how Esme feels," Margie darted in before Ivor could form some reply which would give no offence either to his fiancée or his father. "She wants a baby substitute before the real thing turns up. Do you remember how I used to drool over that boxer dog we had before Ivor was born?"

237

"What happened to the dog *after* Ivor was born?" Esme queried sternly.

"I don't remember . . . Oh yes, didn't we give him to the Chumleigh-Walters because we were going abroad? They took him on. Such a relief really."

"For the dog, I'm sure it was," Esme said quietly and luckily went unheard.

The visit wasn't prolonged much after that. It had been a strain for all concerned. Margie Llewellyn kissed Esme who tried not to go rigid at her touch. Her husband didn't attempt this intimacy but took his son aside for a private word. A stroll around the lawn and labour-saving shrubs.

"I hope you haven't bitten off more than you can chew there, Ivor. Oh, I know, she's something of a charmer . . . But she'll be a handful. Don't say I didn't warn you. I'd guess there's a bit of money there. Am I right?"

"I've never been given that impression," Ivor woodenly returned. His father wasn't listening.

" . . . Tends to make women tricky, does money. Your mother, bless her, never had a bean. And of course, I married her when she was eighteen. That young lady's what? Twenty-five . . . twenty-six? It's pushing it a bit, you know. Give her a family to keep her busy. That's my advice. She'll settle down. You know what your mother says . . . All's right with the world when there are nappies flapping on the line."

Backing the Mustang out of the narrow drive, Ivor's fixed expression was a match for Esme's own. It was she who had to do all the waving to the Llewellyns, who stood framed in the doorway of their home. Edward in his check Viyella shirt with the yellow-silk paisley cravat filling its open neck, leather patches on his worn tweed elbows . . . a grey toothbrush moustache, clipped precisely along his upper lip. Margie in an angora twin set adorned with her enamelled Gunner brooch, and short, tight tartan skirt.

It occurred to Esme that they'd never really left the army. They'd even bought a house that approximated to the kind of quarter they were used to, packing it with Dralon, silver-plated golf trophies and framed regimental photographs.

As a laurel bush obscured the pair from view, Esme turned to Ivor placatingly. "They were awfully kind . . . I hope I didn't behave as badly as I thought I did . . ."

"You'll have to excuse my father," he said. "A man's mind doesn't get much exercise when he retires at fifty. My mother's always spoiled him and let him throw his weight about. He's a tin god and she's never had the heart to knock him down. Sorry, darling."

"Don't worry about it," Esme smiled, completely won by Ivor's understanding. "You haven't met Aunt Alice yet. She can be pretty ghastly. It all depends what mood she's in."

The next weekend when the pilgrimage to Lowlough was made, Alice was in a mood for business. Ivor had no need to ask her for her niece's hand, but she would have taken grave offence had he omitted this ceremony.

His approach, Alice found, was satisfactory . . . his manners smooth enough without being slimy. Where had he been to school? Wellington College. The army's school which Alice considered adequate. Ivor had been under military influence since puberty. He'd been an army pentathlete as a subaltern, could ride, ski and shoot a little. Probably rather better, Alice decided, than he let on. Moreover he cut the cheese from front to back of the wedge in an intelligent and considerate manner. Yobs always cut it selfishly across the narrow bit.

"Will you excuse us, darling," Alice pushed her chair back from the Bedermeir table on the Saturday evening, "while I give Major Llewellyn a little digestive in my office. There're one or two things we should talk over."

Bracing himself to discuss his pay and promotion prospects, Ivor followed his hostess down the hall, admiring the accumulated patina of established, long-term occupation.

"Debts?" Alice rapped, pouring Ivor a stunning quantity of Remy Martin.

"None," Ivor spoke, his eyes fixed apprehensively on the glass Alice pushed towards him. "Look, Dame Alice, that's much too much for me . . ."

"Nonsense, man. By the time I'm through with you, you'll be ready for another. No debts, eh? Family money . . . property . . . savings? Hmm?"

Alice put Ivor through the hoop. He had nothing but his pay, promotion prospects and a few carefully nurtured, very small investments.

Waving these admissions aside, Alice acknowledged she had expected little else. Professional army officers, she said bluntly, were notorious for their poverty. Inculcated early with ideas about their station in life and paid too little to keep it up. Solvency was rare enough.

"This is what I intend to do for Esme," she went on. "You'd better know about it because it may help you with your own financial planning."

"There's really no need . . ."

Alice glared.

"Allow me to finish, young man, if you please.

239

"Under the terms of Esme's father's will, made in London before we all embarked for the Nightjar thing, any child of his marriage to my sister was to have an income of two thousand pounds a year on marriage. An empty promise, actually, quite typical of my brother-in-law. However, thanks to my brokers' management of the few hundred he had in his account, I'm able to deliver on it. Partially, anyway. Esme can have twelve hundred a year to dress herself, buy presents, and so forth. The remaining income I shall retain to augment the capital. I hope you'll find this helpful. I think a woman should have her own money, don't you? So much more dignified than having to hold her hand out for every wretched pair of stockings. Thank God, I've never had to do it."

Ivor found himself blurting thanks for something he himself was not to receive. He was unprepared for this and uncertain how to react. His mind slid past those embarrassing final moments with his father on the back lawn at Andover. How did a wife's money affect a husband's rights? His mother had always asked for everything she needed. She never seemed to mind.

Licking dry lips he said, "Does Esme know about this yet? I suppose she must do . . ."

"No. As it happens, she doesn't. I wanted to see how you took it first. Some men, you know, don't care for a woman to have the means of pleasing herself . . ."

"I assure you, Dame Alice, that I should never think of . . . I'm only too delighted for Esme's sake . . ."

"Good. That's settled then. In a year or two, I thought of transferring a slice of the equity in this place to Esme. Should save you some death duties when I go. Well, it's bedtime for me. You and Esme can suit yourselves. I imagine you'd like the wedding at Woolwich, wouldn't you? Slap up Gunner do. Up to you two, of course. But it'd save me hiring an hotel in Kendal. I'll tell the *Telegraph* to post the announcement on Monday. If you want *The Times* as well, you can pay for it. I don't go in for Communist rags myself."

Esme and Ivor headed the *Telegraph*'s list on the Court page on the day their engagement was announced. No competition from the Household Division. A stroke of luck and an optimistic omen.

The wedding took place in August, following the gracious acceptance of Esme's resignation, an early and excellent report . . . and the news that she was retiring as the WRAC's most senior subaltern.

"In fact," said the AG16 major now doing Philippa's old job. "There are bets on here at Stanmore, Esme, that you're the *army's* senior subaltern. You're quite a prodigy, you know."

240

A prodigy of stagnation, Esme thought.

"Did you know you were marrying the army's most notable nobody?" she asked Ivor on the night before his stag night. They were dining as Philippa's guests, at the Melrose Club with Aunt Alice. On Philippa's suggestion, Alice had taken out temporary membership to enable her to use the club as her own and Esme's pre-wedding headquarters.

At Woolwich there was far too great a risk of Margie Llewellyn attempting to intrude on the bride's party. Between her and Alice there was already considerable abrasion. Inept suggestions on the one side and vigorous set-downs on the other.

Poor Margie meant no harm. Having no daughter herself, she only wanted a share in her daughter-in-law-to-be's bridal preparations. But in the last days of her guardianship Alice was brutal in her possessiveness.

No, Alice firmly ruled, her niece would *not* deposit a wedding present list with any shop. Nor would such presents as the couple got be made available for inspection at the reception . . . An ostentatious habit that, best left to out and out vulgarians. Nor would pieces of wedding cake be posted to three hundred people overseas. Alice was already entertaining close on two hundred Llewellyn guests against her own and Esme's seventy-six. As for the flowers, they had long since been ordered from a West End florist to a scheme devised by Esme. Crimson tea roses, clove carnations, cornflowers and larkspur. Or in other words, the Gunner colours.

"Yes, but I think you'll find Ivor pays for the flowers, so I thought I might . . ."

"You are correct, Mrs Llewellyn," Alice thundered. "Major Llewellyn pays for what my niece has chosen."

Esme's dress? Mrs Llewellyn would surely understand this was a closely guarded secret. She would, however, have only one attendant. An unmarried lady of some consequence. The best man might be glad to know of this to ensure he spared himself any discomfiture by buying her a suitable present. If a hint was helpful, the lady in question had particularly admired a silver and emerald-green enamel powder compact available at Mappin and Webb. And if Ivor's best man stirred his stumps, he might have time to add the initial *P* picked out in diamond chips. At a pinch, Alice sniffed, marcasite might do.

Margie Llewellyn, and more particularly her husband, were quickly disabused of any illusions they might have cherished regarding the development of a familial cosiness with Dame Alice. She gave directions with the hauteur of Buckingham Palace.

"Anyone would think Ivor was marrying Princess Anne," Margie remarked bitterly to her husband after the latest telephone blast from Alice.

"It's up to Ivor to see she doesn't get above herself." Edward surveyed the empty gin decanter gloomily. The cost of living nowadays was monstrous. "He'll know how to handle her or he's not my son."

Margie shot her husband's back a look of loathing.

The wedding itself went off impressively. There is, after all, no bridegroom like a military one. Ivor, his best man and his ushers were caparisoned in blue tunics, tight-fitting trousers with red stripes, gold cross-belts, spurs and ammunition pouches. Esme, fragile seeming in her sheath of ivory lace, was misted in a trailing cloud of matching tulle, anchored by Lady Makepeace's family tiara.

It had arrived at the Melrose Club by special messenger, brought from the vaults of the old woman's London bank. It looked as though generations of Makepeace women had mucked the pigs out in it. A good scrub in gin improved it somewhat.

Departing for Woolwich in the first car with Philippa, Alice turned to Archie, who was to come on later, after seeing Esme herself away with General Vaughan.

"Well, old friend, d'you think he'll do? This Llewellyn fellow. Cast an eye over him for me, haven't you?"

Archie was unable to answer. His eyes were brimming. A wedding and a Nightjar reunion combined was one too many for him.

"Don't blub, man. You'll have me at it."

General Vaughan gave Esme away, a first meeting with him since she had been at school. It came as a surprise to her that he was now on the Army Board. But quizzing him about it didn't seem the most convivial thing to do on her wedding morning. In the small club drawing-room reserved for their use and in the car they talked of other things. Indifferent topics. Fortunately both Esme and her sponsor had seen a lot of plays lately. And of course the General's frock-coat order with sash, sword and gold-fringed epaulettes could be picked over, analysed in all its intriguing details.

Walking up the aisle with her he whispered, "We're going to close that sewer at Coldfleet down, you know. Heads will roll." And gave her arm a squeeze.

It had the right effect. Esme had looked a little forlorn but now her eyes blued over and her smile, when she met Ivor at the altar, was ravishing. She was laughing too, when she walked out on Ivor's arm to pass under an arch of swords, flashing in the sunlight.

In the mess the Gunner servants wore their powdered wigs and famous eighteenth-century liveries. The tables quivered with comestibles in aspic and the speeches were up to standard. General Vaughan had regretfully put aside the idea of telling the story of his first encounter with the orphaned bride. Moving but not funny. Instead he impressed upon the assembled guests the luck the Gunners had in acquiring a wife of Winstanley blood . . . which put a few Gunner noses out of joint. The luck, surely, was at least as much on Esme's side.

Alice, on the other hand, was satisfied. This was not so much an entertainment as a demonstration. A show of force to cow any who might think of undervaluing her niece. At times now, she felt she was getting old. Too old to take up the cudgels as she used to do. She had passed what weapons she had at her disposal into Esme's own hands. Scrimped and saved to do so. Inwardly, Alice celebrated her retirement from surrogate parenthood and blessed the buoyant price of timber. That plantation had stood them in good stead.

One wedding gift everyone could see, and another Esme told everyone about.

The first was the RHA badge that Ivor produced in the car which carried them the short distance between church and mess. Specially made by Garrard's Military and Shows department, it was platinum, *pavé*-set entirely with ten- and five-point diamonds except for the motto which was traced in minute sapphires. The materials weren't worth much, as Ivor pointed out with unnecessary honesty. But at least the piece was quite unique. There wasn't another exactly like it. He'd had the drawings destroyed. It was an exquisite little thing, full of fire and life. Fit for the grandest general's wife.

Worn on the lapel of Esme's going away suit it was eyed with beady calculation by every Gunner wife. Esme herself kept touching it to make sure it was still there. Not only was it precious, it represented so much of Ivor's time and care in planning this surprise. An investment of his confidence. An endowment of his soldier's uncertain fortune. She held his hand very tightly throughout the latter part of the reception, saying her goodbyes.

Philippa's gift was two years' country membership of the Melrose Club. It would give Esme a toe-hold in the capital. Under a roof not provided by the army.

"Change of scene when you want it, cobber."

"I say, Ivor," Edward Llewellyn pumped his son's hand just prior to the couple's departure. "It's not really on, you know. A wife's place is at home. Especially in the early years. I'd never have let your mother gad off up to Town whenever she felt like it. And that brooch, my boy. That's going it a bit, isn't it? Good thing you had that old ring of your mother's to give her, eh? Saved you a packet, I daresay. You'd better take it steady with a family in the offing."

"Thanks for everything, Father," Ivor replied, painfully conscious that his father had done next to nothing and spent even less. Ivor owed his education to a combination of army grants and scholarships.

Esme fought for words of gratitude that would not revolt her aunt. Nothing slushy.

"Aunt Alice, I don't know how to . . ."

"Don't try it, for Pete's sake," Alice interjected savagely. "I don't want to make a clown of myself, do I? Give me a kiss and get off with you."

Their embrace was fierce but not prolonged. Long enough, however, for Alice to mutter a cautionary word in her niece's ear.

"Take care of that husband of yours. He's softer than he looks. That runty little father of his will have the shirt off his back if you don't watch him. Nothing to worry about, just be aware, that's all."

Halfway along the South Circular road, both newlyweds became uncomfortably aware of an atrocious odour. They opened windows casually, at different times. Esme smoked a cigarette. Ivor, who rarely smoked himself, asked for one. The smell persisted.

"Look, Ivor," Esme said eventually, "No human being could be responsible for this. I don't know what's wrong, but it isn't us . . . not unless one of us needs a doctor."

Creased with laughter and relief, Ivor stopped the car amid infuriated honks from passing rush-hour traffic. A lengthy search of luggage resting on the back seat turned up two well-rotted kippers nesting in Ivor's new burgundy-silk pyjamas.

"Bloody puerile . . ."

"It's all right, darling. I should be terrified of pyjamas. Too nerve-racking for words . . . You bursting out at me like Punch and Judy . . ."

"Well, what were you planning on wearing," Ivor snapped, still distressed by the ruination of his lingerie.

"Myself," said Esme. "And so should you."

"I do love you, Esme," Ivor said simply, his anger all diffused.

They were late for their flight but they were first-class passengers and a honeymoon couple. Ivor had seen to it that British European Airways knew of it, not being an officer for nothing. The aircraft could give Major Llewellyn and his bride a few minutes' grace therefore. Arriving breathless on the plane after a sprint along Heathrow's corridors and a bumpy ride across the tarmac on an electric baggage trolley, Esme confided that she had some nighties too.

"Aunt Alice made me have them," she said.

"What are they like?" Ivor laughed at her, grateful that constraint about the looming nuptial night was over.

"Big christening gowns. Oh, Ivor . . . How much more champagne can I drink? I don't even know where we're going . . ."

"Nicosia. Cyprus. Staying at the Dome in Kyrenia. You'll love it."

It was the very last place Esme would have wished to go on her honeymoon with Ivor. There would be no real holiday from the army there. No holiday from lingering memories of Clive. He'd sent her a post card from Kyrenia. Her face fell for an instant but Ivor didn't see it. Ivor was a very happy man.

Esme revelled in the burning heat. Loved the tiny horseshoe harbour where fishing boats and yachts nodded sleepily on their moorings . . . Could have peered for ever from her balcony at the town's only minaret. A pepper-pot beside a dark, tall conifer, rising mysteriously from a private garden. It was the first time, and the first place in which Esme had seen the East play grandma's footsteps with the West. She searched, but never found the garden.

In the daytime she learned to snorkel and scuba-dive. Frolicking with Ivor in an element of mingled aquamarine and sapphire, enlivened with arrows of garnet, gold and green and jolly-striped boiled sweets . . . She cruised, lost to all earthbound ties one day, amid a herd of gentle, pink-finned beasts until her air was nearly out. Ivor was so angry. Frantic with terror and remorse. Why had he ever so much as turned his back on her?

"Oh, but Ivor. Those fish . . . They accepted me. They thought I was one of them . . ."

They dined each night at one of the Greek restaurants which lined the miniature corniche. Surrounded by the sounds of army voices. Drawls and peremptory quacks. It seemed as if the whole place was little more than a private resort for British army officers, their wives and girlfriends. Esme heard Clive's voice a dozen times. When she turned to see from whence it came, it was always from the mouth of a stranger. She saw him everywhere and found him nowhere. He melted into somebody quite ordinary at the touch of her thoughts. Ivor was always meeting people that he knew.

They drove up into the mountains in a hired car and watched the buzzards wheeling. Ivor pretended not to understand the map and said the vehicle was nearly out of fuel. Esme thought the buzzards were vultures and resigned herself to having her dying eyes pecked out.

In a remote village she took a photograph of some old men sitting outside a scrubby café in baggy, Turkish trousers. They were very angry and waved their sticks at her.

"They think you've stolen something from them," Ivor explained. "They want me to give them the film."

"No," said Esme. "I want the picture. Let's get in the car and get out of here."

Ivor gave them money. After some disgruntled negotiation, they let Esme take another picture. The risk to their souls was high but coin was coin. The momentary *frisson* of danger gave Esme a lasting taste for boxing up rare sights and carrying them away.

Sometimes after dinner they played bridge with other residents of the old colonial hotel, beneath the monotonous turning of the electric ceiling fans. Esme's style of play was wilder, greedier, more aggressive than Ivor's. But along with crushing defeats she brought off some brilliant coups.

"How could you bid five no trump with a void in your hand?" Ivor asked her one night as they undressed. "They must have thought you were stark, raving bonkers."

"You mean they were mad when they had to pay up. I'll never forget their faces . . ."

"But how did you do it? No one ever tries it . . . It's impossible . . ."

Esme shrugged her bare, bronzed shoulder coquettishly, stepping into the gritty bath-tub with its verdigris-embellished taps.

"I don't know. I just get a feeling in my water. A smell when they're downwind of me . . ."

"Esme, darling. It has nothing to do with the *people*. The only thing that matters is the lie of the cards."

Esme sucked her sponge and thought about the wiry limbed blond man she had caught staring at her from the stern deck of a yacht which had briefly dropped anchor that day in the middle of the harbour. It had been difficult to see from the quay but nobody had dairy cream coloured hair except Tiggy Johannenloe. That's why the yacht had weighed anchor so quickly and left. Esme was as certain of that on the slenderest of evidence as she was that the critical Queen of Diamonds had lain in the hand of Dummy's partner this evening and given rise to her remarkable triumph in the card-room.

"You mean the whole thing was a fluke," Ivor nagged. "Why can't you admit it?"

Esme offset a feeling of annoyance at having her victory downgraded like this by peeing pleasurably in the bath, a practice, she suspected, that Ivor would regard as grounds for divorce. She blamed her bad temper on Tiggy. If only he had kept away. If only Ivor had asked her where she wanted to go on her honeymoon instead of being so old fashioned and masterful. Of course, it was sweet of him.

Then there was love-making every night. That's what they were here in Cyprus for. To begin, as Ivor said, the learning process. He managed to make it sound like a crash course in grammar. Ivor was a

246

terribly responsible lover. There was nothing he didn't know about erogenous zones.

Towards the end of their two-week honeymoon, a full forty minutes after the by now customary bedtime argument as to whether the old-fashioned, noisy air-conditioning unit was to be switched on or off, Esme said, "Ivor, I am not a central heating boiler and you are not a plumber. Don't tinker with me. Just do it."

"You're not ready yet," Ivor assessed. "Too dry . . ."

"Honestly, Ivor, it's enough." Esme nuzzled him dutifully. "It's my thingummy and I should know."

"Vulva, darling."

The light dew of mild desire evaporated between Esme's legs.

Sitting up, disengaging herself from her husband's arms, Esme tried to explain that the seat of her sexuality lay in her imagination. That was her most sensitive erogenous zone. And no one could help her with it. It was no good. Ivor thought he was listening. Believed that he was trying to understand. But he didn't.

Sex became for Esme the bread and butter portion of her relationship with Ivor. For him it was the jam. A recipe that he continued striving to improve.

"Now then, gents," the Special Air Service sergeant smirked, "a little something to round off with. Very tasty."

Tiggy licked his lips. He didn't know the expression 'sickener' yet, but he was sure this was going to be one. A nasty surprise. There had been several already. These people were out to break his spirit, he knew that. The SAS weren't in business to select, only reject. What ever was good in the army, they'd more or less let on, they'd already creamed it. And it was very unlikely, every glance of theirs seemed to suggest, from trooper to CO, that they could be proved wrong. Still, anyone who reckoned they could carry forty pounds over sixty solitary miles of untracked mountain was welcome to try. And if a man's current CO was willing to back him for that trial and others, the SAS were willing to watch him fail.

There had been thirty such men, of all ranks and arms, here at the Hereford Barracks, a week ago. Now there were four. The rest had gone back to their units.

The four remaining hopefuls stood in an open-air enclosure ringed with hurdles, the circle broken only by some sort of large metal box structure. It betrayed not a clue to its contents.

Tiggy eyed it warily. He had an intense desire to join the SAS. It was an élite that no name or money on earth could buy his way into. The Household Cavalry was all very well and he'd enjoyed the life of a Deb's Delight although it had palled. Particularly after that uncouth business of Clive's.

On the whole, Tiggy was opposed to cruelty. Things were not quite the same between them since his old chum had married the hamster. There had been no need to behave *quite* so caddishly to Essikins. In Clive's shoes – Tiggy had mused over the matter – he would have resigned. Told the Colonel where to go with his rules and his regiment. It had scarcely been a case of King Cophetua and the Beggar Maid, had it? Darling Heart was actually rather respectable. In any case, pleasant as it was in the Silvershods, he'd always intended to hang up his party shoes some time. Get into some serious fun.

Tiggy, foppish in manner, slight of build, had insisted the Colonel put his name forward. He had been lifting weights for months. Very butch.

'A most unusual man,' the Silvershods' CO had written in his half-hearted recommendation. 'Speaks German, claims to know Russian and Serbo-Croat. Anything is possible with Captain Johannenloe.'

Rather damning that, Tiggy had thought, undeterred, when he'd sneaked a copy of the letter from the orderly room. And now this box thing.

"Self-catering, gents," the sergeant slid open the end of the box suddenly, with a grating noise. "Cooking from scratch, as it were."

Tiggy's gaze turned with the rest towards the dark aperture at the end of the box. From within, a rustling hoinking noise issued forth. Something alive. In a moment, an enormous pink pig ambled casually into view, flirting its white eyelashes as it came into the light.

"We've four of these ladies," expanded the sergeant chummily. "One for each of you gents. This one's Emily. Now who's going to kill her?"

One man turned away and vomited instantly. Tiggy closed his eyes. Oh Christ, no. The beast had a name. A nice looking, friendly pig called Emily.

"Come, come, gents," the sergeant was enjoying himself. "We can't always rely on Messrs Dewhurst, can we? Might be separated from our cheque books in the course of an operation. Might have lost our weapons too, mightn't we? But generally speaking a practical man can eat hearty. Let's not be squeamish, now."

Behind his closed eyelids, Tiggy hardened himself to the task. The name was all phooey. A ploy to add an emotional barb to an already unpleasant situation. Pigs, he told himself, were born to die. Alive they had no function. They didn't give milk or eggs . . . How could he possibly do this with his bare hands? Tiggy stepped forward. He had a strategy in mind.

The sergeant watched Tiggy intently while he made friends with the animal. It took a few minutes. In time, however, Emily seemed to rest her head on Tiggy's knee where he squatted, crooning and stroking, tickling underneath her chin with his left hand. Careful to avoid her arc of vision, . . . wider, he knew, than his own, he lifted his right arm high above her, prepared to use the edge of his hand as a blunt axe. *Now!*

"Well done, Johannenloe," a cultured voice on the other side of the hurdles said as Tiggy squirmed helplessly under the weight of the sow. She was snuffling at him stickily with her snout. "Don't worry, Emily is very specially trained. We shouldn't want any harm to come to her. She's part of the selection team. We'll show you how to do the job properly later."

Tiggy blacked out.

"Wot makes you think your so sooperior, Heinrich?" An evil-looking Yorkshireman, a trooper, heckled Tiggy after dinner that evening (not pork). "That's your name, in'it?"

"My Serene Highness, actually," Tiggy replied, outwardly cool. A mistake probably but he really was rather near the end of his tether. He hadn't been warned about this. SAS other ranks, apparently, were allowed to run a harrow over those who might be appointed to lead them. If they gave the thumbs down, the officer wasn't selected. That simple.

"We aren't bothered about yer sodding title here. Rank don't make much difference either. I wanna know if my life'll be safe with you if you and me was to be out on a four-man patrol together . . ."

"I take your point," Tiggy said politely. "However, until I *am* one of your officers, I believe I'm entitled to be addressed in the usual manner. Please don't accustom me to luxuries I may never enjoy in the future. I am so easily disappointed. A boyish weakness of mine."

Scattered laughter and muted cheers greeted this deft recovery. There were many more questions, but they liked him.

16

"Esme!"

Ivor flung his hat and cane on the hall table, his features working with vexation. "Esme! Where are you?"

In the drawing-room Mrs Horsfall, the Llewellyns' daily house-keeper, bent to insert the Hoover plug. The Major didn't sound too cheery. Funny, he didn't normally come home for his lunch . . .

"My wife here?" Ivor appeared, ram-rod stiff, in the drawing-room doorway.

"I think she's having a bath, sir. Came back from riding half an hour since . . . Can I be getting you anything, sir?"

"No," replied Ivor shortly. "No, thank you," he amended. "If you'd just be kind enough to go up and let Mrs Llewellyn know I'd like to see her down here as soon as she's ready, you can take the rest of the day off . . . It's all right, Mrs Horsfall," he added, noticing the woman's disquiet. "It won't affect your hours in any way."

"Right you are, sir. I'll finish the vaccing before I go . . ."

"No, no. Leave it. My wife will see to it. Just tell her I'm here, will you?"

Intimidated, Mrs Horsfall sidled from the room. Poor Mrs Llewellyn was going to catch it from the Major. Probably gone and put him in queer street at the bank. That was usually the way with the majors' wives. It was those joint accounts they had. Mrs Llewellyn was always coming back from auction sales with bits of tat . . . The Major called her Steptoe like that junk man on the telly. Lovely with her, he was, as a rule.

Ivor heard Mrs Horsfall go upstairs, tap on the bathroom door, exchange a few words with Esme and thud softly back down the stairs again. A moment later the bathwater begin to gurgle away down the pipes . . . He imagined his wife putting that rubber duck of hers back on the window-sill. Childish of her to keep the thing. Her moth-eaten teddy bear was as bad . . . Why did she cling to these totems of her childhood, he wondered. She had a husband now.

"I'll be off then, sir," Mrs Horsfall put her scarfed head around the door, anxious-faced and curious.

"What? Oh, yes. Goodbye, Mrs Horsfall."

Ivor sat down heavily, oppressed by the familiarity of the room. He had grown up in places like this. They were all the same or varied so little it made no difference. Two hundred and twenty-two square feet was the mean average allowance for a major's drawing-room.

It was only a major's quarter. Four bedrooms, one bathroom, downstairs cloakroom, two reception rooms, kitchen, larder, garage and garden. Emulsion paint, thin fitted carpets and unlined curtains except the velveteen ones in here. An inventory of G Plan furniture. Printed stretch covers on the sofas to look like chintz. The entitlement, no more.

A quarter like this was what your wife's energy, taste and wedding presents could make of it. Esme had done better than most, considering how little she could change. Bought some old oriental rugs, a few dark oil paintings with voluptuous frames and cracked china bowls fixed with rivets. She filled them with anything from moss to pebbles, sprayed them with water to show the colours. Eccentric but effective.

"How original," commented other wives doubtfully. "Esme's so clever." There were times when Ivor had loyally stifled a regret that Esme was not less original. That she would not plod contentedly along the safe tracks beaten by others. The downstairs loo, for instance, was lined with erotic Indian prints. The usual Giles cartoons and framed text of the Rudyard Kipling poem *If*, had been laughed to scorn by Esme. If Ivor's chums didn't know their creed by now, she said, they weren't going to revise it in her loo.

Esme saw the house with affection as her first married home. To Ivor it represented the deferment of his hopes. Expectations of carrying his bride across the threshold of a CO's residence had been disappointed.

Next time, his AG Branch had promised. They didn't want to burden him with a regiment in his first two years of marriage. There had been talk of getting the honeymoon over . . . Letting young Esme find her feet. Even at twenty-seven or twenty-eight, she would be very young to assume the duties of a lieutenant-colonel's wife. There was plenty of time.

Ivor complained to his patron, Lieutenant-General Chumleigh-Walters, who, fortunately, was commanding Wessex District now, in which Tidworth Garrison and Ladysmith Barracks lay. The current home of the 52 Medium Air Defence Regiment, RA, of which Ivor, with the best exterior grace he could muster, was 2ic.

It was a job he detested more than he could say. Not that he allowed his discontent with propping up an inferior man to show. Jack Cockburn's domineering wife had got him every promotion that he'd had. Managed him and his career as ruthlessly as a child star's mother. Not a woman to cross. And Esme had crossed her in the blaze of maximum publicity.

Did she know what she had done . . . How many months of sheer, tongue-biting endurance she had wrecked? Brown-nosing to that weaseling waste of rations, Cockburn . . . Ivor shook at the memory of the humiliation he had just undergone.

"Oh! Hello, darling. How nice to see you . . ." Esme entered the room sunnily. Dressed in evident haste she wore corduroy slacks and a sweater. "You're in here . . . Do you want a drink? I'll ask Mrs Horsfall to make you a sandwich . . . or an omelette . . ."

"Mrs Horsfall has gone home." Ivor rose to his feet. "I sent her."

Esme's eyes travelled to the abandoned Hoover, with its flex snaking untidily across the carpet.

"Oh dear. Did she feel ill or something?"

"No. I didn't want her here. Sit down, Esme. I have something to say to you. Or rather something to ask you first."

"All right," Esme shrugged fretfully. "But you sit down as well. I don't like being towered over."

"I'll do as I like in my own house!" Ivor turned on her. "You're my wife. Do you have to argue with everything I say?"

Esme paled. He had never spoken roughly to her before. Deep down, she had always known he had it in him. It was the reason, probably, why she had hesitated so long in marrying him . . .

"Please don't raise your voice to me, Ivor."

"I'm sorry," he said, putting his hands into his trouser pockets. "Let's try and deal with this sensibly. The damage is done. No point in shouting. We'd better see what you can do to mend it."

"Me?"

"Yes. What did you say to Cockburn's wife last night?"

"When?"

"Don't waste my time. Immediately after the performance. In the foyer of the Tidworth garrison theatre."

"I didn't say anything to Mrs Cockburn at all. She didn't say anything to me either."

"Come off it, Esme. No smart-arse tricks. You said something to Pauline Chumleigh-Walters and the Brigadier's wife. What was it?"

"Oh, I see. So that's what all this is about. All right. I'll tell you exactly what happened. Once upon a time in Tidworth, it was the fourth and last night of the garrison pantomime . . ."

"Stop it! I know all that. And I know you worked hard to produce it. Just cut out the comedy for once and tell me . . ."

"All right, all *right*!" Esme flung herself pettishly on the sofa and crossed her hands behind her head.

"The General's wife and the Brigadier's wife came over to me and Jennifer Cockburn. They said it had been a fantastic show. Aladdin had been wonderful . . . The Genie had been marvellous. The music had been great, the costumes had been exquisite, the children's chorus had been great and all the rest of it. Lighting effects, sound effects . . . You name it, they praised it. Jennifer said in that syrupy voice of hers, 'Oh, everyone's been *so* co-operative. I'm deeply indebted to my helpers. You can't think how useful Esme's been . . .' "

"So?" Ivor spun round to face her. "She acknowledged you . . ."

"Don't be stupid, Ivor. She was taking all the credit and tossing me a crumb. And I did it *all*. Damn it, she delegated the job to me in the first place. The whole thing. She said she was too busy with those carroty brats of hers and the Brigadier's wife expected somebody to take it on . . ."

"What did you *say*?"

"I said that I must have been extraordinarily useful to somebody who'd never attended a single rehearsal or so much as sewn on a sequin. Then I walked off. You saw the programme, didn't you? *Produced by Jennifer Cockburn* in big letters with *Assisted by Esme Llewellyn* in practically invisible italics underneath. *She*, of course, got the programme printed. The only thing she did do. That's what happened. So what?"

Inside his pockets, Ivor clenched his fists. He'd never previously felt an impulse to hit a woman. He couldn't believe he was feeling it now. He turned away from Esme, alienated by her truculence. She was throwing away their future all for a moment's pique. Criminal stupidity.

Of course, he'd told her to do the pantomime. Told her she'd have to do it. If she hadn't wanted to she should have kept her mouth shut at the Cockburns' dinner party when they first arrived. She'd said then that she'd been an amateur dramatics buff at school. Say anything in the army and you could guarantee it would boomerang. A clever wife cultivated the art of babbling refreshing sounds like a mountain stream. She should never, never say anything likely to be remembered. His mother never did.

254

Esme smarted. The pantomime was her first genuine achievement for years. The only visible end-product since she'd left university. Coldfleet Barracks' closure didn't count. They'd never put her name on that. But in those days she'd been paid. As a wife she did more than she ever had as an officer . . . The Wives' Club, the Thrift Shop, the Gunner Charities Sale of Work Committee . . . The Brigade Gymkhana Committee . . .

Ivor said she had to be on everything the Colonel's wife invited her to join. As the 2ic's wife she had to set an example . . . Free domestic help put her under an obligation . . . A suggestion from the Colonel's wife had the force of a command.

Of course, it was all blackmail, Esme knew. Even Ivor admitted it reluctantly. But senior officers' wives had tremendous influence over reports and promotions. Up to now Esme had gone along with everything to help her husband. The pantomime business had been too much. She couldn't make a doormat of herself for Jenny Cockburn's feet for ever. Surely they were allowed some dignity. Some recognition.

"Well," Ivor gazed out of the french windows overlooking the patch of garden, "I'll tell you what the pay off for your little tantrum is. Cockburn had me in his office just now. Sent the RSM to fetch me. Can you believe that?"

Esme sat up abruptly. Regimental Sergeant-Majors did not round up officers of field rank for the Colonel. Not even the Adjutant did that unless by way of courteously worded message. This really was an insult.

"*Fetch* you, Ivor?"

"Oh, yes. He had me practically frog-marched into his office like a squaddie. And then he told me, in full view of the Adjutant and the RSM that his wife had returned home in tears last night . . . hadn't slept and said she'd never been so insulted in all her life before . . ."

"*Her!*"

"Yes, her. My orders are, that you are to apologise to Mrs Cockburn. I am to order you to do so."

"But, Ivor," Esme was laughing now, "this is absurd. If it wasn't you telling me, I wouldn't believe you. You can't order me to do anything. He must know that. I'm not a Gunner . . ."

"Aren't you, Esme? I thought we agreed you were for any purpose that would help us both get what we want."

Esme's mind moved swiftly to her diamond brooch which lay upstairs in its red-leather Garrard's case. Ivor had a point. But there was a supposition here that she would always want what Ivor wanted at whatever cost. He never meant her anything but good. Only he never saw that her good might be in any way separable from his. Of course, it couldn't be. They were married. Yoked up for life. One turned, the other turned. One fell, the other halted. Esme saw it all so plainly.

She got up and walked across the room to place a hand on her husband's shoulder. Her touch made no impression on him.

"Look, darling, you are an idiot. Cockburn's overreached himself by a long way. He's hopelessly offside. All you do is seek Redress of Grievance. Or say you're going to. He'll back down. He can't go hauling you over the coals in front of junior officers, let alone the RSM . . ."

Ivor swung round, brushing her hand from his shoulder.

"No, Esme. Unlike you, I'm not a barrack-room lawyer. It does no good. You will apologise or we may as well use my confidential report for lavatory paper."

Esme still did not understand. Ivor was not the man to take this sort of treatment lying down. He was the 2ic. A substantive major . . .

"But *you* haven't done anything wrong. So he can't put it in your confidential report, can he? Ivor, it's not like you to be so slow . . ."

"He can do something just as bad. He can fail to mention my wife in my report."

Esme was confounded. Ivor lost no time in telling her, however, that the bearing of an officer's wife was always reported on, albeit in conventional code unless that lady's behaviour was considered unacceptable. In such a case she wasn't mentioned. The kiss of death to a man in line for a command appointment. The omission of Esme's name from the foot of Ivor's next report would sound the death knell for them both.

"You will apologise to that woman, Esme. You must apologise. You'd better get changed, go over to her house and do it now."

"No. I won't. I'm sorry. I've done everything I can. But I won't do that."

Esme made as if to leave the room.

"Where are you going?"

"To change, as you suggested, and then I thought I'd go up to London. Do the January sales . . ."

"You can't. You're not going anywhere."

Slowly, Esme turned back into the room, trembling as she spoke.

"Never tell me what I can or cannot do again. I am not your mother. And I hope to God you're not going to turn into your father."

Upstairs, Esme heard Ivor slam the front door behind him. Their first quarrel in four or five months of married life. There had been disagreements. Tiffs. Differences of opinion, but nothing up to now, that struck so destructively at the roots of their partnership.

Esme apologised. It was a week before she did so.

At least Ivor was able to say she was prevented from calling on the Colonel's wife because she was not at home. Called unexpectedly away on family business. He made her excuses with various hostesses and cancelled their own forthcoming cocktail party. A family crisis.

Nobody believed him.

The story was all over the officers' patch. Up and down the Mall where Jenny Cockburn's residence, Ladysmith House, was situated. Candahar House had it, Connaught House had it . . . Flagstaff House had first-hand knowledge as did the Chumleigh-Walters' palace at Ludgershall Court, a few miles off. Soon it was common gossip in the Naafi supermarket. And dissected by women having perms in the hairdresser's in Station Road.

By the time the story reached the soldiers' wives it had become somewhat garbled. Predictably fruitier too. Mrs Llewellyn had upped and left her husband. Money troubles, according to Mrs Horsfall who was their batwoman and belonged to the garrison Bingo Club. Well, she had those horses and whatnot hadn't she? And some lovely clothes.

She fancied someone else, more like, said others knowingly. Lance-Bombardier Dunwoody's little Terence had been in the children's chorus for the pantomime. And he'd let on that Mrs Esme, as she got the kiddies to call her, had been ever so palsy with the Genie. And who was he if he wasn't a captain in her husband's regiment? Caught them carrying on in the afternoon, had Major Llewellyn. Beaten his wife's bottom black and blue with that stick of his. Young missus hadn't liked it. Her first experience, poor thing.

"She should have my bastard," declared a sympathiser, with three grubby children clinging to her skirts and two in a pram, "Then she'd know all about it."

"S'all right for some, though, isn't it?" another griped. "If you've got a car of your own you can bugger off. Catch mine letting me learn to drive . . ."

Ivor was in the blackest despair. His house was empty, his nights were sleepless and his days in the regiment's headquarters building were torture. Far from ignoring him, Jack Cockburn addressed his 2ic with smiling villainy.

"Brace up, Ivor. Men have made useful contributions as majors, you know. We can't all expect high rank. It takes more than a quick brain and a pretty way with a swagger cane y'know. Got to have a wife with bottom. Bit of ballast in the situation. Get down on m'knees every night and thank the Lord for Jenny."

257

Knees? There were no depths to which the man would not sink in his orgy of gloating.

After an episode like this, Ivor sat alone in his office, ignoring telephones, cataleptic with misery. He could only think of excrement. Ramming handfuls into every orifice of Cockburn's.

He was no longer angry with Esme. She had done only a hundredth part of what he would like to do.

The sub-text of Cockburn's message was easily read. The Colonel could not fault his 2ic with the most devious will in the world. But Esme was his Achilles' heel. She had delivered her husband into his enemy's hands. Served his head up to Cockburn on a dish sweetened with honey.

It was the MO's wife who saved the day, by chance or diplomacy, no one but Esme ever thought to question.

When Esme returned home after an absence of four days, she found Ivor morose but resigned to her decision. No apology. Yes, he admitted, he was depressed. No, he didn't blame her. They would have to think very carefully about his future. Although the army constantly maintained that the skills of its officers would meet the demands of industry, Ivor doubted it. The only officers who'd resigned that he had ever met were pitiable men, reduced to selling insurance. Forced to beg their former friends to sign on Sun Life's dotted line.

"Frankly, I'd rather sweep the roads," he said.

Other ideas were aired. Everything from Ivor buckling down to read for a law degree in his spare time to mercenary soldiering.

At night he tossed and turned. Esme lay awake herself, rejecting and accepting guilt by turns. It took so many lies to keep *esprit de corps* alive.

One morning Esme was getting into the bull-nosed Morris shooting-brake which Ivor had bought to replace the Bean Can, when Mrs Horsfall came running out of the house. There was a telephone call from the MO's wife. As Esme liked her, she went back into the house.

"Were you on your way, dear?"

"Where to?" Esme racked her brains. "I was going shopping and then on to the stables . . ."

"I knew it. You've forgotten. It's my Blue Cross coffee morning today. You will look in, won't you? I know you've a soft spot for animal charities . . ."

Esme was quick to agree. Bored by charities on the whole, she would do anything for animals.

"Of course I will. Now? I've got old jodhs on . . ."

Anything, apparently, would do. This was not a formal coffee morning. Walking briskly across the patch, Esme smiled at the notion of 'formal' coffee mornings. A contradiction in terms to which army women appeared oblivious. 'Formal' meant compulsory. A parade of pearls, Alice bands and p's and q's.

The MO's front door was open and Esme walked straight in . . . straight into Jenny Cockburn. No escape was possible. The little hall itself was crowded, as were the drawing- and dining-rooms. Pauline Chumleigh-Walters was walking down the staircase. Conversation muted noticeably as news of the confrontation spread to those who could not see it. Esme Llewellyn was in social quarantine.

There was only one thing to do.

"Jenny, good morning," Esme thrust out her hand with the passionate sincerity of a Christian martyr committing herself to the flames, "I behaved very badly when last we met and I hope you will forgive me."

Jenny Cockburn, aware of the General's wife, had no alternative but to take Esme's hand. Churlishly she clasped it for an instant, communicating the coldness of her sweat to Esme's palm.

"Quite unnecessary," she said and left immediately. No syrup there.

"I'm glad you did that," Pauline Chumleigh-Walters murmured sweetly, casting a huge, silk square over her crisply-lacquered hair. "It's time we saw you and Ivor for dinner, isn't it?"

Small talk resumed at double volume. Esme was quickly surrounded by a phalanx of supporters now she had no need of them. Nobody, however, referred to the momentous incident. Esme, with her cup wobbling in her saucer, could never remember what was said. A babble of refreshing noises.

That night, while Ivor plunged up and down on her conscientiously, Esme wondered how to fake an orgasm.

When Ivor's confidential was handed him some months later it terminated in the words: *Major Llewellyn is ably supported by his wife, Esme.* The adjective 'charming' had been omitted.

Ivor fought it. 'Charming' was customary. Without the insertion of that word he would not initial the report. 'Charming' went in. Cockburn rocked insecurely on his throne, having put up a few blacks recently. He was in no position to submit to any kind of adjudication between himself and his 2ic. For the time being, at least, Jack Cockburn was well and truly routed.

Esme was humming snatches of the *West Side Story* song, in which the heroine celebrates a pleasing awareness of her own charm, for days afterwards. Habibi and her filly adored the tune, flicking their ears back and forth with delight.

"Cut it out," Ivor told her. "Or you'll have us back in the shit."

Dear Ivor. He took life very seriously. Dinner parties, for example, their composition, frequency and style, were a matter of deep concern to him. There were few weeks in which Esme did not entertain at home and fewer still in which they were not entertained elsewhere in the garrison. Anyone who hoped to be anyone was a remorseless dinner-giver. Esme joined their ranks largely ignorant of the intricate rules of the game. Learning to cook wasn't the half of it.

Mrs Horsfall could not cook what Ivor considered dinner-party food. And Esme found Ivor inflexible over the narrow repertoire he hounded her to perfect.

No venison, he ruled. Older wives would suspect it was horse and younger ones sob into their napkins over Bambi's demise. No veal for similar reasons. Nothing chopped, diced or minced. The army liked its meat joined up. Fish, except as a separate course, put everyone in mind of catholicism . . . Of course some people were left-footers, Ivor conceded testily, but it was better not to dwell on it. Rabbit, no matter how good, was cheap. Hare was too adventurous . . . In fact, better stay off game altogether. It smacked of cruelty and snobbery. Where joints were concerned, there was to be a total avoidance of bones to facilitate carving. Pork? It was too closely connected with tapeworms. It was no good appealing to reason. Toes were not to be trodden on.

That left chicken, leg of lamb and fillet of beef. The same food that everyone else produced.

Esme embarked on a relentless routine of stuffing, boning, and rolling. Many were the mangled chicken's corpses that hit the pedal bin in the early days. Equally numerous were the blackened pastry cylinders enclosing raw, bloody fillets of beef that Ivor sliced and served with apologies. 'Boot', as Beef Wellington is termed in the army, wasn't his wife's strongest wicket.

Root vegetables were not *officers'* vegetables, Ivor stressed earnestly, the evening Esme produced creamed parsnips with nutmeg. Of course they were delicious, but what had that to do with it? If she wanted to be creative, she should work herself off on the puddings.

"I see," Esme snapped on that occasion, eyes filling, "I can give myself a thrill with a sugar thermometer, can I?"

"Esme, *please*," Ivor expostulated. "This is important."

Accepting that, Esme broke out in another direction.

Coming home one late afternoon with thoughts of a gin and tonic before bathing and changing into his dinner-jacket, Ivor was in time to see the barracks men huffing and puffing to carry the G Plan dining-table out of the door. Up a bit, back a bit . . . to the eye of a passer by, quite comedic.

"What the hell are you doing with that?" Ivor was unamused. Two and a half hours to go before his six guests presented themselves at seven thirty for eight . . . and this lot were messing around with his furniture.

"Your lady wife, sir," stated the foreman with dignity, "has haquired han hantique."

"Oh, has she," Ivor muttered grittily. "Put that thing down. Wait here."

"Well, I don't know about that, sir. S'knocking off time for the lads . . ."

"Do as I say."

Ivor entered the house through the back door and called out to his wife.

"In here, darling," Esme answered him happily.

He found her in the dining-room busily arranging cutlery, glassware, napery and candlesticks on a round table surrounded by eight pretty balloon-back Victorian chairs. The G Plan ones were stacked in the hall awaiting imminent removal. Ivor was simply aghast. Esme, standing back to admire the effect of her work, imagined his expression a prelude to joy.

"Much better, isn't it? The chairs were a bit of an extravagance. They always cost more when there's eight . . ."

"What's all this," Ivor gasped. "What on earth's going on?"

Surprised, Esme explained. The table, a bargain she'd bid for at a local sale, was dated about 1840. It was just a little heavy to be truly elegant, perhaps, but a practical size. The reddish mahogany was beautifully figured . . . and in perfect condition with this very nice bit of box-stringing . . .

"You'll have to get that thing out of here," Ivor voiced his disapproval forcibly. "What in God's name do you think you've been doing?"

She'd been buying some furniture that didn't make her sick to look at it, Esme hotly retorted. Something with some personality and quality. She was tired of the institutional stuff and had always wanted a round table. Much more friendly and intimate.

"*Friendly?* What about the seating plan . . ." Ivor was next door to speechless . . .

"No need to worry about that," Esme whipped a piece of paper from a drawer in the G Plan sideboard. "It's exactly the same. It just doesn't feel so stiff . . . You see. Lavinia is still on your right, look. And so on round the table and you end up opposite me . . ."

Kicking the dining-room door shut with his heel Ivor made it clear that not only did he not care for major alterations to be made to his home without prior discussion, but that whatever she said, a round

261

table blurred the significance of the *placement*. The precedence of the guests was less clearly defined . . .

" . . . If they can all see each other and talk to each other at more or less the same time. If the conversation can flow in any direction . . ."

"If you know, why do I have to tell you?"

Esme and Ivor exchanged pugnacious stares like two furiously contending cats. By the time they were done with each other Ivor had won. Time was passing and there was need to attend to the oven. Guests, however unwelcome, could not arrive to find their hosts locked in a dispute over the shape of their table and a total absence of food.

The barracks men, civilians who bowed to no god but the clock, had gone with their van. It was quite a while before Ivor fully forgave Esme for the Laurel and Hardy contortions that followed. The Victorian furniture was inched into the garage somehow, the G Plan restored and re-laid in an atmosphere scenting strongly of sulphur. The guests were on time, Esme and Ivor were changed but only just, and the dinner was late.

Throughout the preliminary cocktails and the meal, Esme ladled on charm spiked with satire and refused absolutely to catch her senior female guest's eye and lead the ladies away to her bedroom before the port circulated. Why should she? They never talked about anything but their ovaries.

"And the men were all that interesting, were they?" Ivor challenged after all the guests had gone home.

"Not remotely."

There was no meeting of minds about either the outdated custom or the furniture until three o'clock in the morning. It was then that Ivor decided that there should be a meeting of bodies. Although the sun had gone down on their anger it had better not rise on it.

Marital problems were best solved in the bedroom, he deposed, putting conciliatory arms around Esme. She persuaded her rigour to melt. Ivor was usually right about everything. She shouldn't have sprung the table on him. He said she could buy an antique one with pleasure as long as it was rectangular. She loved Ivor very much, she reminded herself.

Towards the end of their tour with 52 Medium Air Defence Regiment, RA, Esme and Ivor had entertained and been entertained by everyone who mattered on the Staff List. Husbands with *psc* after their names – (which meant 'Passed Staff College' and was the *sine qua non* of significant promotion) – and quite a few who hadn't. Makeweights whose company Esme generally enjoyed more than that of more ambitious men and their wives. By and large, their speech was less guarded and their interests broader.

Nonetheless, friendship was pretty much of an outsider on the dinner party circuit. It was all about pushing, Esme said. Ivor was displeased with that description of their social activities. Pushing was what captains who attempted to return their Colonel's hospitality were guilty of. The Llewellyns, by contrast, were simply making bridges . . . laying down firm foundations for the future.

In spite of their exalted rank, the Chumleigh-Walters came as family friends. But no one, Ivor dictated, could be invited with them except his parents and the Cockburns. To expose the Chumleigh-Walters to eager beavers of lower rank would put the General in a difficult position.

With such a hideous evening in prospect, Esme drank rather more than she should have done. When Chumleigh-Walters complacently announced that he never read for pleasure Esme said brightly, "What do you do in bed then? Carpentry?"

A crater of silence gaped before Margie Llewellyn, the first to compose herself, changed the subject. Soon the table talk was redirected into its familiar rut. Reminiscences of the autobahns of Germany. The cheapness of motor cars and liquor there. The near impossibility of living without the overseas allowance. Comparisons of ferry ports.

During what Ivor called the 'debrief' later, Esme found it difficult to convince him that her ill-conceived joke had been without prurient intent. Giving her the benefit of the doubt at last he implored her to think before she spoke.

A period of adjustment is how Ivor described their two years in Tidworth. Having prepared for marriage by reading a comprehensive list of manuals, he was well informed. Moodiness was to be expected in women of breeding age. Far less need be ascribed to individual temperament than to hormones, he kindly assured his wife. She shouldn't worry. That business with the table, for example, he told her, had been a classic display of nesting behaviour. It had been mid-month, hadn't it? Probably linked with ovulation. With hindsight he could laugh about it.

Ivor was boundlessly understanding. For nearly every attitude of Esme's he had an explanation until she began to see herself as pre-determined entirely by bio-chemistry. Mind and spirit were immature illusions. Dreams of youth.

Attempting to rediscover them, Esme took up her Greek again. But no span of interrupted hours in which to reacquaint herself with the oddity of the script and idiom was allowed to her. The telephone was always ringing. Between her horses, committees, welfare work and social treadmill, there was no time for immersion. Only shallow paddling. Thoughts of perhaps doing an external MA with London University dissolved and hopes of getting a part-time teaching job were quickly scotched by Ivor.

Jack Cockburn forbade 'his' wives to work. In this he was supported by the Brigadier. Working wives and private housing were against the spirit of soldiering. Women's jobs threatened the cohesion of the military community. Mortgages disabled an officer from spending his money with becoming freedom. Absorbed too much of his energies in selfish home improvements and perpetual trouble with tenants.

"I didn't ask you for a house," Esme countered. "I thought if I could have a job . . ."

"Esme, darling, do try to be realistic. It really isn't possible, you know."

She advanced the case of the captain who had played Genie in the pantomime. His wife was a doctor. And she did locums in the district from time to time. Nor did she make any secret of it. Neither Jack Cockburn nor her husband could expect her to mothball those skills. It would be a scandal.

"It is a scandal," Ivor agreed. "She's ruined him. Her husband may be promoted but he'll never get command if Jack has anything to do with it. Be a little patient, darling. With any luck, our turn will come. It shouldn't be long now."

Biting back a torrent of invective against her enslavement by the Cockburns, Esme faced the fact that it was Ivor, not her, who felt the lash most keenly. He who, hour by hour, felt the harness rubbing and complained much less than she did.

In Tidworth there was no repository into which Esme could safely spill her anger. The majors' wives all knew Jenny Cockburn too well. Older than Esme by ten years on average, they were as friendly as envy of her untrammelled childlessness and svelte figure would allow. Suspicious of her education as of her open-handed way with money, they consoled themselves with the thought that motherhood would change her. They said that to each other and to Esme at coffee mornings with smugly prophetic smiles.

"Wait till you have a baby," they sighed mistily. "You'll be a completely different person. Motherhood makes you far less selfish."

Esme's tart rejoinder was that she did not *want* to be a completely different person. And, privately, yearned to re-establish contact with the person she used to be. A small adjustment to a record stylus slipping in its groove.

The captains' wives, on the other hand, were burdened with very young children, struggling and mostly failing to maintain an appearance of domestic trimness in three-bedroomed, semi-detached houses. The 2ic's wife was a social wild card who didn't share their problems. They liked her but they were wary. Esme had a sharp and ready tongue which she might deploy to their husband's disadvantage in the more senior circles to which *her* husband's rank gave her access. For a time there had been the lady doctor . . . But that couple were posted away to Benbecula in the Hebrides, a million miles distant from the army's epicentre. The direct result, Ivor said, of their defying Jack Cockburn's prohibition on working wives.

Falling back on a correspondence with Philippa, Esme soon refrained from asking Ivor to put her letters in the orderly room post tray. What did she find to write about? Married women, he conveyed without actually saying it, should loosen their ties with female friends. A wife's best friend was her husband.

"But Ivor you never *talk* to me these days . . ."

"What do you want to talk about?" Ivor evinced surprise.

Not the first woman to receive that answer to a plea for mental and emotional communion, Esme was stuck for a reply.

"Well, anything . . ."

"No, you have to give me a definite subject," Ivor sat down opposite his wife, elaborately attentive. "Come on, I'm listening. Talk to me about something."

Defeated, Esme told herself it was her fault. Ivor had made an honest effort. When he was out at mess nights, affairs from which Esme was now excluded, she and Philippa had long chats on the telephone.

Curled up on the sofa in her dressing-gown, fortified by whisky and with all three bars of the electric fire blazing, Esme enjoyed hearing the WRAC parish pump talk. Retirements, postings, promotions, marriages and scandals . . . Discussions about the arbitrary restrictions placed on army wives. Philippa was generous with her condemnation in a way that Ivor wasn't.

"Now, darling, please," he'd said to her one day as they left for a week's holiday in Scotland, to be followed by a few days at Lowlough, "promise you aren't going to go on and on about Jack Cockburn. Give it a rest for the next ten days. I need to get away."

A perfectly reasonable demand on the face of it. It seemed less reasonable when Ivor complained of the phone bill and expressed resentment when Esme admitted that calls to Philippa accounted for much of it.

"I have to talk to someone, Ivor."

"I don't see why. And I don't want that woman involved in our marriage. You're enough for me and I had hoped that I might be able to satisfy you."

It kept cropping up, this mutual sufficiency thing. And every time Esme was cornered. If she didn't reassure her husband that he was all in all to her, he would be devastated.

Attracted one day in the Post Office by a cloth-bound manuscript book, Esme bought it. It was pleasant to handle and its wide, white, feint-ruled pages proffered a welcome of some sort.

"What's this for?" Ivor enquired, picking it up off the kitchen table where Esme had left it temporarily whilst unpacking the rest of her shopping.

"I'm not quite sure, really. I thought I might write in it, you know."

"Oh? What, for instance?"

"Things that happen," Esme shrugged, uncomfortable with this quizzing over her purchase. She really hadn't decided what she might do with the book. "Maybe things that I think."

"I see. A do it yourself confession kit . . . Or another pal to complain to. The Esme Llewellyn Book of Whinges."

"For God's sake, Ivor," Esme took the book from his hand and pushed it into a drawer. "I might use it for recipes . . . Leave me alone."

The excitement Esme had felt in this small, intimate and as yet unformed project was unaccountably spoiled by Ivor's interest. She felt herself to have been caught red-handed in the promulgation of a disloyal liasion. Writing was betrayal . . . playing away.

Ivor's interest in the most mundane aspects of Esme's daily round was omnipresent. He steered or attempted to steer her most trivial activity. There were innumerable instances.

Esme disliked shopping at the Naafi in Tidworth. It never had anything in. The shelves, poorly stocked, were slovenly and the prices outrageous. She went into Salisbury instead.

"Officers' wives are expected to support the Naafi," Ivor hectored her. "It's bad form to take your business elsewhere. Jenny Cockburn's on the Naafi committee . . ."

And: "Why don't you get one of those wicker baskets the other wives have?"

Astounded that her husband should notice such things, Esme remarked that those baskets were useless. You could get hardly anything in them. Pauline Chumleigh-Walters had a pretty one, she reflected aloud, but considering she was usually entertaining parties of up to twenty several times a week, she must shop in relays. Come to think of it, the size of the basket was in inverse proportion to the status of the officer's wife . . .

Ivor bought Esme a basket. It remained in the kitchen, becoming a store place for plastic bags from the supermarkets.

"Why don't you ever wear a headscarf?" He asked her this whilst they walked around the Tidworth Garrison Gymkhana, on a fine summer's day, greeting other men and their wives who were all encumbered with this form of headgear.

"I don't really like them," Esme said. "They don't suit me. I don't know how people keep them on, anyway."

A few weeks later, Ivor bought Esme two very expensive head squares quite as if she'd never mentioned her aversion to them. She wore them like stocks round her neck with a gold stock pin thrust through them. He protested. She said:

"Please, Ivor, don't try and put me into uniform. I don't want to be a copy of somebody else."

But a copy was what she was required to be and not only by Ivor. After a Beating of Retreat, one evening, when Esme had sat with other officers' wives and VIPs in the front two rows of armchairs ranged alongside the parade ground, Jenny Cockburn had kept leaning forward and craning her neck to stare at Esme's diamond RHA brooch fixed to the neckline of her cocktail dress.

Repairing to the powder-room in the mess once the band had marched off, Esme encountered Jenny Cockburn there squirting herself with Madame Rochas.

"Esme," she said, "I know you won't mind me saying this . . . After all, you're so young . . . But it's not really done to outshine senior officers' wives, you know. If you take my advice you'll take that brooch off. I know it was a wedding present, but get Ivor to buy you something quieter until you're further up the ladder. It's just a matter of tact . . ."

Without a word, Esme unpinned the brooch and slipped it into her bag.

"Where's your brooch?" Ivor threaded his way across the crowded ante-room to her, his eyes full of panic.

"In here," Esme patted her bag. "The catch was loose." She had learned not to pillory Jenny Cockburn too much or too often. There was less than two months to go before Ivor's last confidential and posting were due. He'd had as much as he could take. Esme knew it was up to her to help share the load just now when weariness made it heaviest.

She announced her pregnancy to the regiment at large on the night of the last ladies' guest night she was ever to attend in the Ladysmith Barracks mess. At the time of telling, an expedient lie which proved to be the truth within a week.

Jack Cockburn sat over the table till well after midnight as usual. Nobody, male or female, military or civilian, might quit the table for any purpose whatever until the Colonel himself rose. Jack had always enjoyed watching his officers and guests succumb to urinary torment. A test of character.

It was all right for the men. The servants passed them empty claret bottles under the table. On this occasion the captain sitting next to Esme gallantly declined the receptacle, confiding that the noise might set her off when he was powerless to help her. There was no room for prudery on these occasions.

The loyal toast had been drunk over two hours ago. The port had circulated several times. The band had stopped playing. The Band Master had taken his customary glass and departed after a trio of pipers had concluded the musical programme. Liqueurs had come round on a trolley. Coffee cups had been frequently refilled and coffee was now being refused along with every other fluid. Conversation had guttered as low as the candles while the company focused exclusively on bladder control.

Ladies' guest nights happened twice a year, and between one event and the next most people forgot how they would end with Cockburn in the chair.

So desperate was Esme that she decided that if it cost Ivor his career, she couldn't pass water where she sat. Rising, she walked towards the door watched by the horrified gathering. Llewellyn's wife must have a death wish, was the unspoken, universal thought. Meanwhile Esme in her long-sleeved, lace wedding-gown, now dyed royal-blue, was combating a convulsive desire to hobble. A subdued cheer from the subalterns crowned her efforts as she reached the door.

Nobody, suddenly, gave a damn for Jack's authority. In moments the powder-room was thronged with moaning, cross-legged women, thanking God that somebody had done something. Good for Esme.

"I don't think Jack will appreciate this," Jenny Cockburn snapped, pushing past Esme as she emerged from the loo.

"If he's a man at all," Esme said for no real reason, "it might make a difference to him if he knew I was pregnant."

It made all the difference. The army is barmy about babies. Esme's health was drunk in champagne and Jack Cockburn actually apologised. He was apt to forget about ladies' plumbing, he said.

"How long have you known?" Ivor accused her bleakly on the way home. "I wish you'd told me first . . ."

"Oh Ivor, you can be so thick sometimes. Of course I'm not pregnant. But by the time Cockburn hears of it we'll be away from here. What did you want me to do? Dump gallons of pee all over the shop?"

But, to Ivor's unspeakable delight, Esme was pregnant. Had been for a couple of months. She was always vague about her cycle. And to crown it all, he didn't have to do the usual staff job before his next regimental appointment. The CO-designate of a Gunner outfit in Bulford sustained disabling injuries in a car accident and Ivor got the fox's brush instead. Chumleigh-Walters had fixed it.

"I told you it would all be worth it, didn't I?" Ivor buckled on his Sam Browne jubilantly in the hall after breakfast while Esme threw up in the cloakroom. "This won't go on for long, you know," he said sympathetically. "You'll be feeling A1 fit again by the time march out's due."

"March out!" shrieked Mrs Horsfall on her arrival half an hour afterwards. "Gordon Bennet! And you expecting . . . You have a lie down, lovey, and I'll make a list."

The list, when she presented it to Esme, consisted of eight pints of vinegar, five of methylated spirits, a half of petroleum spirit, four bottles of domestos and several pounds of washing soda. All for a cleaning operation, which must apparently begin at once. Unless Esme and the Major were going out tonight, supper had best be cold. A preliminary strip-down of the cooker was essential.

By lunchtime Mrs Horsfall, an experienced army daily, had demolished the cooker with the slickness of a fully-trained recruit dismantling a rifle. Components were soaking in buckets of concentrated alkali by teatime. Army property had to be handed back to Barracks in new condition no matter how old it was. Then the curtain rails came down . . . for a good going over with Brillo. Twenty-five days to achieve total sepsis.

"You'll get used to it, dear," Margie Llewellyn remarked on the telephone. "I did it eighteen times between marrying Edward and retiring."

17

The wife of a lieutenant-colonel in command comes as close to queenship as an ordinary woman ever gets. As her husband reigns over eight hundred men, so do their wives and families look to her for succour and example. Or so the army likes to think.

She has her servants; a staff of five part-timers in those days, provided by the army. She has her coach; an olive-green staff car put at her disposal complete with driver. She has her palace; Kowloon House was three times the size of the old Tidworth quarter. A red-brick Edwardian residence, it sat in an acre and a half of garden behind stone-coped walls with wrought-iron gates in front and wooden ones behind. The latter gave access to a stable-yard comprising three loose boxes, other outhouses and, best of all, an adjoining paddock complete with shade trees and water supply. Perfect accommodation for Habibi and her two-year-old offspring, much handled but as yet unbroken.

And like every other queen, Esme had her court. The 2ic's wife and four other majors' wives roughly equated to ladies-in-waiting. They co-opted lowlier handmaidens from further down the line.

Of officers' wives in total there were thirty. With the senior NCOs' wives, forty-seven names with linked official identities to memorise. Not gradually, not in the course of growing aquaintanceship . . . not if Ivor Llewellyn had anything to do with it. No time like the present for him.

He gave Esme a test, sitting up in bed after a long day spent 'marching' in . . . Removal vans, MFO boxes, barracks men with clipboards and a brouhaha over the vile 'teak effect' issue bookcase-cum-bureau-cum-drinks-cabinet that Esme refused to live with.

The officers' wives would start calling on her tomorrow and then she must visit the senior NCOs' wives, starting with the RSM's. These preliminary ceremonies, Ivor said, should be completed within a month at the most. A fortnight if she could manage it. As Ivor saw it, the fact of Esme's three-month-old pregnancy should not impede her in the fulfilment of her duties so long as she continued fit.

"What's the Quartermaster's wife called?"

"Er, that's Major Finn . . . Doreen."

"Good," Ivor approved, cradling a whisky against his black-furred chest. "The 2ic's . . .?"

"Petra," Esme yawned. That was the easy one. Petra McKinnon would be making her presence felt tomorrow. She would be coming to welcome Esme to the regiment . . . to 'help' with any remaining unpacking and take the measure of the Llewellyns' possessions. By now Esme knew the form.

Ivor was down to the married subalterns' wives when she fell asleep. Getting no reply to his last question, he glanced sideways to where her head lolled on the pillow. Poor old thing. She'd soldiered on all day without a break. Command was going to suit them both very well. She'd have her work cut out and so would he. Lots to do, to make 45 Light Field Artillery the smartest regiment with the highest morale in the whole Royal Regiment. That was the aim, nothing less.

Make a roaring success of this job, he'd told her, and the next step, promotion to full colonel, would come quickly. True, it would be a dreary, pen-pushing staff job next time and for a while they'd lose all this grandeur. But red tabs on Ivor's collar would be a consolation. There was nothing like red tabs. The distinguishing mark of the General Staff, they showed you were really on your way. After that, only three more ranks to lieutenant-general. With any luck, Ivor reckoned, he could do it by the time he was forty-eight. Earlier if only there was war. A pity there was little hope of that.

This new Ulster rumpus was no use. Actions in aid of the civil power fell to infanteers and armoured regiments, not artillerymen. Subduing a civilian rabble was disreputable work for soldiers, in any case. A unit was lucky to get out of a can of worms like that without disgrace, let alone with honour. No, there was nothing for him in Belfast.

Suffering as she still occasionally did from nausea, Esme didn't get up for breakfast. Ivor came up to say goodbye to her. A smooth-chinned, after-shavey kiss and copious verbal memoranda.

He would send her a year-planner chart across from the barracks, then they could co-ordinate their engagements. Weekly diary conferences to start with. Esme had better choose one of the six spare bedrooms for a study. She would need it and he would get her a telephone extension put in there. He would use the downstairs study. He would dine in mess tonight to get to know the subalterns . . . Tomorrow was the brigade cocktail party . . . He was looking forward to seeing her in the new, blue-velvet sack job . . . Could she make a start on roughing out a dinner-party schedule? . . . She would know who ought to come first. Important to establish viable relationships with the armoured division people. She must get a grip of the Wives' Club but Petra McKinnon would give her a steer on that. Remember, delegation was the secret . . . which didn't mean neglect. Oh, and she mustn't forget her exercises. How precise could she be about the baby's advent? Mid-September was likely to be crowded . . . Better pencil the baby in, however, and firm up the details later.

Queasily, Esme grinned. Had he any idea how funny he sounded?

"All right, darling, I'll pencil the baby in."

"Good. Feeling any better yet? You can expect Petra McKinnon round any time after half past ten. I'll send the car back from the office for you if you want to start on the NCO patch after lunch . . . I shan't need it."

"Nor shall I," Esme said. "If I go I'll drive myself. Better to arrive in a friendly way than *de haut en bas*. Anyway, I shall ring the NCOs' wives before I go and ask if it's convenient. They won't want me walking in on them with their husbands' Y fronts draped on the radiators . . ."

"Good thinking. Well, I must get cracking. Right . . . Bye."

Ivor descended the broad, shallow stair-treads whistling. Esme was going to be very good at this. She was really shaping up. Marking time at Tidworth had been a good investment, after all.

He devoted the rest of the morning to a conference with his majors. Pads and sharpened pencils, carafes of water and self-preserving faces were ranged around the board-room table. It rapidly became clear that Ivor intended to orchestrate the regiment's life at a greatly accelerated tempo.

Questioning his officers closely, Ivor winkled out the grey areas, making rapid notes. Changes and improvements. The FFR inspection was two months away, by which time, he informed the meeting, 45 LFA would be running like a Swiss watch movement and be a damned sight shinier too.

The practice of wearing open-necked Vyella shirts with woolly-pully order would cease forthwith. All officers and senior NCOs would wear poplin shirts and ties unless on exercise. Sloppy turn-out meant sloppy work. No officer in future would use his rank to persuade the barrier piquet to allow his car to pass unchecked. All personnel would dismount, open their boots and bonnets whether it was raining cats and dogs or not. Against bombs, as against complacency, there was to be sleepless vigilance.

He went on to outline a brand-new fitness programme aimed at the HQ battery staff. Middle-age spread, the curse of sedentary men, was to be eradicated. Early morning runs until further notice. Ivor himself would run. In the absence of weekend Rugby and soccer fixtures, there would be internal friendly games. Every man and officer was to be on a team of some sort. No exceptions, no excuses.

Ivor would personally conduct lightning swoops on the regiment's obscurest nooks and crannies. Naafi canteen, padre, chippy, sports store . . . No department was too small to interest him . . . and none, Ivor was sure, would require any warning. From now on, every day would be judgement day. Smartness, smartness, smartness.

And finally, Ivor's door was always open. Any officer with a professional or personal problems shouldn't hesitate to confide it. He'd always believed that a CO failed completely in his role of father to the regimental family if his officers were afraid of him.

Everyone was terrified. The regiment crept about its routines, muffling sound as far as practicable and limiting movement. Anything, in fact, which might attract the unwelcome searchlight of Ivor's patriarchal curiosity.

"The king is dead," muttered the Chief Clerk to the RSM, "Long live the effing yard-brush."

Colonel Llewellyn was going to sweep indecently clean. The news, which swept like a forest fire through battery offices and barrack blocks burst upon the families by evening. Husbands of every degree were tense. The old jogging along days were finished. The regiment was about to have its teeth rattled by a military shit. A bloody Horse Gunner.

"What's *she* like?" enquired the mistress of virtually every quarter.

"Dunno," was the specimen reply of Lance-Bombardier Snoddy, "A bloody dragon if she's anything like 'im." He glanced discontentedly round the poky kitchen's streaming walls. "Can't you get that fucking mould off? This place is always in shit order."

Before the night was over the MPs were called out to mediate between the Snoddys.

It was Esme who softened Ivor's impact.

Too driven a man to love, the regiment came quickly to respect him. They nicknamed him Zebedee after the springed puppet on *The Magic Roundabout*. A television programme for children, it had become an army cult. Zebedee jumped high, out of sight . . . and landed when and where he was least expected.

274

Overhearing a gaggle of subalterns refer to Ivor this way, when waiting for her change at a local petrol station, Esme quite often used the name herself among the officer cadre. Speaking of him to soldiers' wives she called him 'Ivor', whereas he alluded always to 'my wife'.

But Esme adjusted the height of her pedestal from time to time and took playful swipes at Ivor's.

"Ivor," she fibbed brazenly to a battery sergeant-major's wife, "is petrified of spiders. Personally, when I feel annoyed with him I pop one in his sock drawer. Do tell your husband. He may wish to follow my example."

The BSM in question had had a wigging from Ivor the previous day and his household, Esme judged, needed cheering up. There was nothing wrong with Ivor's performance as a CO other than a dearth of endearing human weaknesses. Seeing this, Esme astutely invented some.

And indeed, as Ivor imprinted his objective reality on regiment, brigade, garrison and division, he became to Esme more and more of an imaginary concept. She saw very little of him.

Functions of every description, private and official, mess-dressed, dinner-jacketed and lounge-suited, claimed Ivor most evenings in the week. Approximately a fifth of these involved Esme too, as consort. She sat beside her husband in the back of the staff car, going and coming back, dressed in one of the half dozen maternity evening outfits purchased at Elegance Maternelle in Sloane Street. Interaction between them was bland in the presence of the bombardier who drove them . . . non-existent in the myriad messes, private dining- and drawing-rooms to which they were invited. They separated at the door, of course, reuniting only in the act of departure.

It was Tidworth all over again, only more so.

At weekends Esme stood beside Rugby pitches, attired correctly in wellington boots and pearls, trying to remember which goal was which . . . utterly bemused by scrums. Muddy cuddling sessions as far as she could see.

Every second Sunday there was a curry lunch in the mess to which her parents-in-law were bidden. A family affair. Hats were worn and boarding schools compared. Sport, dogs, Fallopian tubes and vasectomies. The usual military fare.

Attempts of Esme's to initiate or join in conversations of a more elevated character were met with vacuous stares, particularly from men. As an officer, her opinion had been sought if not much valued, listened to with amused indulgence. Now, unless she stuck to the limited range of superficial matter proper to army wives, it was as if her lips moved without giving birth to sound.

"I know what the Russians would do if Ireland were their problem," Esme slipped her comment into a short hiatus in the table conversation one evening when no woman of the party had opened her mouth except to slide 'Boot' into it for ten minutes past. "They'd . . ."

"Another slice anyone?" the hostess cut in, flashing a halogen smile around her guests. "Darling, do give Esme some more, won't you? She's supposed to be eating for two and doesn't look as if she eats enough for one. Are you going to put your maternity clothes into the thrift shop, Esme, when you've finished with them? Or will you sell them privately . . ."

Colouring, Esme avenged herself by saying she wasn't an expert on the second-hand clothes market.

Later she recorded what she had been going to say about the probable Russian solution to the Ulster business in the hitherto virgin manuscript book. It became, like the best of friends, a one-way valve for confidences and opinions. It neither interrupted nor disapproved whatever it was told.

Esme was a body. The requisite female shape to occupy a social space. More and more space, she said once to Ivor when changing, puzzled that her brassière no longer fitted.

"You look lovely, darling," he reassured her automatically, slotting in his cuff links whilst peering into his dressing-room mirror. "Everyone says how well you seem. Come on, get a wiggle on. We can't arrive after the Brigadier . . . Don't forget to congratulate him on his OBE . . ."

King and queen of their own small kingdom they might be, but they still had suzerains to deal with.

Once home, rarely before midnight, Ivor would take his habitual nightcap into his study, sending Esme off to bed. She needed her rest, he said. As for himself, he had more work on something called FACE to do. Field Artillery Computer Equipment. This was the future, he explained. Ivor, who'd been involved in the development of the system, was something of an expert and intended to be more expert yet.

Esme read in bed. A luxury, since Ivor had low tolerance of this activity. Beds were for sleeping in, he said. For that and making love. Ivor, who had once again furnished himself with information, knew a number of ways of giving himself and Esme sexual satisfaction as her pregnancy advanced. The rear approach which achieved only partial penetration . . . lying face to face on their sides . . . mutual stroking to orgasm. Esme's enthusiasm for any of these was muted and she turned her light out as soon as she heard her husband's tread in the hall below. If caught out, she put on a decent show. Ivor, as usual, was doing his best for her, leaving no stone unturned.

A loss of libido, the obstetrician at the military hospital said in an odd falsetto, during one of Esme's appointments there, was to be expected. Quite normal. Not normal, however, he thought privately, running an uneasy finger round the inside of his collar, to discuss the sexuality of a lieutenant-colonel in command.

Mrs Llewellyn was under the impression that confidentiality in a military hospital was as confidentiality elsewhere. A sad mistake. He stuck to giving safe advice. "Relax," he squeaked. "Get your feet up."

"Fat chance," Esme remarked to Habibi, standing talking to her horses later. Ivor had forbidden her to ride any more. Another wife might have acceded to his face and disobeyed behind his back. But Esme was not the woman for that. She preferred a clean fight in the open. She was glad too that, for a moment, she was Esme again and no longer 'my wife'. A person to reckon with, not a flawlessly functioning adjunct.

"You can't *forbid* me, Ivor."

"Why must you make such a fuss about semantics? All right, I'm *asking* you not to put our child at risk."

Habibi, defended Esme, needed exercise. The mare had been a part of her life long before this foetus had ever been a factor. At this, Ivor looked very grave and said it was time Esme started getting her priorities right.

"You're talking about your priorities, Ivor. Don't always assume they're the same as mine."

Esme would have said anything just then, to prolong his recognition of her independent being.

"I'm trying to make allowances, Esme," Ivor wore a look of martyred patience. "But do try and pull yourself together. Either lend Habibi to the saddle club or send her and the other one back to Lowlough. I just don't have time for this."

"That's the trouble," Esme shot at his departing back.

He chose to ignore it. Only a fool would be drawn into brawling with a pregnant woman. His father's generation had believed it *infra dig* to argue with the opposite sex at all. These days, however, a man was forced to pay some regard to a woman's education. A crossed thread on the screw of modern life.

Ivor was preoccupied, in fact, with the planning for his regiment's participation in a winter warfare exercise in Norway. The FACE equipment was to be tested on a BV 202 over snow vehicle. He'd be gone for three weeks on that and was determined to come back, Esme knew, with himself and the regiment covered with whatever glory peacetime soldiers could come by.

Before he went, Aunt Alice came to stay. The purpose of her visit was to escort the two horses north in the luxury horse box hired by Esme. Ivor would have preferred the saddle club solution but couldn't interfere with Esme's expenditure or dispute her assertion that use as a livery stable hack would spoil Habibi's mouth and polished responses.

A pity. The horses had lent his establishment undoubted chic, underlining Ivor's membership of the Royal Horse Artillery's superior brotherhood. One wasn't always wearing ball buttons . . . But Ivor had forborne to say it. Esme was increasingly twitchy about window-dressing. A little confused as to where the fine line between bad taste and flair was drawn.

Alice was favourably struck by her niece's smoothly operating ménage and the way Esme's arrangement of her bits and pieces, flowers and books, had tamed the gauntly-proportioned rooms. She had, after pulling rank with barracks, got all the dismal chip-board facias and electric fires removed to reveal Edwardian fire surrounds, hearths and grates. Some had floral tiles. Old brass fenders were cheap to buy then and Esme had purchased several.

Kowloon House was fairly well disguised as a permanent home. Not unlike a rectory in atmosphere. A few good things, a few bad things. Not quite enough of either.

"What about a nursery?" Alice asked when she and Esme ate alone on the evening of her arrival.

"I haven't had time to think about it really. There's the old maids' quarters . . . Nobody lives in here, you know. I've made a list of things to buy . . . I don't really know how one goes about these things . . . Babies seem to need feeding every three hours as far as I can gather . . . It's as bad as having a horse . . ."

"No, darling, worse," Alice observed. "You can't go for rides on them."

Ivor didn't join in his wife's gaiety over this summary of child care when he returned early from his evening engagement to pay his respects to his relative by marriage. Dame Alice, he began to think, was a disruptive influence in his marriage, like Philippa Mayhew. Spinsters, of course. No sense of what really mattered in life.

He went on to dilate on what really mattered in his own life, namely FACE. Interested at first, able to compare what was said with the experience of wartime Ack-Ack colleagues of her own, Alice was an attentive, intelligent audience.

"No more firing for range and firing for effect. All gone."

"Well, going, certainly," said Ivor, impressed. He should have stopped there but he didn't. He went on until both his wife and guest were glassy-eyed with boredom. Each attempted to conceal it from the other, punctuating Ivor's by now incomprehensible monologue with random gasps of amazement.

"Nice to talk to a lady who understands these things," Ivor rubbed his hands after Alice had taken herself firmly off to bed. "Off you go, darling. I'm just going to take a last look at the stores list for Exercise Arctic Fox. See you later."

Looking at him, Esme saw that he was, after a day which had begun at six thirty, still taut with vigour. Power, she had read, and heard it said, was a drug. Too often repeated to have much meaning, Esme realised now, how true the cliché was. Ivor was frankly high, with pupils quite massively dilated; his excitement created a zone of turbulence around him. Stores? Surely that was someone else's job. Ivor's appetite for work was becoming morbid.

"Goodnight," she said. "I'll kiss you now. I think I'll be asleep when you come up."

Before she left very early the next morning but one, whilst the horses were loading into the box sent over by a specialist firm in Andover, Alice told Ivor, who was dressed in a track suit for his run, that she thought her niece looked tired, and was in her opinion both bored and lonely.

"Don't imagine she's said one word to me. But I know the signs. She keeps resurrecting that smile of hers at the beginning of every sentence . . ."

"I think I know my own wife, Dame Alice . . ." He said it in a politely considering tone which offset the prickle of the words themselves.

"I hope you do, Ivor. I hope you do." So saying, Alice opened her handbag to extract a card on which she had listed the names of agencies supplying monthly maternity nurses. "Here, you'd better get on to this. These people get booked up in advance. You're getting the confinement on the army so you can afford it."

Taking the card, Ivor felt aggrieved to be lectured thus on his own doorstep. Given bits of paper when there was no bystanding clerk to hand them to . . . Told how to spend his money. There was flint in his eyes when he excused himself, gracefully enough, from further attendance on the horse boxing procedures. He was needed elsewhere unfortunately, but had very much enjoyed the visit of his aunt-in-law. He pecked her on the cheek, waving without turning his head as he jogged, springily down the drive towards the iron gates.

Esme was nowhere to be seen at that moment. She was inside the horse box adjusting the buckles on the cellular travelling rugs of her two closest friends. Trying not to communicate her sense of desolation. The journey would be stressful enough for them.

"Bye, darling." Alice embraced her niece briefly. "Don't worry about the girls. And don't let that young man wear you out. Stand up for yourself. We don't want you throwing your foal, do we?"

The horse box lumbered down the drive to the sounds of a military band practising on Kowloon Barracks parade square. Esme watched the vehicle out of sight before going indoors to finalise the seating plan for a dinner that night and address yet another letter to the Housing Commandant about the state of the slum accommodation allocated to 45 Light Field Artillery's soldiers. Damp? They were wringing wet. A disgrace. Most of the children seemed to have permanent coughs. Perhaps the Brigadier's wife would take the cause up. There was no point in power if you didn't use it to do some good where it counted.

Caught up in her husband's ever-increasing momentum, Esme heard her aunt's advice but was powerless to take it. She was on a steeply descending slope and all her brakes had failed. No time to think, no chance to stop.

Leaving the men to their port that evening, after spending forty tedious nose-powdering minutes upstairs – army women always make a meal of urination – Esme rang for coffee in the drawing-room. The midsummer light was just beginning to fade and out of habit she went over to the window which gave a view of the paddock. There were no long, gentle faces looking over the gate. No busy rumps turned to her, swishing languorous tails. The two loved silhouettes, the grey and the black, were achingly absent. Esme broke down.

"Oh, my dear! Whatever's the matter?" There was a chorus of enquiry and suggestion. Overtired, possibly. It was a little on the warm side tonight. One felt the heat more when preggers, somebody seemed to recall. Smoked oyster mousse much too rich. Alarming talk about historic miscarriages . . . Should the hospital be contacted . . . No, it was nothing like that. Esme should be taken up to bed and settled with a hot water bottle. Ivor should be called.

"No!" Esme squashed the proposition sharply. "It's nothing," she wiped her eyes inelegantly with the back of her hand. "I miss my horses, that's all."

No one knew what to make of that. It wasn't as if horses were dogs . . . or children, come to that.

The coffee came in, providing a momentary diversion.

"You'll be better, my dear," said Pauline Chumleigh-Walters patting Esme's hand, "when the baby comes. I saw Margie the other day. She's so excited. She, poor woman, had to have a very early hysterectomy . . . I expect Ivor's like a dog with two tails. Well, we know he is, don't we? Hoping for a boy, of course . . . Oh and by the way, I know you won't mind me giving you a bit of advice . . . I have been an army wife so much longer than you . . . Don't push this business about the soldiers' quarters. It's the sort of thing that can embarrass husbands terribly. Politically sensitive. Troublemaking wives don't help . . ."

"But they pay rent for those quarters," Esme exploded. "If it was a civilian landlord . . . Don't tell me. Someone's looking after their knighthood."

Pauline's husband was, indeed, hoping for good things in the New Year's Honours List. A veteran of these skirmishes, she kept her cool.

"Now, now, dear. We all understand. This is a difficult time and you're doing quite splendidly. Ivor's so proud of you. Don't let him down. We're all keen to see him do well. So no hot-head nonsense, *please*."

"She said that to me in my own house!" Esme stormed at Ivor during the dinner party debrief.

He refused to take it seriously. Esme was far too touchy. Nobody had anything but her best interests at heart. She should leave issues like army housing to older and wiser heads. Did she want the dishes taking from the dining-room or would she leave them for the staff next day?

She lay beside him like a stone that night, disturbed by her baby's strengthening punches. Ivor sensed her wakefulness.

"Your aunt wants you to have some kind of nurse."

"Oh yes, she mentioned it. A monthly nurse."

"I'm not sure I can run to it. We spend all the entertainment allowance, as you know, and my father wants me to pay his golf club subscription. They find it difficult to manage, and we have so much."

"Yes," Esme replied flatly. "I'll pay for it, if I'm not overdrawn."

"Don't wave your bloody money at me, Esme."

They had a blazing row in which Esme won on points and Ivor, using his man's ability to be wounded by his mate's refusal to take the blame, won the overall encounter. But even so, Esme would not immediately pull her stumps and they both clung, furiously and uncomfortably to the opposite edges of the mattress. Not an even contest. Moaning, Esme rolled on to her back eventually.

"What's the matter?" Alarmed, Ivor propped himself up on his elbow and looked suspiciously at her in the dark.

"The baby's moving. Feel."

Ivor placed his hand on his wife's stomach and kept it there after he slept. Esme felt like a container. A thing valued purely for its contents. What would this baby be like? It seemed to prefer taking exercise in the small hours.

Soon after the regiment's return from Arctic Fox, they were warned for Northern Ireland. They were to go as infantry for a four-month tour.

At home, Ivor had plenty to say about the wicked waste of his men's expensive training. The custodians of the army's nuclear armaments shouldn't be expected to slog up and down with SLRs. This is what came of cutting the infantry. Imagine exposing a man like Angus McKinnon, who was an authority on Cymbeline mortar locating equipment, to a sniper's bullet. Brave men, infanteers, but nobody could accuse them of having brains to waste. Thick as two short planks.

"Yes, darling," Esme said. "But you know you're really thrilled to bits."

She exchanged a covert smile with Ivor's batman who was helping to pack his kit. Mess dress? No. Service dress, yes. Blues, probably not. Dinner-jacket, yes. Three changes of disruptive pattern combat kit, appropriately accessorised. Rudyard Kipling's poems . . . all a chap needed for moral nourishment. Where were the khaki combat handkerchiefs? Terribly funny those, but terribly necessary.

Whatever he said, Ivor was excited. So were the men. Rubber bullets weren't guided missiles but they were something. The real treat was the whiff of danger. The faint prospect of a scrap. 'Some 'arm, man' was the regiment's one and only black man's metalsome reaction.

Anyone would think they were all packing for a holiday. Esme was glad for them. A long peace dispirits soldiers. Makes training feel as purposeful as scrubbing lumps of coal.

Not every wife shared Esme's understanding and quite a few of the younger, junior wives were sobbing when she went down with all the rest to watch the batteries mustering on the parade ground. Here and there, men were breaking ranks to kiss wide-eyed children, babes in arms and tremulous wives.

Some were hard pressed to conceal glee at escaping glowering helpmeets who resented the withdrawal of their husbands' chauffeuring and porterage services on the weekly shopping trip. The fucking army, declared one woman with skinny arms akimbo, had no fucking consideration. Six years with the colours her hubby had been, and now they expected her to use the fucking garrison bus! Gunner Snoddy, on the other hand, lately busted down from lance-bombardier, was having a vision of hell opened up to him . . . the welcome he could expect if he had the nerve to come home with a dose of the clap. She'd get the bacon scissors to him, she would. The useless article.

"Put him down, Mrs Snoddy, put him down," the unhappy man's battery sergeant intervened, "A harmless wanker, is Snoddy, aren't you, lad? Couldn't poke the Mersey Tunnel, never mind an Irish tart. Get fell in."

No matter what the sideshows, the prevailing atmosphere was one of spree. The officers' wives wore garden party faces, taking leave of hurrying husbands with exemplary sang-froid. Cool discussions of domestic banality. Firm, decisive, last-minute kisses. Teenaged heads received a tousling and canines, protracted farewell caresses.

Enchanted by the scene, Esme stood with her mother- and father-in-law who had driven over specially, watching the untidy squads of human men harden into solid blocks of war materiel. Very cheerful cannon fodder. The order was given to board the four-tonners and the buses.

Edward, dressed as if for an Armistic Day parade, stood absurdly to attention. Margie snivelled delicately into a lace-bordered handkerchief, whether from terror or some more aesthetic emotion, Esme couldn't tell. She rather wished they hadn't insisted on coming. Afterwards there would have to be coffee and probably lunch at Kowloon House, followed by a 'lovely chat' with Margie about anatomical horrors such as breast-feeding and laudings of Ivor's apparently miraculous infancy.

"You're in charge now, darling," he was suddenly beside her. His skin, she noticed, had that opalescent pallor that came with sexual arousal. She felt aroused herself. Too late. How awkward. "Any snags, get on to Ian Swanson." Captain Ian Swanson, given the temporary acting rank of major, was staying behind as Officer in Charge of Rear Party. He was having tendon trouble and missing out because of it.

"Know you'll keep the girls in good heart. Take care." He kissed Esme lusciously on the mouth, one arm around her, the other modishly employed in retaining his swagger-cane. "I'll send you a signal as soon as we hit base. Should be able to co-ordinate R & R with the baby. Goodbye, Mother. Don't worry." He brushed his lips against her cheek, shook his father's hand, stepped back a pace and saluted his family. The staff car arrived with a flourish at that moment, adding to the sense of theatre.

Nothing could have been better done; more cinematographically photogenic. Esme could not help thinking that if Ivor did not come back a hero, he had certainly left as one.

"Good as gold, that boy. What?" Edward, damp-eyed, was milking his gallant old soldier act. "How about a little tincture, Esme? Warmer into the bank, eh?"

An early warmer, since it was only nine o'clock in the morning.

"Yes, why not?" Esme fell in with this suggestion, feeling an inexplicable urge to celebrate. A heady feeling, this waving off to war. Not quite as good as going with the regiment, of course. But the old days when wives lodged within sight and sound of battle were long since gone. There were other people to bind the wounds and do the washing now. Uniformed usurpers.

Esme watched the news that night with very close attention, participating as best she could in this new phase of Ivor's life. A single frame showed 45 LFA disembarking from a clumsy-looking plane. Alone in the empty house, Esme let off a cheer.

There were no more dinners now. A few ladies' luncheons, that was all. An army wife without her husband is no more regarded than a button fallen from his tunic. This thought, along with choleric reactions to news bulletins to which Esme quickly became addicted, were recorded in her manuscript book.

Incandescent one day, after reading that American Irishmen were supposedly bank-rolling IRA activities, Esme telephoned Petra.

"I don't know why you let yourself get worked up about these things," she said with the sound of the washing machine churning in the background. "There's nothing we can do about it, even if it's true."

It didn't seem quite the right answer to Esme, somehow. Madly unsatisfactory. Knowing about things was important in itself, surely.

There was a regimental Wives' Club committee meeting later that same week. From the chair Esme suggested the formation of a current affairs discussion group under 'any other business'.

"Something to counteract the turnip tendency," Esme urged her proposal. "I know I feel very cabbagey at times . . ."

Oratory was unnecessary. When put to the vote, the motion was carried unanimously because Esme was the CO's wife.

Afterwards, Petra took Esme on one side and dissuaded her from taking action to execute her plan. The Gunners' wives would not be interested and amongst the NCO wives, only notorious troublemakers. Furthermore, the Brigadier would interpret this laudable effort at mutual education as an insurrection. Husbands whose wives took part would suffer.

"We can think what we like, but we do have to be very careful what we say. You see, what a wife may say is always taken to be what her husband *would* say if he was allowed. So we can't do it. Think of Ivor's pension."

"But wives and husbands can disagree . . . Dissociate themselves from each others' views . . ."

"Not in the army. Think of yourself as a chattel and you'll never go far wrong." Petra hit the nail squarely on the head as usual.

Esme consoled herself by writing an article about the denial of rights to free speech to a whole class of Englishwomen. She tapped it out painfully on a typewriter borrowed from the orderly room and sent it, under an assumed name, to a half a dozen magazines. The rejection slips, cold and cruel, came without additional comment, except one, which was accompanied by a letter from the magazine's features editor.

Esme's article was nicely written and very funny. However the editor suspected the author was inexperienced. She should make her sentences shorter and ensure the first paragraph encapsulated the entire meat of the story before developing it. If she would revise her work along these lines, the magazine would be happy to consider publication in exchange for the usual fee offered tyro contributors. Fifteen pounds.

There was a lot to do before Esme could settle down to her revisions . . . Walking around feeling distinguished until a work-facilitating exhaustion set in.

When the article appeared many months afterwards, it was substantially edited with a heartless disregard for Esme's favourite phrases. Getting over her disappointment, she found there remained a worthwhile residue of pride in her achievement. They *had* left in her lethal pen portrait of the Brigadier's wife . . . But of the many people, including Ivor, who might have taken a vicarious pleasure in it, none could be told that Esme herself was the scribe. Army personnel, even wives, may not address any military subject in print, no matter how light-heartedly, under a pseudonym or otherwise, without the MOD imprimatur.

The magazine sold well in newsagents in every garrison town that month. Read with squeals of delight, it was passed, too, well-thumbed, from quarter to quarter. It was shown to Esme several times and if her laughter had a peculiar resonance to it, nobody noticed.

Pencilling in the estimated time of Veronica Alice Margaret Winstanley Llewellyn's arrival was a wasted exercise. The child had no sense of military timing. She missed her father's thirty-six hour R & R by a margin of several days.

Esme eventually delivered her in the Bulford Military Hospital, painlessly, by grace of the lumbar injection routinely given to every army wife in labour. This, in pursuance of the military principle that any fool can be uncomfortable – and the QARANC colonel's dislike of caterwauling on any of her gleaming wards. That was the prerogative of wounded soldiers. Although not, apparently, for long.

"One look at me, Mrs Llewellyn, and they soon give over. Had our bowels open this morning, have we? Top-hole. Carry on."

Likened by her staff to the wrath of God, she was a veteran of both Korea and Borneo as the medal ribbons on her crimson shoulder cape proclaimed. She had seen it all, from warty willies to double

285

amputations, personally acquainting every new patient with this soothing fact.

Esme was very well supported by her fellow wives of every rank. When it came to heaping on flowers and knitted garments, Margie found she had a lot of competition. A great many things for the baby . . . fluffy toys, mobiles, packs of soap and talcum powder.

Aunt Alice, who was busy with tupping up in Westmorland at the time, was informed by telegram. The postman toiled halfway up the fell with it on foot.

"Good," she said to her shepherd, Mr Fairbairn, "Never had much time for boys."

Ivor was sent a flash signal . . . an unusual privilege, which, as worded by Ian Swanson, his Oic Rear Party, read: 'Mrs Llewellyn fired a live round at 0400 hours this morning. Female.' A statement which still left many questions. Handed the signal form in the doorway of a Falls Road terraced house, Ivor was pinned down for two hours before he could telephone. Finally they got him a field telephone and patched him through.

"Are you all right?" he shouted.

"Yes, are you? What's going on?"

"A riot. What's the baby doing?"

"Trying to give me a mastectomy. Want to swop jobs?"

"Want to shit bricks for a living? I've got to go. Love you."

Esme was watching the footage of the action on the news that evening when a jeroboam of champagne was delivered at Ivor's behest. Come hell, high water or baton rounds, he was always thorough.

His father drank most of the champagne the following day. Unsuitably, in Esme's hyper-irritable view, he came alone.

"A warmer into the bank, girlie," he said to Esme, "You and Ivor can have a boy next time. What?"

The ballistic imagery failed to appeal to Esme in the context. Did this old fart really mean to compare her body to a gun's cold barrel? To insult the birth of her daughter as a mere priming round . . . And as for calling her *girlie* . . . This time he'd gone too far.

"If you don't lay off my husband and start paying your own bills, there won't be a next time. We won't be able to afford it, will we?"

He was never to address another word to her directly for many years afterwards. Upset by the squalor of her victory, Esme told herself that all she had done was a necessary if dirty job. One that Ivor could not do. They both had little Vonnie, as she was to be called now, to think of.

What others thought of the infant varied. The RSM's wife, a minute oriental, about whose congress with her colossal husband Esme had often wondered, woodenly opined, "She is very atlactive. The Colonel will apleciate her, I think." There spoke a career man's wife.

"Got eyes like 'im, ma'am, in't she?" a junior NCO's wife remarked more incisively. "Like razor blades." An honest woman with nothing much to loose.

"Exquisite! So like you, dear," babbled the Brigadier's wife expectedly. Esme's pseudonymous lampoon of the lady was not yet published. Not that she would recognise herself when it was. Names had been changed to protect the guilty.

Comparing the child with her parents' photograph, Esme could see no trace of the Winstanley or Hansard strain. Or any strain in fact. She was a milk-processing machine. Input eight times a day ... output eight times a day in little yellow pellets. Fairly harmless, those.

They would get worse, Petra McKinnon promised. She *liked* the smell of baby poo. Esme felt the walls of a wet, warm rancid-smelling trap close round her. The worst would be over in six months, they told her. She would get six hours sleep a night. Six months after that, the baby would probably begin to walk ... say a word perhaps. Big deal, thought Esme mutinously.

There was a lot of Vonnie talk. From Margie, from Petra, from everyone at the hospital and everybody else. Not, thank God, from Philippa, who agreed happily to be a Godmother. It occurred to Esme one day that she hadn't heard her own name spoken much lately. She was glad to get out of the hospital after a week.

Immediately she did, Gunner Snoddy, as Ivor put it on the telephone, bought it. They were repatriating the body, if you could call it that. A few bits in a plastic bag. The military undertakers would know how to weight the coffin with stones and Ian Swanson would take care of that. But Ivor relied on Esme to keep Pam Snoddy's mind off any idea of viewing her husband's mortal remains.

What he wanted Esme to deliver to the funeral in Oldham in three days' time was a cried-out, dried-out widow whose comportment would reflect credit on the regiment. Angus McKinnon would be over for a few hours with a party of volunteers to fire a fusillade over Snoddy's grave. No need for Esme to go herself.

"Right," she said. How typical of Ivor to know the widow's first name. He wouldn't have had to look it up or ask for it, he would have known it from memory. The man and the job were fused into an alloy, perfected for its purpose.

"How's my daughter?"

"About to detonate. Ten o'clock feed coming up. Next one's at 0 one hundred hours. It's all right, I can sleep during the day. The staff are wonderful and so is Petra. She really has . . ."

"Good. You'd better liaise with Swanson about the Snoddy situation. Sorry, darling. I have to go."

He always had to go. But Esme could not blame him justly, nor did she attempt to. She and Ivor would have time together when he came home on R & R. He hadn't come as often as he should, pulling strings to stay unhindered with his men. Military mysticism. Poke fun at it and the mystics got unpleasant. Ivor certainly did. For him it would always be the men, and for Esme, at this moment at any rate, it must be the wives.

Pam Snoddy had better come and stay at Kowloon House. Strip the plaster off the walls if she wanted to under Esme's supervision. Get stinking on Ivor's booze . . . that was the least that they could do.

"I shouldn't advise it," Petra said when acquainted with this plan. "What if anything goes wrong?"

But Esme took her own advice and sat up with Pam Snoddy on the first night, feeding the baby at intervals whilst the Gunner's wife said over and over again, "He always was a useless sod." Next day there was an improvement. Pam, hollow-eyed and chain-smoking cigarettes procured for her by Esme, changed her tune. "I'd like to get them fuckers what did it."

"So would I," Esme agreed peaceably. "What would you do to them, Pam?"

What was probably the most creative interlude of Mrs Snoddy's life ensued. Esme listened with interest, beginning to think her idea of female commandos had not been so far-fetched at all. Anyway, they had a very nice time together inventing atrocities.

Much later, after Pam had married a fireman, not being able, as she said, to fancy a man without a uniform, she sent Esme the most touching letter of gratitude. Long, semi-literate and piercingly intimate, Esme kept it but never showed it to anyone. They never met again, but in their thoughts were always friends.

When Ivor came home for a thirty-six-hour break after an absence of two months, the leaves were all off the trees. He was distant now, not from activity but an unshakeable melancholy. He nursed his daughter, staring out of windows and answering Esme's questions in monosyllables.

Were he and the regiment really comfortable in that disused factory divided up with cardboard boxes? No, not very. Had they done any water skiing on the Lough, lately? Some people had. Were the Tankies still next door? No, the Silvershods. Esme examined her own sensations. She must give that rubber duck away before Vonnie touched it. How was the 'hearts and minds' campaign going? Ivor shrugged. Politicians and their phrases. Had Bombardier Chadwick discovered that his wife had burned his entire civilian wardrobe yet? She said flares were in . . . Esme had told her that Ivor himself was an incorrigible straight-leg man. Absently, Ivor smiled.

They walked about the garrison, with Vonnie in her resplendent perambulator, the gift of her great-aunt. Ivor lagged and dawdled. Esme stopped and waited for him several times. He kept looking over his shoulder, scanning the roofs of buildings and top-storey windows.

"Ivor," Esme complained in exasperation, "Do keep up. It's too cold to hang around like this . . ."

"I'm sorry," he said, "I can't believe nobody's going to shoot at me."

That night they made love, very, very carefully. Esme had no stitches and there seemed no reason not to try it. Some primeval instinct must have informed the slumbering Vonnie that she was not top of the list for once. She woke early, and blasted off like an air raid siren just as her father came. A shattering experience.

Shaken, Esme lifted her from the cot and fed her.

"Look, I think you should have that nurse . . ."

"No, Ivor. It's all right. She couldn't feed her anyway. And it's too late now. We'll manage. I'll need the money to buy some thin dresses . . ."

"I was thinking about my money . . ."

Ten minutes passed in the smoothing of ruffled feathers before Ivor fell deeply asleep. Then the baby fell off her mother's breast, similarly unconscious, with all the gratitude and grace of a gorged cattle tick. Babies are like that.

Esme had been asleep herself for an hour when she was woken again by Ivor thrashing around beside her. He was weeping. Tears streamed from his eyes, his face was horribly contorted. There was only the light of an icy moon by which to see this. It was as if he had gone mad.

"Oh shit . . . Fucking Christ! This isn't happening . . . Where's it gone? Get it! Oh shit, shit . . ."

"Stop it, Ivor," Esme switched on the lamp beside her. "Ivor, wake up darling. You're having a nightmare. It's *all right*! Ivor, Ivor . . ."

His eyes snapped open but they were blank. Seeing something, if at all, beyond the bedroom walls.

It took a long while to wake him. It felt so, anyway, in the midst of panic. When at length he lay shuddering in her arms, he said, "Don't ask me."

Despairing, Esme made no answer. She had never loved Ivor more than she did now. Never felt so intensely for him. But he didn't trust her to get even this thing right.

"Is she awake?" Ivor stirred at length, to lean over Esme's hip.

Vonnie's two tiny eyelids were firmly closed. Two neat little ellipses of indifference. She had missed, Esme thought, something of serious interest. Just as well.

Would she have asked about her husband's dream, given the chance, Esme questioned herself. She would have liked to know. What was really going on in Belfast? How did it feel to be there? To be Ivor . . . or Snoddy before whatever hit him changed him into less than half a coffin's load.

Sleeping with soldiers has this facet to it.

18

Vonnie's christening took place in the second week of January, serving to mark not only her own admission to social recognition but the regiment's return to Kowloon Barracks. The combined events would read well in *The Gunner*, as Ivor pointed out. He was becoming an adroit self-publicist.

It was by a narrow margin that Esme established Philippa's right to hold the infant at the garrison church's font. The other Godmother was not of Esme's choosing and in her view, quite ineligible. She and the Brigadier's wife had never cared for one another. Their relationship was purely business . . . a matter of presenting a pleasingly united front at division level, which was what Ivor wanted. This much, Esme said. She couldn't admit that the article she had written, and which had by now appeared, would make Mrs Brigadier's close attendance a painful irony. Authorship, she discovered, be it never so anonymous, is mined with consequences. Enmeshed in her own web, Esme compromised. A Godmother, yes. *The* Godmother, no. A decision with which Ivor had to be satisfied but it didn't prevent him from clarifying the overall implications.

As ever, he wrapped it up in Cellophane. The Brigadier wrote his confidential . . . And a woman like his wife could take any amount of buttering up.

Weary of it all, Esme said it was family life by numbers. Marry suitable girl suitably, impregnate suitable girl, produce suitable baby. Baptise baby suitably. Have another suitable baby . . .

Incredibly, without a flicker of a smile, Ivor said cynicism was unsuitable in women, particularly mothers, and inadvisable in army

291

wives. Rather juvenile actually. Didn't Esme think she was getting a little long in the tooth for this overgrown rebellious schoolgirl act? He had hoped that motherhood would mature her somewhat.

Esme laughed until the high Edwardian ceilings of Kowloon House reverberated with echoes chasing echoes. The sound rang coldly round the house, like a collapsing stack of metal piping.

"*Be quiet*," Ivor ordered, "Must you be so hysterical? The servants will hear you."

"Let them," Esme stopped long enough to say it. "It'll make a nice change for them. Normally all they hear is Vonnie yelling. She's awake most of the day now, you know, and she won't let us take our eyes off her. Mrs Barrow had to peel potatoes yesterday, with her neck screwed round through ninety degrees just to keep Vonnie quiet. It's the same if I put her in her play-pen in my study. I sit sideways at my desk, but if I bend my head to write something, she won't have it. She screams. Look," Esme opened a cupboard beneath some bookshelves, "I put these on in the house if I want to get anything done." She brandished a pair of ear defenders such as were worn by soldiers firing on the ranges. "I got them from Ian Swanson while you were away."

"Don't tell me six adult women can't manage one baby," Ivor made an effort to ignore the significance of the ear defenders. An item of army property not properly accounted for. "I know lactating mothers can be a little tense but you're not feeding her any more. It's time you were over this, Esme. As an excuse it's wearing thin."

"Excuse? I'm not making any excuses, Ivor. Why should I? What is this row about, anyway?"

"It's about your attitude," Ivor snapped back unhesitatingly. "You know what they say, shape up or ship out."

"Do you want me to do that, Ivor?"

"No, of course I don't. The very last thing. I'm simply trying to get you to face up to your responsibilities. You've got the baby now, and a life most women of your age would envy. You don't have to cook or clean . . . Plenty of time to enjoy playing with Vonnie . . ."

Esme clenched her fists until her nails bit into her palms. Why did Ivor never *listen*. He replied to what she said, replies so energetic as to give them a spurious air of logic. That was the effect of masculine voices, Esme noticed. A conjuring trick done with volume and vibration. And Ivor himself was so accustomed now to have his every word received as wisdom, within the regiment at least, that he was both puzzled and affronted by contradiction on the domestic front.

"You say I've *got* the baby now, Ivor. You say it as if I've gained something. Don't you realise it's just the opposite? I've lost something."

"What, for goodness sake? Or is this another of your verbal games?"

Ivor threw himself disconsolately into an armchair and picked the paper up. A gesture that infuriated Esme. "Go on, you'd better tell me. Get it out of your system if that's what you want. What is it that you think you've lost?"

Seizing a porcelain parrot from the mantelpiece, Esme dashed it to the hearth. One of the shreds hit Ivor's cheek, nicking him slightly. He touched his face before looking at a spot of blood on his fingertips.

"My poor Esme," he said quietly. "Would you like to see a doctor?"

"Why don't you stop *talking*, Ivor, and listen for a change. And put that bloody paper down! Half your attention isn't good enough. Don't treat me with contempt."

"As far as I can see . . ."

"I'll tell you what I've lost! It started with the horses going and now I've lost my mind . . ."

"At least we're in broad agreement there . . ."

"No, Ivor, no! I'm not round the bend, or if I am it's with boredom. I don't have the *use* of my mind any more, don't you see. I can't read, I can't think. Can't write . . ."

"Write? What do you write?"

"Oh nothing. Just little things. Diary . . . letters." Esme felt she had made a slip. At least the manuscript book with her printed article pasted in it was always kept under lock and key . . . Why did she have to behave like a schoolgirl hiding *The Perfumed Garden* at the back of her gym shoe locker . . .

"Before Vonnie goes to sleep at six o'clock, I'm just her punch bag unless I'm out or something. And then you come in . . . and you go out again. But you've no idea what it's like here during the day."

"Are you telling me you have no feelings for our child," Ivor's eyes narrowed. "That you don't love her . . ."

"Of course I do. Nature sees to that. It makes it worse. I can't ignore her."

"Well, then, it's bound to sort itself out, isn't it? Give it time. Other people cope. Why don't you talk to some of the other wives? I'm sure they've all had their troubles. Look, I'm sorry but I have to go up and change now. We're dining BK Alamein Battery out tonight . . . I'm going to have a gin and tonic in the bath. Shall I pour you one?"

Too many rows with Ivor ended like that. No matter how tenaciously Esme held her ground or made her points, Ivor succeeded by ending on a reasonable, courteous, even conciliatory note. By Ivor's sleight of hand, Esme's onslaughts came to nothing.

He could leave the house at will too, whereas she, short of making elaborate premeditated arrangements, was imprisoned in it. Impulses are denied to mothers. Doubly denied to COs' wives. No more flights to London. Leave of absence cancelled.

But what Ivor said was true, she was better off than most. As for talking to other wives, he only meant about the baby. The CO and his wife lived in official bliss. To suggest otherwise would be bad for discipline. And morale. He had drilled that into her at an early stage. Kowloon House's dirty washing was not sent out for laundering. Ivor said that as he said most things these days. Decrees for which consent could be assumed.

There was no chance now, as Esme had fondly hoped there might be, that she would able to show off her little venture into freelance journalism. From Ivor's standpoint it would be soiled linen, sent out all right . . . without the laundry mark. Sneaky. Dishonourable and disloyal.

The quarrel was dropped as others had been. The need to put a good front on things in public was too urgent to allow for negotiation. Smile and the whole world insists on smiling with you. Look happy and you are happy. Deny it at your peril. A truthful face attracts few friends, as few as truthful words. Esme wrote the aphorism in her manuscript book, scored out the lines and struggled for an hour to render them in Greek. A hiding place for her anger with a double lock. Having done it, she was pleased.

And so the christening reception passed in a haze of champagne-sipping faces, with Vonnie enthroned in the crook of her father's left arm, a pint-sized idol amid her foaming laces. Apart from the strenuous opposition she put up against actual baptism, arching her back with terrifying rigidity, Vonnie enjoyed her day. She had everything she wanted in the way of continuous eye contact.

"Tough cookie, that one," Philippa, cat-walk beautiful in beige cashmere, commented of her godchild. "Trust you, cobber, to come up with something difficult. Don't let her get on top of you."

"She's on top of me," Esme responded glumly. "My shoulder blades are on the deck and they've already counted ten."

"Why don't you," Philippa paused to wave away a tray of curry puffs presented by a mess waiter, "get a job? Go out to work. Get yourself on the supply list for teaching classics and then you could get a proper nanny in. A professional . . ."

Esme raised a number of nearly practical objections. It wasn't as if she hadn't thought of all this before. And Ivor wouldn't like it.

At this Philippa's gleaming russet eyebrows soared like a pair of gull's wings towards her hat brim.

"Not like it? What has it got to do with him? Is this the heroine of Coldfleet talking?"

Esme smiled. It was nice of Philippa to remind her at this juncture that the whole of her army services hadn't been entirely wasted. She had done something. All Ivor had ever said about that business was that Coldfleet was for the chop anyway. Surplus to requirements. A duplication of existing facilities at Chatham.

"Well," Esme was tentative, "I did say 'obey', you know."

"I noticed," Philippa took two angels on horseback from another tray and handed one to Esme. "Oysters. Full of iron. Why ever did you do it? Why make an unhealthy vow like that? Ought to be declared void in the public interest."

Esme shrugged. "Oh, I suppose it was because we both liked the old marriage service best and if you start hacking a text like that about it ruins the cadences . . . Perhaps I was burning bridges. I don't know."

"Good grief. *Cadences!* Look, this isn't the time or place. But unfortunately it's the last chance we'll have for a while. You need someone around to stiffen you and it won't be me. I shall be out of contact for an indefinite period. If you're afraid of my old mate, Ivor, face it now and fight it now. Don't let him take you over . . ."

Afraid of Ivor? Esme had never even considered this.

"You can't help being affected by his moods but don't let him affect your *actions*. Next time you put the telephone down after talking to me don't tell me it's because Ivor's coming and he's in a filthy mood. Stop talking because you want to or because you're busy."

"Yes, yes. You're right. I'll try to. I'll make myself. But Philippa, where're you going?"

"I can't say." There was a moment's pause before she added, "But you can ask questions which, of course, I shall not answer. Look at me. Remember where my family came from . . . originally."

A split second's computation was all it took.

"Ireland? You've got the colouring . . . Oh, no. Under cover." Questions and statements fell headlong from Esme's lips, before which provocation, Philippa never moved a muscle. "How did it happen? Did they make you? Do you want to? But you're far, far too good-looking . . . You'll stick out like a sore thumb . . . Can you do the accent? Oh, do be careful."

A ridiculous thing to say, she thought, as Philippa turned away to greet Dame Alice. Agents she knew very well were as careful as they could be. But from Ivor's recurrent nightmares and their aftermath, she also knew that Ulster teemed with rival intelligence factions. There were mirages of information, and altered signposts. The civilian met in darkness who produced the credentials of a friend might well leave the stench of stomach contents, blood and cordite behind him when he went.

295

"Philippa's going to Ireland," Esme told her husband that night in bed. "Not in uniform."

"Did she tell you?"

"No."

This negative way of collecting and conveying positive information needed no explanation.

"You know you might never see her again, don't you?"

Esme studied the tones in Ivor's voice, absolving him of any taint of satisfaction. His question was just a balanced statement of the probabilities. Even chances.

"Yes. Hard to take in. In a way, I'm jealous of her . . ."

"Grow up, Esme. You're not a Girl Guide now."

"No, I'm a married woman."

"What's that supposed to mean? Can't we get some sleep now?"

"Yes. Or you can. I'm not sleepy. I think I'll get up and read a bit . . . In my study so I don't disturb you."

She didn't read but switched the portable black and white television on. There was a late night film . . . not much good. The other channel had yet another round and round the houses debate about Northern Ireland. With half her attention on it, Esme watched, thinking simultaneously of Philippa. Come what may, at least she was going to find out what she was made of. A thing Aunt Alice knew . . . knowledge permanently denied to most including, Esme supposed, herself.

There was some retrospective action footage . . . a man in a bullet-proof vest with a microphone, cheerfully admitting to nervousness as brickbats flew around him. A wince, a lopsided grin followed by a thumbnail sketch of his impressions. Lucky thing, Esme thought, to be in the hotspot, doing something . . . *saying* something.

Looking back over the period of her marriage, most of her own public utterances to date had been of the order of 'How fascinating'. Men seated to the left and right of her at dinner parties never tired of hearing how riveting their life histories were. No one she could recall had ever asked her about herself, what she knew about anything or how she might feel about it. Try to tell them, and someone started talking about the flowers . . . or how to make a quid or two on your old maternity dresses.

Esme Hansard had become the charming Mrs Llewellyn under protest. Sand-papered down to fit the slot by Ivor, the army itself and other wives. Or had she dwindled of her own accord?

Vonnie had given up screaming by the middle of June. She crawled now with the speed and sinuosity of a centipede. Hide and seek was her favourite game and it had to be played according to her rules. Discover her too early, if, say, an elongated toe of her towelling babygro should protrude from behind a curtain, and the child grizzled until the game was played again. Leave her too long and Vonnie would play her wickedly abandoned baby card, howling to the point of asphyxiation.

Her father worshipped her, but then he rarely saw her except when angelically asleep. And on the whole, he was smug about her escapades, none of which he witnessed. Vonnie, he said, was a commando baby. Super sprog.

There was a time when she disappeared in good earnest. Mrs Barrow raised the alarm when she went to get Vonnie up after her purely notional nap. The cot was empty. The wretched woman phoned all over the garrison until she could locate the Federation of Army Wives' Club luncheon Esme was attending. Ivor was out on some hillside observing a tactical exercise without troops. Esme came home at speed, frantic with anxiety, searched the house and alerted the police. Why would anyone want to kidnap Vonnie? Not the IRA, the police inspector soothed. That wasn't one of their specialities. Not up to now, at any rate.

Eventually Vonnie was discovered playing happily in the coal cellar. But she couldn't have let the cot side down . . . it had a safety catch . . . and it *wasn't* down. No, she had shifted the mattress aside and lifted the loose-fitting plywood bottom to burrow out that way. A clever little bag of tricks, wasn't she? Case closed.

For Esme and her cook it had been a traumatic interlude. They drank cups of tea together in the kitchen with sizeable slugs of brandy.

"Can't I turn my back for a single minute?" Ivor stormed once the whole thing was over.

"Your back is always turned," Esme sniped without much spirit. "Do you know it's three years since you and I went out to dinner together . . . the two of us, alone. We must have eighteen weeks of leave owing to us . . . I've forgotten what it's like to have you look at me full face for longer than it takes to give me my orders for the day . . ."

"When I get an evening at home, home is where I want to be," Ivor pounced cannily on the side issue. "And I don't want to eat a lot of poncy food in some *chichi* joint . . ."

"You used to like poncy food."

"Well, I grew out of it. How did we get on to this? We were talking about your supervision of our daughter. You'd better get that cot base nailed down tomorrow. And if she doesn't need a nap, don't put her down if this is where it leads . . ."

Within seven days Vonnie indirectly triggered another bout of hostilities.

It was an evening when neither Esme nor Ivor had anything in the diary. An ideal opportunity to discuss the short-list of school fee funding schemes Esme had painstakingly prepared, wading fearlessly through reams of small print over a period of weeks ... a task delegated by Ivor. They had approximately ten years to generate the fees. The sooner a decision was made, the cheaper the whole project would be. Ivor had said it all himself.

Waiting for him in the drawing-room as usual, Esme was ready with the paraphernalia needed for the gin and tonic ritual and a neatly written distillation of the various proposals. It shouldn't take Ivor above a minute to compare the options. Good staff work, Esme congratulated herself. Facts, figures and bottom lines. No unnecessary verbiage.

She heard the staff car's tyres crunch on the gravel drive, Ivor's voice saying goodnight to the driver, the car door slam and the front door open. He came into the room unsmiling.

"Hello, darling. Had a good day?" Esme half-turned towards him, poised in the act of slicing up a lemon.

"Not particularly." Ivor slumped into a chair, running his fingers through his hair. "Two more Gunners want their discharge. It's happening all over ... It's these bloody wives of theirs and their perpetual whining. Women's lib. No loyalty. But the CO always gets the blame. Vonnie okay today?"

"Not bad," she handed him his drink. "Look, about this school fee thing, it seems to me that we have ..."

"Oh, not *now*, Esme. Can't you read the signals?"

"Yes I can," Esme spun round from the drinks tray. "You've had a bad day in the regiment. Why is this supposed to make me tremble and shut up? Can you read my signals? Can you? Or are all our communications to be a one-way traffic?"

Ivor looked completely blank.

"Thought as much. When it comes to my signals you're illiterate. Well, here it is in clear ... I have plenty bad days of my own and I don't make you pay for them. I need your involvement in this," she tapped the pile of papers and her summary, "and I need it now. Don't hang out the closed sign, expect me to read it and creep respectfully away. I am not a squaddie."

"Don't be so bloody silly ..."

There followed a comprehensive row which savaged every aspect of their marriage. Dreadful things were said. About sex, about families, about the motives of one in marrying the other. Ivor even said that Esme's friendship with Philippa Mayhew had always struck him as distinctly suspect. Thank God she was off the scene. In fairness, a not unreasonable counterblow for what Esme had said about her husband's amatory technique. Thanks very much for that, he roared. If what she'd wanted was a husband with balls about the size of frozen peas she'd got her wish. How dare he call her a lesbian, Esme screeched at him. Ivor's trouble was that he couldn't stand a woman of Philippa's calibre treating him with indifference. Couldn't bear her independence. Had he any idea what an overbearing, strutting, pompous, formula-spouting prat he'd become? And so on.

Surveying the carnage after this thoroughly good set to, both partners went into full retreat. Hasty words were retracted and apologised for without reserve. A momentary madness, Esme said, imagining she was imputing the madness to them both equally. Generous of her in the circumstances, as she thought, since Ivor started it.

Mistaken as to the ground on which he now stood, prematurely relieved, Ivor came up with another formula.

"Sometimes I think you're not the girl I married . . ."

"Which is why I'm leaving you."

"Leaving me?" Ivor's eyes went round with horror. "But you can't . . ."

"I can and I must. This is destroying both of us. I just can't face being dragged along in your backwash for the rest of time. It's your life we're living. I want one of my own. Do you know what the latest is? Officers' wives are supposed to go around dissuading soldiers' wives from nagging their husbands to leave the army. So now I'm an unpaid recruiting sergeant on top of every other bloody thing. Look . . ."

Esme showed him the front page of the *Daily Telegraph*. There was an item which said a WRAC corporal had got a Distinguished Conduct Medal for some work in Northern Ireland. A private had got a mention in dispatches. An intelligence operation which, although the piece was maddeningly vague, seemed to have centred round a laundry van.

"What is all this gibberish, Esme," he said. "What has all of this to do with us?"

"Maybe nothing. I'm trying to show you that other women have lives in primary colours. Do real things."

"So do you," Ivor spoke calmly but he was deathly pale, "You're Vonnie's mother and my wife . . ."

"That's not enough. Being Vonnie's father and my husband wouldn't be enough for you, would it?"

Specious arguments, claimed Ivor. Jesuitical trickery. Someone had to bring the bacon home. A different thing altogether. And anyway, what was going on in Esme's head? Did she think she was going to set up as some kind of freelance double agent? At best she'd make a complete fool of herself and at worst get very messily killed.

"No, a freelance journalist . . . a war correspondent, perhaps." The idea came to her in that moment. She could write a bit . . . And she knew about soldiers. Who better?

"*What?* Are you completely off your trolley? Are you seriously planning to castrate me in front of the whole garrison, put paid to my career, desert our child for . . ."

Ivor stopped, got up and walked about the room sunk in concentration. Esme loosened a lock of hair and stroked her nostrils with it. She had never meant to say this now . . . not when plans were still so vague. Actually, brand new. Ivor would shoot her down in flames.

"Esme, you haven't a snowflake in hell's chance. You have no background in journalism. What newpaper's going to give you a job reporting weddings never mind a fiat to go and make a nuisance of yourself in Ireland? You're thirty, for God's sake. A pretty unlikely candidate . . . Women do fashion, cookery and consumer goods comparisons . . . Not war. You'll never get press accreditation . . . You can't do anything without it. The whole theatre's overcrowded. There's an oiky little scruff with a microphone behind every lamppost . . . No, it just isn't on. Forget it."

"I shan't," Esme said with childish vehemence. And then: "Do you want another drink? I'm going to have one."

"Thank you." Ivor brought his glass to her. "I mean, for one thing you won't get on television, which means you'd have to write. Now, honestly, what makes you think you can do that? Hmm? The world is teeming with silly women who think they're God's gift to literature because they used to get B+ for school compositions . . ."

"I wrote well enough to shake Whitehall up . . . to close Coldfleet down. Remember, I never actually spoke to *anyone.*"

Ivor's jaunty, chaffing tone changed at once. He took a swallow at his gin.

"That was a coincidence. I don't care what Vaughan said to you on the way down the aisle . . . He had to think of something to flatter a bluestocking bride, didn't he? My God, how he succeeded . . ."

Esme left the room at this and, early as it was, went upstairs, took everything Ivor would need that night from her bedroom and threw it into his dressing-room. Then she went into her study, unlocked the bottom desk drawer and carefully detached the gummed magazine article she'd written. Going back into his room, she pinned it to Ivor's honeymoon pyjamas, which he'd taken to wearing since Vonnie's birth. Vonnie checked on, she had a bath

300

and went to bed immediately, locking the bedroom door.

She was too knotted up with hurt and rage to regret the lack of supper. A thirty-year-old bluestocking, was she? Past her best and suffering with a congenital defect. He might just as well have said so since it's what he clearly meant.

Yes, she was thirty. Twenty-nine and a half to be exact. And how many of those years had she spent listening to soldiers banging on? Enough for an apprenticeship.

Downstairs, Ivor resisted the temptation to pour another gin. Why did Esme always take everything he said the wrong way? What lurid ideas she got. She'd never do it. She'd never pull the pin on him. It would blow over. There would be a *rapprochement* but it would have to come from her. A husband could only go so far in diluting his authority. Women hated weakness and rightly so. She was testing him.

When finally he went to bed, he came across the thin, glossy page of print. He read the first paragraph or two, slung it aside, retrieved it . . . read it to the end before crumpling it into a ball. A vicious piece of nonsense, written by someone called Iolanthe Legge. A cheap little predator who'd wormed some half-truths out of a discontented, traitorous bitch. Just who that might be, he shuddered to think. It had to be an officer's wife . . . or her mother or sister, to know all this. A subaltern's wife, most likely. They were always hard up. Probably needed the money to pay off the debit on the joint account before her husband got the statement . . . Thank Christ all his officers' wives were sound. Had any of them seen this tripe, he wondered. Must have done. Anyway, he was to understand that Esme agreed with every word of it, was he? With any luck she hadn't gone around sounding off in support of Legge and her informant. Oh, *shit*! What if she had? He would tell her what he thought about it, and her, for sinking to such reading matter, in the morning.

After his run, he did. Esme didn't come down for breakfast so he went up to her when he'd finished. Sausage, eggs and toast hit a curdled stomach. He ate them just the same. A change of habit here, would be giving in. The worst thing a man could do in his position. He must be firm. Fairly kind, but firm.

"Open the door, Esme. I want to talk to you. You can't skulk in there all day."

"The door's open. Come in." Esme's voice was toneless.

"I've read that . . . that *canard* . . ."

"Ooh, *French*," she taunted him, sitting up abruptly, drawing up her knees beneath her chin. "Quite sophisticated for a simple soldier . . ."

"Try keeping your poisonous mouth closed for a moment. If this is what you think about the army," Ivor produced the smoothed article

301

from his trouser pocket, "All I can say is that this woman, Legge, or whoever gave her all this Moaning Minnie muck, has never been in the same army that I and my family have served for generations . . ."

"Oh yes she has, Ivor. She's me, you see." Esme clasped her arms around her legs and put her head down on her knees. In the ensuing silence the sound of the approaching staff car's engine could be heard. Second gear as it turned into the drive off Kowloon Way.

Ivor picked up the house telephone on Esme's side of the bed and dialled the kitchen extension.

"Mrs Barrow? Tell Bombardier Meechie to go away and come back for me in one hour. Yes. Half past nine. Thank you."

Replacing the receiver, Ivor went and leaned against the wall furthest from the bed.

"Say that again," he said quietly.

"I told you. She's me."

"What do you mean? Where did you meet this woman? Or did you ring her up and say you'd give her the lowdown on army life for a fee . . . Or was it all for free, Esme? Tell me."

"Neither . . ." Esme raised her head. "Oh, well, yes. There was money . . ." Ivor's lip curled nastily, she saw. "But I earned it . . ."

"Great. Prostitution. Slack mouth, slack cunt, what difference does it make . . ."

"How *dare* you use that word in front of me! You know I hate it. Hate it, *hate* it . . . You lousy . . . I never opened my mouth to anyone . . . Let's face it, I've probably lost the power of rational speech in this place. I *wrote* it. Iolanthe Legge *is* me! Now have you got it?"

"I'm not sure that I have. Esme, Do you mean to say . . ."

"Yes, yes, *yes*. I wrote it. I got it published and someone paid me. Not much, but it's a large circulation women's monthly. Not bad . . ."

"Not *bad* . . ." Ivor pushed himself from the wall and took a long step towards the bed.

"Are you going to hit me, Ivor?" Esme said quickly, her eyes sharp and eager. "It'll make things so much easier for me, if you do." She started to scramble out of bed. "Walking out on a bully's easy . . ."

He didn't know what he had been going to do. But Esme's expression shocked him, brought him back to his momentarily scattered senses.

"Come on," Esme stood, feet apart in her thin nightgown, head thrust forward, cocked on one side to expose her jaw. "Get it over with . . .What are you waiting for?" She walked towards him.

Menaced by her very courage, it was Ivor who backed away.

"Don't be absurd. I think you'd better calm down. Who else knows about this?"

"Nobody. It's all right, Ivor. You and your career are quite safe."
Ivor looked like a man reprieved.

"Well, I suppose that's something. Some discretion, at least."

"Not to mention self-sacrifice. Don't you think I should've *liked* to have told someone . . . preened a bit?"

"Preened! There's no talking to you, is there? You've lost all sense of decorum . . ." Ivor looked at his watch. "This has all been a very great shock to me," he said primly. "I'd no idea you saw yourself as a bondswoman . . . a geisha girl who never goes off duty. And I suppose this caricature, Mrs Berk, has some real life counterpart?"

Instantly, Ivor knew who Mrs Berk was. A woman who never let anyone finish a sentence unless he was a major-general . . . "No. Don't tell me. Just don't say anything. I need time to think."

Shrugging, Esme got back into bed. "Think about what? Whether to give me six of the best or stop my pocket money?"

Tightening his lips, Ivor said, "Is there anything else? More scurrilous rubbish I should know about?"

"No. That's it. I've done some practice pieces. Some are good, I think. But I've been too busy with the baby and . . ."

"Yes, well, we'll talk about this again later. I have to go now."

Days passed with few words between them. Only the minimum in public. Appropriate smiles came easily. Army people are professional smilers. An appearance of huge enjoyment is the basic standard. Esme could do ecstasy if necessary. 'My wife' was on automatic pilot.

It was in that character that she wrote Ivor a letter of formal resignation. Quite funny really, in the antique form . . . *I have the honour to be, sir, etc*. It had appendices, laying out her proposals for assisting with Vonnie's support. Her army gratuity, which she had never spent, would pay a professional nursery nurse's annual wage . . . her first earnings would follow and as much of her existing and future income as might be necessary. From Ivor she expected nothing except the right to remain in contact with her child and with him in connection with Vonnie's welfare. Nor would she embarrass him by leaving Kowloon House before his tour of duty in command was over. Her going would coincide with 'march out' and his surrender of the regiment.

A joke? From Esme's point of view, partially so, of course. Not to Ivor. Anything formatted on precedents extant in the service writing manual made an irresistible appeal to his understanding.

"I suppose this means divorce," he said after a day spent digesting the contents of Esme's letter.

"Whatever is best for you, darling."

Ivor felt the frozen pea effect in his underpants again. Not only was

Esme dispensing with his services, she saw no reason to replace him. Literally redundant.

The regiment found the Colonel's evident abstraction sinister. Zebedee, prophesied a subaltern on his seventh slice of cinnamon toast in the mess one afternoon that week, was gathering his coils for an almighty spring. Consciences were examined with exceptional rigour, accounts checked and double checked, the contents of pending trays dusted off and re-perused. Manual amendments piling up in cupboards were hastily inserted. Ivor had achieved a fresh reign of terror by default.

At night he bayed like a dog, thinking himself unheard. He had moved to a bedroom at the opposite end of the house and the walls between every sparely furnished room were two bricks thick. Acoustic properties good enough for a symphony orchestra, however, betrayed this private outpouring, half of rage and half of grief.

Hearing him one night, Esme got up and went to him. She knocked on the door.

"Ivor. Are you all right? Are you having a nightmare . . . Ivor?"

The awful, hoarse discordance stopped and there was silence. Rain pattering on the broad, horse-chestnut leaves outside.

"Ivor?"

"Go away," he said.

She went to look at Vonnie whose eyes were open, wide with question. Esme changed her nappy and took her back to bed with her, giving her Rummie, the teddy bear, to cuddle. The child, already wakeful when Esme opened her eyes in the morning, had a tuft of the toy's plush fur between her fingers. An eerie genetic echo. There is something frightening about seeing yourself reprinted.

"Wait till your hair's long enough," Esme muttered, fondling the dark wisps on Vonnie's head that would some day resemble Ivor's. "Whatever is your great-aunt going to say about all this?"

Putting Aunt Alice in the picture was Esme's most immediate test of nerve. She was not best pleased, naturally. Speaking individually to both partners on the telephone she said she'd foreseen a large part of this and had tried to warn them both. Knocking their heads together at this late stage, she supposed, would be a waste of effort.

"War correspondent? Why the hell does she want to be a *war* correspondent?"

"She says she's interested, or could be. And that as a late starter she'll have to have something called a public relations 'hook' to interest editors. As she sees it, being the only woman so far to report the battle zones, that'll add some piquancy. Sex and death. I find it all a bit perverse, quite frankly."

"Can't think why," Alice smacked back at him. "It's what most decent stories are about."

"And all because she managed to get one article printed . . ."

"Good for her," Alice wasn't having anyone denigrating Esme. "Made a start, hasn't she?"

She had more to say. Esme had always had this madcap streak in her and Ivor had known the breeding history. Giddy dam and barmy sire . . . she hadn't been bred for treadmill duties. Ass's work. Well, what *had* she been bred for, Ivor said with some asperity. It hardly mattered, retorted Alice, since she'd thrown off a heavy-handed rider and was now galloping hell for leather towards the guns. If there was a tragedy Alice would hold Ivor personally responsible. It would be nothing short of manslaughter.

"I thought we were talking about horses a minute ago," Ivor yapped crossly.

"There's no difference, you stupid man." Alice banged the telephone down. A minute later she dialled again. "I suppose you'll want me to take Vonnie on. This should leave me free to retire at seventy-six, if I last that long."

To his eternal credit, Ivor never completely lost his temper with his wife's nearest relative. They talked about Vonnie for a while. Alice spotted loose threads in the proposed arrangements. Ivor agreed with her assessment. Not every contingency had been covered. He found himself gratefully accepting her as officer in charge of nursery movements, staffing, and liaision with dodgy formations like nursery schools.

"You know Esme's grandfather was a damned reporter, don't you?" she said suddenly. "Yes, he stayed on in Paris after the Krauts moved in and managed to get some stuff out about the occupation. Left me and m'sister out on a limb, of course. Yup, s'all in the pedigree if you look." And the telephone crashed down again.

Esme's mother-in-law proved a surreptitious ally. At her request they went out to lunch in Salisbury. Not at Snell's but furtively where no one Margie might know would be. Edward had forbidden casual contact with Esme.

"I'm sorry for Ivor," Margie announced with a detachment of which Esme would not have thought her capable. "But he'll get over it. I'm just so glad that you're doing what you think is best for *you*. I would have left Ivor's father as soon as he was born if I'd had your spunk." That was a colourful word for Margie, Esme thought.

"Why don't you leave him now?" she asked.

"I still don't have the courage. I'm such a fool. I hate him, but I'm afraid to be without him. Isn't it silly? But it's just such a pleasure to watch Edward foaming helplessly at the mouth over you. Thank you, dear."

This exchange, over Danish open sandwiches and glasses of warmish hock, haunted Esme for years. Here was no babble of a freshing stream, but the thunder of a sea wall breaking. She could never, ever tell anyone about it. Whilst it was taking place, Edward himself was opening his mind to Ivor on the telephone.

A pity Ivor hadn't listened to his warnings. He called Esme swollen-headed, unwomanly, disloyal, over educated . . . a disgrace to her sex and the service as a whole. An ingrate too. How many women could expect to marry well at twenty-six?

"That's enough, Father." Ivor was finally disgusted. "This is between Esme and myself. She has very interesting plans and I intend to back her all the way."

It was the first time he'd thought of doing any such thing but common enemies make strange allies. And he knew he couldn't keep her. Too much like living in a powder magazine.

The Llewellyns drew closer than they had been since that R & R from Belfast shortly after Vonnie's birth. Since the marriage was to end, better a peaceful death-bed scene, they both agreed, for Vonnie's sake if not their own. It was a time of gentle happiness, qualified by regrets at the farewell that was coming. There was no going back. To live in the sun as Ivor did, Esme knew she must leave his shadow.

They no longer slept together but left bedroom and bathroom doors open, shouting down corridors like two friends away at school in separate dormitories.

"How're the typing lessons going?"

"Fine," Esme called. She had recently enrolled herself on a course in the Education Centre . . . unofficial and ostensibly to facilitate production of her Wives' Club newsletter.

"Did you get that camera?"

"Yes, the Nikon. It's second-hand but it's not too big and it has loads of lenses and things with it. I've been practising on Vonnie . . ."

"Good," Ivor was suddenly in Esme's room, a towel wrapped round his steaming body. He looked over his wife's shoulder at her reflection in the dressing-table mirror. "Have you ever heard of the Sultanate of Oman?"

Esme paused in her application of mascara. "I think I've heard of a place called *the* Oman . . ."

"That's right. That's what the interior used to be called. The capital's Muscat and down south they've got the province of Dhofar . . . they used to own Zanzibar . . . Whole place is closed to foreigners. The

306

ruler's Quaboos. One of ours. Deposed his father in a bloodless coup a few years back with the help of his British officers. Quaboos is a Sandhurst man . . ."

"Ivor," Esme interrupted, amazed. Her husband hadn't been so voluble about any subject not directly connected with himself for years, if ever. "Where *is* this place?"

"Tip of South East Arabia. Controls the Straits of Hormuz . . . a lot of our oil comes through there . . . Hang on, I'll get my stuff and then I can brief you. You don't mind, do you?"

"No, of course not." Esme was bewildered. What was one brief more or less. This one sounded exotic. Something to do with one of the General's guests tonight . . . someone she was to be lumbered with? Probably.

While Ivor crackled into his dress shirt, he gave her a terse résumé of Oman's history. A forgotten, medieval dictatorship which few Europeans had ever seen. Pro-Brit, however. Actually, a client state. The Sultan had a largish army entirely officered by personnel seconded from the British army or officers who'd resigned and worked on contract for the Sultan. Mercenaries.

"It's the gentlemanly end of mercenary soldiering." Ivor went on shoe-horning himself into patent shoes. "It's what I'd have had to do if we'd left after your pantomime fiasco at Tidworth. Remember?"

"Will I ever forget," Esme answered, still in a fog. "You'd better get to the punch line, we're going to be late. Do you mind awfully if I wear my RHA brooch?"

Ivor's answer was delayed a second. He still had not quite forgiven what he saw as Esme's terrible apostasy in that magazine article. Her being right about quite a few things wasn't the point at all. They had discussed it. In the first moment of realisation, he'd told her, he'd have been happy to flip her buttons and rank badges off with the point of his sword, metaphorically speaking. But they had agreed, with difficulty, to understand each other and to differ. The brooch?

"No, why ever not? I hope you'll always wear it. Listen. We're fighting a war in Dhofar. Very few people know about it. No journalists allowed in, see. Occasionally there's a bit of a press release on the back page of the *Telegraph*, which you presumably never read. You don't do the crossword so . . ."

"No, I stop at sport. Go on."

"OK, right. The neighbouring state, the People's Democratic Republic of South Yemen, wants to take Oman over . . . for control of the straits, d'you follow? They're Communist backed, Russian armed, Chinese trained and fairly bloody efficient."

Ivor, now tying his bow tie, hardly paused for breath. He'd been boning up, he said. Not much written about the thing but he'd been asking the odd discreet question here and there. Now, perhaps, Esme understood the usefulness of contacts. You couldn't have too many.

"The enemy have more or less got Dhofar sewn up. Hills are swarming with them and local insurgents who want to see the Sultan out . . . Anyway, the provincial capital of Dhofar is Salalah. We still control it but it's under siege. Surrounded by wire. No way out except by air or sea. And the sea's no good in the monsoon season. The only people who do go out by road are the Sultan's armed forces in the shape of armed patrols, or the air force in Strikemaster jets to do a bit of bombing. Anyway, so far, it's a war of attrition. Nobody's winning. Well, no, that's the PR position. Actually the enemy's winning. But our side's got to pull a rabbit out of the hat or the consequences for the West will be grievous. Ready?"

Esme was. Ivor continued talking into Vonnie's nursery to kiss her goodnight, downstairs to the staff sitting-room to say hello and goodbye to the baby-sitter . . . Mrs Barrow again who liked the extra duty pay . . . back through the hall and into the waiting staff car, nodding briefly at the saluting bombardier.

Careless for once of the man's presence, Ivor talked about the organisation of the Sultan's army. Desert Regiment, Frontier Force, Jebel Regiment . . . Jebel meant mountain and *jebali* meant man of mountain tribe. Oman Artillery . . . Firqat . . . surrendered enemy irregular troops whom the SAS turned round to fight their former friends . . . Oman Gendarmerie very powerful and not under British control, unfortunately, as it was they who issued NOCs. Non Objection Certificates . . . essential for entry into the country and virtually unobtainable for aimless civilians . . . Women? The occasional wife on a visit. It was rare but not unknown.

"But I . . ."

Ivor grasped Esme's hand tightly as she opened her mouth to speak with a warning gesture towards the back of the driver's head whose ears were out on stalks.

The population of Oman, Ivor went on, was composed of many tribes. However, the main distinctions were between the tall Semitic men of the north, the negroid types found in Dhofar especially round Salalah . . . descendants of Zanzibaris, and the slim, small *jebalis* or mountain men. There were also the Sultan's much pampered Negro slaves . . . Yes, slaves. Each with a palace to himself and a couple of Mercedes cars thrown in. The Sultan's mother had been a slave. A grand old lady by all accounts who took a full share in government from behind the harem veil. A sort of Afro-Arab version of Aunt Alice, Ivor said with a rare spurt of humour. Oh, and the workaday language of the place was *jaish* . . . in other words army Arabic.

To Esme it sounded like a tale from the Arabian nights. For the first time in years she thought of Tozo. His mother had been a slave . . . The car stopped in front of the General's hired mansion. The short journey had been a magic carpet flight and now, it was back to official smiling.

"Wake up, Bombardier Meechie, off you go. Ring the doorbell." The man got out of the car with marked reluctance. Did this Sultan geezer want any white slaves, he asked himself indignantly. For a couple of Mercs he'd ring some sodding doorbells . . .

"Now, quickly," Ivor looked conspirational, "We'll have to finish this later, but the point I've been leading up to is this. Forget Northern Ireland. If we can infiltrate you into Oman, it'll get your new career off on a rocket launcher, won't it?"

Esme discovered she was seated next to a Sapper officer at dinner and pointedly devoted all her attention to the Green Jacket on the other side. She was always rude to Sappers and Ivor had never cured her of it.

Later, in their own house, Esme touched a match to the drawing-room fire and blew it out reflectively. No sooner had Bombardier Meechie driven off with Mrs Barrow than Ivor had started again.

Esme stood a better chance of getting into Oman as an unaccompanied woman than anyone, except, possibly, the Queen. She was still on the reserve list . . . Entitled, at a pinch to the use of her army rank. She was his wife, which made her, although she might not think it – he glanced quickly at her here – a somebody.

"Oh, Ivor, of course I know I'm . . ."

"But you're not a journalist . . . *yet*. So there can be no objection to you on that head. I've found out that one of GOC SAF's aides is a bloke I was at Sandhurst with. He's a half colonel now and doesn't mind stacking up favours in the bank . . . Which means, my darling, he'll get you an NOC."

"Does it?"

"Hmm. Well, I'm going to try for you. We'll have to think of some sort of cover story for you and then you'll have to play it by ear. Where you go, how much you do and what you see depends on you. There are risks. This is a real shooting war, Esme. Bombs, mortars, bullets, mines, atrocities . . . empty places at the dinner-table. Can you hack it?"

"I'll find out, won't I. Why are you doing this, Ivor?"

He sat with his ankles crossed, his elbows resting on his parted knees, considering, as it would seem, the fringes of the hearthrug for a while.

"I really don't know how to put this . . ."

"Try straight out," Esme fiddled with a spent matchstick, rubbing the charcoal between her fingers.

"Because," he answered her after some time, "I really can't stand failure, Esme. The sort of girl who can bust her way into a private war is the sort of ex-wife I'm after. Then it'll all mean something or other. And the army'll be able to see that the break up of our marriage had more to do with you than me. You realise that's important, don't you?"

"Naturally," said Esme sombrely, snapping another match in two. Ivor always had an angle.

19

The line shuffled one step forward. Esme pushed her cabin baggage with her toe. One, two. Her overnight bag and her camera case. She hadn't brought the typewriter. Since when did committed amateur bird watchers go around with typewriters? They used notebooks.

She shivered a little in the modern air-conditioning's dry, refrigerated cool. Glistening like an ice-lined cavern, the airport building's white marble spaces echoed with under population. The contrast with the nostril-singeing lemon-yellow heat outside was cruel. It had been like walking from a furnace into an outsize igloo. The air in here crackled with nervous static.

Up ahead, the Omani gendarme seated in his enclosed, elevated box-like bureau seemed to take twenty minutes over every passport. Counting the heads in front of her – passengers off the Gulf Air jet like herself – it looked as though there was another three and half hours to go. No, she must be wrong. Esme glanced at her watch, butterflies in her stomach. Three o'clock, Oman time. Seven hours from Heathrow. Where was her NOC? It was supposed to be here waiting for her. Did the rubber-stamping policeman have it? If he had, he might have given her a signal. But he hadn't and she was the only woman in this queue . . .

Perhaps, Esme comforted herself, he couldn't see her. Most of the men were tall. Military officers, of course. All that was left in the sieve, apart from her, after the last shake out when the plane touched down at Qatar. The dull but friendly electrical contractor whose company she had been so grateful for, had left the plane at Qatar.

"So long," he'd said, shrugging off his transient sympathetic interest in her. "All the best, then. Rather me than you . . . Shouldn't want to spend a night in an Omani police cell personally . . ."

An outcome, Esme thought, that was looking more likely by the minute. Some yards away there were more gendarmes, prowling restlessly, eye-whites whirling in their lignite faces. From time to time one of them caressed the pistol holster at his waist. Pistols for immediate use, not show. Instinctively, Esme kept her eyes away from them. She knew from Ivor's briefings, the Oman Gendarmerie were a capricious bunch. Unpredictable. The army had to flatter them into any necessary action . . . Hence the cat-and-mouse game with her NOC.

There was another shuffle forward as the gendarme at the bureau snatched his next victim's passport. Mechanically, like a closed circuit camera, he commenced a slow scanning of the passport's owner's features. His own face, thin-lipped and narrow-nosed, projected the affability of a steel security door. Feminine charm, Esme guessed, wouldn't work as the master key. Only the NOC.

The men surrounding her exuded a subdued braggadocio special to those who, accustomed to call the shots, are held captive by inferiors. Service rivalry. Nothing to do with colour. One breed of arrogance challenging another . . . Something to do with the SAF's men's pelvic articulation. And the careless way they suspended their blazers over their shoulders with a forefinger thrust through the hanging loop . . . An effeminacy favoured by men with nothing left to prove.

She felt their eyes sweep over her occasionally. Appreciative appraisals. Curious, but not too curious. Not curious enough, Esme felt. Naturally they all took it for granted she belonged to someone else . . . Had a luggage label suspended round her neck. If nothing happened in a moment, she was going to have to make some friends and fast.

She looked upwards to the gallery where acquaintances and soldier drivers in uniform were waiting for passengers in this queue. And nowhere, that Esme could see, was there a face for her. Not one selected her with a flicker of realisation.

How difficult could it be? Ivor's pal at the GOC fort was on leave, but he promised someone on his staff would be here with the NOC. The flight number had been signalled to them here in Muscat . . . She was the only woman . . . From up there, it must be obvious. Her hair was long, held back from her face by her sun-glasses . . . She was wearing slacks because female legs must be covered here . . . But couldn't someone *see*?

312

Another shuffle.

"Excuse me," Esme reached up to tap the shoulder just in front of her, "I wonder if you can help me?"

The man swung round, courteous enquiry cross-hatching his kind and handsome face. Younger than herself, Esme figured. There was a stir of interest from others nearest in the queue.

"I'm sure you *can't* help, actually," Esme went on, hoping her voice sounded more melodious than the tin-whistle notes it was piping in her own ears, "But if you could tell me what to do if my NOC doesn't show up before I have to give my passport to that man . . ."

There were a few questions from the tall, unknown officer, a murmur of commiseration from bystanders, and from Esme a rapid explanation of her status. It was all quite above board, sanctioned by the GHQ . . . She was here to take photographs of migrant birds . . . Actually, in the army herself, or sort of. Allowed to hitch lifts on military planes and other transport . . .

"You'd look sweet in Skyvan made for two," interjected someone out of sight, facetiously. "Whaddya say? Cockpit personalised by Habitat . . ."

"Belt up," a competing voice disparaged. "Can't you see the lady's in distress? She wants a knight in shining armour not a bloody lorry-driver. Can I tempt you to a shiny little Land Rover with a fringe on top, ma'am?"

Esme turned round and smiled, grateful to be flirted with. Already she felt safer.

"Come to Bid Bid," someone crooned. "We've got a swimming pool . . . Fill it with asses' milk, for you . . ."

"Yeah, and you've got frogs in the showers too . . ."

The man Esme had originally addressed had walked away towards the gallery. He was shouting up some words in Arabic, hands cupped around his mouth. She caught her own name. *Rais* Hansard . . . The *rais* element was a bit of poetic licence, she was not and never had been a substantive captain . . . As for her maiden name, well, she'd never been Lieutenant Llewellyn, either. Confusing . . . Anyway there was a heart-lifting tremor of activity above. Something happening. And another shuffle forward.

Esme shoved her own and her benefactor's baggage up again. Oh, please *God*, it must come soon. Before those nice people had to leave her . . .

The handsome paladin was back.

"I've sent a bloke to look in the arrivals concourse . . . He'll go to the Fort if there's no one there and I won't go through the barrier till

313

something's sorted out. Don't worry. We won't let them put you in a dungeon." Brave words to cling to. "Is that your camera? Looks rather swish . . ."

Glad to have any momentary relief from contemplation of her predicament, Esme opened the aluminium camera case and showed its contents. Scenting an opportunity for closer contact, a group closed around her. In a moment, a telephoto lense was being passed from hand to hand. Matt black and somehow phallic-seeming in those capable, long-fingered hands, Esme found herself at the centre of a small cyclone of sensuality. A warmly encircling, protective wind. The gendarmerie, glimpsed through changing gaps in the group, seemed restive. They started talking to each other in snapping, high-pitched Arabic. Esme didn't like the look of them.

"Very professional," an officer who'd said he was in the Frontier Force drawled, playfully suggestive, handing back the extended lens. "But it's how you use it . . . or so I'm told. Any pictures?"

"Umm, not with that lens, no." Esme chose to ignore the innuendo. "Just these." She unbuckled her shoulder bag and took a wallet with snaps of Vonnie and her great-aunt in it, passing them around. Most showed the child astride Habibi's withers perched before Aunt Alice in a veiled top hat and the gash of carmine lipstick she never wore except for hunting. Character shots. "It's my aunt and my little girl. Feel free to laugh. They're both very funny . . ."

"Hey, look, I think this is your fellow coming now . . ."

"*Rais* H'unsa'ad?" An Arab in olive drab fatigues, the green and black Jebel Regiment *shimaag* wound into a loose turban on his head, waved a blue paper up and down the line. He made an attempt at *Sai'eedah* something too. It must have been Llewellyn. More hawking, spitty consonants than a Welshman could have managed.

"That's me," Esme darted forward, eyes feasting on the precious document. "*Shukran . . . Anna Rais Hansard . . .*"

The soldier concealed his confusion behind a lunatic grin, handing the paper to the officer nearest Esme. "*Tafa'dl,*" he muttered the word of welcome, eyes going politely wide of her. He saluted and went away in the midst of another forward shuffle. She was in.

"Thank you very much," she said to the officer who'd been active on her behalf. "I don't know what I'd have done if . . ."

"Pure self-interest," he dismissed her thanks. "Pretty girls are in short supply round here. What I don't understand is how you got this far . . . I'm surprised they didn't stop you boarding the plane at Heathrow . . . You did come from Heathrow, didn't you?"

"Yes. They tried," Esme explained, "But I just fudged it. Threw my puny weight around. I was very grand. I said I was the General's personal guest and expected to attend an official reception on arrival."

"I say, bloody good," he looked at her in admiration. "Ten out of ten for escape and evasion tactics. I tell you what . . . how about an official reception at Salalah Officers' Mess? We'll find you a room along Skid Row, won't we?" He turned to consult with someone else. "She can have Lofty Blackburn's pit. He's on leave, isn't he? No point you going to the Bayt al Falaj," he turned back to Esme. "Your room will be double booked. They always are and then it's just a case of who bribes biggest. Don't hang out with business people. They'll only want to pick you up," he added with a deeply hormonal sincerity. "Much better to come with us."

The next few minutes were devoted to extolling the charms of accommodation on Skid Row. Socially select, but very cosy. Breeze-block cells, each with shower, opening on to a soft sand avenue planted with adolescent banana palms, coriander, tomatoes and somebody's effort at an ornamental water feature. Oh, and bougainvillaea. A bit spindly yet, but thickening up. Wonderful what you could do with camel dung. Eat your heart out, Gertrude Jekyll.

The desert, apparently, brought the horticulturalist out in hired guns.

"Passport." It was Esme's turn with the murderous gendarme. He scowled over her papers for an eternity but could find nothing amiss with them or her. Disappointing for him. "*Yallah*," he snapped. Go on.

The military airfield adjoined the civil facility.

At the foot of a waiting BAC1 11 bound for Salalah and with its engines already screaming, Esme's new-found friends crowded the loading officer. Crisp and cool in the shimmering heat, he consulted a bill board briefly before putting a line through a name on the passenger manifest. A British officer took precedence over a civilian Arab. As simple as that. No liberal sensitivities here. No audible protest either, as Esme ascended the aircraft steps.

"Well, well, well. Look what Allah's brought us . . ."

Blinking black spots away as she entered the cabin, Esme adjusted slowly to the altered light level.

"If it isn't Darling Heart, as I live and breathe."

Disorientated, Esme scanned the faces of the seated men. Some hawkish Omanis . . . Bearded northerners in blinding-white *shimaags*, curving silver daggers centred over their diaphragms. By their demeanour, men of noble family. Englishmen, blue-eyed and tanned in civilian clothes, or in combat kit and berets . . . or the chequered *shimaag* . . . At the rear end, a woman, swathed in black, her face visored by a stiffened mask. 'Darling Heart' ... Who had called her that?

"Knew you'd turn up some time. Come for an adrenalin fix, have you, Essikins?"

The voice came from just beside her. She looked down. Tiggy. Older, thinner, more beak-nosed than ever. His eyes, pale-turquoise slits in his leather-dark complexion. He wore a faded OG shirt, some sort of long, dark-silk plaid skirt arrangement and a greasy-looking *shimaag* wrapped tightly around his white-blond hair. On his feet, green plastic flip-flops. Across his knees an ugly firearm rested. Pleasantly appalled, Esme stared at it.

"Like it? It's a Kalashnikoff. Battle trophy ... You want it? I can always get another ..."

"Tiggy," Esme addressed him in a sharply governessy tone to cover her discomposure, "What are *you* doing here?"

"Firqat. Nice little command on the edge of the Empty Quarter. No interference. Just me, the boys, our goats, the desert and the enemy. 'S lovely. Just like something out of *Eagle* comic. Remember the old *Eagle*? Say, let me give you a hand with that."

He got up to handle her bags without any particular sign of hurry, although Esme was conscious of blocking the progress of a smartly-turned-out, stoutish officer in a short-sleeved SD tunic just behind her. He had red collar tabs. In haste to let him pass, Esme sat down in the seat next to Tiggy's.

"I see you're incorrectly dressed as usual, Johannenloe," the senior officer rapped irritably.

"Confusing me with someone who gives a fuck again, Brigadier," Tiggy taunted lightly as the officer bustled past, mottle-faced.

The phrase was to become current in the next decade, but Esme always swore that Tiggy originated it in Oman.

"Can't stand these seconded clerks," he added for Esme's benefit, from which she concluded that Tiggy offered his services at the higher, contract rate.

"Fancy a little patrol with me, Darling Heart? Say the day after tomorrow if you've got nothing special on. I can lend you some of these things," he plucked at his skirt-like *futtah*. "You'll look horrible. Very novel."

"Stuff it, Tigs," someone a few seats away admonished. "The lady's here to photograph wildlife. Not to go pissing about on suicide missions with you."

"Yah," said Tiggy, glinting sideways at Esme. "Wildlife. Let Uncle Tigs provide."

Esme dug him viciously in the ribs with her elbow, a smile twitching

316

at her lips. Tiggy was a hard man to hate. He never let his friends down. And now he wouldn't have to choose between them. All blood under the bridge anyway.

Years later Esme was to say that in order to join the army, she'd had to leave it. In those days there was no other way.

20

February 1992

"Oh Mummy, do look!" Vonnie whispered quietly in her mother's ear. "What an old darling! Just behind you."

Turning to her, hand outstretched for the cloakroom tickets, Esme thought again how personable her daughter looked in the WRAC mess dress. That fusty gown had now, with the passage of time, acquired something of antiquity's grace. And of course, the new monkey-jacket, just like an infanteer's, with gold braid round the stand collar, had made a world of youthful difference. Vonnie's Gulf Campaign miniature gleamed against the dark, well-tailored felt. Incredible to think they'd let her go. Incredible to think that she was safe. Never, never again. Not for Vonnie, no.

In a sense, they'd been together in the Gulf. Their paths had crossed briefly and only twice. Most of the time Vonnie had been hundreds of miles away leading an RCT convoy of ammunition trucks and their drivers while Esme attended interminable press briefings.

Although still resolutely freelance, Esme was what might be called an establishment war correspondent now. She was too well-known, nowadays, to get away with the tomboy exploits that had made her name. Too valuable. The army loved her for her shameless partisanship. In her eyes, no one could hold a candle to the professional British soldier . . . And when his government or his allies lost their bottle, Esme came right out and said it in her phosphorescent prose.

None of it had come easily or at once. They'd slapped a D Notice on her Dhofar copy. But four years later, when the Communists were beaten, a Sunday broadsheet had serialised Esme's account of the secret war and printed her astounding photographs. Nose to nose encounters with the grotesqueries of war. Visions of the forgotten land of frankincense. The Queen of Sheba's fiefdom.

"Mum*mee* . . ." Vonnie nudged her sharply. "Please look."

A small backward jerk of Vonnie's dark head indicated the direction of her interest.

"Just a moment, darling." Esme took the three pink tickets from the woman behind the wooden counter, placed them in her evening bag, thinking mainly of Aunt Alice's fur, Vonnie's splendid velvet cloak and her own new evening coat. People stole things these days. She supposed Guildhall's set up was bomb proof . . . "Now, where? What do you want me to look at?" She stepped aside to let those behind her hand in their wraps.

"There . . ."

Esme saw. A very old lady. Somebody she knew? No. Too old even for her to remember. She was discarding an ancient squirrel cape. She was tall, or had been, judging by the largeness of her frame. Her body, misshapen now and sagged with age, was encased in a graphite-coloured evening gown which dripped bugle beads like drops of rain. There was a small rent under the arm, of which she could not possibly be aware . . . A paste aigrette quivered bravely in her sparse white hair, scraped, as it was, into a defiant top knot. Her putty-pale face was held in some semblance of its former shape by clenched jaws and pride. If there had been beauty there, it had long since gone.

"Her *feet*," hissed Vonnie, between immobile lips.

Yes. The lady wore grubby tennis shoes. Esme glanced quickly down and back to the row of medals pinned to the graphite dress. Like all the rest of them, whether she was in pain or poverty or both, this great old lady had come to say goodbye.

Esme's throat thickened, and her eyes prickled dangerously. It was going to be that kind of night, she feared.

"Don't stare," she took her daughter's elbow and marched her firmly away. "She could've been your great-aunt Alice's boss in the FANY. Probably was, for all we know. We'll ask her."

But Esme didn't see the old lady again that evening. Among eight hundred women officers, serving and retired, together with a bare dozen men, people were soon swept away, lost in conversational eddies at the margins of the flood.

This was the last headquarters' mess night the Corps would ever have. Latest of the women's army services, it was disbanded now. The women were to be badged with the men, at last. A good thing . . . the logical end to the story. Esme had always thought so. Suddenly, she was not so sure. Who would now care for old warriors like that one in the cloakroom?

As for Vonnie and her contemporaries being trained at Sandhurst alongside the boys . . . Well, Esme had not, after all, been happy about it. She had opposed Vonnie's wish to join the army. She was too young. Why not go to university first? The army was an easier place for women with technical specialisms . . . But youngsters came of age at eighteen these days and her daughter had been one too many for all of them. Esme, Ivor, her great-aunt Alice and her Godmother, any of whom might have pulled some strings to keep her out . . . had found their own strings ably manipulated by Vonnie.

So the whole unexpurgated programme at Sandhurst had begun, culminating in the Sovereign's Parade and a wild commissioning ball. During the latter stages of that, if Vonnie could be believed, couples had been seen copulating on the lawns within sight of Old College. A step too far beyond the bounds of acceptable bad behaviour.

Esme had longed, then, for the ladylike futilities of Camberley. But it had closed some years ago, an abolition which predicated the entire Corps' demise.

Women in the army were no longer an expensive optional extra. They were badly needed. Recruitment across the board was down. There wasn't much to pick from. Lower levels of educational achievement, smaller hearts, softer feet, lower stamina. Among male officer candidates it was a question of choosing the likeliest from an uninspiring lot.

The girls were the young Turks now. More intelligent, better qualified, better-looking . . . more ambitious . . . They were the ones the army was forced, reluctantly, to look to. They were going to get everything they wanted. They were in a position to insist. Even Ivor said so.

With her hand on her heart, Esme couldn't say she liked it. Where would it end . . . with the Chiefs of the General Staff all in skirts?

"Oh, Caroline . . ."

Caroline Clough was middle-aged and still the same. Esme was shocked to see how recognisable she was. She must be fifty now . . . One crown, two pips . . . a full colonel. General Service Medal, two bars . . . Married? Marriage was no barrier to promotion these days. Even the Corps' Director was married.

"Someone you know, Mummy?"

"Mm. Yes, we were at Camberley together. She came to my wedding and to your christening but then she disappeared into GCHQ in Cheltenham. Or so Philippa told me. Never mind. I'll find her later . . ."

321

A group of handsome, laughing girls came up to them and greeted Vonnie. There was something about them Esme could not quite put her finger on. Something that made them different from the way her vintage had been . . . Not brash, exactly, but very, very certain of their value.

"Come on, Von. Aren't you going to introduce us?"

Vonnie was not allowed the chance. The girls, all full lieutenants, introduced themselves. They had guessed she would be coming . . . They had loved her report on the breaching of the sand ramparts . . . she must have been terribly close to know all that detail.

"Oh, no," Esme lied. "I got it all from a REME sergeant. He was close . . ." She bit her lip, hoping Vonnie would buy it. That adventure had been extremely difficult to arrange . . . "I don't take any foolish risks these days, you know. Much too old."

Well, it would be the last time for her. From now on it would be armchair reflections on whatever conflict was coming next. Safe overviews from way behind the lines at most. She'd seen more action than most people here tonight, including General Sir Ivor Llewellyn, bless him. He was retiring, she was retiring . . . Philippa, who had never become Director of the Corps, was retired already. Aunt Alice would never retire from being Aunt Alice.

Waiting in the vast antechamber with her former son-in-law, Alice was wearing her medals too. Ivor, by unremitting labour in gymnasiums, had avoided adding a bay window to his torso. None the less, at sixty, the ballet-dancer tightness of his mess dress was a strain. Imminent retirement had prevented him from ordering a new one. His hair, still densely black from widow's peak to nape, was widely winged with silver at the sides. There were still a few around who, remembering him from way back, called him Zebedee when they thought him out of earshot. Anyway, his spring had slackened off considerably in the last five years.

Recently Ivor had married a natty little naval widow and bought himself a commodious cottage close to Farnham. All set for Blimphood. What was it Esme used to call them? Crusties. That was it. Here she came now, arm linked through Vonnie's. He studied the pair appreciatively, his attention wandering from Alice's remarks.

How lovely Esme was still. Erect and slender in her green velvet gown, her face was not yet deeply engraved with lines. But at forty-nine, indentations, shallow yet, had prepared the place for age.

"Hello, Daddy." Vonnie kissed him. "Here's Mummy. Doesn't she look stunning? Hello, Aunt Alice . . . Good evening, ma'am," she wisely said to Camilla Crump who, retired, was in civilian evening dress and medals.

322

"Go and get us something fit to drink, Vonnie," Alice commanded. "Your father looks a fool drinking this pink tart's tipple . . . Oh damn. Your Colonel-in-Chief's here now. Aren't you on the presentation list? What a perfect nuisance."

Vonnie was taken away to meet the Duchess of Kent, who, oddly, in Esme's view, had chosen to wear a civilian gown. Shouldn't she have worn mess kit tonight of all nights? The Duke, with less reason, was wearing his. Had she been entitled, Esme would have done so, much as she had always detested it.

"I'll go, Aunt Alice," Esme volunteered to pursue a waiter peddling white champagne. "I'll see if I can see Philippa . . . Did you hear, Daphne Deveril's dead?"

"Three cheers," Alice greeted this news robustly. "Serves her right. Ivor," she added. "Camilla's just been telling me that our Corps funds are to be given away to any Tom, Dick or Harry. Can't you *do* something? It's barefaced theft . . ."

Esme wove her way through clumps of elderly women in the midst of similar conversations. The Corps silver was to be auctioned off . . . the Headquarters Mess was to go. Monstrous. They'd be lumped in with the *Pay* Corps, for heaven's sake. You could call it the Adjutant-General's Corps till the sky fell in, but *really* . . .

The army's tribalism was alive and well. Everyone could still find someone to look down on.

There were volatile groups of excited youngsters looking forward to the changes. Sniffing power appreciatively. The army as a sweet shop . . . The infantry was smartish, of course and influential. Lot to be said for the logistics outfits. The coming thing, some said . . . Cavalry? Not yet, but they'd give in eventually. The Silvershods had a WRAC assistant-adjutant. Hadn't she ridden side-saddle at the Queen's Birthday Parade last year? Definitely a MUSK . . . Major Unit Sex Kitten.

Esme knew about that. It gave her an uncomfortable pang that someone else had realised a fantasy of hers. But they should have revived the old FANY mounted dress . . . And if it had been her, she would have had a nice *little* charger . . . Darling Habibi would have been perfect. The wrong colour, of course but she would have stood out better. She was dead. Buried along with Oberon in a corner of the paddock at Lowlough. Aunt Alice never had her horses taken to the knackers. Lowlough would be Vonnie's now, when Aunt Alice died. She loved the place . . .

"Hi, Miss Hansard."

Esme turned to see a television news technician she knew setting up a camera in a kind of elevated alcove. A thick-set man in a dinner-jacket, squatting to readjust the twisting cable, had his back turned.

"Oh, hello . . . Are we going to be on television? I didn't know." Esme stepped up the shallow stair tread.

"Might be. Depends what else there is . . ."

The man in the dinner-jacket rose to his feet and turned to face her. Esme didn't hear the rest of what the technician said. She was looking at a face she knew. Almost recognised. It was just the name that wouldn't come. Face and name stayed obstinately separate . . . like two near-identical photographic images before a stereoscope combined them into leaping significance.

He took a pace towards her with his hand held out. It looked so big in Esme's dream-like, distorted vision. Like Mickey Mouse's . . .

"Hello, Esme. In the thick of things as usual . . . You don't know me, do you? Clive Campbell-Carson."

The sheet of muscle dividing Esme's lungs and heart from her colon fell in like a collapsing ceiling. She could feel the hollowing space. Where did the Campbell come from? Oh yes, the Lady Roxanne . . .

Why she shook his hand she never knew. It was as if a stun grenade had exploded in her mind. Everything shook and shimmered with the shock waves. He held her hand too long . . . Esme pulled hers away. This couldn't be Clive. He looked down at heel and flabby . . . His eyes too eager in his coarsened features. He had a wheedling, seedy way with him, foreign to her memory.

He talked. A stream of patter. Not the old Clive. He had never talked except in fits and starts. Something about being with the army's PR team. Laughable pay but kept him busy. Kept him in London too. Never could settle to turnip management. What a name she'd made for herself . . . He always meant to look her up . . . They ought to get together . . . In the same business, weren't they? Plugging the army with the media . . .

From all of which Esme gathered that Roxanne had ditched him.

He reached into his inside pocket and handed her a card. For a moment, Esme studied it. Two addresses. Trust Clive for that. East Lodge, Stromnor Castle, Kincardineshire . . . A dog kennel for a discarded husband . . . And a flat in Camberwell.

"It has been a long time, hasn't it?" The empty phrase plopped down soggily between them . . . "Excuse me, won't you? I must join my family."

Her head swimming. Whatever Clive had had before, it had left him. He was impotent, a nullity. Holding out his beggar's tin for alms.

A moment later, stopping to speak to a Mill Hill chum, while the walls continued to revolve, Esme hoped that someone would take care of him. She couldn't be the one. It was too late to wash her hands . . .

324

cleanse the necrosis of his touch. They were moving into dinner. Clive would have no seat at this table.

Service dinners are not designed for conversation. A cacophony of noise disguises psychic communication. All is ritual. Liturgy and rubrics. Clothes, objects, procedures, music, food and drink, even silences, pertaining to the sacrament of unity. The dullest companion on earth is dear, wearing a similar or friendly uniform.

Ivor and Philippa sat at the top table. Esme, her daughter and Aunt Alice sat close together at another set at right angles to it. Within hailing distance, were it not for the gusty performance of the band. The WRAC Staff Band was better than Esme ever remembered. It filled the soaring Gothic vaults. The atmosphere, from the grace to the loyal toast, was electric. A locked grid of memory, grief, triumph, regret and hope.

Where was Ursula Spotteswoode? Had anybody seen her? She would never miss this night . . . She was dead, someone said. Oh *Ursula*, Esme thought. *You would have loved this. You must be here . . . somewhere.*

And her parents too. Vonnie's grandparents. They should have been here with them. A pity Vonnie couldn't wear their medals for them . . . What an array they all had between them . . . Except me, Esme thought. She was just an observer here. As so often down the years, a hanger on, invited to the feast.

Easy to get maudlin. She stopped herself before the tears spilled over. It wouldn't take too much to start the whole gang off. A bad way to get the event on television.

There were speeches. The young Director was feisty. She spoke of the Adjutant-General's Corps, the newly formed administrative organisation was to incorporate the majority of her officers to start with. "Dominate it," she enjoined them. "Take it over." Fighting talk. No submissive pussy-footing, now.

Other grandees spoke. Ivor added a word or two. His Whitehall job had had something to do with recruitment last year. Feminism had crept up on him, he said. No getting away from it. The movers and shakers in today's army were the women. And he was proud to have a daughter among them. It was the end of a long day for women in the army, but a victorious one. He knew they'd be up and running with the ball again tomorrow. Mixed metaphors or not, Ivor always said the right thing. Force of habit.

The royal couple left, and after that the night belonged to the children. The shining, clear-skinned subalterns.

The band played 'Cagney and Lacey' . . . Only once in fact. But it rang so long in Esme's head that she thought they'd played it over and over again. A better, fiercer, more passionate march, than 'The Lass of Richmond Hill'. Another day, another tune. There were the young Jordanian princesses in those pretty uniforms of theirs, wondering whether or not this was too public a place in which to join the mischief. Did they stand on the tables? Esme couldn't remember quite, recalling the scene to her memory later. But there was a natural amount of horseplay. An inflammable gas billowing off the top of a cocktail made from adrenalin, rampant hormones and alcohol.

Had she ever, Esme wondered, sowed a single viable seed towards this harvest? Maybe yes, maybe no. It was enough to see it reaped with such glorious *élan*.

"Is he still up?"

Esme stepped over the threshold of Tiggy's house in Eaton Close. A broad smile tore a strip from the huge Fijian's face as he held the door for her. Name of Griller, for domestic purposes. His great-grandfather had preferred this method of preparing missionaries for the table. No lie. He had been Tiggy's sergeant in the SAS, and his close companion ever since both had left to pursue careers as soldiers of fortune. Now they were co-directors of Global Surety. One of those 'go anywhere, do anything dangerous' organisations that incurable soldiers found.

"Sure he is," Griller acceded. "Waiting for you. Are you hungry? Got some cold woodcock in the kitchen . . ."

Tiggy's electric wheelchair hissed across the hall's black and white marble tiles.

"Knew you'd come. Was it a real chandelier swinger? You look good, Essikins. Very good. Green's your colour. Your old mob's, of course. Appropriate."

Squinting up, he scanned her from head to toe with one eye. The other was temporarily patched. He had a leg entombed in plaster and was wearing a rigid corset under his shirt. Part of a long and expensive repair job which was entering its final phase. He was lucky to have kept his leg.

Tiggy had taken one risk too many. Not his fault really. A question of ensuring customer satisfaction. A trooper had bugged out of an operation at the last moment and Tiggy, knowing full well his own reactions were past their best, had taken his place. Hong Kong . . . fourteen months ago.

"I suppose it might have been," Esme laughed at him, "If we could have reached the chandeliers. Long way up at Guildhall . . ."

Tiggy spun his chair manically on the spot.

"No excuses, please. Come on. Come in. Tell me all about it. The Hine Antique, I think for this, Griller. Special occasion."

"Count me out," the Fijian swung away to the kitchen. "I'm going to have me a couple of wads and watch my new baseball video in bed."

"Good," said Tiggy, "That's got rid of him."

Esme took no notice. The two men, she knew, were mutually devoted. Griller had saved Tiggy's life on innumerable occasions.

"Anyone there we know?" Tiggy sped himself to the decanters in the drawing-room.

"Only Caroline Clough that you might remember. Oh, and Philippa Mayhew, of course." Esme unscrewed her earrings, looking in the glass above his chimney-piece, wondering why she lied.

"Do you want soda? Because if you do I'm going to give you cooking brandy . . ."

"Tiggy, I wasn't telling the truth. Clive was there." She hadn't meant to say it. What would be the point? If Tiggy knew anything of Clive's history she didn't want to hear it.

"I hope you were strict with him." Tiggy, incapable of surprise, spun himself around with the glasses.

"I think I was . . . a bit."

"Nice work."

They did, after all, talk about Clive for a while. A necessary catharsis for both of them, too long delayed. A sifting of cold ashes. Throughout this interlude, Esme had to poke a skewer up Tiggy's cast several times. His leg itched more in the evenings.

"He touches me for money from time to time . . . That's good. No, more to the left . . ."

"Heavens, do you give it to him? Is that better?"

"Yes to both. You can stop now. Thank you, Darling Heart. About a thousand quid a time. Can't see the boy embarrassed, can I? We were at school together and in the regiment . . ."

"Quite right," Esme found herself saying, her heart and mind agreeing. As much as anything, she realised, she had fallen in love with Tiggy and Clive's brotherhood. A third, transcendent entity, it had been a thing of specifically English beauty. It deserved no blame.

"Do you see him much?" Esme picked up her coat to go.

"Hardly ever unless he wants some cash to tide him over. Once a year on average. As little as possible, anyway. He never stops talking about you . . ."

"But Tiggy, that's utterly bizarre. Does he know that you and I . . .?" Esme put down her coat again, rocked by the news that Clive spoke of her. And to Tiggy of all people. "He used to tell me not to talk about *you* . . . because it was boring."

327

"Used you to talk about me, Essikins?" Tiggy held out his hand to her. "Did you?"

"Yes," Esme nodded, slipping her hand into his. And I used to think about you, too. You were always interesting.

Tiggy squeezed her hand, dropped his face and kissed it. "Don't go. Name your price."

"No, you're not fit. And how do you think you're going to do anything with that pot leg on . . ."

"I can think of a million things."

"I don't do specials. You know that." Esme was very familiar with this old game. They hadn't played it since Tiggy was injured. And, in her opinion, it would be many weeks yet before it would be feasible to play again.

"Well, I think you might, Essikins. I have been a very good customer . . ."

"Client," Esme corrected huffily. "I'm a high class tart, remember."

"Greedy bitch," said Tiggy sunnily. "How much?"

"Nothing doing. I don't need this class of trade, mate. A girl's got to have her sleep, you know."

"So's a boy," Tiggy yawned hugely. "Come and sleep beside me."

"What do I charge for that?" Esme, weakening, stroked his white, white hair.

"Nothing. Love's buckshee. Even I know that."

"Romantic little sod, aren't you?" Esme said, installing him in the special stair lift.

"As an officer, this becomes me. Aagh," he grunted. "Scratch my ankle."